A Great
Catch

Books by Lorna Seilstad

LAKE MANAWA SUMMERS

Making Waves
A Great Catch

LAKE MANAWA SUMMERS, BOOK 2

A Great Catch

A NOVEL

LORNA SEILSTAD

Revell

a division of Baker Publishing Group
Grand Rapids, Michigan

© 2011 by Lorna Seilstad

Published by Revell
a division of Baker Publishing Group
P.O. Box 6287, Grand Rapids, MI 49516-6287
www.revellbooks.com

Printed in the United States of America

Library of Congress Cataloging-in-Publication Data
Seilstad, Lorna.
    A great catch : a novel / Lorna Seilstad.
        p.   cm. — (Lake Manawa summers ; bk. 2)
    Includes bibliographical references.
    ISBN 978-0-8007-3446-6 (pbk.)
    1. Manawa, Lake (Iowa)—Fiction. I. Title.
PS3619.E425G74 2011
813'.6—dc22   2010048770

Scripture is taken from the King James Version of the Bible.

Published in association with the literary agency Books & Such, 52 Mission Circle #122 PMB 170, Santa Rosa, California 95409.

11 12 13 14 15 16 17   7 6 5 4 3 2 1

To my father,
who taught me to love
history, family, and the Lord

In all thy ways acknowledge him, and
he shall direct thy paths.

Proverbs 3:6

1

Lake Manawa, Iowa, 1901

Three blind mice.

Three little pigs.

Three days in the belly of a whale.

Emily Graham stifled a moan. Some of the worst things in life came in threes, and she was facing her favorite meddlesome trio right now.

"The right to vote won't warm your bed at night, dear." Aunt Millie poured fresh lemonade from a crystal pitcher into four glasses, then blotted her round face with a handkerchief. Even though the table, complete with an heirloom lace tablecloth, sat in the shade of the Grahams' cabin at Lake Manawa, the late May heat brought a sheen to her aunt's crinkled brow.

Emily pressed the glass of lemonade to her cheek and watched the sailboats on the lake lazily glide across the rippling surface. "As hot as it is, the last thing I want is a warm bed."

"Honestly, what are we going to do with you?" Aunt Ethel, rail thin, stiffened in her chair, and Emily imagined her aunt would launch into a tirade concerning Emily's character flaws at any minute.

Aunt Ethel turned toward her older silvery-haired sister, Emily's grandmother. "It's your fault, Kate. You filled her head with all those ridiculous notions of changing the world, women voting, and all that other nonsense. Now look at her. She's twenty-three years old, and she's still not married."

"I'm twenty-two, Aunt Ethel."

"But your birthday's just around the corner."

Emily rolled her eyes. "It's six months away."

"So sad. Almost a spinster." Aunt Millie shook her head and smoothed her apron. "If we don't do something soon, no man is going to want a woman that advanced in years."

"I guess it's up to us." Aunt Ethel tsked and patted Emily's hand. "Even though you're no great catch, don't worry, dear. With the three of us on the job, we'll have a man on your arm in no time."

"Three?" Emily felt a millstone sink to the pit of her stomach. She turned to her grandmother. "I thought you were on my side."

Grandma Kate smiled. "I am. That's why I'm going to help. If I leave it up to your aunts, they'll have you married off to some spineless simpleton you'd have henpecked in a matter of days, or some bald, solid member of the community that every other bright girl has already discarded."

"Do I even want to know what these two have in mind?"

The corners of Grandma Kate's crinkly mouth bowed. "Probably not."

"Trust us, dear. We have your best interests at heart." Aunt Millie held out a plate. "Prune cake?"

"No thank you." Emily checked the watch hanging on the chain around her neck. "I have to go now. I promised to meet some friends to go roller-skating."

"You're not going out in that abysmal outfit." Aunt Ethel's face pinched. "It's hardly proper."

Emily held out the sides of her sporting ensemble, complete with a shorter-length, divided moss-green walking skirt. "I can't very well skate in a full skirt. I'd kill myself."

"You probably will anyway," Aunt Ethel said solemnly.

"Ethel!" Grandma Kate shot her a warning glance. "It's not Emily's fault she struggles a bit in the art of gracefulness."

"A bit?" Aunt Millie chuckled. "That's like saying I'm a bit old."

"Aunties, Grandma, we'll talk about all of this later."

Aunt Ethel squeezed Emily's forearm. "No need to thank us, dear. It's our pleasure to help."

❧

After buckling the metal roller skates to her boots, Emily pulled the straps tight and dabbed her upper lip with a handkerchief. Patrons of the roller-skating rink, the newest addition to Lake Manawa's Midway and ever-growing resort, lined the bench beside her.

"I can't believe you two talked me into this again." Emily set her feet on the paved brick sidewalk, shook the wrinkles from her skirt, and smiled at her two dearest friends, Lilly Hart and Marguerite Andrews.

"You're the one who said we should challenge ourselves to grow." Lilly, formerly Marguerite's personal maid and still her best friend, grabbed Emily's hand and pulled her to her feet.

"I said we needed to challenge our minds, not break our necks." Emily wobbled, and Marguerite caught her arm.

"Careful."

"You both realize that you are putting yourselves at great risk. It's common knowledge I could trip over a chalk line drawn on the sidewalk."

"You were a little shaky when we started last time, but you caught on just fine." Lilly kept a firm hold on Emily's elbow. "Besides, teaching you to skate is the best excuse Marguerite and I have for getting a break from our children."

Keeping a hand on the door frame, Emily rolled in behind her friends. Her lips turned downward as the excitement soured. "Did you have to ask your husbands for permission to come today?"

"Tate takes a long afternoon nap, so Trip doesn't mind." Marguerite paused to give the clerk her coin. "Did Ben give you any trouble about coming today, Lilly?"

"Nothing I couldn't handle. Besides, Levi's with my mama." She deposited her nickel on the counter. "And probably being spoiled rotten."

Emily fished a coin from her chatelaine purse attached to the wide belt at her waist. "I can't imagine having to ask a man if I can go somewhere. How utterly degrading."

Marguerite stepped onto the smooth wooden floor of the rink. "That's what I used to think."

"And now she's just a plain old married woman." Lilly laughed as she followed her onto the floor.

"And you're not?" Marguerite countered. "Emily, it's not that I ask permission, really. Trip and I share our lives. It's more of a common courtesy."

Emily eased out onto the rink, pausing to adjust to the feel of the wheels on her feet. "But what if Trip told you no? If he said he didn't want you to go, would you be here?" She wavered on the uneven floor and narrowly avoided the boy in front of her. His brows knit in anger, and she shrugged in apology. Why did skating and speaking at the same time have to be so difficult?

"The right answer is probably 'no,' but I can't honestly say I'd obey him. I'm not sure what I'd do." Marguerite smoothed a crinkle in her skirt.

"I am." Lilly spun backward with ease. "You'd be here now and fight with him later."

"That's why I'm not sure marriage is for me. Obey? Even the word irritates me."

Lilly laughed. "You just need to find the right person—like we have." Emily started to lose her balance, and Lilly caught her hands. "Relax. Don't fight it. Think of the skates as wheels on your feet."

"Remember, I'm not graceful on my feet *without* the skates."

They giggled, and Marguerite linked her arm in Emily's. "You're your own worst enemy. Smile. Act like you're having fun."

"It would certainly be acting." Emily adjusted her hat, set askew by her last near fall. "I'm holding you two back. Why don't you two go skate together awhile and let me practice on my own for a few minutes?"

"We couldn't do that." Lilly twirled in a circle.

"Please. It's hard for me to talk and concentrate on the task at hand. I need about ten minutes to get used to this."

"Are you sure?" Marguerite worried her bottom lip between her teeth.

Emily reached for the wall to steady herself. "Yes. Please, I'll do better on my own. I certainly couldn't do worse."

"Ten minutes," Lilly said. "And no hugging the wall."

Like birds set free from their cage, the two friends sped off.

Lilly skated with such ease she made it look as if she'd been doing it all her life, and Marguerite looked angelic floating around the rink with her blonde hair surrounding her head like a halo. Emily felt a stab of jealousy but pushed it away. It wasn't their fault she'd been born without an ounce of athletic prowess.

She let go of the wall and shoved off, determined to master at least one lap around the rink. It might not be fair that fear pulsed through her every time another skater whooshed by, but that wouldn't stop her. It never had before.

Despite her worries, her wobbly legs seemed to solidify as she rolled down the length of the maple floor. The soft *thunk, thunk, thunk* of her skates passing over the boards caused her confidence to grow. She rounded the first corner by pressing her hand to the wall and grinned. Perhaps she'd get used to this yet.

Relax. Don't think about the skates.

Maybe if she concentrated on something else, like the Council Bluffs Equal Suffrage Club. With the recent failure of the Iowa legislature to amend the state's constitution, the women were despondent, tired after losing a hard fight. As their local president, she needed something to rally the troops—something they could put their wholehearted efforts into. They couldn't quit before they'd won the right to vote. She wouldn't let them.

Would a husband complicate all she hoped to accomplish? Marguerite and Lilly had been able to participate in the fight, but having young children affected the amount of time they could commit to the cause. As a single woman, she was free to give the effort her undivided attention.

She reached the end of the rink and bit her lip when she crossed her right boot over her left, as she'd seen Lilly and Marguerite do many times.

Suddenly her feet tangled. Arms spinning like the paddle wheels of a steamboat, she teetered precariously to the right, then the left. Strong hands tightened around her waist and attempted to move her out of the way. Instead, she gave an ungainly kick and fell hard against the person holding her. Air whooshed from her lungs as they tumbled together onto the floor, a heap of knotted limbs and skates.

2

Emily hurt. She just couldn't figure out where.

The man regained his footing and crouched in front of her. A mass of coffee-colored curls tumbled from beneath his cap and over his chestnut brown eyes.

"Carter? Carter Stockton?"

"Emily Graham? I didn't figure I'd bump into you here." He shoved the locks away. "Are you okay?"

"I think so." A sharp pain shot through Emily's wrist as she struggled to sit up. She clutched it to her stomach. Trying to ignore the sting, she smiled weakly. "I haven't seen you since high school."

His gaze dropped to her wrist. "You're hurt, aren't you? How bad is it?"

"I'm okay. I'm so sorry. This was all my fault."

"Nonsense." He smiled, and the cleft in his chin deepened. "Come on. Let's get you out of harm's way before some of these other skaters do more damage."

Carter skated behind her, slipped his hands under her arms,

and lifted her to her feet. Then, to her surprise, he kept his hand locked on her elbow until they had safely skated off the rink. He lowered her onto a bench and dropped down beside her. "Is your wrist broken?"

"Oh, heavens no."

"Let me see it."

"Honestly, I feel bad enough having taken so much of your time."

He gently pried her arm loose and examined the puffy area. "It's already swelling. Does it hurt to move your fingers? Wiggle them."

His cool touch made her skin tingle in a most alarming way. Emily tried to tug her arm free, but he held her elbow fast. With an exasperated sigh, she gave a tiny wave with her digits. "See. I'm fine."

"Humph." He scowled and rubbed his chin.

Lilly rolled toward them and used the back of the bench to stop. "Emily, we saw you fall. Are you all right?"

Marguerite joined them, out of breath from rushing across the rink. "Carter, are you the man she crashed into?"

"No, I crashed into her." He laid Emily's hand back in her lap and stood up.

"That isn't true, and you know it." Emily winced when she jostled her arm. All this fuss. It was bad enough to make a fool of herself in front of all the skaters, but now they were all drawing added attention to her embarrassment.

"She needs someone to take a look at that wrist. My carriage is outside, so I'll be glad to take her home. Is she staying here at the lake?"

"Her grandmother has a cabin on the south side." Lilly checked the watch hanging off her belt. "I can ride with you. It's on my way."

17

Marguerite elbowed her side. "You're not going in that direction. Remember, you have to pick up Levi and your mother at the Grand Plaza. She's waiting for you."

Puzzled, Emily eyed her best friends.

When Marguerite tilted her head toward Carter, realization seemed to explode across Lilly's face. "Ooooh, yes. Sorry, Emily."

Emily's eyes widened in disbelief, and her cheeks flushed hot. They were abandoning her on purpose.

"You really don't mind taking her home, Carter? It would be such a help because Trip is expecting me soon. He has a sailing lesson to give in half an hour."

"Actually, I insist. I want to make sure I didn't do any lasting damage."

"In that case, we leave you in good hands." Marguerite flashed Emily a winning smile. "I'll talk to you tomorrow."

Emily's eyes shot fire. "You can bet on it."

"Take care of her, Carter." Lilly squeezed her shoulder. "She's one special lady."

Emily watched the two betrayers skate away and turned to Carter. "Thank you for your kind offer, but I really can get home on my own." She bent to unbuckle her skate and let out a tiny yelp.

Without a word, he knelt in front of her and scooped up her boot. He slipped off the heavy skates and set them on the bench beside her. "Emily Graham, I can see one thing hasn't changed. You are as stubborn as ever. Still trying to change the world?"

"Someone has to."

"Indeed they do." He chuckled, stood, and offered his hand. "But even crusaders can get a lift. Come on. Your carriage awaits."

Every rut and bump along the dirt-packed service road made Carter flinch. The road wound behind some of the buildings and cabins lining the lake's edge. Usually, resort patrons rode the streetcar to Lake Manawa, but Carter was glad he'd chosen to take his own carriage today. If not for the sporty two-seated phaeton, Emily would have had to walk home, and her pale face told him she wasn't up to that.

He glanced at her and found her jaw clenched against the pain caused by the jostling. Having been in his own share of scrapes on and off the ball field, he sent up a silent prayer on her behalf. A lock of silky, soft brown hair had slipped from her bun in the collision and now danced across her forehead and landed on her nose. She struggled with her good hand to tuck it back in place. When the strand refused to comply, she finally puffed it away from her face.

She caught him watching her and rolled her eyes. "I must look a mess."

"You look fine." Truth be told, she looked more than fine. The Emily Graham he remembered from high school was all arms and legs with no obvious curves. This Emily had grown into her arms, legs, and curves quite nicely.

He shook his head and forced his gaze back to the road. What made him notice that? This was Emily, Martin's little sister. Martin had played on some of the same ball teams with him in high school. Emily and Carter had simply been acquaintances, due in part to their positions on the school's literary magazine staff. Even though she was a year younger than he, she was selected editor of the publication, a fact that still both riled and impressed him.

"So, Emily, what's your brother up to?"

"He's running Graham Implement Company while my parents are out of the country."

"I'm sure he's good at it. I remember he had quite the competitive streak in high school."

"You're telling me. I don't think he let me win so much as a game of checkers growing up." With a wince, she adjusted her hold on her wrist. "I believe my father's company banks with your father. If you're joining his business, it looks like you and Martin could be on the same team again."

"Not unless he's playing baseball."

"Excuse me?"

"My father is semiretired. My brother Nathan is the vice president who runs everything now. So unless Martin is playing baseball, we won't be on the same team. Though my brother expects me to join him this fall."

"And until then?"

He drew his left index finger over the red letters on his striped wool baseball jersey. "I'm pitching for the Manawa Owls in the field they put up a couple of years ago."

"I didn't realize the owls at Lake Manawa gave a hoot about pitchers." She giggled, a soft, full, infectious sound that rolled off her lips, not a high-pitched twitter so many girls tried when flirting.

Carter chuckled too. "Of course they do. Whooooever it is, they have to be the best."

"I see. But he'd be wise to keep that news to himself."

Her drawn face relaxed, and a warm feeling spread in his chest. It appeared he'd managed to keep her mind off the pain.

The two-seated rig hit another bump, and she gasped.

Carter grimaced, snapped the reins, and the horse picked up speed. "Sorry. It won't be long now."

"Good. I can't wait to be out of this rig. I'm sorry. It's

20

not that I don't enjoy your company. I do. I mean—" She huffed. "Oh bother, listen to me. I sound like my great-aunts. I apologize, Carter. None of that came out right."

He couldn't stop the corners of his mouth from lifting at the sight of her looking flustered, her cheeks turning crimson. Sucking his lips together to make the grin go away, he turned the horse to the right. "So, how long have you been roller-skating?"

"This was only my second time, but I suppose that was obvious." Despite her pain, she managed to laugh at herself.

"As soon as your wrist is better, you can tackle it again."

"I'm not sure you should use *skating* and *tackle* in the same sentence where I'm concerned."

"You need to have a little faith."

Carter slowed the horse as they approached the cabins. Last summer, only tents had lined the seven-hundred-acre lake—a virtual sea of white on the grassy areas. Now a handful of whitewashed cabins had been constructed off the shore's southwest edge. Farther down the shore on this side of the lake stood Louie's French Restaurant and the soon-to-be-opened grand Kursaal. He pulled the rig off to the side of the service road, climbed down, and secured the horse to a tree.

"Easy." Carter helped Emily out of the phaeton.

"Thank you for seeing me home."

Ignoring her dismissal, he took hold of her elbow and urged her toward the cabins. "Which one is yours?"

She sighed. "The fourth one."

He led her around to the lakeside, and they followed the gravel path in front of the cottages. Carter scanned the row of cabins. Reading the wooden signs posted over the doors, he recognized they'd been built for the best families in the area, such as the Wickhams, the Kimballs, and the Officers. Of course, the Grahams would be among that elite group.

If Carter remembered correctly, Emily's grandfather had made his fortune mining silver in Colorado and had left his wife and son a significant sum upon his death. Emily's father, James Graham, had then built one of the most successful implement companies in the Midwest.

An elderly woman sat in a wicker rocker bent over an embroidery ring. She looked up as they approached and craned her neck forward as if she didn't recognize the two of them. "Emily?"

"Yes, Aunt Millie. It's me."

Her aunt struggled to her feet. "Is that a man with you?"

"Yes, ma'am."

Carter chuckled at the disbelief in the older woman's voice. "I brought your niece home. She was injured at the skating rink."

A grin plastered on her wrinkled face, Aunt Millie wobbled closer. Her gaze raked Carter from head to toe. "Isn't he a dandy?"

Carter sucked in his cheeks to keep from laughing at the comical aunt.

"Aunt Millie," Emily hissed.

"Relax, child." She patted Emily's cheek. "Are you really hurt?"

Carter pointed to her arm. "Her wrist may be broken, ma'am."

The elderly woman's eyes grew as large as baseballs. "Ethel! Kate! You need to come out here and see who Emily brought home."

"Aunt Millie, I d-d-didn't bring him home. He b-brought me." Red-faced, she stumbled over the words. "And he was just about to leave."

Carter crossed his arms over his chest. Now was not the time for ridiculous concerns. "Not until I know if I need to summon the doctor on your behalf."

"Oh bother." Emily rolled her eyes.

The door swung open and two more elderly women stepped out.

"Emily, you're injured." Concern filled the green eyes of a stately white-haired woman. She examined Emily's cradled arm. "Thank you for seeing my granddaughter home."

Carter shifted his weight from foot to foot. "If it's all right with you, I'll stay until I'm certain she's okay."

"We'll keep him company," Aunt Millie volunteered with a girlish giggle. "I think Britta just made some fresh lemonade, and I believe we have a nice selection of cookies."

"Yes." The slim elderly woman eyed him with suspicion. "I think keeping your gentleman friend company would be an excellent idea."

"Stay at your own risk," Emily muttered as her grandmother directed her inside. She paused at the door. "And don't say I didn't warn you."

❦

Carter swallowed hard and eyed the wide smiles of Emily's two aunts. Like buzzards preparing to attack a fresh kill, they stared at him, sizing him up for dinner. He glanced around and spotted a white dining table, a few straight-backed matching chairs, and a rattan rocker situated in the shade.

"Would you ladies care to join me on the lawn? I believe someone said something about fresh lemonade."

Aunt Millie's face lit up. "Yes, I did. Please, do sit down. I'll go ask Britta to bring some refreshments."

"That's very kind of you." After she'd waddled inside, he swept his arm toward the empty chairs. "After you, ma'am."

He followed the slight aunt to the table and watched her settle in the wicker rocking chair. He sat down at the table.

"Young man, perhaps you should introduce yourself."

"Yes, ma'am." He paused when Aunt Millie stepped through the doorway balancing a tray bearing a pitcher of lemonade, three glasses, and a plate of cookies.

"What does she think she's doing?" the aunt beside him squawked. "Millie, let Britta tend to that."

Carter hurried to relieve her of the burden. As soon as he delivered the tray to the serving table, the thin, pinch-faced aunt began again.

"Why didn't Britta bring the tray?"

"She was helping Kate with Emily. Her wrist doesn't look good at all." Emily's round-faced aunt sank into a chair.

Carter swallowed, hoping she'd share more about her niece's condition.

"Very well. Emily's gentleman caller was about to introduce himself."

"Oh, of course. Do go ahead. I beg your pardon for interrupting." She poured him a large glass of lemonade and set it before him.

"No pardon necessary, ma'am. I'm Carter Stockton."

"What delightful manners." She clasped her hands to her bosom. "If my sister isn't going to introduce herself, I will. As you heard Emily say, I'm her aunt Millie, and this grouch is her aunt Ethel."

"It's a pleasure to make your acquaintance, Miss Millie." He turned toward the other aunt. "Yours too, ma'am."

Aunt Ethel scowled. "Now, please tell us how you came

24

to be stepping out with our niece, unchaperoned, down the service road this afternoon."

"They were not stepping out." Aunt Millie jerked and spilled lemonade on the tablecloth. She blotted it with a napkin. "Now see what you've done. Clearly Mr. Stockton is a gentleman, and Emily was simply in need of his assistance."

A smile itched to break through, but Carter managed to keep it in check. "I meant no disrespect in escorting your niece home, ma'am. She was injured while skating, and I couldn't let her attempt the journey back here alone."

"See." Aunt Millie held out the plate of cookies to him. "I like the lemon best myself."

He selected a lemon cookie and grinned at her. "I'm partial to things with a little tartness too."

"You ought to get along with my sister quite well then." A girlish giggle escaped.

"Millie, please contain yourself." Aunt Ethel unfolded her napkin in her lap. "I apologize for my niece's clumsiness. She should know better than to try something as foolish as skating."

"It wasn't her fault, ma'am. I ran into her. I tried to avoid the collision, but I'm afraid I failed miserably."

"And, like a knight of the Round Table, you gallantly brought her home." Aunt Millie picked up the fan beside her and waved it in front of her flushed cheeks.

"I'm no knight, Miss Millie."

Aunt Ethel eyed his clothes and frowned. "No, but apparently you are an Owl."

"You're familiar with Manawa's baseball team?" Carter set down his glass. "I'm impressed, Miss Ethel."

"I make it a point to be aware of all the current rages." Aunt Ethel broke off a piece of her cookie and slipped it between her crinkled lips, which curled at his compliment. "How else will we steer our niece in the proper directions?"

Another smile tugged at the corner of Carter's mouth. He couldn't imagine steering Emily in any direction. He took a sip of the lemonade. "I'm the pitcher."

"A hurler? How exciting." Aunt Millie bounced in her chair.

"Perhaps you two ladies will do me the honor of attending a game soon."

Aunt Millie clapped her hands. "That would be delightful."

"But hardly proper." Aunt Ethel turned to Carter, paused, and frowned. "Did you say your last name was Stockton?"

"Yes, ma'am. I went to high school with Emily."

Her brows drew close. "Are you related to Angus Stockton?"

"He's my father." Carter traced a rivulet of condensation on the outside of his glass as it trickled onto the tablecloth. What was taking so long with Emily? He was half tempted to fetch a doctor without her grandmother's request. He took another bite of cookie.

Aunt Ethel stood. "If you are that man's son, then I'm afraid you are no longer welcome at this table."

3

The cookie lodged in Carter's throat. Coughing and sputtering, he choked until his eyes watered.

Aunt Millie passed him his lemonade and pounded on his back. "Ethel, now look what you've done. You've nearly slain Emily's knight."

The cottage door creaked opened, and Emily's grandmother made her way to the table. Carter rose from his chair as she approached, downed the rest of the lemonade in his glass, and finally found his voice. "Is Emily okay? Do I need to bring the doctor?"

Her grandmother waved her hand in the air. "It's a bad sprain, but she'll be fine. Thank you for seeing her home, Mr.—"

"Kate, this is Carter Stockton, and before Ethel throws him out, you might as well know he's the son of Angus Stockton."

The grandmother, clearly the oldest of the threesome, raised an eyebrow toward her sister. "Throw him out?"

"Angus Stockton is no friend of this family's. You remember

what he did after you lost your Ethan?" Aunt Ethel's tone was terse.

"That doesn't make his son our sworn enemy." She turned toward Carter and smiled warmly. "Thank you for assisting my granddaughter today."

"I'm glad she's going to be all right. Please tell her I wish her a speedy recovery." He tugged his pillbox baseball cap from his back pocket, pulled it on, and adjusted it. "Now, if you ladies will excuse me, I have to get to practice. We have a big game tomorrow."

With every step away from the Grahams, the tension eased from Carter's shoulders. What had his father done to cause such ire? Nothing would surprise him. Angus Stockton treated business as war, and he didn't care who got hurt in the process.

At least Emily would be fine. She'd tried to be so brave, so tough. If he wanted to, he could forget her now and go on with his summer.

The problem was he didn't think he wanted to. He'd been praying to meet a girl who was different, who made him laugh and knew her own mind. The sight of her biting her lip to keep from crying out lingered in his thoughts. Maybe it was no accident he'd crashed into Emily Graham's life.

⁂

Peering out the window of her cottage bedroom, Emily spied Carter Stockton jogging back down the path toward his rig. The sleeves of his red and white striped jersey were rolled up to the elbows, revealing a contrasting red undershirt. The bright color, the matching stockings, and his broad shoulders made him stand out against the background of the shrubs surrounding this part of the lake.

She recalled the red letters of the word MANAWA stitched on the front of his collared jersey as he knelt before her. But it was the image of his caramel-colored eyes filled with concern that robbed her of breath. No one had ever looked at her in that manner.

Her cheeks heated, and she stepped away from the window. Her wrist ached, but not nearly as much as her pride. Why did she have to make such a fool of herself in front of someone she knew? She could only imagine what he was thinking right now. An athlete like Carter Stockton would never have landed in a heap at the skating rink if it wasn't for her, and now she'd have to face him over and over again this summer, reliving the humiliation every time.

A knock on the door startled her.

"Heard my sister took a spill," a familiar, deep voice boomed.

She flung the door open. "Martin! I didn't hear you come in."

"Unlike some people"—he tapped her nose—"I can manage to cross a room without tripping."

She shot him a glare. "I was skating."

"So I heard." He leaned against the door frame. "I realize you're injured, but why don't you let me walk you down to the beach? It's as hot as—"

"Martin."

"What? I was going to say as hot as an oven."

"Of course you were." She slapped her brother's arm and followed him out.

He held the door, offered her his arm, and helped her cross the lawn to the beach. "Careful. We don't want you tripping over a twig."

She fired an elbow into his ribs.

29

"Ow! For an invalid, you're still pretty tough."

"And don't you forget it."

He laughed and led her to the water's edge. "Would you care to go wading? It might feel good."

"I don't think I could manage my stockings one-handed." She sat down on a fallen log, and he joined her.

"Does your wrist hurt?"

Cradling her tea-towel-turned-sling with her free arm, she shrugged. "Dull ache."

"Grandmother said you ran into Carter Stockton—literally."

"If you're going to tease me about this, I'm going back inside." She moved to stand.

Martin caught her good wrist. "I'm sorry. Stay."

She resumed her seat and gazed at the glassy surface of the lake. If only a breeze would wrinkle its surface and cool her skin. From her position on the lakeshore, the sands of Manhattan Beach, now deserted for the day, seemed nearly a half mile away to her left. The new elaborate pavilion, called the Kursaal, extended from the shore into the lake. It would be open next month, and she couldn't wait to go into the two-story building that seemed to float on the water. The Midway's upbeat music, equal distance in the other direction, echoed in the stillness of the evening. Across the way, the Grand Pavilion, a crisp white against the tree foliage behind it, served as a backdrop for the long boardwalk along the lake's northeast shore.

She sighed. Only a few days at the lake and already she'd gotten hurt. What a summer this was going to be.

"Has Carter finished college then?"

She shifted on the log. "I didn't ask. I would assume so."

"How much has he changed?"

Emily felt a warm sensation in her stomach. How did she

tell her brother what she'd noticed? Carter had always been athletic, but now solid muscle filled his uniform.

"Emily?"

She swallowed. "Well, he's older, of course, and he's playing baseball for the Owls."

"Is he? I'm surprised Nathan Stockton is allowing his little brother to do that."

Since talking about Carter unnerved her, Emily decided a change of topic was in order. She rose from the log and walked to a thicket of gooseberry bushes heavy with green-striped berries. "We should pick these. Britta might make you a pie."

"I hate the thorns, and with one of your arms out of commission, there is no 'we' in the picking part."

"A little hard labor won't hurt you. You're getting soft sitting in Daddy's chair."

"Am I now?" He joined her at the bush. "I bet I can pick more than you."

She propped her free fist on her hip. "You've got two hands."

"I'll only use one."

She plucked a large, ripe berry. "You're on."

In minutes, Martin had a fistful. He shrugged out of his jacket and laid it on the ground to carry the delicacies.

Emily deposited her collection in a neat pile beside his. "So, how's the business going? Are you making Daddy proud?"

"Naturally." He grinned and plopped one of the sour berries in her mouth. She puckered and he laughed. "After he and Mother get back from England and he sees how great things have gone in his absence, they'll probably arrange an excursion to China."

"I certainly hope not. I miss them so much already I'd have to stow away in one of Mother's trunks."

"And miss the opportunity to see Iowa's own Carrie Chapman Catt in her second year as president of the National Woman Suffrage Association?"

Emily smiled. "You remembered."

"Of course I did."

"I still can't believe someone from our own state is in charge of the women's suffrage movement. It's hard to imagine."

Martin bent and gathered up the edges of his jacket filled with over a pint of gooseberries. "I can imagine it quite easily. Only, the person I pictured in charge of those suffragists was you."

Arm in arm, they made their way back to the cottage. Their grandmother and aunties sat beneath the oak with reading materials in hand. With a flourish, Martin deposited the berries in an empty basket and presented the prize to his grandmother.

He kissed Grandma Kate's cheek and sat down beside her. "Did you want me to take your ledgers with me? I know I'm behind in managing your finances like I promised."

She patted his hand. "No, no, Martin. I can see to my own investments."

Emily eased into the chair opposite her grandmother. "If you needed help, why didn't you ask? I'm good with figures."

"Because I'm perfectly capable of overseeing my own affairs. I'd like to remind you both I managed fine after your grandfather's death and before your father decided he would relieve me of the burdensome task."

Martin rose to his feet. "And it is a burdensome task I also will be glad to relieve you of by the end of the week."

"No, Martin, you've got your plate full with the company."

Emily grinned at her grandmother's use of her don't-argue-with-me tone.

"And if I need any assistance"—she patted Emily's hand—
"I've got a perfectly capable grandchild right here."

With a practiced glance toward first base, Carter wound
up for the pitch and sent the ball toward the batter. As soon
as it left his fingers, he knew the pitch was wild.

Dale "Ducky" Winslow, the team's catcher, lunged to the
right to catch the errant ball. His heavily padded leather mitt
hit the dirt, and dust flew.

Ducky stood and threw the ball back to him so hard, it
stung Carter's palm despite the glove. "What are you thinking, Stockton?"

Tempted to remind Ducky it was only practice, Carter bit
back the retort. It wasn't his best friend's fault he was dis-
tracted. That honor went to Emily Graham. No matter how
hard he tried to focus on the game, he kept wondering if she
was indeed all right. He could still see the tears, barely held
in check, lacing the lashes of her moss-colored eyes. Would
her grandmother have lied to set his mind at ease?

While some girls would play on a fellow's sympathy, he
was certain Emily wouldn't. In fact, she seemed mortified by
the incident more than anything else. If only he'd been able
to gently move her out of the way instead of plowing into
her like some big oaf. He shook his head. Some athlete he'd
turned out to be.

Sending up a prayer for her quick healing, he raised his
hand in the air and made a circular motion. "Let's take a
break!"

The eight other players jogged off the field, eager to get
a cool drink in the ninety-degree afternoon heat. Of course
the four batters already in got to the bucket first. Waiting his

turn, Carter whipped off his hat and swiped his forearm across his brow, the wool uniform scratching his face. May was too early for such high temperatures, but the good Lord didn't seem interested in consulting with Carter on such matters.

Ducky tucked his catcher's mitt under his arm and passed the pitcher a tin cup of water. "What's got you addled? Have you forgotten tomorrow's our opening game?"

"And the Merchant Browns have been looking good. They'd be quite happy to best us on our own field." Carter downed the cup's contents.

"Which they will easily do if you don't rally."

"I know."

Ducky cocked an eyebrow at him. "Who is she?"

"What?"

"Carter, we played college ball together for four years. You don't make rookie mistakes like that unless you've got your mind on a girl."

"Don't be ridiculous. We've only been here a couple of days."

Ducky clapped Carter's shoulder. "That's never stopped you before."

Carter stuck his thumb and forefinger in his mouth and gave a short, ear-piercing whistle. The team crowded round. "Let's get back to work. Taylor, your pickups are looking a little sloppy in right field. When the sun is in your eyes, block it with your hand or something. Mac, make sure you watch Reynolds. It's the only way you'll know if someone's trying to steal. And I need to focus."

He tugged his hat back on and glanced at the wooden bleachers on the side of the infield. A spattering of men and boys sat in the hot sun. A familiar gentleman in a smart linen summer suit approached the stands.

His brother. Come to check up on him or, more likely, to try to get him to give up this "childish" game. Fine. In a few minutes, he'd see exactly why Carter belonged on a ball field and not behind a desk.

Carter forced Emily Graham from his thoughts. She only complicated things, and the last thing he needed was complications.

Nodding to his brother, Carter spoke to his team. "Looks like we have some spectators. All right, men. Let's give them a reason to spread the word that the Manawa Owls are the best players west of Chicago."

❧

The dull ache in Emily's wrist had awakened her over an hour ago. Not wanting to rouse Aunt Millie, who shared the room with her, she remained abed. Finally, she could tolerate it no more and swung her feet over the side. The iron bed creaked, but Aunt Millie's snores continued their raucous crescendos in the tiny room.

The morning sun filtered in through Emily's east-facing window, leaving sun spots sparkling on her cotton nightgown and sling. Dust motes danced in the early morning crisp air. Thankfully, yesterday's warm temperature had taken a milder turn.

She considered starting the day off with a prayer of thanks, but she pushed the thought aside. Prayer would still be there later. God understood the pressing matters on her mind. Right now she needed to dress and prepare for today's suffrage meeting.

Easing a ruffled white shirtwaist and powder-blue skirt from the wardrobe, she gathered her stockings, underpinnings, and shoes, nestling as much as possible in the sling.

35

With nowhere else to put her broad-brimmed hat, she clamped it in her teeth and slipped from the room, closing the door behind her.

"What in the queen's name are you doing?"

Emily spun to find apron-clad Britta, her grandmother's matronly housekeeper, blocking the hallway. Britta tugged the hat from Emily's mouth.

"I didn't want to wake Aunt Millie, but I needed an early start to the day."

"A steam engine thundering through your room wouldn't wake your aunt." Britta relieved Emily of the blouse and skirt too. "Your grandmother is awake and out having her morning tea. Why don't you dress in her room?"

"I'll need your help to do up my dress."

"Of course you will, pumpkin. And I'll have a gander at that wrist while we're at it."

Thirty minutes later, Emily had won the battle with her silk stockings and lost the battle of whether the sling was still necessary. Britta insisted she continue to wear it for at least a few days. Truth be told, as much as the injury ached, she didn't mind the inconvenience.

Britta adjusted the sling. "Now, you join your grandmother under the oak, and I'll bring out a fresh plate of waffles for you."

"With strawberries?"

"God's smiling on you today, young lady. One of the local boys was selling big, juicy, ripe ones yesterday. The warm weather brought them on early this year, and I bought a pint basket with your name on it."

"You're too good to me, Britta."

"I certainly am." She chuckled, a deep, full-bellied laugh, and propelled Emily toward the door. "And I plan to put some meat on those skinny bones of yours or die trying."

"I know I'm too thin."

"No, pumpkin, you've become a beautiful young lady right before our eyes."

Emily nudged the screen door open with her foot and stopped short. Dressed in a tawny-colored linen suit, narrow striped tie, and checkered sportsman's cap, Carter Stockton sat at the rattan table with her grandmother. Suddenly her corset felt cinched too tightly. Even the cool morning breeze wafting off the lake didn't provide enough air. What was he doing here?

Her grandmother waved her over. She smoothed the side of her skirt and touched her hair, then smiled and took a deep breath. With no other options, she crossed the lawn and joined them.

Carter stood and pulled out a chair for her. "Good morning, Emily."

Emily took the seat and forced a weak smile. "Good morning."

"Mr. Stockton came to see how you were doing." Her grandmother spooned sugar into her tea.

"I'm fine." Emily's voice quivered, and she paused to swallow. "Thank you for your thoughtfulness."

"It's the least I can do after plowing you over."

"As I said yesterday, I accept full responsibility for the fall."

Her grandmother smiled and picked up her cup of tea. "I told him you'd need to keep your arm in the sling for a few days."

"Will it inconvenience you terribly?" Carter forked a bite of waffle.

"My biggest concern is finishing the articles I have due."

"Articles?"

"For the *Woman's Standard*."

37

His mouth dipped in a frown. "You believe women should have the right to vote?"

"You don't?" She stiffened. She shouldn't be surprised. Most men disapproved of her work. "Why should they not be granted suffrage? Because women aren't capable of intellectually dealing with the political arena? I'll have you know, Carter Stockton, women can think just as well as any man."

"Darling, need I remind you of James's admonition?" Grandma Kate's voice grew stern. "'Let every man be swift to hear and slow to speak.'"

Emily's chest tightened at the mention of the Scriptures. Guilt pricked her like thorns on the gooseberry bush every time her grandmother brought up the Bible. From the beginning, she'd not consulted the Lord regarding her suffrage work. She hadn't dared. It was too important for her to risk. What if God told her no?

She glanced from her grandmother to Carter and let her anger grab hold at yet another man's lack of support for the cause.

"I didn't say I was against women's suffrage, Miss Graham, although your little outburst does seem to lend itself to the 'too emotional' argument many men use." Flecks of gold sparkled in Carter's brown eyes. "But I'm willing to overlook that given your condition."

She shot him a scorching look.

Britta delivered Emily's plate of waffles topped with a generous helping of strawberries. The berry syrup cascaded down the side of the stack, and Emily's stomach rumbled.

"Perhaps we could hold off on suffrage discussions until after you've eaten your breakfast and are in a more cordial frame of mind." Emily's grandmother paused to allow her the chance to say grace. "Are you aware Carter graduated

38

this last spring from Iowa State College of Agriculture and Mechanics?"

Emily blinked and shot a puzzled look in her grandmother's direction. Carter? What happened to calling him Mr. Stockton? While her grandmother had never been one to adhere to strict social rules, the two of them could not have become so familiar in such a short time.

"Congratulations. I'm sure your parents are very proud." Emily forced the words out and eyed the pile of waffles, her mouth tingling. The empty gnawing in her stomach reminded her she hadn't eaten supper last night, and the plump berries begged to be plucked from the plate.

Carter blotted the corners of his mouth with his napkin and laughed. "My family would be happier if I put my education to work in my father's bank."

Emily picked up her fork and contemplated eating the waffles left-handed in front of Carter. Her skin prickled as she imagined a trail of strawberry syrup cascading down the ruffles of her pristine blouse.

"Aren't you going to eat, Emily?" Grandma Kate asked. "Your waffles will get soggy."

"I like it when the syrup soaks in."

"Nonsense." Her grandmother waved her hand in the air, shoved her own empty plate away, and set a leather-bound ledger on the table.

Emily bit her lip and used the side of her fork to try to cut off the corner. Ah. Success.

She glanced up and caught Carter grinning at her. Heat flooded her cheeks, and she dropped her gaze back to her breakfast. Even without looking, she knew he was still watching. She'd show him she was a woman who could tackle anything—big or small.

Her grandmother thumbed through the ledger. "And Carter studied finance, Emily. Since your brother is busy running your father's business, I've asked Carter to help me manage my assets."

"But I thought—" Emily jerked. The bite of waffle on the tip of her fork, drenched in strawberry syrup, went flying across the table.

4

Instinct alone propelled Carter to catch the chunk of waffle midair. The contents squished in his palm, and he grabbed his napkin from the table. When he'd managed to scrub the worst of the berry stain off, he looked up and met Emily's horrified gaze. Laughter rumbled in his chest, but with great effort he kept it in check.

"Carter, here are the current investments. As you can see, they are quite diverse." Grandma Kate nudged the open ledger in his direction, clearly unaware of the entire waffle fiasco. "Of course we'll have much to discuss, which means you'll have to join us for breakfast on a regular basis. Will that be a problem?"

He grinned at Emily and watched her cheeks bloom pink. "Not at all, ma'am. Not at all."

Grandma Kate glanced at Emily's plate. "Why haven't you touched your waffle? Oh my, I forgot. You can't cut it."

"I can take care of it, Grandma."

"Nonsense, dear." She pulled the plate over and began

to cut neat squares. "We wouldn't want any mishaps, now would we?"

Carter snickered, and Emily shot him a glare. His midair catch obviously hadn't won him any favor in her eyes. If he had to guess, she'd tried and convicted him of being a cocky baseball player, not worthy of thinking beyond the field. Fine. He'd change her mind. He enjoyed a challenge. And she should realize he wasn't used to losing.

She pushed back from the table, stood, and pressed a hand to her stomach. "Never mind, Grandma. I'm not hungry anymore. Besides, I need to prepare for my meeting this afternoon."

Carter rose to his feet beside her. "I enjoyed having breakfast with you, Emily. I'd offer my hand, but . . ."

Her cheeks flamed afresh, but she met his gaze defiantly. "You should be more careful about that syrup."

"Maybe so." He pushed a nest of curls off his forehead with the back of his berry-stained fingers. "I don't mind a little mess, even when things get sticky. What will you be discussing at your meeting?"

"Renewing our efforts—not that you'd care."

"I don't think you have any idea what I care about, Miss Graham." He turned toward Grandma Kate. "Ma'am, I'll be here tomorrow at the same time, and there's a game tonight if you and your sisters care to attend. We're playing the Merchant Browns."

Grandma Kate glanced from Carter to Emily. "We might come watch, and thank you for coming to check on Emily."

"Yes, Carter, thank you for your concern." Emily gathered her tablet. "But I really must be going."

"In that case, I'll walk with you since we're going the same way."

"The baseball field is on the opposite side of the lake from the Yacht Club."

He gave Emily a lopsided grin. "Is it? I hadn't noticed."

Before she had a chance a respond, Aunt Millie waved from the doorway of the cabin. "Oh, Emily, wait for Aunt Ethel and me. We have a new prospective suitor we wish to discuss with you."

Carter's lips tugged into a grin as a crimson blush infused Emily's cheeks.

Emily lifted her chin. "Well, apparently I won't need a walking companion, so you can be on your way."

"Just like that?"

"I know you're a busy man."

Even though he didn't expect Emily to let him be privy to the details her aunts would be giving, his curiosity had been piqued. The don't-you-dare-ask look in Emily's eyes told him, however, now was not the time to broach the subject.

He touched the brim of his ball cap. "All right, I'll leave you in your aunts' capable hands."

Nodding to the ladies, he spun and jogged down the path away from the whitewashed cottage. He chuckled as he pictured the horrified expression on Emily's sweet face when she realized he'd caught the piece of waffle. Things were probably always exciting around that little spitfire.

He flexed his sticky fingers and shook his head. If he wasn't careful, he could get stuck thinking about her a lot more than he should.

No girl—certainly not one who'd already made up her mind about him—could be in his plans for this summer.

❧

Dragging another set of chairs over to the center of the Yacht Club's upstairs meeting room with her good arm, Emily completed the seating arrangement. In moments, the Council Bluffs chapter of the Iowa Women's Suffrage Association would arrive for their first lakeside meeting of the summer. She hoped the change of venue would give the ladies a much-needed boost in their enthusiasm for the cause. Marguerite Andrews had arranged for them to use the second floor of the usually men-only Yacht Club for their meeting. That alone should give the ladies' spirits a lift.

"Emily, you're early." Marguerite breezed through the doors and tugged off her gloves. "I said I'd help you set up. How's your wrist?"

"My pride aches worse than the sprain. I came early because I needed to escape."

"From your grandmother?"

"Among others."

"Are your aunts bothering you again?"

"They have designated themselves my personal matchmakers, as I am fast approaching the age where no one could possibly want me. I have to meet their newest prospective suitor after our meeting."

Marguerite chuckled. "They mean well."

"Humph."

Lilly Hart strode in and took a seat. "Why does Emily look as if she swallowed a lemon?"

"Her aunts and grandmother have decided to take her lack of matrimonial bliss into their own hands."

"Mercy me, Emily. Are you going to let them?"

"I don't see how I can get out of it without hurting their feelings." She tugged the string hanging from the electric ceiling fans and listened for the whir. Slowly the blades began to stir the humid air. "Aunt Millie and Aunt Ethel are basically harmless, and they mean the world to me."

A few more members filtered in, most of them married. Emily let out a wistful sigh. It wasn't that she didn't appreciate her aunts' efforts, but she'd made her choice. Gaining the right to vote for women was worth the lonely nights. It had to be. No man would tolerate the long hours she put in toward the cause, and they shouldn't have to.

"Who knows? Maybe they'll actually find you the perfect match." Lilly removed her hat and set it beside her on the chair.

Emily adjusted the sling. "Lilly, be serious."

"Well, the Lord does move in mysterious ways."

Marguerite glanced toward the oak-framed doorway, where Mrs. Olivia DeSoto paused to make a dramatic entrance, wearing yet another new frock. "Speaking of mysterious ways, look who's coming."

Emily moaned. "I thought you'd said she was ill."

"Wishful thinking?" Marguerite raised her eyebrows. "She certainly keeps you on your toes, Madam President."

"She hates me." Emily rubbed the ache in her wrist.

"Only because you bested her in the election," Lilly said. "She thrives on being the center of attention, and you thwarted her plans."

The middle-aged beauty, flanked by two of her cohorts, glided across the room and immediately readjusted the carefully placed chairs. "There. That should do nicely," she said. "Marguerite, Lilly, so glad you could make it. Emily, you aren't going to be carrying on again, are you?"

"This is a suffrage meeting, Olivia. Not a social club."

"Of course it is, but you do seem to drone on and on and on." She spoke loudly and looked around as if to see who was listening. When it appeared she had the attention of one of the newcomers, a smile played on her lips.

"Olivia, why don't you come sit by me?" Lilly patted the chair beside her. "Let me hear about your attractive new skirt. Where did you get it? It's a lovely color."

Emily moved to the window, anger simmering inside her, but grateful Lilly had deflected Olivia's hurtful intent. Taking a deep breath, Emily sent up a silent prayer for a smooth meeting. Why did she let Olivia get to her? Simply because the woman tried to make the meetings more about her own popularity than about the cause, that was no reason to let it chafe her so.

Staring down from the second-story window, Emily saw the electric launch docking. While the steamers still ran once in a while, resort guests were now most often transported by the new boats that had to be plugged in and recharged every night. She recognized a few fellow suffragists disembarking and waited until they'd made their way upstairs before she started the meeting.

"Ladies." Emily rapped the gavel on the podium and knocked her notes off in the process. She dove for the fluttering papers, but with only one useful arm, they scattered like autumn leaves on a windy day. Holding her breath, she counted to ten as the papers settled. Lilly scooped them up and offered them to her.

Ignoring the twitters filling the room, Emily straightened her shoulders and fanned her burning cheeks with the papers in her good hand.

"Welcome to the first lakeside meeting of the season. Before we begin, I want to remind you of our demonstration on the pavilion steps this Saturday. As we voted at our last meeting, I will be speaking, and everyone needs to arrive wearing their banners. It is an excellent opportunity to educate the large weekend crowds here at the lake as to the advancements made in the movement."

"Advancements?" Olivia scoffed in a shrill voice. "Need I remind you the petition before the Iowa assembly failed? A petition, I believe, you assured us would make the politicians finally listen."

"And they did listen." Emily slapped the papers on the podium. "We barely lost the fight, and there were over a hundred thousand signatures from Iowa's citizenry. I understand this is an unfortunate setback, but we should be proud of our efforts, and now more than ever we should press onward."

Mrs. Gertrude O'Neil clucked. "Why? It will be two years before the legislature meets again to even discuss amending the state's constitution."

Emily took a deep breath. "If we slow down now, then we lose whatever ground we've gained. In most states, women now make up a fifth of the workforce, but they make less than half the wages of a man who does the same job."

Chatter broke out among the ladies, and Emily had to call them to order again. "The difference in wages is what makes it vital we encourage the women who are working in places like Woodward's Candy Factory to join the cause. I believe they are the key to the future and will be quick to lend their support if they are invited to do so." She studied the faces before her. "Do I have a volunteer who feels comfortable talking to the ladies working in the factory?"

Lilly raised her hand, and a few women gasped. She silenced them with a glare. "I haven't been married to Benjamin Davis Hart long enough to have forgotten what it was like to work for a living. I'll speak to them. I'll go every day if I have to."

"Thank you, Lilly." Emily smiled.

"I don't see how that is going to make a difference." Olivia waved a silk fan before her face. "Perhaps what we need for this organization is some new direction and leadership."

The ladies in the room fell silent. Emily clenched her fist tight inside the tea-towel sling. "That very well may be, Olivia, but my term is not over until the end of the year, and I have no intention of giving up this fight—or any other."

"I'll second that!" Marguerite applauded, and like dominoes, soon the other ladies joined her.

Olivia snapped her fan closed and rose to her feet. "This room is stifling. I need some air. But before I go, I want to remind you ladies of the spring tea at my home less than a month away. Your invitations should have been delivered already. I thought some of you"—she raked her gaze over Mrs. Tjaden's wrinkled skirt—"may want to have something new made. I've got a lovely crepe summer dress ordered for myself."

Emily's heart tugged at the deliberate snub. No invitation had come for her, but she kept her expression frozen, unwilling to give Olivia DeSoto the satisfaction of ruffling her.

"Oh, and did I mention Mrs. Mary Jane Whitely Coggeshall has agreed to be our honored guest? I believe you all recognize the name of the past president of the Iowa Women's Suffrage Association." Excited chatter filled the room, and Olivia cast a smirk toward Emily. "She says the future of the suffrage movement in Iowa lies with *married* women such as myself."

The now-silent ladies awaited Emily's response. With a mouth as dry as wool batting, Emily swallowed. "She should be a delightful and informative guest. I hope she will be able to share what is truly imperative in this cause, and the importance of rising above petty differences."

Olivia huffed, swung her lace-trimmed floral skirt in a circle, and whooshed from the room.

5

Exiting the front door of the Manawa Yacht Club, Emily paused and scanned the throngs of lake visitors for her doting aunts. Not spotting them, she headed toward the Grand Plaza. Maybe her aunts had given up this ridiculous notion.

A soft breeze made her skirt swish against her ankles, and a contented warmth spread across her chest. She loved everything about Lake Manawa. Having come to the resort since she was in high school, it was truly her summer home. She smiled at the husbands and wives, linked arm in arm, as they strolled along the boardwalk with children in tow. A baby's cry made her turn. Lilly lifted Levi from the pram, and immediately the baby quieted. On the lake, a sailboat glided over the rippling surface. Maybe Trip Andrews was testing another of his creations. Off to the side, a family of picnickers began gathering up the remains of their lunch and folding a tartan blanket.

A perfect day.

"Emily!" Aunt Millie waved at her from a bench in the shade. "Over here, dear."

So much for perfect.

Sidestepping a cyclist, Emily stepped toward her aunts.

Then she saw him.

Previously blocked by the trunk of a sturdy oak, the apparently balding man situated between her two aunts now stood as she approached. A Cheshire cat grin nearly reached his sideburns and made his large ears fan out from his face. She stifled a grimace.

Aunt Ethel hurried to her side, linking her bony arm in Emily's free one. "Looks can be deceiving, dear. Let's not make any hasty judgments."

"Does he at least have teeth?"

Aunt Ethel leaned closer. "Emily, Marion might be a few years older than you, but—"

"Marion?"

Waving her arm in a circle, Aunt Millie indicated they should hurry. Aunt Ethel quickened her steps. "We don't want to keep Mr. Wormsley waiting."

Emily moaned. Wormsley? With her luck, he'd be a bug collector too. She shivered. Even thinking of spiders made Emily's skin crawl. A nasty experience with an overly friendly wolf spider in the root cellar had left a lasting impression.

"Ah, here is our lovely niece." Aunt Millie wrapped her arm around Emily's waist and drew her close. "Mr. Marion Wormsley, I'd like you to meet our niece, Miss Emily Graham."

Mr. Wormsley tipped his hat, and the sun shone off his scalp. "It's a pleasure to make your acquaintance. Your aunts have told me all about you."

Certain they'd left out most of the qualities that usually sent suitors running—her lack of gracefulness, outspoken manner, determination to use the brain God gave her—Emily smiled politely. "It's a pleasure to meet you too, Mr. Wormsley."

Emily Wormsley. The ridiculous name caused a tickle to rise in the back of her throat. It erupted in a half-hiccup sound. Face hot, Emily covered her mouth with her gloved hand. "Excuse me."

"You need something to drink." Marion shifted nervously from foot to foot. "Why don't I, uh, get you a beverage?"

Emily thanked him and waited to speak to her aunts until he'd gone toward the pavilion. "Whatever made the two of you think I might be interested in Mr. Wormsley?"

"Dear." Aunt Millie patted her arm. "He's such a sweet man. And he's a marksman."

The stooped shoulders of the slight man in the distance made that hard to believe. "He shoots?"

"No, dear."

"Archery?"

"Of course not." Aunt Ethel shook her head. "Mr. Wormsley is an expert horseshoe player."

"Horseshoes?"

Aunt Millie clapped her hands. "Yes, aren't you lucky? Luck. Horseshoes. Get it?"

Emily rolled her eyes. It was going to be a long afternoon, and right now she saw no escape. Perhaps she could trip over a bench.

"That one's a leaner." Marion pointed to the horseshoe he'd tossed, which had landed upright against the stake. "It's almost as good as a ringer."

"Oh, and we certainly encourage rings, don't we, dear?" Aunt Millie squeezed Emily's arm.

"He said *ringer*, Aunt Millie."

"Why don't you give it a try, Miss Graham?"

"Do call her Emily." Aunt Ethel adjusted her hat. "Emily doesn't stand on formalities."

Emily's mouth gaped. What were her aunts thinking?

Actually, she knew exactly what they were thinking, and she didn't like it one bit.

Marion offered her the horseshoe. "Give it a try—Emily."

"I don't know, Mr. Wormsley. I'm not very athletic."

Aunt Millie nudged her. "Do try for that ring, dear."

"Ringer." Emily sighed and accepted the proffered U-shaped metal. Stepping up to the line Marion indicated, Emily swung her arm back with force. When she raised her left arm to swing the horseshoe, the weight of it surprised her, and she lost her balance. The horseshoe flew high into the air, flipped three times, and came down with amazing speed. Before anyone could react, it conked Marion Wormsley on top of his derby-covered bald head, and he slumped to the ground.

Emily stared at the dazed man lying prone at her feet. Slowly he sat up, drew off his hat, and rubbed the egg-shaped swelling on the top of his head.

She squatted beside him. "I'm so sorry, Mr. Wormsley."

He looked at her, eyes glazed. "Who are you?"

"Oh my." Aunt Millie wrung her hands.

"Don't stand there, Emily," Aunt Ethel snapped. "Get the poor man a drink or something, or better yet, get someone to help us."

Wadding her skirt in her fist, Emily raced toward the nearest concession stand. Patrons lined up in front of the counter. Drink. Her aunt said to get Mr. Wormsley a drink. One-handed, she fumbled with her pocketbook and in her haste dropped it. The coins clattered as they rolled across the boardwalk surrounding the stand.

"Oh bother." She stooped to retrieve the few that hadn't slipped through the cracks.

"Need some help?"

She tipped her head up, and her eyes met Carter's. He held out a quarter in his palm, and a grin spread across his face.

Plucking the coin from his grasp, she started to stand, only to find another gentleman's foot on the hem of her skirt, holding her in place.

Carter caught her arm. "Excuse me, sir. I believe your boot is on the lady's dress."

The long-faced man grumbled an apology and stepped away.

"What's going on, Emily?" Carter scanned her face. "You look flustered."

"I have to get a drink for Mr. Wormsley."

Carter frowned. "Why would you be buying refreshments for a man?"

"I hit him in the head and knocked him out."

"Why?" The furrows deepened. "Did he try to hurt you?"

"Heavens no." Worry knotted in her stomach. "Carter, please. I need to hurry. He needs help." She turned to leave, but he caught her arm.

"Not so fast. You wait here and I'll get the drink."

Glancing back and forth from the concession stand to the horseshoe pit area, Emily absently rubbed her injured wrist through the towel sling. Surely Marion wasn't hurt badly.

Within a minute, Carter returned. "The owner wasn't happy about us leaving with the glass. I promised we'd return it. Lead the way, Slugger."

Emily shot him a fierce glare and marched toward the horseshoe pit with the glass in hand.

Carter fell in step beside her. "Hey, easy, or you'll get there with no water left. Is that him?"

Like heavy dumplings, dread and shame weighed in her stomach. Emily nodded.

Carter wasted no time in reaching her two aunts, who were attempting to assist Mr. Wormsley to his feet. "I'll get him, ladies." With one swift motion, Carter lifted the smaller man from the ground and deposited him on the bench beside the pit. "Good grief, Emily. What did you hit Marion with? A baseball bat?"

She lowered her head and mumbled the answer as she passed Mr. Wormsley the glass of water. Only a slight glance at the offending curved piece of iron, and Carter's ever-so-slight smile told her he'd heard her.

"I'm very sorry, Mr. Wormsley. It slipped."

He rubbed his head. "I thought this was a safe game."

"I'm sure it usually is." Guilt washed over her. *Unless I'm around.*

Carter squeezed the man's shoulder. "Not every day you get knocked off your feet by a pretty girl, eh, friend?"

"Are we friends?" Marion blinked owlishly.

"Of course we are. You work for my dad." Carter brushed the dirt off the man's sleeve.

"If I'd have known stepping out was this painful . . ."

"Ah, but the company of the right girl is worth it."

Emily felt her cheeks burn. Did Carter believe she'd step out with Marion Wormsley? "We need to get him home."

"I'll take him," Carter offered. "I have to go into town anyway. That is, unless there's more between the two of you . . ."

"No!" Marion sat up straight. "I'm sorry, Miss Ethel, Miss Millie. I'm not sure courting your niece is going to work out."

Emily balled her fists. Dumped by Marion Wormsley! Could anything be worse?

Carter snickered.

So, it could get worse. Embarrassment flared to anger. It wasn't her fault she didn't have a graceful bone in her five-foot-seven-inch body.

If the horseshoe wasn't so far away, she might try for another ringer. Only this time she'd ring Carter Stockton's athletic little neck.

6

Carter hopped off the open-air streetcar, tucked his leather glove beneath his arm, and jogged toward the dock. If he missed the electric launch to the other side of the lake, he'd be late for the Owls' opening home game. He shouldn't have offered to take poor Marion home, but he couldn't imagine Emily and her aunts managing the ungainly man on their own.

"Hey, hold up!" He waved his hat in the air, and the deck assistant paused in releasing the ropes. After thanking him, Carter hopped on board the launch and took an empty seat in the stern. The boat jetted away from the dock, the loud whir of the motor drowning out the conversation of the two ladies beside him.

Carter glanced at the shore in the distance and then at his pocket watch. He groaned. He'd missed most of the time the team used to warm up, but the jog to the boat had to count for something. The trail of sweat trickling between his shoulder blades confirmed it.

His insides heated a bit more as he pictured Emily's

flustered face, haloed by wisps of hair blown free in her haste to help poor, injured Marion. Did she have any idea how cute she was when her dander was up?

Shaking his head, he pushed away the thought. This was Emily Graham, Martin's little sister and an all-fired-up suffragette ready to take on the world. Besides, this summer was about baseball, not courting. His team was counting on him, and he had his own reason to focus on delivering an undefeated season.

His brother.

"You one of those Owls?" an overly freckled man asked above the din of the engine.

Carter nodded toward him. "Yes, sir. Opening game tonight."

"Then what are you doing here?"

"It's a long story." Unbidden, Emily's image took shape in his mind once again. The corners of his mouth lifted. A horseshoe. He couldn't imagine how she'd managed that. And what was someone as talented and lovely as she was doing stepping out with Marion Wormsley, of all people?

"You boys any good?" the man called.

"Sure hope so." Carter rubbed his hands together, itching to get on the ball field. He sent up a silent prayer to get there in time.

"What position do you play?"

"Pitcher." Carter eyed the field set nearly a quarter mile from Louie's French Restaurant. Nerves tingling, he berated the launch's speed as it devoured every precious minute he needed to warm up for the game. It skirted around the nearly completed, man-made peninsula of a pavilion, which they'd named the Kursaal. Since there'd be little time to do much before the game, he stretched his arm over his head and pulled the tense muscles. The launch chugged into place at the dock.

Unhurried, the captain closed the throttle and tossed a rope onto the dock. A dockworker caught it and secured the boat in place.

Carter jumped to his feet but paused to let the ladies disembark.

"Son, we understand you're in a hurry." The woman who'd been seated beside him stepped back. "You go ahead."

"Thank you, ma'am, but I couldn't." He took her elbow and helped her ever so slowly step out of the vessel. After assisting four other women from the launch, Carter raced down the path past the Kursaal and the restaurant toward the ball field. Sweat trickled from his brow. If they lost this game because of him, his team would never forgive him. More importantly, he'd never forgive himself, and it would ruin all his plans.

Finally, red and white striped uniforms dotted the field in the distance. Good, they were still warming up. Since they were playing another local team, maybe he'd get lucky and his team would be able to bat first. Carter sprinted the last few yards onto the field and met Ducky at home plate.

"Where have you been?" Ducky punched his catcher's mitt.

Carter sucked in a lungful of air. "It's a long story."

"Hope she was worth it."

Carter shot his best friend a glare. "Just give me the ball."

"You haven't warmed up."

"Ducky, we don't have time."

"Now you're worried about time? Don't be a fool. You can't pitch without warming up. Go on. Ned can keep pitching till you're ready." Ducky turned. "Pauly, go catch for Stockton."

Pauly trotted off the bleacher and met Carter on the outskirts of the field. He punched his thick leather glove. "Ready?"

Carter nodded but stopped to watch the start of the game. Spinning his arm in a wagon wheel–sized circle, Ned sent the first pitch of the season toward the batter of the opposing team. Carter's heart sank like an anchor when a crack echoed across the field as the bat made contact with the ball. Shielding his eyes from the sun, he watched the ball sail past Elwood Taylor in right field and land in the grass. Half the crowd cheered.

He motioned to Pauly. "Step back. I'm mad as a hornet right now."

"At Ned?"

"No. Myself."

❧

"This is ridiculous." Emily stepped over a puddle in the path leading from their camp along Lake Manawa's south shore. "By the time we get there, the game will be over."

"Then you don't have anything to complain about." Grandma Kate gave her a half grin.

Emily swatted a mosquito buzzing around her wide-brimmed straw hat. "There won't be any seats left."

"We'll see."

"Grandma, sometimes . . ."

"I can be as stubborn as you? Where do you think you came by that trait, dear?"

Emily smiled. If there was anyone she wanted to emulate, it was her grandmother. While she loved her own soft-spoken mother dearly, ever since she was a little girl she'd admired Grandma Kate—the fighter, the strong, independent woman who didn't let anyone or anything stand in her way. Grandma didn't need a man. She took care of herself, or at least she did now.

"What was Grandpa like?" Emily's grandfather had died before she was born, and she often wondered about the man. Every time she asked her mother about him, her mother would tear up and say they'd talk later. Fearing she'd upset her grandmother as well, Emily didn't speak of him often.

"Why do you ask?"

"I was thinking about how you don't seem to need a man."

They reached Louie's French Restaurant, and Grandma Kate stopped by a thicket of burgundy peonies. "Emily, don't confuse what I've had to do with what I want."

"I don't understand." Emily adjusted her sling and bent to sniff the honeyed perfume.

"I can handle business matters without your grandfather, but I would much rather have him here."

"To do them for you?"

Grandma Kate laughed. "Sometimes that would be nice."

"But Grandma, you do an excellent job with your affairs." An ant crawled onto her hand, and she shook it off. "Don't you enjoy making your own decisions? Thinking for yourself? Not answering to anyone?"

"We all answer to someone. I answer to God, and so do you." Grandma Kate started walking down the path again. "In some ways, your aunts are right. I have filled your mind with ideas about women being equal to men."

"But you're right."

Grandma patted her arm. "Yes, it's true. But equal doesn't mean identical. Men aren't unnecessary, dear. I miss your grandpa terribly. He was a part of me. We faced the world together. That's how God planned it."

The deep sadness mirrored in her grandmother's pale eyes broke Emily's heart. "What do you miss the most?"

Grandma Kate didn't answer for several minutes. When

she did, her voice was soft and far off. "I miss being the most important person in the world to someone."

Tears pricked Emily's eyes, and she let the poignant words soak in like a soft rain. She wanted to argue that her grandmother was the most important person in the world to her, but she knew that wasn't what Grandma Kate meant. A longing, so deep and painful it made her heart ache, forced her to press her hand to her chest. She wanted that kind of love.

But it wasn't going to happen. No man would ever make her the center of his world. Not too-plain, too-clumsy Emily Graham.

She swallowed the longing and sighed. It was just as well. She had her own fight to concentrate on. If she had her way, she'd be doing it on a national level someday, right alongside Carrie Chapman Catt. Like her grandmother, she was a fighter, and no one was going to stop her.

Emily glanced up and paused on the path. The fan-shaped baseball field, which she'd thought was still a good distance away, seemed to have sprouted from the earth. The Manawa Owls, sporting their red and white uniforms, had one man on second base and another at bat.

Grandma Kate stopped beside the packed wooden bleachers beneath a canopy for spectators and squeezed Emily's hand. "Only God knows the plans He has for you. He made you. Let Him direct your path."

Guilt swept over Emily. How long had it been since she'd asked God to direct her path or light the way? Of course she prayed. This morning she'd asked Him to bless her meeting with the suffrage league. He'd put the desire to do this work in her heart. Surely that was a good indication she was doing exactly what He'd have her do. Wasn't it?

Carter Stockton rose from the bench when he spotted them,

waved, and jogged over. "Well, if it isn't Slugger. Maybe we could use you on the team."

"And maybe you could use some manners, Carter Stockton."

"Emily." Her grandmother scowled at her. "And Carter, why on earth are you calling my granddaughter 'Slugger'?"

"Never mind, ma'am. I apologize. You two need a place to sit?" In three long strides, he walked to the bleachers, then spoke to two men in the front row. Seconds later, they vacated their spots. He swept his arm toward the empty seats and bowed. "Ladies."

"You shouldn't have made those men move." Emily hung back, but Grandma Kate nudged her forward.

A broad smile creased Carter's face. "They volunteered. Enjoy the game."

"Wait. Who's ahead?" Emily asked as he jogged off.

"They are," Carter called over his shoulder. "But not for long."

7

"Play ball!" Umpire Harvey Hill, a former classmate of Carter's, pointed at the Owls.

Emily and her grandmother had been there for nearly two hours now, and the sun was casting shadows on the field. The game was tied at 2–2. Carter had not allowed a single hit since he'd taken over on the pitcher's mound. But that was seven innings ago. How long could he keep that up?

Carter drew the ball to his chest as he squinted at the catcher. He looked away, both hands hugging the ball to his chest, then he kicked and wound his arm like a windmill before hurling the ball toward the batter so fast Emily lost track of it.

"Strike three! You're out!"

The batter glared at Carter and threw down his bat. A glimmer of a smile broke through Carter's stoic expression as he ran in from the pitcher's mound. The others joined him on the bench.

First to bat, the Owls' shortstop connected on the second pitch and made it safely to first base.

Carter stepped to the plate next but was facing a different direction than the shortstop. Emily couldn't see his face. He balanced the ash bat in his hand and hit the dirt a couple of times. The breeze carried the dust cloud away. Then, setting his stance wide and sure, he held the bat aloft over his left shoulder.

The opposing pitcher threw the ball directly at him. Carter jumped out of the way. The ball whizzed by him and landed with a thud in the catcher's mitt.

"Strike one!" the umpire shouted.

Carter shook his shoulders and stepped back to the plate. He swung at the second pitch. The ball flew toward right field and landed in an open spot. Carter raced toward first base.

"Not bad for a southpaw," a man behind Emily said.

"And for a hurler," his friend added.

Although Emily knew southpaw referred to Carter being left-handed, she was tempted to turn around and ask why they doubted his batting abilities. But she chose to remain silent. A lady could learn much by listening to those around her.

"Yeah," the first man agreed. "Most pitchers are the weakest batters on the team."

So, Carter Stockton was a bit of a wonder. Why didn't that surprise her?

The Owls took the lead by the end of the eighth inning. As the game continued, Grandma Kate pressed her hands to her back. "It's getting late, Emily. Perhaps we should go."

Carter sent the baseball sailing toward the batter, and the umpire called the second strike in a booming voice.

"Now?" She glanced at Carter.

A smile graced Grandma Kate's wrinkled face. "I thought you didn't want to come."

"I never said that."

"You implied it would be a complete waste of time."

Emily wanted to cheer when Carter struck out yet another one of the Merchant Browns. "Although I still believe I could have used my time more wisely, I must say, this has been invigorating."

"It has at that." Her grandmother flicked open a Battenberg lace fan and waved it in front of her face.

"And it's almost over. I don't think a slight delay in our departure will make any difference in what I complete today." *Or don't complete.* A familiar tug of guilt pulled on her. Responsibilities, forgotten for the last two hours, suddenly felt heavy on her shoulders again.

The batter stepped back in place, and Emily held her breath as the ball sped over the plate.

"Strike one!" Hill called.

Applause and cheers erupted around her.

Carter glanced at her and nodded. She could practically see the win going right to that cocky, curly-haired head of his. If he won, he was going to be insufferable. He already had an air of confidence about him. And why shouldn't he? He was good-looking, athletic, and wealthy. He could play all summer long even if there was work to do.

She, on the other hand, couldn't afford to play. After all, it was her job to find something that would unify the ladies in their fight. They needed something to get behind, and it needed to be public, where the community could see a woman could do anything a man could do.

If only she could teach men like Carter a lesson. Wipe that smirk right off his chiseled face. *Lord, okay, I'm trying to turn to You first. Do You have any ideas?*

"Think they'll pull this off, Lyle?" the man behind her

commented to his buddy. "If they do, I'll be back to watch every game."

"You know what I'd pay to see? These boys up against one of those Bloomer Girls' teams."

"A girls' team wearing their bloomers in public?"

"Yeah, ain't you heard of them? They were in the newspaper the other day. They're teams of girls as good as men, and they travel around the country doing exhibition games against men's teams. They put on a real show."

"In bloomers?"

"Well, they can't very well run around bases in a dress."

A smile spread across Emily's face. *Thanks, Lord. That was fast.*

❧

With her healed wrist finally freed from the sling, Emily padded down the path, a rubberized swim bag swinging from her wrist. Only four days ago she'd attended the Owls' game. Now, armed with all the information she needed about one of the Bloomer Girls' teams, excitement bubbled inside her. She could already picture Marguerite's and Lilly's faces when she shared her idea. If the Council Bluffs Equal Suffrage Club could sponsor this game, it would speak volumes for what women were capable of.

Bright sunshine, clear skies, and friends—could the day get any better? She'd even managed to avoid Carter this morning. And since it was the weekend, the beach would be crowded enough that she wouldn't see him there either. A row of honking geese waddled single file across the gravel path as she neared. She giggled and stopped to let them pass.

Marguerite waved at her from the door to the ladies' bathhouse on the lakeshore.

"Where's Lilly?" Emily glanced across the way at a clump of men, who appeared to be laughing uncontrollably in front of the men's bathhouse. She thought she recognized the Manawa Owls team members, though it was hard to tell with them out of uniform. But she knew Carter was not among them.

"Lilly's inside getting ready."

"Good," Emily said. "I have an idea for the club I want to talk to you both about."

Marguerite opened the door to the changing facilities and waited for Emily to pass through. "Can't you just enjoy yourself for one day?"

"I can enjoy myself and still get done what I have to. It's called efficiency."

"It's called boring." Marguerite nudged her toward one of the curtained dressing areas. "Now hurry up. I haven't been swimming all summer."

Drawing a striped serge skirt over her bloomers, Emily talked to her friends through the curtain, explaining her plans for the Bloomer Girls' competition. She pulled the curtain aside and peeked around it. "Wouldn't it be a great way to show women can do whatever a man can do?"

Lilly tied a yellow ribbon below her knee around her black stockings. "If you can get the Owls to agree. I'm not sure most men would want to be shown up by a group of women."

"The women aren't guaranteed to win." Emily stepped from behind the curtain and held out a flower-bedecked bathing cap to Marguerite.

Marguerite helped Emily slip the cap over her bun. "But you sure hope they will. Do you think Carter's team will say yes?"

"I was hoping you'd ask him." Emily tucked the fringe of curls around her face inside the cap. "No one can say no to you."

"It seems to me if anyone has any pull with Carter Stockton, it's you, Miss Emily Graham." Lilly adjusted her sailor collar. "The way he was fawning over you after you fell."

Emily placed her hand on the bathhouse door but didn't turn the knob. "Believe me. Carter thinks I'm more trouble than I'm worth."

No watch was needed for Carter to know he was late again. The boys on the team planned to meet to swim at one this afternoon, and it had to be nearly half past. He hadn't been to this section of the beach in a couple of summers, and chances were, they'd not waited for him. He'd have to change quickly and find them in the water—probably at one of the toboggan slides out in the middle of the lake.

He hurried to the men's bathhouse and swung open the door.

Emily's eyes, wide as saucers, stared back at him from beneath a hat with way too many flowers on it.

Then, before he could react, she slapped his cheek so hard he saw stars.

8

Girls screamed.

Emily gaped at him. "Carter Stockton, what in heaven's name are you doing?"

Marguerite pushed her out of the doorway, and she and Lilly joined Emily outside the bathhouse before slamming its door shut.

Carter rubbed his bright red cheek. "What are you doing in the men's bathhouse?"

Emily propped her hands on her hips. "From the screams of the ladies inside, clearly this is not the men's facility."

Loud guffaws erupted around them as a group of men converged on Carter. A mustached man with black hair parted down the center slapped him on the back. "Good one, huh?"

"Ducky, is this some kind of joke?"

A freckled redhead lifted the sign reading MEN from the nail on the door and replaced it with the sign reading LADIES. Holding his sides, he doubled over in laughter again. "You should have seen your face, Stockton."

"You know these miscreants?" Emily scowled at them.

"They're my teammates." He glared at each of them. "My soon-to-be-deceased teammates."

"Ah, you have to admit it was funny, and no harm was done," the red-haired man managed between chuckles.

Marguerite giggled beside Emily and pointed to the men's bathhouse. "If you boys don't hurry, I think Mrs. Neville is about to get the surprise of her life."

Like crabs on sand, the team members scrambled to the building. Marguerite and Lilly followed to watch the show.

Emily started to leave as well, but Carter caught her arm. His gaze swept her from head to toe, and an appreciative smile seemed to curl his lips. Heat rushed to her cheeks even as she chided herself for such foolish thoughts. Carter Stockton was *not* looking at her that way. Still, she pressed her hand across the exposed flesh above her white sailor collar.

"Since I gave you that scare, Emily, maybe I can make it up to you with some ice cream after we swim. It's the least I could do. I feel really bad about this. Between your wrist and the bad luck with Marion, you've had quite a week."

Her jaw tightened, and she glared at him. Did he feel sorry for her again? *Poor Emily. The girl who couldn't even get a man like Mr. Wormsley to be interested in her.* She didn't need his pity, she didn't need his help, and she certainly didn't need the questions his attentions would elicit from her friends and aunts. She jutted out her chin. "I don't need your mercy social outing."

"But—"

"Go back and play with your friends, Carter. That's what boys do, isn't it?"

Carter wanted to punch something. He'd struck out, and Emily marched away as if he'd threatened to kill her firstborn. The form-fitting striped bathing costume hugged her narrow waist, and the bright yellow, pink, and red flowers on the ridiculous cap bounced with every step. What was with that woman? He'd asked her to join him for ice cream. Simple. Easy. Fun. And she'd called him a boy. A boy!

Fine. If that's how she wanted it. From now on, he'd keep his mouth shut.

"What'd you do?"

Wheeling around, Carter found the diminutive Lilly at his side. "Excuse me?"

Lilly rolled her eyes. "Well, Emily steamed off like a hot teakettle, and it doesn't take a genius to figure out you said something."

"All I did was offer to take her out for ice cream."

"And?"

"I said it was the least I could do. You know, to make up for my mistake after she's had such bad luck this week with Marion Wormsley and her wrist. I feel sorry for her."

Lilly lobbed him on the side of his head with her palm.

He jerked back. "What was that for?"

"Someone needs to knock some sense into you."

"Why? I didn't do anything wrong. I mean besides the door thing, which was an accident."

Lilly sighed. "I'm not going to spell it out."

"What? Why?"

"That"—she poked him in the chest—"is what you need to discover on your own."

Then, for the second time in less than three minutes, a woman stalked away from him.

Emily waded in the waist-deep water toward the toboggan slide with Marguerite and Lilly flanking her. Complete with a bathhouse attached for sled rental and refreshments, the thirty-foot-tall structure sat off the shore of Manhattan Beach, ready to thrill bathers.

As they paddled toward the slide, Emily let the ripples carry away her anger and humiliation. *The least he could do.* The words echoed in her ears. Carter felt sorry for her, and it stung. She didn't want it to, but it did. She hated pity. Everyone felt sorry for her. She could hear them now. *Poor Emily can't cross a room without tripping. She'd drop her own head if it wasn't attached. She'll probably trip down the aisle at her wedding.*

She bit her lip, silencing the voices. No one needed to worry about her wedding. There wasn't going to be one. Marriage was a complication she didn't need, and she had more important things to consider. Later this afternoon, she was speaking on the pavilion steps. The other ladies were joining her, and a rousing speech was necessary for both them and the community.

They reached the dock surrounding the slide's bathhouse and climbed the wood ladder onto the platform.

"Stop right there." Marguerite put her hands on Emily's shoulders. "You need to get rid of whatever it is you have going on in your head. The next hour is for fun."

Emily shrugged. "Maybe I should head back and work on my speech."

Lilly linked her arm in Emily's. "No, ma'am. Marguerite and I don't get away without our little ones very often, and you need a break. Before all your suffrage work, you used to be the one dragging us off to have a good time."

Marguerite's blue eyes sparkled, and Lilly's no-nonsense

expression left little room for argument. Emily laughed. She'd never win with either of them. Besides, they were right. More and more, the suffrage fight had consumed her time. "Okay. Let's go enjoy ourselves."

Plopping a dime on the counter, the three ladies rented a long toboggan from the clerk to share. Giggling, the three of them carried the heavy toboggan through the passageway and up the staircase leading to the slide. At the top, Marguerite sat in the front, and Lilly wiggled into place behind her.

"Your turn." Lilly tilted her head, looking back. "No bolting to practice your speech."

Emily rolled her eyes and eased one stocking-covered foot onto the toboggan. She froze when she heard a familiar voice behind her. Her heart thundered against her rib cage. Carter and his teammates were climbing the stairs. Heat rose from her sailor collar to her flower-covered cap. She grabbed Lilly's shoulders. She couldn't face him again—not yet.

"Emily, be careful."

Lilly's warning came too late. Slipping on the slick wood, Emily shoved the toboggan forward with her foot. Her friends careened down the chute, and she landed with a thud on the deck. Tears pricked her eyes. Her bottom hadn't hurt this bad since her father caught her putting a frog in her brother's pocket.

Laughter surrounded her, accusing her of what she already knew. She was clumsy, plain and simple.

"Emily?"

With hooded eyes, she peered up at Carter standing over her. What she wouldn't give to sink into the water below and never resurface.

He offered his hand and pulled her to her feet. "Everything okay?"

"Yes. I slipped getting on."

"I sort of guessed that." His eyes danced with amusement. "It happens sometimes."

The cleft in his chin deepened with his grin, and he stood there, broad-shouldered and so male she couldn't breathe. Escaping him became a necessity. She whirled, intending to head back down the stairs.

Carter caught her wrist. "You can ride down with me."

More heat flooded her face, and the afternoon sun seemed to pour down with greater intensity. She considered walking away, but the pain in her backside predicted a less than lady-like gait. He'd see her waddle, and her humiliation would double. But riding down the toboggan run with him?

"Carter, I'm not sure."

His eyes darkened. "Is it because of earlier?"

"Aw, ease up on her, Stockton." Ducky stepped forward. "It's not her fault if she doesn't want to be around a cad like you. Walking into ladies' bathhouses and all." Comfortable teasing laced his voice. "She can take my toboggan, and I'll ride down with you." He flopped the toboggan down on the deck and held out his hand. "Will that work, Miss Graham?"

"Yes, thank you very much." She took his hand and gingerly seated herself. Picking up the reins on the toboggan, she turned to nod to Ducky to release her. Instead, she found Carter. Her eyes widened.

"Hold on." The smile had crept back into his voice. "You're about to go on the ride of your life."

The sled lunged forward and her stomach lodged in her throat—not from the ride as much as the unspoken promise Carter's words seemed to hold.

"Do I look all right?" Emily pressed a shaky hand to her stomach. From inside the pavilion, she could see folks gathering at the foot of the stairs. Apparently, word had gotten around about today's speech. She swallowed hard. "I think the butterflies in my stomach have butterflies."

"You look fine." Lilly straightened the patriotic red and white satin banner that lay diagonally across Emily's chest with VOTES FOR WOMEN sewn on in bright blue letters. "And you'll do great. I think this is the biggest crowd we've had so far."

"That's not helping." Emily filled her lungs with lake-scented air. "I guess it's time. Wish me luck."

"You don't need luck, but I'll pray for you." Lilly nudged her in the direction of the steps.

Emily stepped out of the pavilion and scanned the crowd. Although it contained mostly women, a few men stood with their arms firmly crossed over their chests. This wasn't going to be easy, but she hadn't expected it to be.

She lifted her voice. "Ladies and gentleman, or should I say sisters and brothers, hear me. There are wrongs in this country we have in our power to right, and change is within our grasp. It is up to us to reach out and grab hold of the opportunity."

"Go home to your babies!" A burly man in his fifties pushed to the front. "A woman's place is in the home."

Emily stiffened. Should she respond to him, tell him she had no children, or continue with her plans? Deciding it best to ignore the comments, she pressed on. "Allow me to tell you why this fight is of the utmost importance.

"A woman in Davenport who had been repeatedly beaten by her husband, fearing for her life, chose to separate from him. He now has her children, and she has no right to see them.

"A woman in Tabor killed a man in the presence of her husband. She cannot be tried for what she's done, but her husband can.

"A woman, a sister, in Des Moines inherited her parents' farm, and her husband drank it away. He died from his consumption of alcohol and left her penniless."

"That's his God-given right!" the heckler shouted. "She belongs to him."

Nerves and anger tangled inside her. How dare the man? If he kept this up, he'd ruin her speech. She'd never dealt with a heckler before.

Then she spotted Carter shouldering his way through the crowd. He stepped directly behind the heckler. "Let her talk," he said loudly. "I want to hear what the lady has to say."

Emily blinked. What was he doing here? He didn't believe in suffrage. She swallowed hard and willed her voice to come out strong. "You all know of someone who is similar to one of these women. Perhaps you are one of these women."

She let her gaze rest on the woman standing beside the heckler. He lunged toward the stairs. Instinctively, Emily moved away.

Carter clamped a broad hand on the man's shoulder and yanked him back.

Emily's gaze locked on Carter's, and he nodded for her to continue.

She licked her lips. "Personally, I've met many men who would die before they would let anything happen to their wives, sisters, or mothers. Men like those of you listening with an open mind." Her eyes met Carter's for the briefest of seconds, and the butterflies took flight again. "The women in your lives do not worry about being provided or cared for.

"Perhaps your husband fits in this rare category as well—a

man who sees you first as a human being, his partner, his equal. Or perhaps your husband is one of the selfish men who sees his wife as his property to do with as he pleases.

"Until women as a whole are elevated to equal status with men, our country will never become all it should be." Emily punctuated her words with examples of women who had made remarkable contributions and achievements: reformers, artists, entrepreneurs, and career women. Her confidence grew as she spoke, and her voice rose. "These women dared to step out of the sphere assigned to them. They made a choice, and so must each of you—a choice to fight for our right to vote and have a say in our country, our state, and our communities. Only you can take this message back to your towns.

"For a woman to vote is to elevate her in the scale of humanity. And that will carry with it the elevation and well-being of the entire race. So we believe, and so we pray, God speed the day when a woman can stand beside a man and cast her vote!"

Applause erupted along with a few jeers, but to her surprise, the heckler remained quiet. Emily lost sight of Carter as she accepted the well wishes of several women.

"You make me want this as much as you do." An elderly woman pressed a dollar into Emily's hand. "For the fight, dear."

"Thank you, ma'am." Emily started down the steps. Olivia DeSoto, with her two ever-present followers, waited at the bottom. Seeing no way to escape, Emily smiled a halfhearted acknowledgment.

Olivia closed her parasol. "I must admit I was surprised you managed to handle this so well."

"If that's a compliment, I'll take it." Even Olivia's rudeness wouldn't crush her buoyant spirit this time. "Perhaps next time, you'd care to speak."

Olivia glanced at her two cohorts. "I wouldn't want to dishearten you, dear."

Ooooooh, that woman! How could she shatter the moment with one jab? Emily lifted her chin, refusing to let Olivia see that the hurtful words had touched her. "I'm sure, if you're the speaker, I'll have no worry, but thank you again for your support."

"Humph." With the dramatic flair of an actress on stage, Olivia spun and strode away.

A man chuckled behind Emily and she turned. Carter. She should have guessed.

He walked over to her, his gait wide and easy, and leaned casually against the banister. "Guess you told her."

"She has a way of bringing out the worst in me."

"And here I thought that was my job." He rubbed his cheek and grinned.

A smile curled her lips. "You came to hear the speech."

"And you're surprised." He plucked a long blade of grass from beside the steps. "You made some excellent points."

"Enough to convince you to change your mind?"

"Not necessarily." His eyes sparkled with mischief in the afternoon sun. "Sorry about the heckler."

"I could've handled it myself, but I still appreciate your intervention."

"Do you appreciate it enough to have supper with me to-night at Louie's?" The cleft in his chin deepened with the crooked grin.

"Alone?"

He glanced toward Olivia and her two friends now speaking to Marguerite and Lilly. "Unless you'd like to invite Mrs. DeSoto."

"Carter, I . . . I . . . can't." Her cheeks flamed. Part of her wanted to leap at the offer, but only moments before, he'd admitted he hadn't changed his mind about suffrage. And earlier today he'd asked her to join him out of pity for her blundering ways. He was out of her league, they didn't agree on the important matters of life, and she'd only embarrass herself further if she accompanied him.

"I don't understand."

"That's the problem."

Hiking up her skirts, she hurried up the pavilion's steps. She had to get away before she said yes to the biggest mistake of her life.

Carter thrust his hands into his pockets as Emily disappeared inside the pavilion. Asking her had been a mistake—an enormous mistake.

"Hey." Ducky strolled down the sidewalk. "I've been searching for you. What have you been doing, and why do you look like you just struck out?"

"I guess you could say I did. I asked Emily Graham out for supper. She turned me down."

"Then ask her again. That's what I always do. I guess this is a new problem for you, though, huh?"

Carter shrugged. "I asked her to ice cream earlier today too. I can't get her out of my head, but it's probably better this way."

Ducky chuckled. "Maybe so. Maybe not. But I think you've got that count wrong. Sounds to me like you have two strikes. You've got one more time at bat."

"What's the use? She'd rather shoot me than spend a moment alone with me." He punched his palm. He hated not winning. If he could get her to say yes just once, then she'd see he wasn't the ogre she made him out to be.

"In that case, want to come with some of the boys and me to the Midway?"

That was it. The Midway.

"Ducky, you're a genius!"

He'd make her an offer she couldn't refuse.

9

Perched on a park bench, Carter watched for Emily's re-appearance. She couldn't stay inside the pavilion forever.

He didn't have to wait long. When she emerged, she paused at the top of the stairs before beginning her descent. Afraid his sudden presence might frighten her and cause her to slip, he waited beside the last step with his back to her. Once she was firmly on even ground, he faced her. "Hi, Emily."

Her breath caught. "Why are you still here?"

"Walk with me?" When she hesitated, he quickly added, "Please."

Despite her obvious misgivings, she fell in step beside him. "You didn't answer my question. What are you doing here?"

"We're going somewhere together."

She halted. "We most certainly are not!"

He grinned and met her wide, moss-green eyes. "I'm not taking no for an answer this time."

"Carter—" The resolve in her voice weakened. "We can't do this."

"We can, and we are." He took her hand and tucked it in the crook of his elbow.

She yanked her hand away. "Just where do you think you're taking me?"

"To the shooting gallery." Carter crossed his arms over his chest. "Then, if you want to kill me, at least you'll have a gun."

"Does it shoot real bullets?"

"Yes."

She raised an eyebrow. "In that case, it sounds fun."

❦

Nestled at the east end of Lake Manawa, the Midway wasn't far from the Grand Plaza and pavilion, but to Emily it seemed like a mile as they walked in silence. Lively organ music from the Midway contrasted with the anger pumping in her chest. The audacity of Carter Stockton. She'd told him no—not once, but twice. Now, mixed with the irritation, her nerves tingled in the sweetness of his presence.

Even without looking, she could feel his confident gait and broad shoulders beside her. And she hadn't forgotten the feel of his muscles beneath her hand when he'd placed it in the crook of his arm.

She risked a glance at his face. As usual, coffee-colored curls tumbled from beneath his hat. Carter Stockton was too handsome for his own good. She should have flatly refused. Although the more ill at ease she felt, the more the prospect of shooting him tempted her.

Why was he doing this now? She'd made it clear she didn't need or want his well-intentioned offers. So why did he insist on her company?

"I'm glad you came." His baritone voice, warm like hot chocolate on a cold day, broke the silence, and his lips curved in a genuine smile.

Emily pressed a hand to her uncooperative throat. "We'll have to hurry. My grandmother will be worried."

"No, she won't. This morning I asked her for permission to take you out for ice cream or to supper, whichever opportunity presented itself. I wanted to spend some time with you. She agreed as long as it was still daylight."

This morning? Her mind reeled. But that was before the swimming incident. He'd planned this. He actually wanted to be with her.

"Do you want one?" He pointed toward one of the booths.

Blinking, she took a moment to consider his question. Around them, hawkers shouted for the crowds to come try their games of chance. One claimed he could guess anyone's age. The hawker nearest them held up a porcelain figurine and tried to get the men to win one for their lady by throwing a baseball at three stacked milk bottles.

Carter grinned. "Say the word and it's yours."

"That would hardly be fair—you being a pitcher and all."

"Step right up!" The man pointed at Carter. "You look like a fine young man. Don't you want to impress your girl?"

"Impressing her might be harder than you think, but I'll give it a try." Carter winked at her. "What do you say?"

Unable to resist the boyish grin on his face, she nodded.

Carter passed the man a nickel, picked up the baseball, and bounced it a few times in his palm.

The hawker set two more balls on the plank in front of him. "You get three tries to knock them all down."

With a knowing glance at Emily, Carter drew his arm back and launched the ball. The milk jars clattered off the wooden pedestal onto the straw below.

The gap-toothed hawker shook Carter's hand. "Good job, son. Here you go. Give this to your gal."

Carter accepted the prize and turned to Emily. "You heard the man."

She traced the fine features of the porcelain match holder with her finger. It depicted a boy trying on his father's boots. "It's lovely. Thank you." She tingled inside. No one had ever won her any of the trinkets before.

A freckle-faced boy darted between them, knocking the figurine from her grasp. Both Emily and Carter lunged for it, and their heads collided. The figurine tumbled to the dirt and one of the boots broke off.

Emily gasped and pressed her hand to her head.

Rubbing his own head, Carter scooped up the broken pieces. "I'll win you another one."

"No, that's all right." She bit her lip as she adjusted her hat, set askew in the collision. "I'm such a butterfingers. The next one would probably slip through my hands too."

"It wasn't your fault, Emily. It was the boy's. Are you okay?"

"I'm fine. I've got a pretty hard head."

"I can believe that." Chuckling, he deposited the two pieces in the pocket of his coat and offered her his arm.

This time she held her breath and slipped her hand in place. Her pulse quickened, but she didn't let go.

"Hawkins Shooting Gallery is down the street. Still want to shoot me for dragging you here?"

She couldn't let him off that easily. "I'll settle for a small flesh wound."

"Make sure you hit my right arm then. I need the left to pitch."

They strolled down the Midway until they reached the long, narrow brick gallery at the far end. Carter held the door, and she stepped inside. The report of rifles made her step back, but Carter pressed a hand to the small of her back and urged her forward.

An outdoor mural lined the back wall of the gallery. In front of it, a row of cast-iron ducks, squirrels, and rabbits moved steadily on a chain while two young men took aim and fired. A bull's-eye spun in a circle behind the figures. The explosion of gunpowder overpowered the sound of the engine, which kept the chain moving, and filled the air with a peppery sulfuric scent. An occasional metallic ping indicated the men had hit the target.

Emily gasped. "What's the boy doing out there?"

"That's Mr. Hawkins's boy. He keeps the steam engine going."

"But he could get hurt."

Carter laughed. "Only if you shoot him. Have you ever fired a gun before?"

Emily shook her head. Suddenly she found the idea of a weapon in her hands quite terrifying. With her luck, she might end up wounding Carter for real or, worse, accidentally shooting the child. "Maybe I should just watch."

"Not on your life. Come on. I'll teach you." As soon as the two patrons left, Carter led her to the plank where the guns lay. Reaching in his pocket, he furnished the owner with two dimes. "Hello, Mr. Hawkins. We need two of your best rifles."

"They're all the same, Carter."

"Ah, but you and I both know some are sighted better."

Mr. Hawkins gave a full-bellied laugh and pointed to the second and fourth ones lying on the divider. "Those two ought to work for you."

Emily took a step back. "Why don't you go first?"

"I don't think so, Miss Suffragette." Carter picked up his gun and pushed a second rifle into her hands. Immediately, he angled the barrel of Emily's gun toward the ground. "The first rule of using a gun is never to aim at anything you don't plan to shoot. And while we joked about you killing me, I'd really like to take you to supper tonight, and I can't do that if I'm dead."

"Sorry." Her cheeks warmed again.

"That's okay. These are Winchester pump rifles, which means to shoot them, you have to push the magazine forward like this." He shoved the wooden cylinder up on the barrel and put a bullet in. "They shoot .22 shorts. They'd shoot a hole through a man, so remember to keep it aimed at the targets."

"You do realize you're taking your life in your hands."

"You'll do great. Ready?"

When she didn't move, he turned her. "Emily, you need to spread your, uh, stance and stand more like a man."

She shifted her feet wider apart. "This isn't very ladylike, Carter."

"But it will help you hit the little squirrels."

She flinched.

"Let me guess. You like squirrels."

"And bunnies."

He chuckled. "Now, put the butt of the gun against your right shoulder."

"Like this?"

"Sort of." He stepped behind her and raised the gun to the correct position, his large hands covering her own.

Her back pressed against his chest, and she felt every breath he took. Emily's stomach warmed and lurched all at once. Never before had she been this close to a man.

"Relax," he whispered in her ear.

She jerked and fired a shot in the air. The bullet pinged off the ceiling, and the rebound threw her against Carter.

He caught her and turned her around to face him. "Emily, what are you doing?"

"I—I—"

Mr. Hawkins roared with laughter. "I think a better question is what were *you* doing?"

Carter shot him a glare. "Let's try again." He resumed the position behind her, his breath hot on her neck. "This time, slowly squeeze the trigger."

Clamping her eyes shut, she complied.

The shot ricocheted off the ceiling.

A loud guffaw erupted from Mr. Hawkins. "Hey, Carter, you'd better give her rule two." The owner shielded his eyes with his palm.

Releasing her, Carter came around to face her. "Did you close your eyes?"

"You didn't tell me not to."

Carter grinned and shook his head. "Emily, keep your eyes open. Go ahead. Try again."

To her relief, he took a step back. She lifted the rifle in place, aimed at the bull's-eye, and fired. A familiar *ping* sounded, and then a little organ began to play a joyful tune.

"I did it!" She bounced up and down.

Carter grabbed the barrel of the gun. "Emily, remember rule one about how to use a gun?"

"That wasn't rule one. Rule one was never to point at anything you don't plan to shoot."

He lifted his eyebrows and nodded toward the boy who had stood in her line of fire as she celebrated.

"Oh, I see what you mean. I wouldn't want to shoot him by accident." She lowered the barrel of the gun and pointed it toward the floor. "Now that I can shoot, do you want to have a contest?"

"Emily, you made one shot. It doesn't make you a marks-man."

"Markswoman." Emily raised her gun again. "And I think I like shooting things."

He laughed. "Why doesn't that surprise me?"

10

"Stop right there, Katherine Graham!"

Kate picked up her pace, but Ethel's skirts continued to swish with tick-tock precision behind her.

"Don't you dare ignore me."

With a sigh, Kate stopped and turned. She spotted Millie trying to catch up. Kate released a slow breath with more patience than she felt. Sometimes her sisters tended to mind everyone's business except their own. Holding out a wicker basket on the tip of her finger, she let it swing back and forth. "I'm not ignoring you, Ethel. If you two would like to join me in gathering flowers, then come right along. I want to get a bouquet before the rain comes in."

"Flowers for the table?" Panting, Millie waved a hand in front of her perspiration-dotted face. "What a wonderful idea."

"I thought so." Kate continued down the path until she reached a thicket of wild rosebushes, their five-petaled pink blossoms winking at the sun.

Ethel propped her hands on narrow hips. "Katherine, enough. I want to know if you are encouraging Emily's carousing with that Stockton boy."

"She is not carousing." Kate snipped a stem and tucked the bloom in her basket.

"But you gave him permission to court her?"

Kate glared at Millie, who shrugged. Only her youngest sister had been around when Carter spoke to her concerning Emily. She should have known she'd not keep the information to herself. "He asked if he could take her out for ice cream or supper, depending on when the opportunity to ask developed."

"And you agreed?" Ethel pursed her lips. "You, of all people, should know better."

"What I know is Carter has been kind to Emily." Kate pointed the tip of her scissors at her sister. "And he's expressed an interest in getting to know her better. Aren't you the ones who want her to find a husband? I'd think you'd both be quite happy with this turn of events."

"But that boy's father did everything in his power to destroy your security after Ethan died."

"You're absolutely right. Angus Stockton was a ruthless businessman, but that does not mean his son is like him."

"And it doesn't mean he's not."

Millie held out a well-shaped bloom for Kate to snip. "Perhaps his plan was to finagle his way into our family."

"By deliberately knocking Emily down? Yes, that makes perfect sense." She rolled her eyes, and her curt tone bespoke of the irritation grating on her. "I would certainly be more apt to let him see to my financial affairs because he injured my granddaughter. Listen to yourselves."

Ethel divided the bush with her hands and came face-to-face with Kate. "But he does have control of your finances now."

"He is overseeing them *because I asked*." Kate straightened and thrust her scissors in the basket.

Pinning her sisters in place with her gaze, she studied each of them. All their years together made them easy to read. Ethel, lips pulled in a thin line, had judged Carter, tried him, and found him guilty. Millie, worry creasing her brow, obviously feared Kate had made a grievous error in judgment.

Kate sighed. She couldn't convince them Carter Stockton was worthy of their trust. Only he could do that.

She squared her shoulders. "As for Carter and Emily, I hope they have a good time."

"Oh, so do I." Millie sighed wistfully. "He's such a sweet boy."

Ethel sniffed. "But remember, dear sisters, the apple doesn't fall far from the tree."

❧

By the time Emily had finished her pulled pork sandwich from one of the Midway's lunch counters, the sun sat low on a bluff. Hues of pink and purple stained the dusky sky. A breeze twisted the silvery leaves of the maples and carried a whiff of popcorn from one of the street vendor's carts.

"I guess I'd better take you home." Carter, who sat beside her on a park bench, wadded the waxed paper from his sandwich into a ball and stood up. "After all, I did make a promise, and the last thing I want right now is to get your grandmother angry."

She dabbed her mouth with her handkerchief. "Right now?"

He held out his hand and kept hold of Emily's after he

pulled her to her feet. "I want to be on her good side since I'd like to see you again. That is, if you want to."

She dropped her gaze to the cobbled path at her feet. "I've truly enjoyed today, but I don't know. We're so different."

"Emily." Placing a finger beneath her chin, he tipped her face up. "Differences can be good."

"And sometimes they can drive a wedge between people."

"I'm willing to take a chance, aren't you?" His caramel eyes flickered with the dare.

She ducked away, taking a few steps toward the path.

He fell in step beside her. "You're just contrary by nature."

"I am not."

He raised an eyebrow. "Prove it."

"How am I supposed to do that?"

"Say yes."

She stopped on the path and turned to him. "To what?"

"Go to a play with me Monday evening." He paused. "Unless you're afraid."

"Me? Of you?" She yanked her gloves on and met his eyes. A cocky grin creased his face. Emily sighed. "Fine. I'll go."

"Good." He chuckled, soft and low.

"What?"

"That was easier than I expected."

She slapped his arm. "Carter, I was being serious. We're very different."

"I happen to think we're more alike than you realize." He took hold of her elbow and urged her toward the dock.

"How?"

"That's what we're going to start finding out—Monday night."

No amount of prodding made Carter disclose what he meant as they made their way to the dock. Once seated beneath the canopy of the electric launch, she glanced at him. Sure of himself, he sat with his face to the wind as the boat left the shore. It wasn't an arrogant confidence, though. Rather, it was a quiet acceptance of who he was, and it made her like him all the more.

Her heart skipped a beat. Was she making a mistake? Her head told her yes. He was everything she was not. Their beliefs, their futures, even their families were so different. But the warmth pooling in her heart told her to take a chance.

When he cocked his head in her direction and grinned, the last of her resolve melted with the dying daylight. She knew her answer. This once, she'd cast her vote with him.

11

"There must be some kind of mistake." Carter pushed the ledger across the Grahams' outdoor breakfast table. The canopy of trees overhead rustled as Mrs. Graham leaned close, and a few maple seeds whirled to the ground. He pointed to the column of figures. "The bank's quarterly statement isn't matching the book here at all."

Mrs. Graham poured a second cup of coffee from a pansy-covered china pot. "I'm sure my books are correct. Perhaps the bank is in error."

"I certainly hope so. I'll check into it tomorrow." Even the breeze, fresh this morning after last night's rain, did little to chase his concerns away. Carter closed the book and glanced toward the door of the cabin as it squeaked open. Aunt Millie and Aunt Ethel, each dressed in printed cotton morning dresses, stepped off the stoop and hobbled across the damp grass.

He kept his gaze on the door, waiting for Emily to join

them. No sign of her. Disappointment hardened his jaw. He stood and pulled out chairs for the two women joining them.

"Emily's not here. She got up with the chickens this morning." Aunt Millie beamed like a schoolgirl. "Not that we have chickens. We don't, of course."

Aunt Ethel sipped from her cup. "I'm not sure where Emily was off to."

"Suffrage work," Mrs. Graham answered and smiled at Carter. "You enjoyed your time together?"

"Yes, ma'am. Is it obvious?"

Aunt Millie patted his arm. "I noticed at the tent services yesterday. You seemed to pay more attention to her than you did to Brother Fossen. Besides, we have a lot of years of experience observing young love."

"I wouldn't go that far." Carter's cheeks burned.

"No, of course not." Mrs. Graham seemed to be stifling a smile. She dumped a generous spoonful of sugar in her cup and stirred.

"Not yet anyway." Aunt Millie twittered.

Clearing his throat, Carter leaned forward. "Ma'am, in view of this conversation, I'd like to ask for permission to escort your granddaughter to the play at the Dohany Opera House this evening."

"So, you would like to court our Emily?" Aunt Ethel's mouth formed an upside-down *u* as she spread her starched napkin across her lap. "Do you think that's wise, Kate?"

"I believe my sister is concerned with your intentions." Mrs. Graham poured cream into her cup.

"I assure you they are honorable, ladies. I've met very few women as remarkable as Emily."

Aunt Millie clapped her hands. "A marvelous declaration, and I volunteer."

"Volunteer?" Carter blinked.

"To chaperone, of course. If you're going out after dark and into town, Emily must have a chaperone."

Aunt Ethel huffed. "I'd hardly call your presence adequate supervision. You'll get so involved in the play, you'll forget to protect Emily's virtue."

Carter swallowed the bubble of laughter threatening to surface. He was the one who needed protecting—from the two of them.

"I will not," Aunt Millie protested. "And Carter, wouldn't you prefer my company over my stuffy sister's?"

"I'd be honored if all three of you ladies would join us."

"Nonsense." Mrs. Graham waved her hand in the air. "Ethel and Millie can both attend with you if they must, but I will be here—enjoying the peace and quiet."

Exchanging a knowing grin with Mrs. Graham, Carter tapped his pen on the table. It was hard enough to handle Emily's feistiness, but adding her two aunts to the equation certainly complicated matters. This may not turn out to be the evening of discovery he'd been hoping for.

Maybe it wasn't worth all the trouble. After all, he should be concentrating on baseball. They had another game coming up in a few days with a tougher team than they'd faced yet.

As if on cue, Emily strolled up the lakeside path toward the cottage with a daisy in one hand and a parasol in the other. Beneath a wide-brimmed hat topped with a fluffy black plume and satin roses, Emily's long, fawn-colored hair, streaked by the sun, hung loosely down her back. Her black and white striped walking skirt swung with each step, displaying both her ankles and heeled shoes. A wide belt cinched the ruffled white shirt and hugged her narrow waist.

Her steady, carefree stride stuttered when she caught sight

of him. She stumbled but caught herself and readjusted her shirtwaist. Then she marched toward him as if the near mishap was entirely his fault.

He grinned and his heart pounded in his chest. Nothing stopped this woman. Nothing.

So she liked daisies. What other secrets did she have?

A most unsettling truth took hold. He wanted to discover them all. And not only was it worth a few minutes of discomfort under the meddlesome aunts' scrutiny to be with Emily Graham, but he also had a sneaking suspicion she was worth a whole lot more.

He crossed the grassy area to join her.

"Carter." Her momentary anger seemed to have ebbed, and the corners of her lips curved sweetly. "I'm surprised you're still here. I thought you'd be at practice by now."

He tugged his baseball cap off his head and held it in his hands. "I wanted to speak to you about the play tonight. Your aunts have graciously offered to accompany us."

The blood left her face and her voice came out squeaky. "Both of them?"

He chuckled. "It'll be fine. I promise."

"You don't know them like I do."

Dipping his head slightly, he peered into her moss-green eyes. "Do you love them?"

"Of course I do."

"Then I look forward to getting to know both of them better—and you." He nodded toward the table. "I'll pick all three of you up at six thirty. And Emily, have a little faith."

❧

Rolling her stocking over her calf, Emily gently tugged on the wool toe until the undergarment gave way and slipped from her foot. She tossed it on the bank beside the other. She lifted her hand to shield her eyes from the sun and scanned the beach in front of her. Manhattan Beach, as the area had been named after its famous Eastern cousin, was dotted with bathers. A couple of pink-cheeked children caught her eye. Two boys giggled as they buried their sister neck-deep in the sand. Their mother lounged in a deck chair, watching them.

"Over here, Emily!"

She followed the sound and spotted Marguerite and her four-year-old Tate wading along the lake's edge. Tate, as blond as his mother, grasped a stick in one hand and sat on his haunches in the water. He seemed intent on spearing something.

Emily balled her skirts in her hand, crossed the sand, and dipped her toes into the tepid water. "What are you looking for, Taters?"

He jumped up when he heard the familiar nickname and threw two wet arms around her legs. "Aunt Emily!"

"Tate!" Marguerite laughed and pried him off. "You mustn't get Aunt Emily all wet."

"I'm okay. Besides, his hug was worth it."

"Want to help me catch minnows?" He grinned at her hopefully, revealing two dimples set deep in his chubby cheeks.

"You're catching them with your stick?"

"No, ma'am. I got a can."

She laughed and felt one of the silvery fish brush her ankle. "Maybe later. I need to talk to your mama for a minute first."

"Okay." Tate swung the stick in the water, sending a spray on both of them.

Marguerite wiped her face. "Tate, be careful!"

"Mama, it's water. You're supposed to get wet at the lake. Just like baf time."

Both women grinned and watched him resume his search with stick and can in hand.

A gust of wind blew a section of hair across Marguerite's face. She tucked it behind her ear. "I heard you spent Saturday afternoon with Carter Stockton at the Midway."

"Who told you?"

"So it's true?"

Emily's cheeks flushed hot. "I guess I can't deny it."

"Let's sit down on the sand and talk. Like when we were girls." Marguerite admonished Tate to stay close before she selected a spot in the sand.

Emily sat beside her, arranged her skirt, and dug her toes past the hot top sand, deep into the cool, wet layers. Within minutes, Marguerite managed to prod all of the pertinent details out of her concerning her outing with Carter. She lapsed into a fit of laughter when Emily said she'd nearly killed him by accident at the shooting gallery.

Marguerite wrapped her arms around her knees and sighed. "Oh my, Emily. I did need this good news today."

"Why? Is something wrong? Is Trip okay?"

"Yes, he's fine." She glanced at Tate and wiped a tear from her cheek. "Remember when I told you we've been trying for quite a while now to have another baby?"

"Yes."

"Well, it's not going to happen again this month."

"Oh." Emily drew a stick figure in the sand. "I'm sorry. What does Trip say?"

"You know him. He says, 'Maggie, I realize this isn't your usual way of doing things, but you've got to let God be God.'"

Emily smiled at her friend. "Does that make you mad?"

"Because he's right?" Marguerite tucked the strand of blowing hair behind her ear again. "No. It's still not easy

99

to let go of control, but I'm learning God does a better job putting my life together than I ever did." She released her knees and leaned back on her elbows. "Now, before I let you sidetrack me completely, I want to know how you feel about Carter and when you're going to see him next."

"I don't know if I feel anything about him. It's not like I think about him all the time."

"Is that a fact?" Marguerite pointed to Emily's stick figure drawing. Around the original drawing, a baseball diamond lay etched in the sand.

"It's simply a sketch." Emily blurred the picture with her hand. She met her friend's grin and matched it with one of her own. "He's fun to be with, and I have to admit I enjoyed our time. But—"

"But what? He's handsome, intelligent, and clearly thoughtful. What is there to stop you?"

"We're so different. He's hit home runs, and I've done mortal damage with a croquet mallet. He has this unnerving calm about him, and I can rant about an injustice at the drop of a hat. And worst of all, he doesn't believe in a woman's right to vote."

Tate trotted across the sand with his can and jabbed the can under Emily's nose. A set of bulging eyes stared back at her, and a loud croak made her jerk back.

"I named her Croaky 'cause she's so loud."

"You think this bullfrog is a girl?" Emily ruffled his hair.

"Yep, and now I'm gonna go find her a husband, 'cause I don't want her to be lonely. You get lonely, Aunt Emily? I can find you a husband too."

The image of a bullfrog groom filled her mind, and she chuckled. Did everyone have to make her lack of marital bliss their business?

100

Marguerite hugged his waist. "Tate, Aunt Emily is fine like she is. You go on now and find Mr. Croaky."

Emily watched the boy, so much like his father, skip down to the water. "Do you really believe I'm fine like I am—even without a man? You don't see me as not being complete?"

"You? Heavens no! Look at you, Emily. You've got a whole world of work to do, and I can see you working for Carrie Chapman Catt herself in Washington DC, like you've always wanted." She stood up and shook the sand from her skirt. "Now, about Carter and suffrage. You could always convince him. He was at the rally. Even if he doesn't support the cause, he seems to support you."

Emily took the hand Marguerite offered and stood up as well. "We're going to a play tonight—with Aunt Millie and Aunt Ethel."

"That ought to be fun." She snickered. "Next time, why don't you ask Trip and me to go with you as chaperones? The four of us would have fun together."

"If there is a next time. It's hard for me to imagine what he sees in me or how we'll get past our different suffrage views. I could never be with anyone who didn't understand how important it is for women to have the right to vote. It means too much to me."

Marguerite draped an arm over her shoulders. "Emily, this is going to be hard for you to hear. But, my friend, you have to let God be God."

<hr>

The three-story Dohany Opera House mocked Emily from the corner of Broadway. The theater's fine arched windows and Italianate, brocaded cornice only reminded her of how inadequate she felt in this world—a world where fine ladies like Olivia DeSoto reigned.

It wasn't a matter of wealth. Emily had that. Her orchid silk gown, with its exquisite gold piping curling in loops on the front, was as fine as any woman's could be. It wasn't a matter of upbringing. Her mother had patiently instructed her in all of the social arts, and she'd been to this very theater dozens of times. Even now, if she closed her eyes, she could picture the parquet floors, the sparkling gas jet chandeliers, and the heavy velvet curtains.

No, that wasn't what made her feel like an outsider. Her discomfort came from not wanting to wrestle for the same things as the Olivias of the world. She didn't want material things or prestige, and she didn't understand those who did.

Give her a soapbox any day with a worthy fight, and then she'd feel at home.

She sighed and smoothed her skirt. At least tonight she'd better be as good an actress as those on stage.

"You look beautiful, Emily." Carter pulled the carriage to a stop, climbed down, and came around to her side.

Though it was hard to take his compliment at face value, his dark eyes brimmed with honesty. As he lifted her down from the carriage, Emily caught sight of the playbill posted on the front of the theater. "We're seeing Ibsen's *A Doll's House*? But that's about—"

"I know." His tone held a hint of mischief, and his lips turned up at the corners in an easy grin. He turned to assist her aunts. "Ladies."

"Well, I don't know what it's about." Aunt Ethel humphed. "And it had better not be one of those tasteless vaudeville acts."

"It's not, Auntie. It's a dramatic play."

Aunt Millie nearly threw herself into Carter's arms. He caught her and easily set her on the ground.

"How perfect." Aunt Millie continued to cling to his bicep. "You know, I once performed the part of Juliet in Shakespeare's *Romeo and Juliet*."

"Performed?" Aunt Ethel's tone was terse. "You read the part aloud at school."

Hurt marred Aunt Millie's round face, and Emily's heart pinched for her dear aunt.

"And I bet you were wonderful." Carter winked at Aunt Millie after he handed the reins to one of the stable boys.

Emily fought to contain a giggle.

Aunt Ethel scowled. "Well, let's not stand around lollygagging."

"You heard your aunt." Carter offered Emily his arm. "Besides, I can't wait to show you off to everyone."

Finding his last statement both hard to believe and hard to ignore, Emily's cheeks warmed. Moments later, with her two aunts in tow, Emily entered the theater on the arm of a handsome athlete . . . only to come face-to-face with Mrs. Olivia DeSoto.

"My, isn't it a surprise to find you here, Emily?" Dressed in a showy pink gown, Olivia raked her gaze over Emily's attire, then studied Carter from head to toe. "And who is your escort? A cousin from out of town?"

Without thinking, Emily dug her fingers into Carter's arm. He covered her hand.

"Darling, don't you recognize Angus Stockton's son?" Mr. DeSoto, a stout man with a thick beard, stuck out his hand. "I don't believe we've been formally introduced. I'm William DeSoto. I work in your brother's bank."

The muscles of Carter's arm tensed beneath Emily's hand.

"I've seen you there during my visits home from college, but I must correct you. It's my father's bank—not my brother's."

"Technically, I guess that's true. For now. And what do you do, Mr. Stockton?"

"I'm a baseball player with the Manawa Owls. The pitcher."

"Honestly? And you're out with . . . Emily?" Olivia made no attempt to hide the disbelief in her voice.

Emily opened her mouth to speak, but Carter interrupted. "Yes, I've been lucky enough to snag the beautiful and mysterious lady of the lake. Now, if you'll excuse us. We should be going. I'd hate to miss the opening curtain."

"Yes, of course." Mr. DeSoto looked over Carter's shoulder. "Darling, can you wait here a minute? I believe I see someone I need to speak to."

Olivia stuck out her lip. Tears filled her sapphire-blue eyes. "But what about—"

He patted her arm dismissively and strode toward another group.

"I'm sorry." Emily reached for her hand. "I'm sure he'll return momentarily, before the opening curtain."

Jerking away, Olivia tipped her chin in the air. "My husband is an important member of the community. He has other obligations." She glanced at Carter. "As a Stockton, I'm sure you understand the importance of such connections. Oh, I forgot, you don't work in your father's bank, do you?"

If Carter hadn't tugged her away, Emily would have delivered a dissertation that would make Olivia DeSoto think twice about insulting anyone she cared about. Sure, her words were sugary sweet, but the implication that Carter was somehow a failure because he didn't work at the bank came through all the same. Someone needed to teach Olivia some manners.

Wait a minute. Did she just defend Carter? Hadn't she herself referred to him as a boy playing games? When had those feelings changed?

The truth struck her and spread like a creeping vine inside. Her feelings for Carter had not only taken seed, they'd taken root. The warmth spread through her, and she realized his presence seemed to be the only sunlight the feelings needed to grow.

Carter stopped at the door dividing the foyer and theater and handed the usher their tickets. The man bowed slightly. "This way, sir."

Aunt Millie huffed behind them as they hurried down the aisle. "Is Mrs. DeSoto one of your suffragists?"

"I'm afraid so." Emily released a slow breath. The last thing she wanted to do was let anger ruin the evening.

The usher directed them toward the rows in front of the gilded stage. "You have two seats in row four and two in row eight."

"Thank you." Carter waited until the usher departed. "I believe Mrs. DeSoto suffers from the green-eyed monster."

Aunt Millie applauded. "Shakespeare's *Othello*, Act 3. 'Beware, my lord, of jealousy; it is the green-eyed monster which doth mock.'"

"Her eyes were blue." Aunt Ethel scowled. "And her manners were insufferable."

Emily let her hand drop from Carter's elbow. "You think she's jealous? Of what?"

"You really don't know, do you?" He chuckled and held up the four tickets, two in each hand. "So, would you ladies like the seats in row four or eight? I'm sorry I couldn't secure four side by side at such a late date."

"I think we should take the ones behind." Aunt Ethel studied the two areas. "That way we can properly chaperone."

Aunt Millie slipped two tickets from Carter's hand. "We'll take the front so you two can have some privacy. Come along, Ethel."

Emily waited until her grumbling aunt departed before she giggled. "You have truly been a good sport about all this. First them, and now Olivia."

His gold-flecked eyes bore into hers, melting her concerns. "Emily, it's all worth it."

She swallowed. "Maybe we should sit down."

With a sweep of his arm toward their seats, he smiled. "After you."

•

Slipping into the plush velvet seat beside Emily, Carter removed the playbill from the inside pocket of his tailcoat and opened it. He glanced at Emily, who appeared to be nervously fiddling with her program, and his heart warmed.

How refreshing she was. So many of the young women he'd met used their wiles to promote their personal agendas. They had their futures all neatly wrapped up with a wedding ring–sized bow.

But not Emily. And while she looked lovely in her purple sleeveless gown and long white gloves drawn up to her elbows, it was her unassuming nature that captivated him. She seemed to have no idea why Olivia DeSoto was jealous of her, but he certainly did. Emily faced everything with an infectious passion.

His lips curved upward. If he hadn't dragged her away from Olivia, he might have seen that passion released full force.

"Carter, why did you pick this play? There are two other theaters in Council Bluffs and more in Omaha. Not to mention the shows at the lake."

"You don't like Ibsen?"

"No, I do. The point is, I don't think you will."

He closed his playbill. "Do you remember what tonight is about?"

"Being mortified by my aunts in public?" Her eyes sparkled in the chandelier's light.

"No, it's about us discovering our similarities."

"And you think a play addressing how unfairly a woman is treated in the home will do that?"

The lights dimmed and the crowd quieted. As the heavy velvet curtains spilled open, he pressed his lips to her ear. "I guess we'll see."

12

"That was the most ridiculous piece of drivel I've ever witnessed. Nothing is more holy than the covenant of marriage, and that play made a mockery of it." Aunt Ethel's nonstop diatribe continued.

Emily suppressed a moan. Since it was growing dark, Carter had opted to leave the carriage in town and take the ladies back to the lake by streetcar. Now they were making the final leg of the journey across the lake in one of the electric launch boats.

She shivered as the lake breeze licked her heated skin.

"Are you cold?" Carter asked, slipping his arm around her shoulder.

Aunt Ethel cleared her throat and frowned. "We'll have none of that, Mr. Stockton."

He withdrew his arm—after pulling Emily a bit closer to his side and taking her hand. Her aunt didn't seem to notice.

"I know you paid a handsome price for those tickets, Mr. Stockton, but I think you should go demand your money back," Aunt Ethel droned on. "I find it simply incredulous Nora abandoned her husband and children."

Emily pressed a palm to her churning stomach, her emotions as mixed up as those of the main character her aunt mentioned. While she found the play thought provoking, something about it unnerved her. She actually found herself agreeing with her aunt on some level.

"Leaving her children has folks everywhere up in arms," Carter said. The boat dipped, and he squeezed Emily's hand. "What did you think?"

Her voice came out shaky. "I'm not yet certain."

"It sure makes you look at things differently."

His words faded as the captain piloted the launch next to the dock, called out orders, and tossed a line to a waiting dock assistant.

Once the boat was secured, Carter stood and extended his hand to Aunt Millie. "Here we are. Safe and sound."

The elderly lady wobbled, and Carter caught her thick waist.

Aunt Millie giggled. "You're a wonderful companion. Thank you for letting us tag along."

"It was my pleasure." He helped her out of the boat and then assisted Aunt Ethel before returning for Emily.

Emily slipped her hand in his and relished the feeling of it. She'd not slip or fall with Carter by her side. He'd see to it.

The four of them gathered on the dock. Aunt Ethel snapped a fan against her arm. "Come along, dear. We'll see you home, and Carter won't have to make the long walk."

"Ethel! Leave her be." Aunt Millie looped her arm in her sister's. "You two take your time walking back. Ethel and I will go on ahead."

With cheeks flaming, Emily bit her lip, grateful for the darkness swallowing her.

Carter chuckled. "They're quite a pair."

"Yes. A pair of jokers."

"Best watch your step." He offered her his arm.

She took it when she stepped off the dock, linking her arm in his as they began to walk home. "Thank you for the evening. I truly enjoyed it."

"I couldn't tell for sure. You've been awfully quiet. Did the play disappoint you?"

"Hardly. No, I guess I'd have to say it was disturbing in some ways."

"I thought you'd find it empowering. After all, Nora goes from a scatterbrained, childish wife to a woman who discovers herself."

"And leaves her children and her husband."

"And that bothers you." His words, more of a statement than a question, drifted into the sound of the lake lapping the shore behind them.

"You won't understand."

"Try me."

"I'm not sure I can explain it. I agreed with so much of what Nora talked about—men who refuse to sacrifice their integrity but expect hundreds of thousands of women to do so every day. She was his doll, his plaything, not his wife, and when she used her brain, she was wrong. Can't you see that's exactly why women must have the right to vote? If they're never elevated to the same place as men, they will always be treated as possessions rather than equals."

Carter covered her hand with his. "What else bothered you about the play?"

"I know it was only a play, and I understood why she had to go, but I hated it too." She sighed. "Nora's decision felt selfish." She was filled with thoughts of Marguerite's little boy and Lilly's baby. "I can't believe I'm saying this, but Aunt Ethel is right. A marriage, a family, is too sacred to abandon."

Carter didn't respond. With each passing moment, Emily's chest clenched more tightly, and her corset pressed hard against her rib cage. Why had he grown so quiet?

Finally, he stopped on the path and turned to her. "I told you we'd discover some of our similarities tonight." Emily started to speak, but he pressed a finger to her lips. "I've not been honest with you, and it's time I told you the truth."

13

Without any moonlight, it was impossible for Emily to see Carter's face. The whir of locusts and the chirping of crickets mixed with the pounding of her heart against her rib cage. She held her breath, waiting. What was he about to tell her? Surely he didn't have a wife and child he'd abandoned. No, not Carter.

"Breathe, Emily. I didn't mean to scare you. I'm not confessing to a heinous crime or anything."

The air whooshed from her lungs, but she worried her lip between her teeth. "What is it?"

"When I said I hadn't been truthful, I was talking about the cause near and dear to your heart."

"I see." In a split second, the gap between them became a chasm.

He took hold of her hands. "No, you don't. Emily, I do believe women should have the right to vote. I believe they should have all those things you do. That's why I chose that play. To show you I wasn't against what you're doing."

Excited shivers shot through her. He wanted what she did? Could it be possible?

"But when we met, you frowned when my grandmother brought it up."

"I know, and you jumped to conclusions." His voice softened. "My mother was a suffragist. She was a lot like you—driven, determined, wouldn't let anything stand in her way."

"Was?"

"She took ill at an Iowa convention but didn't come home. She kept going and grew sicker. She ended up dying of pneumonia a few weeks later."

Tears burned in Emily's eyes. "Carter, I'm so sorry. I don't know what to say. How old were you?"

"Fourteen." He turned to continue their journey but kept her gloved hand in his. "After that, my father threw himself into his work with my brother remaining faithfully by his side."

"So you really lost them both."

He laughed a humorless laugh. "In a manner of speaking. So you see, Emily, we are more alike than you thought. I wouldn't abandon my family either." His voice hardened. "No matter what."

⊷∞⊷

After volunteering to accompany Britta into the city, Emily rose early and donned a pleated white shirtwaist, brown skirt, and plaid vest. She drew her fingers along the quills of the duck feather on her hat. So soft when rubbed the right direction, but rubbed the wrong direction, it bristled.

Was she like the feather? She had bristled at Carter when she sensed he was against her. But last night, his words and his tender touches had definitely smoothed her ruffled feathers.

113

As he said good night, his voice had gone gravelly in a knee-weakening sort of way, and all too soon Aunt Ethel was calling to her from the cabin porch.

Britta knocked on her door, startling her. "You ready, pumpkin?"

"Coming." Emily jammed the hat on her head and stuffed two pins in place. While Britta checked on the upkeep of the Graham home, Emily would attend to some errands.

Once outside at the breakfast table, she downed a muffin and a cup of coffee much more quickly than her aunts deemed appropriate, then left with Britta. They crossed the lake on the launch and then boarded the open-air streetcar into Council Bluffs.

Britta sat beside her, penciling grocery needs on a pad of paper, while Emily watched the open fields give way to civilization. The streetcar slowed inside the city, and Emily scanned the streets for changes since she'd last been there a few weeks ago.

The lilacs and tulips in Bayliss Park had faded, and columbines, irises, and purple coneflowers now brightened the center. Kresge's Five and Dime had a new sign, and the People's Department Store was advertising a sale on beds.

Passing by the Stockton Exchange, Emily went over Carter's words last night. She'd slept little after his revelation concerning his mother's death, and her heart squeezed as she thought about Carter alone in his grief. And why did she hear such a bitter edge in his voice when he spoke of his brother?

She sighed. A minute later, a smile tugged at the corners of her mouth. That hadn't been Carter's only disclosure last night. He believed in a woman's right to vote, and if the telegram she hoped to receive arrived soon, she'd find out for sure how far he was willing to go to support her and the cause.

Britta stepped off the streetcar at the corner of Broadway and Main, saying she'd meet Emily back at the Graham home before noon. Emily continued on for another couple of blocks and exited at the telegraph office.

"Morning, Miss Graham." Roy Chambers leaned against the counter. "I bet you're wanting your reply."

"It came?" Emily couldn't believe it had arrived so quickly. She'd only sent her request four days prior.

"About an hour ago." Mr. Chambers reached into a box and withdrew a slip of vanilla-colored paper. "Here you are, Miss Graham."

Emily scanned the reply quickly.

"I take it from the pretty smile on your face it's good news."

"The best, Mr. Chambers. Thank you." She stepped to the door and turned. "You won't say anything about this, will you?"

"Not a word."

Emily thanked him again and strode into the morning sunlight. Turning toward the Council Bluffs Savings Bank, she began to compile a mental list of things she needed to do now that she had her answer from Chicago. Contacts had to be made, advertisements designed, and articles written.

She reached the corner and stepped into the street.

Suddenly the pounding of horses' hooves jerked her away from her thoughts. Someone grabbed her from behind and pulled her to safety on the sidewalk.

"What were you thinking?" Carter's chest heaved beneath his summer suit.

"My . . . my thoughts were elsewhere."

"Apparently." He motioned toward a bench, and they sat down together. "I'm sorry I was so abrupt. Are you okay?"

Still rattled, she nodded. "I . . . I guess I didn't look."

He locked his gaze on her, studying her face. "You were obviously deep in thought. So what's so important it almost got you killed?"

"If you don't mind, I'd like to talk to you about it later." Lowering her gaze to her lap, she hastily smoothed her skirt. "Where did you come from?"

"I was speaking to the bank about the discrepancy with your grandmother's account." He leaned forward and placed his elbows on his knees. "You know, you scared the wits out of me. I think my heart has finally stopped racing." He drew in a long breath. "So, where were you headed?"

"Home."

"Home on the lake?"

"No, Britta's purchasing a few items and checking on the house here in town. I'm planning to meet her there to pick up a few things before we head back to Lake Manawa."

"How about I walk you over?"

"You don't have to do that."

"I know, but I'd like to." He grinned. "Besides, someone has to save you from wild horses."

She slapped his arm. "You're not going to let me forget this?"

"Nope." He stood and pulled her to her feet. "It's fun having something to tease Miss Perfect about."

Her face flushed, and she stuffed the telegram into her pocket. "Me? Perfect? Hardly."

"You're smart, beautiful, kind, and can get up in front of a crowd and speak your mind with the elocution of a statesman. I'd say few women can rival that."

"Carter—"

"Don't argue with me on this. It's one fight you won't win. Just say thank you."

She giggled. "Thank you."

Several blocks later, they climbed the steep bluff to the Victorian-style Graham home. At the sight of the shades of pale blue and yellow decorating the home, sadness touched her. The house shouted her mother's influence, and Emily instantly missed her terribly. What would she think of Carter Stockton?

"Are you going inside?" Carter asked.

"No, I thought I'd stay out here for a while."

He pointed to a swing hanging from a spreading oak on the side of the front yard. "Why don't you sit over there?"

She rolled her eyes. "Carter, I haven't been on that swing since I was a little girl."

"Then it's about time you do it again." He took her hand and pulled her toward it. After he tugged on the ropes, he patted the seat. "Still safe. Go on. Sit down and tell me what you wanted to talk to me about."

He held the ropes in place while she carefully positioned the narrow board beneath her. "Did you mean what you said last night? About supporting a woman's right to vote?"

"Yes."

She dug the paper from her pocket, smoothed the creases, and passed it to him. "Read this."

He read the words aloud. "'Bloomer Girls available in one month for game. Go ahead with arrangements. J. B. Olson. Manager.'" He looked up. "Okay. What does this have to do with me?"

"I'm not sure yet." She let her shoes brush the ground as the swing swayed.

"Hold on." Carter stepped behind her and pushed the swing in the air.

She clutched the ropes and giggled as the swing took flight.

"What aren't you sure of?"

"Are you familiar with the Bloomer Girls' baseball teams?"

"Sure, they're teams of girls that travel around the country challenging men's teams." He pushed the swing high in the air. "I read in the paper once that five college boys from Tennessee University got expelled for playing them."

"But it wasn't the ladies' fault." Her stomach leaped as he pushed her again. "It was the narrow-minded college dean who forbade the underclassmen from participating. Can you imagine a grown man being so threatened by a group of girls?"

He chuckled and gave her another solid push toward the branches.

"Carter, I need something for the ladies of the Council Bluffs Equal Suffrage Club to be able to get behind. Something exciting. And I need something that will show the people of this area that women are capable of doing anything a man can."

"So you invited these Bloomer Girls here?"

She nodded.

"It's a great idea. Those ladies should draw quite a crowd."

"I certainly hope so, and I'm glad you see how important this game is because I need your help." She paused, hoping he'd figure it out for himself. When he didn't appear to, she said, "The Bloomer Girls need a team to play."

The swing flew backward, and Emily waited for another push. It didn't come as she arced forward again. The swing slowed, and she wished she could see Carter's face. Was he angry? Considering it? Perhaps even as excited as her?

In a few moments, he captured her waist with his arm and brought the swing to an abrupt halt. Marching around to face her, he crossed his arms over his chest, a twitch under his right eye the only thing that moved on his stone-set face. "Absolutely not. Not my team."

"But Carter—"

"No, Emily. I won't put them through it. My team will be the laughingstock of the state."

She stood up, expecting him to take a step back. "I told you we were too different."

"You're asking too much." He held his ground.

"One little game." Tipping her chin up defiantly, she didn't flinch. "That's all."

"My team will never go for it."

His team or him? The words her grandmother had told her so often echoed in her mind. *It is one thing to say you support something. It's something else altogether to fight for it.* Well, if he wouldn't do it, she'd get a team that would. She shoved her shoulder into his chest, moving past him.

He caught her arm. "Where are you going?"

"To find another team."

"Fine."

She yanked away. "I'm glad I have your permission."

"No, I mean fine, we'll do it."

"Really?" Her voice came out squeaky.

He chuckled. "On one condition."

"I'm listening." She swallowed, the I-dare-you glint in his eye unraveling her.

"There are always one or two men on those Bloomer Girls' teams, right?"

"Usually."

"Then, to be fair, we need a woman on ours."

Relief flooded over her. "That wouldn't be a problem. I'm sure one of the suffrage league women would do it. Several, like Lilly, are quite athletic. I can ask this afternoon for volunteers."

119

He cocked an eyebrow, and a grin spread across his face. "No, Emily. My condition is *you* have to play for the Manawa Owls."

"Me?" The breeze picked up, and Emily had to press her hand to her hat to keep it from blowing off. "But Carter, I'm not an athlete."

The amber flecks in Carter's eyes flickered with a strange amusement. "Take it or leave it."

The cockiness in his tone irked her. "I've never even held a bat."

"I'll teach you."

"You're serious, aren't you?"

"Dead serious."

"That's not funny. You realize I may accidentally kill you."

He chuckled. "I survived the shooting gallery, and you had a gun in your hands there. I think I'll be safe on a ball field."

"I doubt it," she mumbled. Why didn't he see it? Her on a ball team? Her brother was going to have a heyday with this. "Carter, this is insane."

"Maybe, but I like a challenge. So you agree?" Jaw set firmly, he met her gaze. He didn't show the slightest indication of backing down.

What if she said no? Could she find another team to play the Bloomer Girls? Probably not. And the cause in Iowa needed this. Her local girls needed it, and so did she.

Her stomach knotted. "I can't very well say no. It means too much."

"In that case, I'll see you at the ball field the day after tomorrow at noon."

"What about lunch?"

"Good idea, and nice of you to offer. We'll have a picnic after we practice."

Before she could protest, he jogged off, every athletic muscle doing exactly as he told it.

As Emily watched him go, her corset felt tighter than ever, and tears burned in her eyes. When Carter saw how clumsy she truly was, all his interest in her would disappear.

14

Gathered in the shade of a grove of sky-reaching cottonwood trees, the Council Bluffs Equal Suffrage Club sat at picnic tables enjoying almond cake provided by Lilly's mother. Roses tumbled from a nearby planter, and Emily fought the urge to skip the meeting and go soak in their fragrant sweetness. Her idea, which had seemed so perfect, now made her palms sweat and her pulse quicken.

She touched her flowered straw summer hat self-consciously, rapped the gavel on the table, and called the meeting to order. "Good morning, ladies." Heads turned in her direction, and she continued. "I believe we have two fights on our hands at this point in the suffrage movement."

"Two?" Greta Wilson asked.

"Yes, two. As many of you are aware, my grandmother was dear friends with Amelia Bloomer, the suffrage leader from our very own town. Allow me to share one of Amelia's thoughts. 'The human mind must be active, and the thoughts of a woman's heart must find vent in some way; and if the garden of the mind instead of being highly cultivated, so that it may produce a rich harvest of fruits and flowers, is suffered to run to waste, it is not surprising that it yields nothing but weeds, briars, and thorns.'"

"What's your point, Emily?" Olivia DeSoto waved a fan in front of her face.

"My point is . . ." Emily paused and smiled at the women. "As we sit here at this lovely lake, soaking up all of God's beautiful creation, it is easy to see what Mrs. Bloomer was referring to when she spoke of gardens. So, to begin our meeting today, I wanted to say if every woman here represents a blooming flower, then we have indeed already started to cultivate a rich garden free of weeds, briars, and thorns."

The ladies applauded.

"Now, as Mrs. Bloomer said, we must also cultivate the garden of our minds. I'd like to discuss how each of us is trying to enrich our minds."

Olivia's brow scrunched and her lips pursed. "You are pushing us to read again, aren't you?"

"Books are certainly one of the best ways to enrich your mind. My grandmother told me this was the reason the Bloomers were strong advocates of the library."

"Amelia Bloomer thought wearing pants like a man was a good idea." Olivia turned to her group of friends and waited for them to agree. "That little experiment certainly failed, and we don't need her telling us how to live in 1901."

"Mrs. Bloomer simply advocated a change of dress for women—something allowing more freedom of movement, like the divided skirts and Turkish pants we now wear today for cycling, riding, and other sports. I don't think you can say she failed when we in fact enjoy the product of her labors in our own clothing. We should applaud her for having the fortitude to actually follow through on what she said. She didn't let ignorance hold her back."

Emily waited, hoping her words stung as much as she intended. Olivia didn't want to change. What she really wanted was the prestige of being a member of the suffrage association. The right to vote would be lost on women unwilling to think beyond petty rivalries.

Olivia glowered, but Emily didn't flinch. "I'm reading *The War of the Worlds* by H. G. Wells," she announced. "I find it fascinating."

"A book about Martians?" Olivia rolled her eyes.

"It's eye-opening and makes you consider a world of possibilities." Not that Olivia would understand. Emily swallowed a giggle.

Soon the women had launched into a discussion of their current reading selections, including *Captains Courageous* by Rudyard Kipling, *Tom Sawyer* by Mark Twain, and *The Wonderful Wizard of Oz* by L. Frank Baum. Delighted by the breadth of their choices, Emily listened intently to each of them as they shared. Finally, she pounded the gavel and announced it was time to move on to her second point.

"While most men have more physical strength than women, when we set our minds to a job, we find a way to accomplish the same goal. Ladies, I believe we must make the community aware of our ability to overcome all obstacles."

"Oh, for goodness' sake, that is simply not true!" Mathilda Henningsen, a railroad vice president's wife, cried out. She glanced at Olivia for affirmation.

"Let Emily speak." Marguerite sat up in her chair. "She has a marvelous idea, and I for one want you all to hear it."

"Thank you, Marguerite." Emily pressed on. "I believe we can tell the citizens that women are capable of doing the same things as men over and over until we're blue in the face, but if we *show* them what we mean, they may get the message. For this reason, I've arranged for the Chicago Stars, a Bloomer Girls' team, to join us here at the lake on the Fourth of July for an exhibition game."

Expressions on the club members' faces ranged from nervousness to excitement to disgust. Such a vast assortment almost made Emily want to laugh.

Elderly Mrs. Bradley beamed. "And who are they going to play, dear?"

Emily smiled at the gray-haired woman, who was always willing to do whatever was necessary to get the job done. "This morning the Manawa Owls agreed to participate, on one condition."

"Which is?" Greta asked.

"Since all the Bloomer Girls' teams have a couple of men on the team, the Owls insist a woman play on their team as well."

"Lilly would be excellent at that." Sally Nesmit nodded in Lilly's direction.

"She would, but unfortunately, the condition the men's team has put on participation is that *I* must play with the Owls."

"You?" Olivia erupted into laughter. "Do they want to lose?"

"Olivia!" Lilly glared at her.

"It's all right, Lilly. It gives me a chance to make my final point. I've had some time to think about this. I said a woman can do anything she puts her mind to, so I have every intention of working hard and not making a fool of myself."

"Good luck," Olivia said under her breath.

Emily raised her eyebrows. "Thank you. I'm going to need it."

Sleep evaded Carter like a fly avoided the swatter. Outside the Manawa Owl Club, where he and some of the other team members rented rooms, a few stars blinked against the inky sky. With the window open, the breeze ruffled the flimsy curtains. He jammed his fist into his feather pillow, wadding it into a ball, and rolled on his side. If he couldn't get his mind off Emily, it was going to be a long night.

In the cot beside him, Ducky snored with a soft quacking sound. Carter would have laughed if he wasn't so annoyed about not being able to sleep. The last few days blurred in his tired mind, and yet he remembered every detail—about her. The smell of her rose-scented hair, the sound of her bubbling laughter, and the feel of her soft, velvety hand in his. His insides jellied.

He whacked the pillow again.

Somehow she'd gotten him to agree to a baseball game with a women's team! How was he going to tell his boys about that? They'd probably use him for batting practice—literally. For certain, they were going to tell him he'd been hit in the head with one too many baseballs.

And what would his family say if they heard he was seeing someone? Although his father seemed to ignore him most of the time, Nathan had an uncanny knack of showing up whenever he didn't approve of Carter's decisions. It didn't take a genius to guess seeing a Graham would not be a choice Nathan would like.

Carter flopped on his back and stared at the shadows playing on the ceiling. Tree branches waving in the wind seemed to laugh at him. Even the crickets chirped mockingly. He'd let it all happen. From asking Emily to the shooting gallery that first day, to the play, to the episode on the swing. All his ideas. And when she stepped into the path of those horses earlier today, he'd known the truth when his heart stopped.

He'd been licked.

But what a way to go.

After stretching and warming up, the team members took their bases for practice. Hours spent in prayer had left Carter with an extra lift in spirit despite the lack of sleep. He'd woken early and arrived at the baseball diamond with a calm in his heart concerning Emily. God had brought them together for a reason, and he'd let the Lord show him how and when to proceed.

Carter stepped on the mound, scanned the basemen, and eyed Ducky behind the plate. Their fifth man to bat was up—Elwood Taylor, the Owls' best batter. Carter wound up and let the baseball fly. He waited to hear the familiar crack of the bat. The man swung, met only air, and swaggered in a full circle.

The ball whacked into Ducky's padded catcher's mitt. He jumped up and threw both the ball and his glove on the ground. A cloud of dust puffed as he shoved Elwood away from the plate. "Taylor, what was that? You keep this up and we're going to get trounced."

Carter ran in from the pitcher's mound.

Elwood drew back his fist, but Carter stepped between the two men before Elwood could deliver the blow. Elwood staggered.

Carter whirled on Ducky. "What in the blazes do you think you're doing?"

Ducky's chest heaved. "Look at him, Carter. Smell his breath. He's been hitting the bottle again."

Turning back to the right fielder, Carter stared in his eyes. It was only ten in the morning, but the telltale signs were there. How had he missed the bloodshot eyes, the unsteady stance, the red nose and cheeks? The answer hit him hard. He'd been too preoccupied with Emily and her Bloomer Girls' plan.

Carter shoved Elwood toward the bench. "Get out of here, and if you come back like this again, you're off the team."

Elwood staggered and stopped. "Aren't you going to tell 'em?"

The other teammates had circled around them.

"Tell us what?" Ducky asked.

"Stockton's got us playing them Bloomer Girls." Elwood's words slurred together.

A chorus of chuckles and disbelieving guffaws surrounded them.

Ducky sliced the air with his arm. "You don't know what you're talking about."

Glaring at Elwood, Carter crossed his arms over his chest. This was not the way he had planned to let the team in on the situation.

"Tell 'em, Stockton. I heard it from my girl, Greta. You said yessss to spunky little Emily Graham 'cause you're ssssweet on her." He stumbled, and the shortstop grabbed his arm.

"Get out of here and take your stories with you." Ducky scooped up the baseball.

"They aren't stories," Carter said.

The team's laughter died, and with puzzled faces, they stared at him.

He sighed. "I said yes to the Owls playing an exhibition game against the Bloomer Girls from Chicago next month, and Emily Graham will be playing on our team."

"You've got to be kidding," Fred Brunner, second baseman, said in his nasally voice.

"Anyone have a problem with it, they can talk to me."

"I got a problem with it." Joe Powel, the burly left fielder, stepped forward. "I don't happen to like playing with a bunch of girls 'cause you got your eyes set on that know-it-all Graham girl and her family's money."

Coal-hot anger burned in Carter's gut. "Powel, you better make sure your mouth doesn't get you in more trouble than you can handle."

"Yeah?"

"Yeah." Carter struck his mitt with his fist.

"Take it easy, boys." Ducky situated himself between the two of them. "Joe, how'd you like it if someone was spouting off about your Belle?"

Joe yanked off his hat. "I still don't like the idea of playing girls."

"You don't have to like it. You just have to play." Ducky clapped him on the shoulder. "We're a team. Carter brought us together, and if he thinks we should do this, we should trust him."

"Carter, no disrespect intended to Emily," Fred said. "But in high school, everyone knew she was so uncoordinated, she made bungling Bill Hancock look good. Does she have to be the girl on our team?"

"Yes." Tired of their attitudes, Carter leveled his gaze at his teammates. "Emily is playing and so are we."

Judging by the glares he received, clearly most of the team did not like the idea, but he didn't back down. Let them be mad. The idea would grow on them. He glared right back, not even blinking. Some things his brother had taught him came in handy.

Carter glanced toward Elwood weaving his way down the path. He could also decide who deserved to play and who didn't, and he imagined Emily would try harder during one game than Elwood Taylor would in a month of Sundays.

Yanking off his cap, he knocked it against his thigh and jammed it back on his head. "All right, boys, let's play ball!"

15

As the afternoon sun swung high into the sky, Carter's stomach began to protest. Based on the slow response of the outfielders, he knew he wasn't the only one ready for lunch. With a wave of his arm, he called them in and watched his team file off the field. Muttering under their breath, they headed toward Manhattan Beach without waiting to see if he planned to have lunch with them.

Only Ducky remained. Carter's best friend downed a dipper of water from the Red Wing crock they'd brought along, then wiped his wet mouth on the sleeve of his jersey. "The boys had a point."

"Not you too. I've about had enough!" Carter yanked off his hat, took the dipper, and poured its contents over his head. Water streamed over him, cooling his face but not his temper. He shook his head, and water splattered into the air.

Ducky jumped back. "Hey!"

With a sigh, Carter sank onto the bench. "Sorry."

"For what part? Getting me wet or getting angry at me

because I think the boys had a point?" Ducky tossed a baseball into the air.

"Both."

"I reckon if you're going to teach her to play, you might need some help."

"But you said—"

"I said they had a point—not that I agree with it."

"And you're willing to help?"

"What can I say? I'm a sucker for lost causes."

"Is that a fact?"

"I'm friends with you, aren't I?"

Carter chuckled and then grew silent. Whippoorwills called from the trees, and the sun beat down on his head. Truth gnawed at his gut. "I couldn't tell Emily no. She wants this game so much."

"That's why she offered to play?"

His lips curled and he stood. "Nope. That part was my idea."

Ducky lifted an eyebrow.

"If you spent one evening with her aunts as chaperones, you'd understand why I jumped at the chance to see her without them around."

"That bad, huh?"

"Worse." Carter picked up the baseball bats and stowed them in a gunny sack. "Besides, it will be fun to see how she does when she's not calling all the shots."

Ducky drew his hand down the sides of his mustache. "For some reason, I don't think your little suffragist would like the sound of that."

Slinging the gunny sack over his shoulder, Carter grinned. "Trust me. It's for her own good."

After exiting the streetcar in Council Bluffs' Haymarket Square, Emily waited while Lilly disembarked with ten-month-old Levi in her arms. Storefronts with one, two, and three stories stretched the length of Main Street. The steady clopping of horses' hooves on the paved brick streets mingled with the voices of the patrons on the sidewalk.

Lilly bounced her squirming baby. "When did you say your grandmother and brother were meeting you for lunch?"

"In about an hour. At noon."

"Good. Then we have enough time to get you a few baseball-playing essentials."

The mention of baseball set Emily's nerves tingling. "Like?"

"A sensible pair of shoes." She plopped Levi on her hip and strolled down the sidewalk. "Do you even own a pair of laced-up Oxfords?"

"What do you call these?" Emily paused and lifted her skirt to display her bow-topped shoes.

"They have heels."

"Of course they do."

"Do you plan on running in those?"

Emily dropped her skirt, and they resumed walking. "Guess they do make it hard."

"Let's stop in at Ben's office. He lets me keep a pram in the back room. We'll have a little time to shop before lunch."

Shielding her eyes against the sun, Emily scanned the street for Lilly's husband's law office. The building, one of the newest, featured gothic brickwork and arched windows. Five years ago, she'd have never guessed Lilly would marry into one of the city's most influential families.

Lilly tickled Levi under his chubby chin. "If we're lucky, Ben will offer to keep this little wiggle worm while we shop."

"How likely is that?"

"It depends on if he has any pending cases. Between his father and the railroad, there's always something going on."

"You've done so well fitting into his world. Has it been hard?"

Lilly switched Levi to her other hip. "Yes and no. For example, I find it hard to turn over my Levi to anyone else's care even though he has a perfectly wonderful nurse. Of course, Ben's mother handpicked her. She couldn't let me do something so important."

Emily smiled at the sarcasm in Lilly's voice.

Levi pulled on the brim of Lilly's hat, and she pried his chubby fingers free. "I simply like having him with me. And it's been hard to go from being Marguerite's maid to having maids of my own, but people are people. They want the same things."

"Like?"

"To love and be loved."

"What about the people who only want to make a difference in the world? The people who are willing to forgo their own needs for the good of mankind?"

"Or womankind?" Lilly gave her a sidelong glance and opened the door to Ben's office. "If you get right down to it, they still want to be loved."

"I'm not sure a person can always have both."

An hour later, with Levi sleeping in the pram and new shoes purchased, Emily and Lilly went their separate ways to their lunch appointments. Emily hurried to the restaurant Martin had suggested. Inside, he and Grandma Kate waited at a table in the center of the dining room.

Martin drew Emily into a warm embrace. "How's my little sister?"

Emily swatted his arm, then bent to kiss her grandmother's

cheek before sitting down beside her brother. "Have the two of you been having a nice chat?"

Grandma Kate laid her crinkled hand on Martin's arm. "It's been good to catch up. With your father away, Martin's been so busy I've hardly talked to him."

"I'll second that." Emily smoothed her napkin across her lap.

Within minutes, a waitress appeared and took their order. No one needed a menu. While not as fancy as Louie's *poisson en papillote* on Lake Manawa's Manhattan Beach, the Main Street Café's pot roast, complete with carrots and potatoes, couldn't be trumped. Soon the three of them were feasting on generous portions and chatting between bites.

Martin pointed to Emily with his fork. "Grandma tells me you're planning an exhibition game with Chicago's Bloomer Girls."

"I am. The Manawa Owls have agreed to play against them."

"And she says you've elicited the support of your club and contacted the team manager to arrange the whole thing. Very impressive."

"Thank you. Now I simply need to find a business to sponsor their traveling expenses."

He leaned back in his chair. "I should have guessed you had a reason to request lunch with your big brother."

"It's a hundred dollars. If Daddy were here, I'm sure he'd offer to cover it." She speared a carrot and popped it into her mouth.

"But he's not." Martin steepled his fingers over the remnants of his pot roast. "I'm not certain this is a viable business venture. If some men find out our company supported your suffrage association's game, they might be inclined to stop doing business with me."

"Martin," Grandma Kate said as firmly as a schoolmarm.

"Someone has to tell her. Dad gives into her whims at the drop of a hat."

"Oh, for heaven's sake, do you have to be so difficult? This is important to her." Grandma Kate turned to Emily. "I'll give you the money. When do you need it?"

Martin slammed his napkin on the table hard enough to make the water in the glasses ripple. "Don't make me the bad guy. The company isn't doing that well, and I daresay neither are you. Have you looked at your finances recently?"

Emily blinked. Was her grandmother in trouble? Carter hadn't said anything.

"As I told you before, that discrepancy is being handled with the bank. It's none of your concern." Grandma Kate broke off a piece of bread. "I'll hear no more of it. Now, Emily, tell Martin the rest of the story about the game. He'll be proud of you."

Martin's eyebrows furrowed. "There's more?"

"She's going to play with the Manawa Owls." Her grand-mother smiled proudly.

His eyes narrowed. "Play what?"

"Baseball, of course."

"Emily? Our Emily? She can't walk a straight line, let alone run bases." He laughed and appeared to wait for his grand-mother to join him. She didn't. "Who are you kidding, sis? The only thing you can throw is a fit. Tell me how you got into this. I'll take care of it and get you out. No need to make a fool of yourself publicly."

"I'm going to do this." Emily pushed back from the table, opened the chatelaine purse clipped to her belt, and withdrew a dollar. She tossed it in the center of the table.

Martin grabbed her wrist. "What do you think you're doing?"

"I'm buying lunch, as I'm certain you don't have enough money for that either." She yanked her arm away and turned to her grandmother. "I'll meet you at Bayliss Park, Grandma. I need some air."

Grandma Kate nodded. "I imagine you do."

Kate watched her granddaughter exit the café, then released a long sigh. "You hurt Emily's feelings."

"I'm only trying to protect her. Someone has to." Martin downed a glass of water.

"Protect her from whom?" Kate laid a wrinkled hand on his arm. "She's an adult now. Not your little sister. She has dreams. They're real. She puts her heart and soul into everything she does—especially this fight for women to have the right to vote. But this time, she has another reason to do this as well."

"Such as?"

"Carter Stockton."

"She fancies him?" He laughed, long and hard. "You're kidding."

"No, but I believe he did the fancying first."

"Carter? But Grandma, how could that be possible? He's—"

"Not another word, Martin." She folded her napkin and set it beside her plate. "Let her become the woman God intends her to be, and stop trying to make her back into your little sister."

16

Even though Emily prayed for rain, bright sunshine and perfect temperatures greeted her as she stepped out of the cabin. A goldfinch landed on the grass in front of her and tipped his tufted head. He too probably thought she looked ridiculous wearing dark blue bloomers gathered at the knees. They showed off her black stockings and the laced-up Oxfords she'd purchased with Lilly yesterday. Perhaps she should change back into a skirt, then at least she'd have an excuse when she tripped.

Martin was right. She had no business doing this.

"Emily," Aunt Millie called across the lawn. "Come join me for breakfast."

She pressed a hand to her quivering stomach. The girls often complained of having butterflies. Hers were more like big, hairy moths. Maybe toast would settle the queasiness. Then again, so would an unexpected thunderstorm, which would prevent her from meeting Carter to begin practicing.

As she made her way to the outdoor table, she glanced toward the sky and sighed.

Not a cloud in sight.

God was not listening.

"Don't you look sporty," Aunt Millie said, pouring her a cup of tea. "I asked for tea this morning. I didn't feel like coffee. I hope that's all right."

"Perfect." Emily sat down and sipped from the cup her aunt poured.

A few minutes later, Britta sauntered over. "Everyone else has already eaten, but if you're ready, I'll bring you some pancakes hot off the griddle."

Emily stifled a moan. Imagining the heavy flapjacks sitting in her stomach like a weight—a dead weight—made her even more nauseous. "I think I'll just have toast."

Britta scowled. "Do you think a piece of toast is going to hold you over if Mr. Stockton has you running around bases all morning?"

"I'll take an apple with me too."

"At least I've got the picnic lunch packed you wanted." She clicked her tongue and returned to the kitchen inside the cabin.

Aunt Millie leaned closer. "Dear, I'm glad we have a few minutes alone. I bought you something, and it arrived yesterday."

"Aunt Millie, you shouldn't have."

"Oh, but I had to do something." She dug in her pocket and removed a tin. She held it out like a prize on her crinkled hand for Emily to see the label. "I ordered it from the catalog before you met Carter, and now that you have, I do believe there's all the more reason to use it."

Heat infused Emily's cheeks. "Aunt Millie, that's—"

"Sears Bust Food for, uh, enlargement of the bust. A wonderful blessing for a girl like you that isn't as endowed as some."

"You expect me to use that?"

"Absolutely, dear. You have to understand the male of our species. Your uncle Josef had quite a fondness for my ample bosom. You see here, it says it is 'unrivaled for feeding and developing the bust, arms, and neck.'"

Emily swallowed hard. What was she going to do with this? She couldn't refuse a gift, but this was no ordinary gift. And while she wasn't as voluptuous as some of the girls in the club, she certainly wasn't a flat-chested schoolgirl in need of Aunt Millie's bust food.

Britta returned, and Aunt Millie thrust the tin onto Emily's lap. Quickly she slipped it into the pocket of her bloomers seconds before Britta set a plate of buttered toast on the table.

"I packed a good lunch for you and the young Mr. Stockton. Fried chicken, biscuits, apples, and chocolate cake. Now, Miss Emily, you let Mr. Stockton choose first. I don't know if he's a breast man or a leg man."

Emily spewed tea across the table and covered it with a series of coughs. "I'm sorry. I choked."

Aunt Millie patted her hand. "It's okay, dear. It's all this talk about b—"

"Baseball," Emily said. "It's because I'm so nervous about my first practice."

Her aunt's eyes twinkled. "Whatever you say, dear. Whatever you say."

❦

"You want me to say what?" Emily stared at Carter. They stood beside first base on the Owls' field, where he tossed a ball in one hand, a smug expression on his face.

Anger simmered inside her. He was out of his mind. She didn't care if she needed his Manawa Owls to play the Bloomer Girls' team, she was not going to repeat the "o" word to him or anyone else.

"It's for your own safety." His arms now barred his chest like a fortress. "I need to know you're going to listen to me out here."

"I already told you I'll listen."

"Not good enough." His voice dropped deeper. "You don't say it, you don't play."

She could finish the unspoken words herself. This was his world, and the cocky athlete wanted her to know he was in charge. If she didn't play, then his team didn't play. Without an opposing team, there'd be no game.

Her willingness to do anything for the cause wavered. This was asking too much. But a fraction of a second before opening her mouth, she stopped. Perhaps she was wrong. What had the others given up in the fight? Families? Comfort? Acceptance? Was it her turn to sacrifice?

"Well?" He thumped his forefinger against his bulging bicep.

She glowered at him. "Fine."

"Then say it."

"I'll obey you." She nearly choked on the words.

Carter gave a chuckle and squeezed her shoulder. "There. That wasn't so hard, now was it?"

She shrugged off his hand. "Did I hear you say something about going back to the shooting gallery?" She forced a sickeningly sweet smile. "I'm pretty sure I wouldn't miss this time, Mr. Stockton."

His chest rumbled with laughter. "Emily, I really do need you to do what I say out here. You might not see a ball coming your way, and if I yell directions to you, I need you to obey without a second thought."

"And you received no satisfaction from making me say that word."

He held up his finger and thumb pinched together. "Maybe a wee bit. Ready to start?"

"Why don't you just order me to do it?"

"Okay, okay, I get it. I pushed you too far, but surely you realize I'm not like that. I wouldn't be here if I was." He tossed the ball from his right to his left hand. "Let's start with something easy—catching."

"Carter, you might as well know that nothing requiring my mind and the rest of my body to cooperate is easy for me."

"Then we'll take it slow. I promise to be a patient teacher."

"I think I could try any man's patience."

He grinned. "I don't doubt." Moving several yards from her, he held up the ball. "Now, we're going to warm up slow."

Carter tossed an underhanded throw toward her. Emily's heart quickened. The ball flew through the air like a bat swooping in on an insect, and Emily closed her eyes. The ball thudded at her feet. Did she hear Carter moan?

"Emily, a great catch starts with keeping your eyes open."

"That's easier said than done." She picked the ball up and lobbed it back. It fell short of him by a good yard.

Carter sighed.

"What was wrong with that?"

"You throw like a girl."

"I am a girl, in case you haven't noticed."

"Oh, I've noticed." He gave her a cockeyed grin and bounced the ball in his hand. "Keep your eyes open this time, okay?"

"You." She pointed a finger at him. "Throw nice."

Carter tossed the ball in a high arc, and she stepped forward with her hands outstretched, eyes wide. The bulky leather glove he'd given her refused to move fast enough. Instead, the baseball bit into her sweaty right hand. She winced and dropped the ball. "Ow!"

"Use the glove to catch the ball. Use your other hand to throw it."

"But this thing is huge! How can I catch anything?"

Carter jogged over to her. "Ninety percent of any game is knowing you can do it." He tapped her head. "You need to believe you can do this."

She dug the toe of her shoe into the soft dirt. "Carter, you don't understand."

"Look at me." He lifted her chin. "I'm not going to give up, and neither are you. That was the first of a hundred throws you're going to miss today."

"I won't miss every one of them!"

He laughed. "See, you're already thinking like a winner."

An hour later, Emily felt like she had indeed missed at least a hundred throws. But she'd also managed to catch enough that her confidence grew a fraction. Her throwing, Carter insisted, was still pathetic, but he said they'd work on that tomorrow.

Emily rubbed her aching shoulder. Why would anyone want to do this every day?

Carter jogged over and glanced up at the sun. "Ready for lunch?"

"I thought you'd never ask." She trudged to the basket, the new shoes pinching with each step. Surely at least two blisters had formed on each foot.

Carter lifted the basket from her hand and led her to a spot under an oak with a view of the rippling lake.

She caught a whiff of the tangy water on the breeze as he spread the tartan blanket in the grass and set the basket on top. Then, offering his hand, he helped her settle beside their lunch.

Her body protested at the movement, but she tried not to wince.

"You're going to be sore tomorrow. Maybe we should go for a swim later on. The water would help ease your muscles."

Emily opened the basket's lid and took out the chicken Britta had packed. "I'd like to, but I can't. The girls are meeting to discuss publicity for the game."

"Are you coming to our game tonight?" He spread a napkin over his lap.

"I don't know if I'll get back from town by then."

He gave her a mock frown. "I guess I can't have all of your time."

"I'll try to do both." She withdrew two apples, tossed him one, and bit into her own. Sweet juices burst on her tongue and a drop eased its way down her chin. She hurried to catch the liquid with her napkin.

"Emily, don't you want to ask a blessing before we eat?"

"Oh." She dropped her hands, apple and all, into her lap. "You've worked me so hard, I'm muddleheaded."

"Sure, blame it on me." He took her hand in his.

The warmth of his touch made it hard to concentrate on the words of his prayer. She forced herself to focus as he thanked God for their new friendship and the food. When he asked God to give them both patience, a smile played across his lips. He was certainly going to need an extra helping of that.

She held out the chicken, and to her secret delight, he selected a leg.

The next hour passed all too quickly. Carter regaled her

144

with stories about his teammate's antics, which left her sides aching. Emily shared a few stories of growing up as Martin's younger sister. A true prankster, Martin always had a habit of bending the rules, and Carter seemed to enjoy hearing about his former classmate's antics.

Bit by bit, Emily found herself forgetting she was in the presence of a man and thinking simply about being with Carter. When he laughed, his dark curls bobbed. She ached to brush them off his forehead and to see how springy they were.

"So how long have you known Ducky?" She pushed a strand of her own windblown hair out of her eyes.

"Since the first day of college. He was my roommate. When we graduated, neither of us was ready to give up baseball."

"Would you like to play professionally?"

"Sure, along with every boy in the country."

"Why didn't you try?"

"Who says I'm not trying now?"

"Are you?"

"Not this minute." He grinned and took a swig of lemonade from his tin cup.

"What would your father say if you were successful?"

"I doubt if he'd care. He's got Nathan, big brother extraordinaire. The perfect businessman and the perfect son. According to Nathan, I'm expected to join them in the family business after the season." He forked the final bite of his chocolate cake.

"But that's not what you want."

With a shrug, he deposited his dappled blue and white enameled plate into the basket. "You can't always get something simply because you want it."

"But you're so good."

"It's been my experience that being good at something is seldom enough."

"So you're not going to try? You'll never get there if you don't fight for it."

He bristled. Tossing in her empty plate, he closed the basket with a huff.

"Carter, I'm sorry. I overstepped."

"No, you said what you were thinking. I want you to be honest with me." Irritation edged his voice. Then, with a sigh, he continued. "What made you such a fighter? And don't tell me it was that women should have the right to vote. Remember, I knew you back before you were involved in suffrage work."

"I'm not sure. Martin says I was always a scrapper. I think life didn't always seem fair to me."

"And it's your job to right all the wrongs."

"Something like that." The difficult strand of hair broke free again. She reached for the pins tucked in at the nape of her neck to secure it in place.

"Don't." He stilled her hand.

"Pardon?"

"I like the wind blowing your hair that way. It matches you. Unpredictable. Alive. Resilient."

He stood and pulled her to her feet. Bringing her hand to his lips, he brushed her knuckles with a kiss. "You can't fix every problem in the world. Especially mine."

"Carter—"

Pinning her with his gaze, Carter silenced her words. Her chest tightened at the sadness she saw swirled within the caramel depths of his eyes, and she wanted to say or do something to ease the pain he wasn't yet willing to share. But what could she say that she hadn't already said? No matter

146

how much Carter might want to play professional baseball, it seemed he felt it was beyond his grasp. Why was that?

Suddenly she realized how little she actually knew about Carter Stockton. He'd always seemed so capable and sure of himself, but this was a different side. The desire to know everything about him flooded over her—to know what he thought, where the pain came from, and what he dreamed his future would hold.

"Enough serious talk." A smile creased his face, and his gaze dropped from her eyes to her lips. "Lunch with a beautiful girl should end with a taste as sweet as the dessert."

Heat infused her cheeks like a potbellied stove in the winter, and her heart beat wildly against her ribs. Would he kiss her? The depth of the wanting surprised her. She held her breath.

"Hey, Stockton!" Ducky called from the diamond. "Ready to play some ball?"

Carter blinked and his Adam's apple bobbed. "Sounds like the boys are here."

He stepped back and released her hand. They bent to gather the blanket. Each grabbed a corner, and a lighthearted tug-of-war ensued. Emily pulled hard and, for a moment, made progress, only to realize too late that Carter was allowing her to win. He gave her a mischievous grin and let go of the blanket. She toppled to the ground and giggled. He dramatically fell down beside her.

"Hey, what's this?" he asked.

When he held up the tin her aunt had given her, the laughter died on her lips.

17

Whatever the tin was that Carter held in his hands brought horror to Emily's beet-red face. Though tempted to read what it contained, something deep inside told him it would be the worst mistake of his life.

"I think this fell out of your pocket." He passed it to her, catching the title by accident. He forced his lips to remain rod straight.

Even though he considered himself fairly well-versed on women, this product was new to him. Bust food? Did women have to feed those?

Emily jammed the tin in her pocket, refusing to meet his gaze. She gathered the blanket against her chest. "I'd better hurry. I'll be late as it is."

"Yeah." He cleared his throat. "I'll get the basket and walk you home."

"No need. I can get there on my own."

He didn't argue with her. Whatever had occurred here in the last couple of minutes had her wound as tight as a spring, and maybe she needed some time to herself. He collected the basket and helped her fold the blanket. "Tomorrow I'll provide lunch. And remember, I'd love to see you cheering for me tonight at the game."

A bit of sparkle returned to her moss-green eyes, and a smile curled her lips. "I'll try to come, but who said I'd be cheering for you?"

❧

"Okay, boys, let's call it a day."

Due to the game against the Neola Knights tonight, Carter planned only a short practice for the Manawa Owls. He'd heard the town of Neola had five hundred citizens planning to board a special excursion train to come see their team play. He hoped some of them brought blankets to sit on, because if they all showed up, there wouldn't be enough room on the bleachers.

Even with that excitement, the time on the field seemed abysmally long. After he called the practice, he gave his usual pregame pep talk and followed the boys toward Manhattan Beach for a well-deserved swim.

Once he changed into his bathing suit, he dove off the end of the pier and plunged deep into the cool lake. Surfacing, he treaded water. A few of the guys called to him, asking if he wanted to join them on the toboggan run. He waved them off. Today he wanted to be alone.

With a crawl stroke strengthened by hours of pitching, he cut through the water, his thoughts churning like the waves. Why did he let his brother's success get to him?

His conversation with Emily had hit home. He was a good baseball player, plain and simple, and it wasn't a matter of pride. In fact, he felt humbled whenever he thought about it.

God had given some people the ability to carry a tune, but He'd given Carter the ability to throw a ball.

Thankfully, it was the one talent He hadn't given Nathan.

At least on a ball field, Carter could be somebody. A picture of Mrs. Sylvester, his fourth-grade teacher, pointing to his arithmetic paper formed in his mind. Though he'd received 100 percent on it, she still frowned. "You do realize your brother was doing sixth-grade math by your age."

Even now the words stung.

He pushed his body harder, his heart pounding in his ears with every stroke. *Nathan's so good. Nathan's the best.* At home. At school. Even at church. It never stopped.

Nathan. Nathan. Nathan.

❧

With papers sprawled on every table of the Yacht Club's upstairs room, the ladies of the Council Bluffs Equal Suffrage Club sat divided into the work groups Emily had dispersed. The air crackled with excitement. Never had she seen the women get so energized by one of their efforts.

Everywhere she turned, Emily heard discussions about the upcoming game. She'd placed Greta in charge of seeing to the Bloomer Girls' meals. Marguerite took the lead on publicizing the event here at the lake, while Lilly took charge of putting ads in the newspaper. To Emily's surprise, Olivia volunteered to oversee the poster designs. She even offered to pay for printing them and said she'd distribute them.

Emily picked up her notebook and pen. They'd still need to construct additional bleachers to deal with the crowds, arrange a welcoming ceremony of some sort for the ladies upon their arrival, and determine a way to bring a woman's right to vote to the forefront of the entire event. So much to do, but at least this was an excellent beginning.

150

Greta scurried over and handed her a menu. "Do you think this will work?"

Emily smiled. "I think that'll be enough food to feed an army."

"Like you said, we don't want any of the Bloomer Girls to leave our city and say we weren't good hostesses."

"In your hands, I think there's no danger of that, Greta. Thank you."

"Emily." Olivia waved her over. "The girls thought you should be the one to decide which design to use."

Olivia's ever-present cohort, Mrs. Penny Poppleton, turned over the designs, and a little thrill surged through Emily when she caught sight of them. A beautiful pencil drawing of a Bloomer Girl adorned each poster. One sketch sported the female baseball player in a pair of loose-fitting trousers, and in the other, the player wore a skirt.

"Who made these? The artwork is wonderful."

"I did." Olivia raised her eyebrows. "Don't look so surprised, Emily."

"I—I—I didn't know you could draw. That's all."

"Well, now you do. So, which picture do you prefer, Madam President?"

Did she detect a note of teasing in Olivia's voice? Emily picked up both posters and held them out. The comical one would never do, but she'd play along for a moment. "I could never choose which to use. They both are delightful. Do you have a favorite?"

Olivia seemed pleased to be asked. "As a matter of fact, I do. The one on the right is better. The player seems more lifelike, less silly."

Suddenly Emily recognized the face on the more cartoonish poster on the left. It was her own! Olivia had drawn her upended with her feet in the air, bloomers displayed beneath her skirt for all to see, and a ball bouncing off her head.

Emily's cheeks burned along with her anger. It would most certainly garnish attention, but not the kind Emily wanted. How could she ever be taken seriously if she was the subject of cartoon drawings?

"Use this one." Emily thrust the first poster back at her grinning nemesis. "I'll keep the other one for my scrapbook."

18

After hauling her Underwood typewriter outside to the table beneath the shade trees, Emily settled herself in a straight-backed chair and ratcheted a sheet of paper into the machine. The stark white paper stared back at her. But instead of words, only Carter's face appeared in her mind, along with the fear about the upcoming baseball practice tomorrow. She'd missed his game Thursday night, but he hadn't seemed too miffed when she showed up for practice on Friday.

They worked on throwing, and she'd shown improvement. Not nearly enough, but it was a start. Then he'd announced it was time to tackle batting, and her fears multiplied faster than the lake's mosquitoes after a rain. He must have noticed because he'd whisked her off for lunch at one of the Midway's lunch counters and kept the conversation far from baseball. Afterward, she returned with him to watch the Manawa Owls practice, and following that, he'd quizzed her mercilessly about what he'd taught her so far.

She took a deep breath of the crisp, morning lake air and released it slowly before turning back to the typewriter. These articles were overdue now. In an effort to get them done, she'd risen before everyone else and snuck from the cabin. Between her work with planning the game and spending time with Carter, she'd neglected her obligations this week. She couldn't let it happen again. Her personal life could not interfere with the cause. Nothing was more important than that.

A twinge of guilt tugged on her heart.

God was.

Why did it have to be Sunday? Surely He understood how much she had to do and the importance of it all. There simply wasn't a choice. Besides, God wasn't going anywhere. He'd still be there when she finished the articles.

She set her fingers on the ceramic-topped keys. What should she write about this month? Two recent arguments she'd faced came to mind. One man had told her that because all women did not support a woman's need for the right to vote, the suffrage claim held no merit. This, of course, was ridiculous. Many women had yet to realize they were important factors in the government of this nation.

Another argument she'd heard recently was that men had already given women the right to have an education, to own property, and to work in professions once closed to them. "So," one man had asked, hooking his thumbs in his vest pockets, "why do they now need to vote? What do women hope to gain from that?"

She could answer that question easily. While it was true some of the country's best colleges had opened to women, many still did not admit them. Owning property still had its limitations, and while there were women doctors, lawyers, and scientists, they were not as accepted as their male counterparts. Giving women the right to vote raised them to equal status, and future rights would then be harder to deny.

The cabin's screen door creaked open. Grandma Kate hiked up her skirt and crossed the dewy grass. "Emily? What are you doing? Church services begin soon. There's no time to write."

"I can't go this morning. I need to finish these articles."

Grandma Kate sat down across from Emily and placed a hand on her arm. "Dear, that's hardly seeking first the kingdom of God."

"God understands."

Her voice was soft and warm. "I'm sure He does, but do you?"

Before Emily could return to typing, Britta arrived bearing a tray with a pot of coffee and a basket of fresh sweet breads. She poured them each a cup.

"Thank you, Britta." Grandma Kate stirred a spoonful of sugar into her cup. "Ethel and Millie will be along directly."

Emily took a sweet roll from the basket and slathered it with butter. The first bite of spicy cinnamon and apples melted on her tongue. Her favorite. It was gone before her aunts even stepped out the door.

Her grandmother cleared her throat. "You still have time to get ready."

"Grandma . . ." The plea in her voice came out more like a whine. Why was she acting like this? Her grandmother was right. Still, how would she get it all done if she forfeited this opportunity for an empty camp, free from all distractions?

Her grandmother swept her hand over the typewriter and papers. "This will all still be here when we get back."

"I guess you're right." Emily stood, gathered her papers, and lifted the typewriter into her arms. "But this afternoon, you have to help keep Aunt Ethel and Aunt Millie busy so I can complete my work."

Grandma Kate laughed. "And who will keep Carter Stockton busy?"

❧

Kate watched her granddaughter balance the typewriter and attempt to open the screen door with her right index finger. The typewriter started to tip, but Emily managed to recapture it before the impending crash.

Releasing the breath she'd been holding on Emily's behalf, Kate pressed a hand to her heart. What was she going to do with that girl? When she was younger, Kate had been constantly driven too, but willing to skip church?

Deep inside, concern fanned into worry. This morning was only a symptom of something she'd seen growing in her granddaughter. Should she confront her? Kate sighed and picked up her teacup. No, it wouldn't do any good. Emily needed to see this hole in her faith for herself.

❧

The canvas edges on the meeting tent flapped in the breeze. Carter eyed the row of chairs he'd been trying to save. Services were set to begin in minutes, and if Emily and her entourage didn't hurry, someone would snag them.

Then he spotted her, a vision in a white gauzy dress, walking beside her grandmother with her two aunts in tow. Emily's hat seemed to bloom with pink roses, while her grandmother, in soft blue, paled beside her. She walked slowly to accommodate the older women, but the ladies seemed to have no trouble keeping up with the conversation.

She spied him and shyly wiggled her gloved fingers in

his direction. A few minutes later, they approached and he stood.

"I saved some seats for you ladies." He motioned to the row of wooden folding chairs.

Aunt Ethel's lips curved downward. "I don't like to sit this far back, but if I must . . ."

"It's a perfect spot." Aunt Millie winked at Carter. "Ethel, why don't you take the aisle seat so you can see better?"

This seemed to appease Ethel, and the women filed in. Chuckling, Carter took his seat beside Emily. "You look lovely. It was getting so late, I wasn't sure you were coming."

"Neither was I."

Before he could ask what she meant, the service began, and they stood to sing. He held the hymnal for her and found her sweet soprano a perfect match to his sometimes off-key baritone. Neither of them would be asked to perform, but he was certain the sound of two believers lifting their hearts in song brought a smile to the Lord.

Somewhere between the preacher's opening words and the conclusion, Emily's rose-scented perfume reached his nose. He wondered what the preacher would say if he kissed her right in the middle of the sermon about Haggai. It was hard to concentrate on how the Israelites were too busy to rebuild the temple when he was entertaining thoughts of building a life with the special lady beside him.

"God didn't dwell in their hearts back then," Brother Fossen said. "He dwelt in the temple. And when the Israelites said they were too busy to do His work, it was like saying they were too busy to have God in their lives."

Emily fidgeted beside him and opened her fan. Odd. It didn't seem warm to him.

Brother Fossen's deep voice rose. "Mark my words, brothers

and sisters, if you don't let the Lord make your paths straight, you'll spend most of your life running in circles."

Following the chorus of "amens," the congregation rose. Emily again sang beside him, but not with the same exuberance. The words seemed to come out strained from her lips. Glancing at her face, he found her eyes closed, and when she opened them, they glinted with unshed tears.

With a sigh, he chastised himself for not listening closer to the sermon. Now he had no idea what the preacher had said that had moved her.

And one thing he'd learned about Emily. Asking her may or may not yield an answer.

19

"Don't I get a day off?" Waving her lacy fan in front of her face, Emily couldn't believe her ears. Carter wanted to give her another baseball lesson today? Besides being Sunday, the noonday's stifling humidity made her cotton dress cling to her skin, and dark clouds gathering in the sky promised a shower later in the day.

Carter had joined them for lunch after church. As soon as he'd polished off the last bite of Britta's apple cobbler, he announced they'd better get going if they were going to beat the rain.

"Honestly, Carter, I have an article I need to write." She glanced at her grandmother for support. Having already challenged her sisters to a game of whist, Grandma Kate gave Emily an I-told-you-so grin.

Maybe Carter was the problem.

Carter downed the rest of his lemonade. "There're only a few weeks until the game, and you've yet to hold a bat."

"But you're not dressed to practice."

"I can fix that." He removed his jacket, draped it over the back of a chair, tugged his tie loose, and rolled up his sleeves. "All set. Besides, I'm not the one who'll be doing the work."

"If you're teaching me to hit a ball, I promise it will be work." Emily glanced at the sky. "What if it rains?"

"You'll get wet." He chuckled, then tapped her nose. "But I'm already quite certain you aren't made of sugar, so you won't melt."

"Oh, all right." Emily rolled her eyes, folded the fan, and set it beside her plate. "For a little while, but I have to get back here and work on that article."

"I won't keep her out all afternoon, Mrs. Graham. I promise."

"Please, call me Kate." Grandma Kate grinned, her eyes twinkling. "And take your time, Carter. Who knows how long it will take for our Emily to perfect her swing."

Less than half an hour later, Emily stood on the field with the tapered bat in her hands. Carter encouraged her to take a few swings in the air to get a feel for it. The first time, she nearly toppled from the weight.

He laughed—a full-bellied, enjoying-the-moment laugh. "Well, I can see I have my work cut out for me."

"Might this be a good time for me to say 'I told you so'?" She sighed. "Carter, it's hopeless. I'm hopeless."

He stepped behind her and rested his hands on her shoulders. "Let me be the judge of that." He worked the muscles in her neck, kneading them gently. "Relax. Tension is your worst enemy when it comes to swinging a bat."

With his touch firing through her, relaxing seemed impossible. Still, she leaned into his warm hands and found some of the tension easing.

"Good." He slipped in front of her and held out the bat. "Let's start with your grip."

After wiping her sweaty palms on her divided skirt, she grasped the heavy ash bat.

"Choke up, Emily."

"Why would I do that?"

Laughter rumbled from his chest. "I didn't mean you had to choke. I meant"—Carter pointed to the bat—"move your hands up higher. It's called 'choking up.' There you go. Good. Now line up your middle knuckles on each hand. See, you did it."

"If that's all there was to this, I'd be a happy lady."

"'Fraid not." His gaze dropped to her feet. "Next is stance. Remember how you stood when you were at the shooting range? Try that."

She shifted her feet farther apart. "Like this?"

"Yes, only now you need to bend your knees a little."

She complied. "I look ridiculous."

"You look like a beautiful baseball player." He paused and grinned. "And that blush looks lovely with your outfit."

She rolled her eyes. "Have you forgotten I have a bat in my hands?"

"Ah, but can you use it?" He backed away toward the pitcher's mound. "We're going to start with a nice, easy lob. All you have to do is watch the ball and swing at it."

Emily kept her gaze on the baseball from the moment it left Carter's hand. As the ball barreled toward her, she raised her bat in the air and brought it down like an axe chopping wood. The ball landed with a thud behind her.

"That was—uh—interesting." Carter managed to contain the laughter obviously wanting to erupt.

"You said you were going to make it an easy one."

"It was." Carter grabbed the ball and then moved behind her. He stepped close to her, his hot breath warming her neck.

"What are you doing?" she squeaked.

He slipped his hands over hers. "I'm going to show you how to swing. Relax, Emily. Remember? No tension."

"I'm trying." She swallowed hard. Who was she kidding? She'd never relax with Carter so close.

"Now, when you hit the ball, concentrate on driving through it." As he spoke, he moved her hands and the bat in a horizontal line. "Keep it nice and even. Got it?"

His breath tickled her ear, sending chills coursing through her despite the June heat. "Huh? Oh, yeah. Nice and even."

When he removed his support from the bat, it started to fall. She caught it and quickly resumed her batting position. If Carter noticed, he didn't say anything.

Determined to master this, she took a couple of practice swings. Nice and even. Sweat beaded on her upper lip. Why didn't the heat seem to bother Carter?

"Ready?" Carter lifted his hands to his chest before tossing the ball underhanded in her direction.

She swung, catching only air, and spun in a circle.

"Toss the ball back, and we'll try again. That looked a lot better." He caught the poorly thrown ball with ease. "You need a break?"

"No. I'm going to do this."

"Good girl."

Twenty pitches later, she'd yet to make contact. Still, Carter didn't seem daunted. With every pitch, he reminded her of how to stand, hold the bat, or swing. He never failed to add a word of encouragement.

Emily dropped the nose of the bat to the ground and leaned

on the handle with one hand. "Maybe I could use that break now."

"Not until you hit one."

"Carter—" She lifted the bat back into place and took a deep breath. "You're right. So, what do I do when I hit one?"

"Run to first base."

"Here? Now?"

"Sure, why not? That's what you'll do in the game." He held the ball up in front of himself. "You're going to hit it out of the park this time. Right?"

She got into position and nodded. The ball came toward her. Her nerves tingled. She swung. The solid connection reverberated down the length of the bat and tingled up her arms. The ball came off the end and flew toward the infield.

"Run!" The ball dropped to the ground in front of Carter and bounced toward third.

Halfway to first base, she realized she still held the bat. She heaved it into the air, took two more steps, and came to a complete stop. End over end, the bat flew through the air—right toward Carter on the pitcher's mound.

❧

"Carter!"

The hurler heard Emily's words of warning but didn't need them. He took a step back from the pitcher's mound, and the bat clunked to the ground with a puff of dust.

She ran across the field to him, tears making her eyes glisten like mossy pools. "Carter, are you all right? I'm so sorry. I threw it without thinking. I should have known better."

"Hey." He captured her hand. "It's fine. I've coached enough kids to realize a bat can be thrown anywhere when you're first learning. It's nothing to get upset about."

"But it is. What if I'd hit you? What if I did that in a game?"

"You didn't and you won't." He retrieved the ball and jogged back to her. "Now let's go celebrate."

"Celebrate the fact you survived another day of practice with me?"

"No." A few raindrops splattered the light blue fabric of her shirtwaist. "You deserve to be rewarded for your first successful hit, and it looks like it's the perfect time to call it a day before we both end up getting soaked. I'll get the bat and we can go."

While Emily made her way to the edge of the field, he picked up the discarded bat and tossed it in the air. Catching it with ease, he grinned. He had the perfect reward in mind for Miss Emily Graham, and he couldn't wait to give it to her.

"Ready?" He stuffed the bat in a burlap sack and swung it over his shoulder.

Emily shielded her face with her hand from the now-steady sprinkling and turned in the direction of her cabin.

He caught her arm. "Where are you going?"

"Back to the cottage."

He glanced at the sky. Like overfilled wineskins, the gray clouds threatened to burst without notice. "We'll never make it. Let's head toward Manhattan Beach."

"But Carter—"

"Trust me."

She sighed but let him lead the way.

As the rain started to fall harder, the two of them jogged toward the buildings lining the shore's edge.

He pointed to the upscale Kursaal, the newest pavilion on the lake, still being constructed. The walls of the two-story pavilion were sided and painted a pristine white, but Carter knew the building's interior was not yet completed.

"We can't go in there! It's not open yet."

"Emily, you're getting drenched."

Leaves whipped from the ground and spun in a dizzying dance. The weather vane on top of the building whirled and clacked in the gusts.

"But it's trespassing." Emily hugged her body.

He could pick Emily up and carry her inside if he had to, but that wouldn't start the rest of the afternoon off like he hoped. "Technically, my dad's bank handled the financing, so it's not trespassing. Besides, aren't you the least bit curious as to what it's like inside?"

Even with rain-dampened tendrils framing her face, a spark lit her eyes at his unspoken dare. Home run.

Emily hiked up her shortened skirt. "Last one there is out!" she called, bolting ahead of him.

With a grin on her face, she took to the path at breakneck speed, but sliding into second would have been easier than running on the freshly soaked dirt.

"Emily, be careful!"

❧

For once Emily held victory within her grasp. Sure, the race wasn't completely fair, but she had to take whatever advantage she could get. At least she was running, and Carter could see she was changing. Hadn't she hit that baseball? And hadn't she learned to throw it?

In a fraction of a minute, the clouds opened, releasing the burden they'd been carrying all day in a torrential downpour. Blinded momentarily, Emily caught her foot on what felt like a protruding root. She fought to catch herself with outstretched arms, but when her hands hit the mud, they simply slid. She lost her battle, landing face-first in the fresh sludge.

Carter quickly pulled her to her feet. "Are you hurt?"

"Only my pride." She wiped the mud from her mouth with the back of her hand and licked her lips. She grimaced at the grit on them.

A bolt of lightning lit the sky and thunder followed on its tail.

"Inside. Now." Carter held her elbow, and Emily didn't resist as he propelled her down the remainder of the path, up the steps, and inside what would soon be the grandest building on the lake.

Fitting she should enter it, covered in mud, on the arm of a handsome man.

She wiped a muddy tear from her face. Why had she let herself believe things could change? She was still the same clumsy girl she'd always been. Now all Carter had to do was look at her and have it confirmed.

He led her to a pile of lumber and motioned for her to sit down. After finding a rag, he tossed it to her.

She missed it, then retrieved it from the sawdust-covered floor. While she made a feeble attempt at cleaning her skirt, Carter found a crock filled with drinking water and brought her a tin cup.

In silence, he walked around the skeleton insides of the building for several minutes. "It's going to be something, isn't it? Some people think it's hard to picture something all completed when they see the bare bones like this. But it's not for me. Maybe it's a gift, but I can already see you dancing upstairs in that new grand ballroom, wearing a fine emerald gown."

"I don't have an emerald gown."

"Yet." He shoved a fistful of wet curls from his forehead. As he raked his eyes over her disheveled appearance, another grin tugged at the corners of his lips.

166

"What?" she snapped.

"Well, based on what I saw, you should be a natural at sliding into a base."

She wiped her hands on the rag. "Carter, this isn't funny. Look at me. I make a mess of everything I do."

He chuckled.

She threw the rag at him. "I said it wasn't funny."

His laughter echoed in the empty building. Apparently, he found her circumstances quite entertaining, even though they irritated her to no end. The humiliation was bad enough, but knowing any minute Carter would wake up and realize she was—and would always be—the same clumsy person, was far worse. She marched to the window, her wet skirt clinging to her legs.

Before her, the lake churned like the anger burning inside her. It wasn't fair. If she hadn't run . . . if God hadn't let it rain at the wrong moment . . . if Carter hadn't insisted she learn to play baseball . . .

She whirled toward him. "Why are you doing this?"

"Doing what?"

"Making me play this game." Tears, traitorous and frustrating, fought their way down her cheeks. "Why can't your Owls simply play the Bloomer Girls without me on the team? Even if we worked day and night, I won't be an asset. This"—she pointed to the mud clinging to her—"should prove that."

Carter shrugged. "It doesn't prove anything. Emily, you tripped. It happens to everyone at one time or another."

"No one trips like I do."

Another chuckle rippled through the room. "You may have a point." He crossed the space between them and leaned casually on the window casing beside her. He stared out at the lake and then slowly turned toward her. "No one does anything quite like you do. That's what I love."

A new warmth spread inside her under the intensity of his gaze, replacing the heat of anger she'd felt only moments before. Had he used the word *love*? She couldn't move, could scarcely breathe.

He stepped closer and cupped her grimy face with his hands.

"Carter, I look awful."

"You look beautiful to me." The pad of his thumb traced her cheek, then moved over her lower lip.

Her heart whirled like the weather vane on top of the Kursaal in the midst of the storm. Did he mean it? She studied his eyes, the truth laid bare in their caramel depths. How she wanted to believe him! Despite her tear-streaked cheeks and mud-caked clothing, for once in her life she let her heart take flight.

The thunder outside paled in comparison to the resonance beating in her chest.

Carter bent his head and brushed her lips with a kiss. He drew back, looked into her eyes, and kissed her again, long, slow, sweet—chasing away her last remnants of doubt.

20

Kate studied the playing cards fanned in her hand and arranged by suit. Not a bad dummy whist hand, but a truly tiresome afternoon.

Outside, the rain rat-a-tatted against the roof, forcing Kate and her two sisters to squeeze into the cottage's tiny parlor.

"How much did I bid?" Millie asked for the hundredth time.

"Three," Ethel snapped.

"I did not. Tell her, Kate."

"I have it right here." Ethel tapped her pencil so hard on the paper that the tip broke. "Now look what you made me do."

"Ladies." Kate let out an exasperated sigh. If the apostle Paul had been confined in prison with her sisters instead of Silas, he certainly would not have been singing. "Perhaps we could call this one hand a do-over since we have a discrepancy."

A rain-scented breeze ruffled the curtains. Ethel frowned but shuffled the cards again. She dealt to each of them and placed the dummy hand where Emily usually sat. "I do wish you would have told Emily to stay home this afternoon."

Picking up the hand she'd been given, Kate arranged her cards. "Only because we need a fourth. I bid one."

Ethel upped their bid to two, but Millie announced she believed she could turn three. Ethel dutifully recorded each number.

Finally, Millie turned the cards of the dummy hand over and smiled. "Delightful cards!" She led by playing the ace of hearts.

"If Emily were here, the four of us could practice our bridge whist instead of playing this dummy whist." Ethel followed suit and laid a ten.

"I'm still surprised bridge has become the rage of the season." Kate set her two on the table. "Although it is more scientific than old-fashioned whist."

"And far more exciting." Millie scooped up the first trick. "Emily is simply a natural at it."

"So I should have kept her here to entertain you?" Kate shook her head.

"Yes. No. I mean—"

"Play your card, Millie." Ethel laid down an eight of hearts after Millie played a king. "Kate, the reason I said you should have insisted Emily remain here this afternoon has nothing to do with card playing or the storm."

Kate took the trick with a trump card. "Then what is it?"

"I find it hard to believe you're encouraging a relationship with that Stockton boy."

"Haven't you noticed how happy Emily is?" Kate adjusted the cards in her hand. "Carter has been so good to her, and she clearly enjoys his company."

"But look what he's reduced her to. She parades around

like a man, catching balls and swinging bats and wearing those bloomers."

"She has a point, Kate," Millie said. "How will Carter notice her womanly ways if she acts and looks like a man?"

Kate stared at them. "I don't think he's having any trouble remembering Emily is a woman."

"But you've forgotten he's a Stockton." Ethel played a trump card, swiped the cards from the table, and neatly arranged her trick in a stack to her right.

"I don't want to talk about this."

"I know you don't, but you're going to have to. We all care about Emily, and you're handing her over to that boy."

"That boy has a name." Kate prayed her no-nonsense tone would end this discourse. "It's Carter."

"Stockton," Ethel added. "Son of Angus Stockton, the man who almost reduced your husband's business to bankruptcy only days after his death."

Kate slapped the remainder of her hand onto the table. "When are you two going to let that go? I forgave Angus long ago."

"So much so, you left your money in his bank." Millie folded her hand and smiled at her older sister. "Katie, dear, are you sure that was wise?"

"How many times do I have to tell you? I understand why Angus Stockton called in the implement company's loans when my Ethan died. He didn't trust me to run the business, and James had yet to prove himself."

Ethel sat up straighter. "So you've said."

"He was protecting his business. After we spoke at length about it, Angus agreed to let James continue with the loan payments as scheduled."

Ethel pointed her pencil at Kate. "And in a show of good faith, you left all of your accounts with that scoundrel."

"Angus wasn't a scoundrel." Kate rubbed her neck as the beginnings of a headache took hold. "He was a young bank president who wanted to impress his investors. When I was able to show him how it was in his best interest to extend the loan, he agreed."

Millie touched her arm. "After you showed him your larger investments, including your share in the Colorado silver mine."

"And after you agreed to a higher loan rate than any other bank would have required," Ethel said.

"But it all worked out. Angus has been nothing but fair to me ever since. And he's extended the same courtesy to James and now Martin."

A percussion of thunder shook the cottage. Kate glanced out the window where branches swung in the wind. Concern lumped in her throat. At least Emily wasn't out in this alone. Carter would take care of her.

Kate cleared her throat. "I think it's time the two of you forgave Angus and stopped worrying about Carter."

Millie wobbled to the window and shuttered it against the rain blowing in. "You're not the least bit concerned?"

"About her out in this? Perhaps a little. But not about Carter. Besides, if I remember right, weren't you the ones determined to see Emily married?"

"Yes, but we have a number of eligible suitors." Ethel pulled a list from her pocket and peered at it through the spectacles perched on the bridge of her nose. "I've been collecting names. Ralph Lingenfelter, Cecil Arbuckle, Horace Throop, Oly Smelby, and Walford Lindeen."

"And don't forget Marion Wormsley." Millie tapped the paper. "He may be willing to give her a second chance if the dizziness has worn off."

Kate held up her hand. "I can already tell I don't want to

know the rest of that story." She pinched the bridge of her nose, her headache now pounding incessantly. "I'll make you two a deal. If Emily decides to stop seeing Carter of her own accord, you can resume your matchmaking attempts to your hearts' content. Until then, leave her alone."

Ethel's lips pinched together as if she'd been given some bitter elixir.

Millie squeezed Kate's hand. "We only want what's best for her."

"As do I." Kate sighed. "And Emily deserves to find out if that best is Carter Stockton."

❧

Emily plucked a piece of dried mud from her skirt and flicked it into the sawdust. After the kiss, Carter had found comfortable spots on the second floor of the Kursaal where the two of them could sit and watch the rain dapple Lake Manawa. Not willing to risk another drenching, they'd agreed to remain inside the Kursaal until the rain stopped.

"I hope Grandma Kate isn't worried." Emily touched a finger to her lips. "But I don't want this afternoon to end."

"Me either." Carter grinned and looked out the window. "And apparently God thinks we should get some more time to talk."

"Then it's my turn. Tell me about Ducky."

"Do I have competition? You asked about him the other day too." Carter chuckled and Emily shot him a mock glare. "Fine. What do you want to know?"

"You told me before that the two of you were college roommates. Where's he from?"

"He's a farm boy from somewhere around Red Oak. His parents had a place there, but they've moved west."

173

"And he stayed?"

"Yes, to go to college. Since he lives here, his tuition was free."

"Did he play baseball before college?"

Carter chuckled. "Sort of. Every Sunday afternoon, a group of boys came out to the ball field so I could teach them how to play ball. It started with four or five and grew until there were more than enough for two teams. Ducky showed up one week and pitched in." Carter drew his hand through his moisture-kinked curls. "He was a natural."

"Maybe you were a natural teacher and coach."

"Don't tell Ducky. He thinks making the team was all his doing."

Conversation continued for another hour as the rain beat down on the new building. All too soon, the sun peeked from behind the clouds, birdsong filled the air, and they had yet to leave.

"I could talk to you all day." Carter kissed her fingertips.

"I think you already have." Emily glanced out the window. "How late do you think it is?"

He shrugged. "Five o'clock, maybe."

Oh no! With a cry, Emily jumped to her feet. "My article! I completely forgot."

"Relax, Emily. You'll get it done." He climbed to his feet and brushed the sawdust from the back of his pants. "How hard can it be to throw some words on a page?"

She frowned. "I need to get home. Now."

"Whoa." He caught her waist and pulled her close. "I didn't mean to offend you. I know what you're doing is important. How can I help?"

She placed her hands on his chest. "Take me home."

"Can I kiss you goodbye first?"

She giggled. "Well, you'd better do it here or my aunts will probably skin you alive. On second thought, they might anyway when they see me. Perhaps we should say goodbye at the halfway point."

"No way. I'll take my chances." He raised his eyebrows. "And by the way, you look good in mud."

"But I'd look better in an emerald-green ball gown?"

"Different. Not better." Beneath her hands, she felt laughter rumble in his chest. "But speaking of ball gowns, you know they're having a big grand opening here in two weeks. Would you like to go?"

"With you?" she teased.

"Or I guess you could go with Marion Wormsley."

"Oooo, do you have to remind me?" She looked up into his eyes. "Yes, Carter Stockton, I'd be honored to go with you."

"Good. Now, about that goodbye kiss." His gaze dropped to her lips.

As he dipped his head, her heart skipped a beat, banishing thoughts of anything but him.

❦

After lighting the wick of the kerosene lamp, Carter sat down at a small table inside the Owl Club and opened the ledger containing Kate Graham's financial information. The clock on the wall struck an ominous three o'clock. What was it about this ledger that had startled him out of his sleep and driven him to reexamine it?

His lips curled as he thought of Emily, splattered with mud and looking beautiful. Never in his life had he met anyone who captured him so, nor anyone he'd wanted to kiss as much. She fell and got back up. She failed and kept trying. She saw a wrong and refused to quit until it had been righted.

Unsinkable.

And he was drawn to her spirit like a five-year-old to a peppermint stick.

He shook his head. But why had his dreams of her turned to nightmares involving her grandmother's ledger? He'd awakened with a sense of urgency he'd learned not to ignore. God had a way of getting his attention, and he feared this was one of those times.

After locating a piece of scratch paper, he added the columns again and listed the total. But the quarterly statement from the bank differed by nearly three thousand dollars. How could that be? If it had been exactly three thousand, he would have guessed someone had erred in figuring it, but not this odd sum. When he'd spoken to the bank clerk, the man had insisted their recording ledgers had been signed by Nathan himself.

And Nathan didn't make mistakes.

He rubbed his sleep-filled eyes. Could Kate Graham somehow have forgotten to record a significant withdrawal? Worse, maybe she was forgetting things and didn't record several. His chest tightened. Poor Emily. This afternoon she'd told him about her grandmother—her courage, her determination, and her intelligence. If he had to tell Emily her grandmother's mind might be slipping, Emily would be devastated.

But until he knew the answer, he was not telling anyone anything. He flipped the pages back to the beginning and began to recalculate every column. Even if it took all night, he'd find out if there was a mistake. Maybe Nathan had messed up for once. If by morning he hadn't found it, he'd begin to look elsewhere.

Something was definitely not adding up.

"You're late."

Emily stiffened at the gruff voice. "I know, and I apologize." She held out her article to the newspaper's editor, Irwin Fletcher. "I had to finish it up this morning, and I wouldn't ask, but it really needs to go in this week."

A shiny spot on the bald man's head glinted as he wiped his hands on his printer's apron and took the article. "I'll accept it this time, but don't let it happen again."

"I won't, Mr. Fletcher." She offered him a broad smile. "And I do appreciate your willingness to print the articles about women's rights. You're a grand supporter."

"I'm not a supporter." His tone serious, he sat down at his desk and opened the article. "It's news, Miss Graham. Some folks care about ladies voting and some don't. I just give them what they want to hear. Take your Bloomer Girls' game, for example."

"You've heard about it?"

"Folks all over town are talking about it. Personally, I don't think a woman has any right to play a man in a game of checkers, let alone baseball, but I'll be there to report on it because people want to know."

Her eyes narrowed. "And you'll do so fairly?"

"Goes without saying." He dipped a pen in an inkwell and motioned toward the door. "Thanks to you being late, I'm behind."

"In that case, I'd better bid you farewell." The words came out clipped. "Again, I apologize for my tardiness."

"You're a woman. You can't help it. That's how God made you females."

After slamming the door harder than any lady should, Emily marched toward the bank. She could imagine Mr. Fletcher grumbling about emotional women, but she didn't care. If she didn't need the free press opportunity his newspaper offered, Emily would happily never grace Irwin Fletcher's presence again.

Council Bluffs First Bank stood out among the buildings on Broadway. Six stories tall, the building sported a corner turret. Emily smiled at the gentleman who held the heavy walnut door while she passed through. The heels of her shoes clicked on the shiny floorboards as she crossed the foyer to the teller's desk. Spotting Jim Wilson, Greta's brother and one of the bank's clerks, she approached his window.

"Hello, Miss Graham. What can I do for you today?" The nervous sort, Jim wrung his hands while he waited for her answer.

"I'd like to make a withdrawal for my grandmother." Emily placed a bank draft on the counter. "She wants to purchase some new wicker furniture for the lake cottage."

"Give me a second, and I'll get that right out to you." With an overly polite smile, Jim walked to his desk and flipped through a ledger.

Suddenly someone covered Emily's eyes with their hands. "Guess who."

She pulled the large hands away. "Martin! What are you doing here?"

"I'm a businessman, remember?" He glanced behind the clerk's counter. "You here for Grandma?"

"She wants two new wicker rockers. She's tired of Aunt Millie and Aunt Ethel fighting over the one we have." She looped her arm in Martin's. "And I want lunch. If you can be civil, I'll let you treat me."

He chuckled. "I apologize for last time."

"Apology accepted."

Jim returned, his brows creased in worry. "Miss Graham, I

regret to inform you there doesn't seem to be sufficient funds in your grandmother's regular account. Do you want more transferred from her savings?"

"There must be a mistake." Emily glanced at Martin for confirmation. "According to Grandma, there should be plenty."

Martin squeezed her arm. "I'll check into it, sis. For now, Jim, please transfer over the necessary funds."

A few minutes later, he returned with the cash and counted the bills into Emily's palm. "I apologize for the confusion, but I'm sure we'll get it straightened out soon. Carter Stockton was in this morning speaking to his brother, our vice president, about it."

"Carter?" Surprise registered on Martin's face.

"Yes, sir. He said he's working for your grandmother. He had a letter of proof stating that fact—not that he'd need one here." He leaned forward and spoke to Martin. "He and Nathan had words." He stopped, and guilt clouded his features. "I'm sorry. I shouldn't have said anything."

Offering Jim a weak smile, Emily thanked her friend and bid him goodbye. After leaving the bank, she walked beside her brother in silence. Martin was so quiet. Maybe he was mulling over the same information as she. Carter and Nathan had argued. From what Carter had told her, arguments between the two brothers occurred regularly. She suspected this one had more to do with baseball than her grandmother's finances.

Martin rubbed his chin. "Tell Carter I want to talk to him."

"Let him handle this. Grandma has faith in him and so do I."

"I didn't say I didn't believe he could do it." He held the door to the café for her.

"You didn't have to. I can see it on your face." She started to enter and stopped short. On a nail by the door, a poster advertising the Bloomer Girls caught her eye. However, it was not the artful one she'd approved. Instead, the caricature of her, with feet in the air and bloomers displayed for all to see, loomed large.

Her cheeks grew iron hot and so did her anger.

Martin pointed to the poster. "You okayed that?"

"Of course not!"

"Let me guess. Olivia?"

"Who else?" She ripped the poster down from the nail, shoved it at his chest, and marched up the sidewalk.

"Where are you going?"

"To tear down every single one of those."

He caught up to her. "Wait a minute. You don't want to do that."

"And exactly why wouldn't I?" She yanked another poster from an undertaker's storefront.

Martin tugged it from her grip and rehung the poster. "Because if she knows she's rattled you, she wins. If you laugh at it, then you win. The ability to laugh at yourself has always been one of your best qualities."

She stopped and spun toward him. "Do I look like I'm laughing?" The hurt flamed. What would people think? What would Carter think? Every time he went anywhere with her in town, that poster would be reminding him what people thought of her.

Martin placed his hands on her shoulders. "Emily, trust me."

She huffed but finally met Martin's eyes, solid and strong. For twenty-two years he'd never let her down. Even though she was often irritated because he still thought of her as his little sister, his advice had always been sound.

She released an exasperated sigh. "So what do I do now?"

He smiled. "That's my girl. Let's start with lunch and move on from there."

21

"Lunch time!" Carter waved his cap in the air to signal the team. Skirting the puddles left by yesterday's rain, he jogged off the field.

Ducky passed him a dipper of water from the crock the team carried to the field every day. "When are you going to bring Emily to practice with us?"

Carter gulped the cool water. After plunging the dipper back into the crock, he poured the contents over his head. "She's not exactly ready for that."

"Like she ever will be." Elwood Taylor plucked a blade of dry grass from the earth, stuck the end in his mouth, and leaned against a post.

Carter shot him a glare. Why hadn't he left with everyone else? "She tries hard, Elwood."

Elwood flicked the piece of grass at Carter. "I think what she's trying is to wrap you around her little finger."

"Drop it, Elwood." Ducky tossed the burlap gear bag at the right fielder. "Make yourself useful."

With a sneer, Elwood left to gather the bats.

Ducky turned to Carter. "He's trouble."

"Tell me something I don't know. You think I should let him go?"

"He's the best batter we have. If you do, our perfect season will probably be over."

Carter picked up his glove from the bench. "I can handle him. He's just trying to rile me."

"I know you won't let him get to you, but what about Emily? What if he bothers her?"

Carter jabbed his fist into the mitt so hard his knuckles stung. "She'll probably handle it better than I will."

Behind home base, Elwood stuffed the various bats into the sack. What was with him? Everyone knew that when Elwood had been drinking, he got a little crazy, but today he was as sober as Emily's aunt Ethel. Was his anger directed at women in general, or Emily in particular?

Elwood returned and tossed the equipment bag at Carter's feet. "I'm coming to watch the girl play this afternoon, Stockton, and you can't stop me."

Ducky snagged the sack from the dirt. "Leave her alone."

"It's okay, Ducky." Carter's gaze never left Elwood's face. "You can come. You can use the extra practice 'cause you looked a little sloppy out there today."

"*I* looked sloppy? Have you taken a look at your clumsy girlfriend? She should be throwing tea parties, not baseballs. I'm telling you, Stockton, that woman is going to make us the laughingstock of the city."

"Watch it, Taylor." Carter crossed his arms over his chest. "And for your information, Emily can hit."

His gut clenched. The words were out before he could yank them back in. Connecting once was hardly being able to hit, and if she had someone watching her, who knew how she'd perform.

Elwood pushed his sleeves up. "All right, Stockton, I'll make you a bet."

Carter raised an eyebrow. "I'm listening."

"If the girl can hit a ball into the outfield, just one ball, I'll . . ."

Ducky moved alongside Carter. "You'll what?"

"I'll do whatever Stockton wants. But if she doesn't, he tells her she can't play in the game after all."

"Whatever I want?" Carter let the idea bounce around. Elwood Taylor deserved to be taken down a peg, but at Emily's expense? Then an idea made his lips curl. "Okay, here's the deal. If Emily can't get a decent hit this afternoon, I'll tell her she's not playing. But if she does, you'll dress up like a woman for the Bloomer Girls' game."

Elwood held up his hands. "No way."

Ducky laughed. "You made the deal. You can't go back on your word now. You said whatever Carter wanted."

"But—"

Ducky walked around Elwood, raking his gaze over the man's stature.

"What are you doing?" Elwood whirled to face him.

"Trying to decide what kind of skirt to get you."

Elwood grabbed his cap from his back pocket and jammed it on his head. "She hasn't hit the ball yet, and I don't think she ever will."

With a deep chuckle, Carter clapped him on the back. "There's something about Emily you ought to know. She likes a good challenge, and I've not seen her fail at one yet."

After Elwood skulked away, Ducky slung the bat bag over his shoulder. "Is she going to have your hide for this?"

"Probably—if she finds out about it." Carter tossed the baseball in the air as he walked down the path.

"You're not going to tell her?"

"I haven't decided yet."

"I just hope you know what you're doing."

He launched the ball high in the air. Using his glove to shield his eyes from the noon sun, he moved to the right and waited until the ball landed with a satisfying thud in his glove. "So do I, Ducky. So do I."

❧

"I don't have a clue what I'm doing." Emily stomped her foot on the first base bag. Carter stood on the pitcher's mound like a Greek god, not even breaking a sweat, trying to explain under what conditions she should run the bases. "If I hit the ball, I run here. But what do you mean about stealing second? Why would I want to do that if I'm safe here?"

Ducky laughed from home plate.

"Emily, if the pitcher throws to home, you can take advantage of it and steal the base," Carter said. "It puts you one step closer to scoring."

"But you said if they see me, I have to run back to first base."

"Or . . ." He closed the distance between them and gave her a roguish smile. "You can slide into the base. I know you know how to do that."

Her cheeks warmed, and she imagined them turning as red as the letters on his jersey. "Can I just go back to hitting practice?"

"Batting practice." He ran his hand down the length of her arm and squeezed her hand. "And yes, you can."

A shrill whistle made her jump. Ducky grinned and nodded toward another approaching Owl.

Emily stiffened. "Who's that?"

"Elwood Taylor. Another one of the Owls. Don't worry about him."

"But you said I wasn't ready to practice with the team."

Carter nodded toward home. "Go get your bat and show him what you can do."

Rolling her eyes, Emily sighed. "Oh, that ought to be impressive."

When she reached home plate, Ducky handed her the bat. "Carter said you've been doing really well."

"He lies."

Emily assumed the still-awkward stance over the plate. Carter threw an easy ball in her direction. She swung and missed.

"Keep your eye on the ball, Emily." Ducky tossed the ball back. "You can do this."

The second ball whizzed by and slapped into Ducky's glove. A man nearby chuckled. She turned. It was that Elwood fellow.

"Go back to your preaching!" he called. "This is no place for a lady."

She glared at him. How dare he? She'd show him.

Setting her jaw, she eyed Carter and nodded. The pitch barreled toward her. She drew back the bat and swung it hard. The solid connection rumbled through the bat to her hands and reverberated up her arms. The ball ricocheted off the end.

"Go!" Ducky yelled.

Drop the bat. Drop the bat. She tossed it and sprinted toward the first bag.

Carter met her, grabbed her waist, and swung her in the air. "You did it!"

Emily shrieked and held her cap on with her hand. Finally, Carter set her down, and she noticed for the first time where the ball had fallen—on the edge of right field. Joy sent her heart soaring.

Then she spotted Elwood Taylor jogging over. Her lips pulled downward.

"Was he hassling you at bat?" Carter nodded toward Elwood.

"A little. Called me a preacher. Told me I didn't belong." Carter chuckled. "You showed him."

Elwood stopped in front of them. "Don't look so happy. I would have caught her on first."

"Taylor, she did it, and I'm proud of her." Carter kissed her cheek. "And for your information, I'm the only one who'll be catching Emily—on first or anywhere else."

With a smile as bright as the late afternoon sunshine, Emily paraded beside Carter on the boardwalk toward the electric launches. Reaching the dock, she tugged her skirt lower on her hips. She should have insisted he take her back to the cottage to change. Her loose blouse and divided skirt, while perfect for practicing baseball, were hardly appropriate on the Grand Plaza and showed far too much of her ankles.

She smoothed the sides of her hair with her hands.

"You look beautiful." Carter squeezed her hand. "And you're dressed perfectly for what I have in mind for the rest of the day."

"I didn't agree to spend the whole day with you, Carter. I still have work to do." She took the hand he offered and stepped down into the boat.

Carter sat down beside her. "And what did you have on your save-the-world agenda today?"

"I have letters to write to Iowa's senators and representatives, I need to plan tomorrow's suffrage meeting, and I really need to see about some new advertising posters."

"And that can't wait for one day?" He gave her an impish smile, his eyes dancing with pride.

She shook her head and laughed. "You're insufferable."

"You can't blame a guy for wanting to go out and celebrate with his girl. Besides, Ducky volunteered to go tell your grandmother I'd have you home by nightfall."

Her breath caught. His girl? Sure, she sort of considered herself his girl, but to hear him say the words sent her heart fluttering.

A broad grin creased his face. Did he realize what he did to her?

She swallowed. "As long as I'm home by dinner."

"I'll do my best."

"Carter." She placed her hand on his arm. "Please, I have responsibilities."

The launch's engine roared to life, and the boat pulled from the shore. Carter pressed his mouth to her ear. "I promise I'll have you home in time to check all those things off your list."

The breeze from the ride fanned Emily's cheeks. Carter nodded toward the Kursaal, where men worked feverishly on the decking surrounding the building. He turned back to her and grinned. Emily's cheeks warmed under his gaze. From the center of the lake, the pavilion built out in the water seemed odd.

"See the men hanging the electric lights?" Carter pointed to three men on the roof. "The entire building will be lit at night like a Roman candle."

"How can they do that?"

"The streetcar company's electrical generators." He draped

his arm behind her. While he didn't touch her, the heat from his presence seeped through her blouse.

The launch bounced on the water, and he pulled her close.

Emily's gaze darted around the boat. No one seemed to notice. His closeness was intoxicating. She sighed, tucked a windblown tendril behind her ear, and let herself relax against his shoulder.

She should be working, but how could she with him around?

Fifteen minutes later, the electric launch docked and the captain cut the engine.

Carter pressed a kiss to the top of her head. "Ready?"

"Could we simply ride around on this all day?"

"And miss the fun I have planned?" He pulled her to her feet and assisted her out of the boat. Once on the boardwalk, he directed her toward the Grand Pavilion. "I know you said you'd like to be home by dinner, but would you like to get something to eat at the Grand Pavilion?"

She glanced at her clothes. "I'm hardly dressed for that."

"How about at one of the Midway's lunch counters?"

She agreed, and half an hour later she found herself seated at a counter, enjoying a pulled pork sandwich and a glass of soda.

"Can I get you two some pie for dessert?" The plump lady behind the counter pointed to the pies on the shelf. "We have apple, peach, and rhubarb."

Carter raised his eyebrow. "You pick."

"Rhubarb."

"Rhubarb it is. One piece, please, with ice cream if you have it, and two forks."

"You expect me to share?" Emily giggled. "Rhubarb is my favorite."

189

"Hmmm. We may have a problem. It's mine too." He took a swig of soda and waited as the server placed the pie between them. He forked a bite and held it out to her. "Let me guess—you like it because it's sweet and still a little bit tart."

"Exactly." She accepted the bite he offered.

"It reminds me of you."

Before she could ponder his words, a burly man approached and slammed a newspaper on the counter beside her. She jumped.

"Did you write this trash?" the man demanded.

Carter stood up, stance wide, his right eye twitching. "That's no way to address a lady."

Placing a hand on his arm, Emily glanced at the folded paper and spotted last week's column. "Sir, if you're asking if I wrote the article containing the reasons women should serve on juries, then the answer is yes."

"This is a bunch of rubbish. You can't expect women to be able to make those kinds of hard decisions. Women don't have the common sense."

"Sir, as you must have read in the article, since women commit crimes, they should be judged by their peers. The only way that can happen is if women serve in the capacity of juror. Furthermore, even the Bible speaks of a woman judge—Deborah."

He slammed his fist on the counter. "Stop filling my wife's mind with this nonsense."

"Your wife has a mind, sir. Obviously, however, you are lacking one."

The man turned to Carter. "You just gonna stand there?"

"Actually, no." Carter grabbed the man's wrist and twisted his arm behind his back. "I'm going to see that you take your rude self out of here." He pushed the man toward the door.

Another gentleman held it for him, and Carter heaved the man onto the sidewalk.

Carter returned, drawing his hand through his thick curls. "You okay?"

"You didn't need to trouble yourself."

"How often does that happen?"

"Once in a while. I'm used to it." She shrugged, but when she lifted her soda, her trembling hand betrayed her.

Carter dropped thirty cents onto the counter. "Come on. Let's get out of here."

Outside, he paused to make sure the man was gone before leading Emily off to the side of the lunch counter. He drew her into his arms. His chest heaved beneath her cheek.

"I'm okay, honest," she said, only a slight tremor in her voice.

"I'm not." After a few moments, he took hold of her shoulders, and his gaze met hers. "You were great in there."

"So were you." Her smile faded as fast as it appeared. She dipped her head. "I'm sorry about this."

He kissed the top of her head. "It wasn't your fault. Do you want to go back to the cottage?"

"And miss out on whatever you planned? I don't think so, mister."

The tension eased, and he grinned. "In that case, may I escort you?"

She took the arm he offered. A short while later she found herself standing in front of the Midway's bowling alley.

Her gaze darted from the sign to Carter's face. "You are kidding, right?"

"It'll be fun."

"Did you forget what I did with a horseshoe?"

"That was before."

"Before what?"

"Before me." He chuckled and held open the door.

Emily hesitated at the doorway to let her eyes adjust to the indoor lighting. Five alleys lay across the length of the room. A rack holding a row of bowling balls divided each alley from the next. Despite the wide ventilation opening between the top of the wall and the ceiling, the room reeked of cigar smoke. She spotted the reason hanging like a limp sausage out of the proprietor's mouth. Carter dropped two dimes in the man's hand. Emily squinted at the men calling to Carter.

"Is that Ducky? Is your team here?"

"Looks like most of the boys came." He placed his hand on the small of her back. "They want to meet you."

"I suppose it's too late to take you up on that offer of taking me back to the cabin."

He laughed. "You have to meet them sometime."

"All right, lead me to the lions' den." She took a deep breath and slipped her sweaty hand into the crook of his arm.

"They don't bite, and if any of them try, they'll answer to me."

She stiffened. "I can take care of myself."

Shaking his head as if he wanted to say something, he finally chuckled. "Of course you can."

"Anything I should know?"

He covered her hand with his own. "They are going to love you."

Despite the raucous laughter of the Owls, Emily's footsteps seemed to echo on the waxed floorboards. The group silenced as she approached.

She searched their faces. Some, like Carter, she'd known in high school. Others must have moved to the area since then, or like Ducky, they'd come to play ball on Carter's team.

As Carter introduced each player, she tried to commit their names to memory.

"There are a few more of us." Ducky's warm smile set her at ease. "Joe Powel wasn't feeling too well after practice, and Elwood Taylor was taking his girl to the vaudeville show."

"I'm afraid it will take me awhile to remember all the names."

"With Carter yelling at us every few minutes during practice, you'll catch on faster than you think."

The one she'd learned was Digger Hall slapped a hand on Carter's shoulder. "You going to stand around all day, Stockton, or are you two going to bowl?"

Emily tugged Carter's arm. "Carter, I've never done this before. Why don't I just watch?"

"Never?"

She shook her head.

He grinned. "One more thing I get to teach you. You'll do fine."

"But—"

Carter didn't let her protest further. Instead, he took her by the hand and pulled her to an open alley. "Wait here."

Seconds later, he returned with a hard wooden bowling ball. "This one should be light enough. Put your fingers in here." He pointed to the two holes. "And thumb in this one."

She positioned her hand.

"Not those fingers. Your middle and ring fingers."

"Did I hear you say something about a ring finger, Stockton?" Digger guffawed at his own humor.

Emily's cheeks flamed as she put the correct fingers in the holes.

"Hey, just ignore him, okay?"

"Carter, I can feel them all watching me," she whispered.

193

"You can't blame fellows who can't take their eyes off a beautiful girl." He winked and turned her to face the pins. "Okay, now you're going to take about four steps, bend down, and roll the ball at the pins as hard as you can. I'll go first, and you can watch."

Standing on the edge of the alley, she held the heavy ball in her hands and watched Carter. After he selected a ball, he held it near his chest. He took four steps while drawing his arm back, and then thrust the ball forward. The ball smashed into the stubby pins, and they flew into the air with a massive clattering of wood against wood. Not a pin remained standing.

The Owls hooted behind her.

"A strike on your first throw?" Digger called. "No one should be that lucky."

"Got my lucky charm right here." Carter placed his hands on her shoulders. "As soon as the pin boy gets it set back up, it's your turn."

"What if I get it in the trough thing?"

"It's a gutter, and you get no score for that." He squeezed her shoulders and then stepped back. "Ready?"

The loss of his touch set her nerves jittering. How many steps did Carter say she should take? What if she dropped the ball or sent it into the gutter thing? The last thing she wanted to do was embarrass Carter in front of his friends.

She pulled her fingers from the holes and wiped her damp hand on her skirt. Then, taking a deep breath, she stood before the pins and repositioned her fingers. *Please, Lord, don't let me fall.*

Hiking up her skirt with her free hand, Emily wobbled a bit on her steps. She managed to reach the line, dip low to the boards, and release the ball with a solid push. The ball spun first toward the gutter. Then, in an arc, it wove back and crept toward the pins. She bit her lip as it seemed to be on course for the other gutter. It tapped the first pin and slowly forged a path through the others.

Unable to watch any longer, she closed her eyes.

"Strike!" Carter grabbed her by the waist and hoisted her in the air. He spun her in a circle before setting her down. She glanced at the fallen pins and a thrill surged through her. Maybe her luck was changing after all.

An hour later, she and Carter said their goodbyes. She still found it hard to believe she'd actually thrown the ball backward once toward the fellows. Thankfully, Carter's teammates were good sports and moved lightning quick. Taking out the shortstop would not have been a good start to her participation on their team. Carter dismissed the event by saying it happened all the time.

Now brushstrokes of purple and pink over the lake told her the lateness of the hour. If they didn't hurry, she'd get home after dark and her aunts would berate her for hours.

With the sun sinking behind the bluffs, the air grew cooler. She welcomed the relief from the heat and the smell. A roomful of sweaty baseball players and a cigar-smoking proprietor did not make a rose garden.

Reaching the dock, she and Carter climbed on board the electric launch, seated themselves among a spattering of passengers, and waited for the captain to disembark.

Carter slipped his arm around Emily. "You were incredible tonight."

"Even when I almost bowled over your teammates?"

"It did put new meaning to the word *strike*."

She elbowed his ribs.

The boat puttered out onto the lake, and he leaned closer.

"You only had one gutter ball, and this was the first time you've ever played. Don't you think you should be proud of yourself?"

"Pride goeth before a fall, and in my case, that is a dangerous thought."

"Emily." His tone lost its playful edge. "Enough."

She swallowed hard. What had she said to annoy him? It was the truth. Wasn't it?

An uncomfortable gap in conversation followed. Finally, Carter pressed his lips to her ear. "Sometimes I wish you could see yourself through my eyes."

Her heart fluttered, and tears burned hot beneath her lids. Sometimes she wished she could too.

As quickly as it had flared, the serious moment evaporated. Holding her closer than he ought to in public, Carter seemed to relax. The tension in her own muscles seemed to slip away as well. The lull of the boat bobbing on the waves made her eyelids ache to close. She'd been up before the sun to write the article, had a heavy lunch with Martin, and had followed that with Carter's grueling practice. The altercation with the man at the lunch counter had taken an emotional toll, and she'd finally ended the day with two hours of tenpins. Surely resting her eyes for one minute wouldn't hurt anything.

Her head bobbed, and Carter gently pulled it toward his shoulder. She should sit up. Ladies didn't allow young men such liberties, but she was so tired. Cracking one eyelid open, she spotted a disapproving glare from an elderly lady about the age of her great-aunts. She smiled. Aunt Ethel would be horrified if she saw her right now.

Oh well, Aunt Ethel was never going to find out.

22

Soft, steady breath against Carter's neck signaled Emily had dozed off. She stirred and settled again. Warmth spread across his chest as he realized how significant this moment was. Emily trusted him enough to let her guard down and relax in his presence.

The ancient woman seated across from them stared with a disapproving frown permanently fixed on her sagging face. Carter glowered at her. Why couldn't people mind their own business? The lady didn't know Emily from Adam. She hadn't seen her step up to the plate today and hit that ball into the outfield. She hadn't seen how Emily didn't back down from the cad at dinner. And she certainly hadn't seen Emily take on the tenpins, fight her own demons, and triumph.

Even more, she hadn't witnessed Emily win his teammates over one by one, minus the two who hadn't joined them. They'd taken to her almost as easily as he had. They laughed with her, teased her, and made her feel like one of the Owls. More than once, he'd caught a teammate trying to share some embarrassing story about him. She'd listened and given them the warm smile that never failed to set his insides on fire.

He pressed his cheek against the top of her head, still nestled on his shoulder. How could he describe what was different about her?

Genuine.

There wasn't a false bone in Emily Graham's body.

As the boat docked, he touched her cheek with his free hand. "Hey."

She jerked her head up and blinked. "Please tell me I did not fall asleep."

"Then how could I tell you that you look even more beautiful that way?"

She rolled her eyes and tucked an errant strand of tawny hair behind her ear. "You sure you don't mean with my mouth shut?"

With a chuckle, he drew her to her feet. "As soon as I get you back to your cottage, you should probably get some sleep."

Her eyes widened. "Tomorrow!" She attempted to scramble out of the boat before he could help her. Still drowsy, she teetered and he steadied her. As soon as he released her, she stormed down the path like a line drive to second base.

"Emily, what's going on?"

"The meeting, remember? I need to organize it. All those things I told you I had to do, and I completely forgot."

"Relax. It'll be okay."

"No, Carter. It won't." Her pace picked up. "Those women are counting on me, and there's no way I can get it all done now."

"Even if you don't, it'll be all right."

"Carter, you don't understand. I've worked as hard to earn their respect as you've worked to earn your team's."

"And you don't want to lose that."

Even in the dimming light, he caught her glare. "I should have told you no."

"Whoa." He caught her arm and stopped. "Are you blaming me?"

She yanked her arm away. "No, I'm blaming me."

A sheet of silence hung between them for the rest of the walk. He could almost sense Emily ticking off her mental lists, planning how she'd get it all done through the wee hours of the morning, making herself sick—just like his mother.

❦

The words on the paper blurred. Emily rubbed her eyes and blinked to clear her vision. In the midst of her furious composing, morning had overtaken the night. Now, facing the day without sleep, she squinted against the sunshine pouring into the cottage's tiny parlor. Even the sweet twittering of the birds grated on her nerves.

"Good morning, dear." Aunt Millie laid a hand on her shoulder and squeezed. "Burning the midnight oil?"

"I'm afraid so."

Aunt Ethel entered the room, her shoes clipping against the hardwood floor. She cocked her head to the right and studied her reflection in the framed wall mirror before weaving a tortoise shell hat pin into her festooned bonnet. "That's what happens when you're out till all hours with that boy."

"Carter," Emily corrected.

"Yes, Ethel, the boy's name is Carter. And by the looks of him, he's hardly a boy." Aunt Millie giggled and sat down beside Emily at the table. Suddenly her aunt's demeanor changed. Her brows drew together in concern. "And you weren't out all night, were you, dear?"

"No, Aunt Millie. I was home before dark."

Her plump aunt's lips bowed in a broad smile. "I trust you had a good time."

"Mostly." Emily refused to lie. Even though she might be avoiding daily contact with God, she still didn't want to incur His wrath. "But I had a lot to do and probably should have told Carter I couldn't go bowling with him."

"Bowling!" Aunt Ethel spun from the mirror, her eyes flashing. "Ladies do not frequent bowling alleys. The very name sounds so . . . inappropriate."

Nerves worn thin, Emily hit the table with her palm. "When are you going to open your eyes, Aunt Ethel? Women can do anything a man can do. They can bowl. They can shoot. They can play sports. They can become doctors and lawyers and own businesses."

Aunt Ethel's lips thinned. "And apparently they can be insolent with their elders."

"Emily, who else was at the bowling alley?" Aunt Millie asked, apparently trying to ease the tension.

"Carter's team."

A deafening silence filled the small room. Finally, Aunt Ethel spoke. "You mean to tell me that you, a single woman, spent an entire evening with not only one man but a whole team? And unchaperoned to boot?"

Emily sighed and pinched the bridge of her nose. She did not need this aggravation this morning. "We didn't do anything wrong. Other bowlers were present too, including other men and their wives, and I was home before nightfall."

"Did he kiss you good night?" The hope in Aunt Millie's voice was hard to miss.

"No, he didn't." The frosty conclusion to their evening had only added to her drive to not attempt sleep. When Carter had left without so much as a "see you tomorrow," Emily's eyes stung. Only by forcing herself to stay on task had she avoided the tears still on the brink of falling.

"Well." Aunt Ethel joined her hands in front of her, ready to pass judgment. "I will speak to your grandmother about all this when she returns from town. You're spending far too much time with him, and it doesn't look good."

Emily doubted her aunt needed to trouble herself. She'd spoken rashly to Carter, and he'd not be back. Maybe it was just as well. She would never be a woman who could hold her tongue. And if it wasn't that particular characteristic, she'd do something sooner or later that would send him running. She didn't deserve Carter.

She pressed her hand to the ache in her chest. But oh, how she missed him already.

Leaning against an oak a few yards from the front door of the cottage, Carter waited for Emily and her entourage to emerge.

The screen door creaked, and a funny feeling rumbled in his chest. He'd heard the raised voices from inside. Maybe Emily hung on to her ire as tenaciously as she held on to the suffrage fight. If she wasn't happy to see him, showing up here this early could be a big mistake.

"Carter." Emily's breath caught as she stepped out of the cottage.

Behind her, Aunt Ethel scowled, but Aunt Millie tugged the thin-framed woman inside before the screen door banged shut.

Keeping her distance, Emily clutched a stack of papers and periodicals to her chest, covering her lemon-yellow blouse. She'd carefully done her fawn-colored hair and topped the bun with one of her overly flowered hats. He frowned when he spotted the telltale dark circles rimming her eyes. Guilt washed over him.

He took a step forward and pointed to the papers. "Are you on your way to your meeting?"

"It's at the Yacht Club at ten o'clock."

"Then let me walk you there." He slipped the stack from her hands. "We can talk on the way. Please."

Emily nodded.

When they reached the last bend in the path, Carter cleared his throat. "I'm sorry. You were right to blame me."

"No, I wasn't." Emily wrapped her arms around her middle. "I was angry with myself because I should have insisted on going home and working."

"You told me what you needed to do, but I was selfish and wanted you with me." He held up his hand when Emily started to protest. "I spent a lot of time praying about this, and I'm sure you did too." He waited for her to agree, but she remained silent. "This is all new, and it will take us awhile to figure out the best use of our time. But I believe if we keep praying about it, God will show us the way."

They reached the dock, and a cool morning breeze drifted over the surface of the water. He glanced at the electric launch still in the middle of the lake. Turning toward Emily, he crooked a finger under her chin and lifted her face to his. "You don't have to tell me. I can see it. You look exhausted."

"Carter, it's not your fault." She stepped away and turned toward the water. "I'm not good at balancing things. I wanted to go with you last night, but there's so much to do."

"Do you have to do it all?"

"I'm the president. It's my responsibility. Would you say the same thing about your team? What if they were counting on you?"

"Easy, Emily. I only meant there has to be something you can cut back on."

The launch neared, making the waves lap against the shore. She turned around and shrugged. "I like to be busy."

"This busy?"

For the first time, she smiled. "Maybe not quite this busy. But I'll manage. I always do."

The launch's captain tossed a rope toward the weathered boards. The dock assistant caught it and secured the awning-covered boat.

Carter squeezed Emily's gloved hand. "Want me to ride with you across the lake?"

"Don't you have practice?"

"I'm already late. Being a little more late won't hurt."

"It won't help either." She kissed his cheek. "I'll see you this afternoon at the ball diamond."

"Skip it today. You need a nap."

"But the game's so close."

"Hmmm. I remember a little word you promised me. It started with an *o*."

"Carter—"

With a chuckle, he helped her into the boat and passed her the papers and periodicals. "I want you rested so you can go to our game on Saturday."

"I'm not making any promises," she called with a wave as the launch putt-putted out into the lake.

Remaining on the dock until the boat was a spot on the blue water, Carter wrestled with a thought he couldn't shake. He hadn't planned on making any promises to anyone this summer, but he found himself considering a few to Miss Emily Graham.

23

Standing before the ladies of the Council Bluffs Equal Suffrage Club, Emily glanced at her checklists before looking up and scanning those gathered in the Yacht Club. Even Olivia DeSoto wouldn't find fault with her preparations. She'd considered every possibility, every nuance, and every detail.

Her lips curved in a smile. She could do this. She could balance Carter, baseball, and her suffrage work. She could do it all and still not leave anything out.

Tapping her gavel on the podium, she took a deep breath of the tangy lake air. "Good morning, ladies. I'd like to start by going over—"

"Excuse me." Olivia shot from her seat, waving a handkerchief in the air. "I move we elect a new president."

Lilly grabbed Olivia's sleeve and tugged on it. "Sit down. We don't have time for your nonsense."

Yanking her arm free, Olivia squared her shoulders dramatically. "I have proof Emily is letting her relationship with

Carter Stockton and the Manawa Owls interfere with her duties to our association."

"What proof?" Wizened Gertrude O'Neil scowled beneath her overly plumed hat.

Olivia waved the newspaper. "Emily's weekly article should have been in today's edition. However, it's missing. When I inquired about it, Mr. Fletcher said she turned it in late."

A knot the size of Lake Manawa formed in Emily's stomach. Olivia was right. She had failed the ladies.

Mrs. O'Neil's scowl deepened. "Is that true, Emily?"

"I—I—I was late, but Mr. Fletcher indicated he'd still print the article."

"Emily." Marguerite smiled. "How late was it?"

"Only about half an hour. But it was my fault. I take full responsibility."

"Poppycock." Lilly propped her hands on her hips. "Our esteemed editor must have had something come up and used your tardiness as an excuse to bump your story."

"But you heard her," Olivia whined. "She admitted to missing the deadline."

"And you've never been half an hour late to anything?" Marguerite joined Emily at the front of the room. "I think we all know better. All in favor of dismissing Olivia's motion, say 'aye.'"

Feminine voices called out the response, filling the room.

Olivia's pitch rose above the din. "Mark my words. Emily's attention is divided."

The ladies chattered among themselves.

"Ladies." Emily struck the gavel again and cleared her throat. "Let me assure you the passage of suffrage in Iowa and in this great nation of ours is of uppermost importance to me. I would do anything to see that it happens." She paused and took a slow, deep breath, allowing the ladies to weigh her words. "Now, if we can avoid any further distractions, we have a lot to accomplish and a very short time to do so."

After Emily received reports from each of the Bloomer Girls' committees, the ladies went to separate tables to work. Chatter rose, and the heat of the stuffy room made Emily's head throb. She sat down at an empty table and rubbed the kink in her neck.

"Emily." Olivia's loud, singsong voice signaled trouble. "You didn't say anything about the posters I designed."

Lifting her head, Emily sighed. "Let me take another look at them."

"Here's one." Olivia held up the rectangular sheet of paper, displaying an upended Emily for all to see.

Several ladies giggled, but Emily didn't miss the frown on Lilly's face or the anger on Marguerite's. Martin's advice popped into Emily's mind. *Don't let her get to you.*

Emily took the poster from Olivia and perused it at arm's length. "I will say one thing, Olivia. It certainly gets a person's attention. And your idea is brilliant. Get them there with humor and then sock them with the seriousness of the subject. I'll gladly give my likeness to accomplish something so important for the cause."

The women erupted in applause and praise for Emily's good sportsmanship and selfless efforts. Joy pushed Emily's nagging headache to the side momentarily. For so many years, self-doubt had plagued her. But now, between Carter and these ladies, a sense of pride filled her. She wouldn't be parading her accomplishments down Broadway, but it did feel good to matter.

You've always mattered to Me.

The words pressed on her heart. Was God trying to tell her something? She shook her head. No, not her.

She touched her throbbing temple. Sally Nesmit appeared with a list of supplies needed to build the additional bleachers for the Bloomer Girls' game. Emily took the pencil from behind her ear and jotted notes in the margin.

There'd be time to think about God later.

⤜⤛

"Well, if it isn't my brother."

Carter stiffened as Nathan, broad-shouldered and impeccably dressed in a crisp summer suit, approached him on the boardwalk. "What do you want, Nathan?"

"Can't I enjoy the resort, or is it reserved for those of you intent on not growing up?"

"Nathan, let it go." Carter tossed his beach bag on the bench beside him. "Why are you really here?"

"It's about the discrepancy in Mrs. Graham's account you came to see me about."

"You found the error?"

Nathan raised an eyebrow. "Yes and no."

Making no effort to hide the grin spreading across his face, Carter sat down on the bench. He motioned to the other side in invitation. "So, the great Nathan made a mistake."

"No." Nathan remained standing. "There's no error on the bank's part. The error is hers."

"Why are you so certain?"

"It's obvious, isn't it? The old woman is daft."

Carter bolted to his feet, fists cocked at his side. "You don't even know her! Mrs. Graham is more quick-witted than you'll ever be."

"Honestly, Carter, can you say you haven't considered the possibility that Mrs. Graham's senility is to blame?" He paused and then laughed. "That twitch beneath your right eye tells me you have. I take it, then, you're thinking with your heart again, and that your reaction comes from your connection to her granddaughter."

"How did you hear about her?"

"News travels fast from the lake. Did you think you could keep the fact you're seeing a Graham from me?"

"Leave Emily out of this." Carter intentionally struck Nathan's chest with his shoulder as he walked to the railing. He stood there inhaling the fishy lake air for several seconds before turning around to face his brother. "Did you come all this way to tell me you believe you're still perfect?"

"No, I came to meet some friends for a business lunch. Finding you was a bonus." He shoved the bag from the bench into Carter's chest. "And it appears you're off for another day of frolicking in the sun. Eventually Dad will get tired of supporting you, Carter."

"What I do is none of your business."

"Really? You don't think your decisions reflect on our family? That my associates question me regularly as to why you haven't started working at the bank yet?" He crossed his arms over his chest. "Rest assured, it may seem your life isn't my business now, but it will be when you come work for me. Then I'll be able to straighten you out like our father should have done a long time ago."

Jaw set, Carter tossed the bag back on the bench. "I won't be working at the bank."

"Be careful what you say, little brother. I can tell you're awfully sweet on Emily Graham. So much so, I daresay you've entertained the idea of marrying her. Do you believe you can provide for a wife by playing baseball?"

Carter's heart thudded against his ribs, and he clenched his fists again. "Didn't you say you had a meeting to get to?"

"I did." Nathan nodded his head. "But mark my words, little brother. If you keep seeing Miss Graham, you'll be sitting at a desk in my bank within the year."

"Dad owns the bank."

He chuckled. "For now."

∞

Kate snipped the rosebush stem beneath a node. She stood back up and cocked her head, squinting at the oddly shaped bush. No matter how much she clipped, it seemed unbalanced and looked more like a flamingo than a vase, as it should. Some things were hard to fix.

"Hello, Grandma." Emily shifted her stack of papers from her right hip to her left. "Isn't it a little late in the season to be pruning?"

"Yes, June means I'm a bit tardy, but I need to teach this overzealous rosebush who is in charge." She tugged off her gardening gloves and sighed. "But I'm ready for a break. Why don't we go have some lemonade and you can tell me how your meeting went?"

Kate pointed to a silver tray bearing a pitcher of lemonade situated between the two new wicker rocking chairs. The chairs, selected from the People's Department Store, had been delivered earlier in the day. Since Millie and Ethel would most likely plant themselves in the two chairs for hours, Emily would seldom have the opportunity to sit in them.

"Where are Aunt Millie and Aunt Ethel?" Emily placed her papers beside the tray on the rattan table and sat down.

"Playing bridge with Mrs. Alamander and Mrs. Wendell." Kate filled two of the glasses and passed one to Emily. "I think they're quite taken with the game."

Leaning back, Emily appeared to relax against the ornate

weaving. She dug the toe of her shoe in the ground and gave the chair a push. As she rocked, lemonade splashed on her chin. She came to a stop and giggled as she dabbed at the liquid. "I can't believe I did that."

Kate smiled. "I can."

Emily took another swallow. "I don't think I know Mrs. Alamander or Mrs. Wendell."

"Oh, but I bet Millie and Ethel have made sure they know you." A smile played on Kate's lips. "Well, we don't get much time alone these days, so tell me about your meeting, or better yet, tell me how things are between you and Carter."

"Grandma, you're almost as bad as Aunt Millie." Pink tinged her granddaughter's cheeks. "The meeting was fine except for Olivia. That woman delights in making me look bad."

"I'm guessing she thinks it makes her look more important. We all want a place of significance, Emily. Our own insecurities drive us to do things our heart knows are wrong." She let her words soak in for a moment before continuing. "And Carter? Did you work things out?"

"How could you tell we had a spat?"

Kate sipped her drink. "Your aunt Millie said he looked quite penitent this morning. I assumed you'd had a tiff."

"It was my fault as much as his. I had a lot to do and should have insisted he bring me home. Instead—"

"Instead you got angry at him."

Her head dropped in shame. "Between learning to play baseball, my suffrage work, and Carter, I'm meeting myself coming and going."

"Why do you do it, dear?"

"Excuse me?"

"I'm not saying it's not important work, but I wonder if

you know the real reason you insist on staying so busy. Even before the Bloomer Girls' game, you seemed to have a need to not have a minute to spare."

"But the fight for a woman's right to vote is important."

"It is important. I'd always hoped you'd see that." She set her glass down. How could she make her granddaughter understand the truth? She took Emily's hand. "But there are other things even more important."

"Grandma, when we've won the right, when this is over, then—"

"Then what, Emily? Who will you be then?"

Tears laced Emily's long lashes. Only birdsong and the sound of the wind ruffling the trees filled the silence between them. Finally, a yawn escaped Emily's lips, and Kate patted her arm. "If you hurry, maybe you can get a nap in before your aunts' return."

❧

Raised voices outside her window called Emily from a most delightful, Carter-filled dream. Propping herself on one elbow, she strained to hear who was speaking.

Aunt Millie's singsong voice came through first. "Helen Alamander was quite certain it was our Emily."

"I'm telling you, Kate, it's scandalous." Aunt Ethel sounded mortified.

Fear gripped Emily's chest. What on earth could they be referring to? The time she'd spent alone with Carter in the Kursaal? But who could possibly have known about that?

Emily stuffed her feet into her shoes, reset the pins in her hair, and hurried outside.

"She's ruined!" Aunt Millie wailed. "Our sweet Emily is ruined."

Emily gasped and stopped short. She pressed her hand to her chest. "Aunt Millie, how can you say such a thing?"

"Come sit down, dear." Grandma Kate pointed to one of the empty rocking chairs.

Emily lowered herself into it and folded her hands in her lap. Unfortunately, all three members of her meddlesome trio remained standing. "What's wrong?"

"Emily," her grandmother began, "this morning, while your aunts were playing bridge, your name came up."

"It did?"

Aunt Ethel stepped forward, and the sharp lines on her face declared her harsh judgment. "Helen Alamander said she saw you with the Stockton boy."

Emily's heart beat faster. The refuge from the rain. It had to be. What else would upset the three women so? Emily swallowed the lump lodged in her throat. "That's quite possible."

"Don't you want to know where she saw you?" Aunt Ethel pointed in the direction of the lake. "Out there. In one of those electric launches."

Emily breathed a sigh of relief. This whole thing had to be some kind of mistake. "And?"

Grandma Kate sat down in the wicker rocker beside her. "Sweetheart, she says she saw you sleeping with Carter."

Emily's jaw dropped and her face heated. "Sleeping with Carter? And you believe I'd do something so improper?" Then, in a flash, realization exploded and Emily began giggling.

"This is not funny!" Aunt Ethel snapped.

"I'm sorry, but are you sure she said 'with' and not 'on'?"

"What difference does it make?" Aunt Millie dabbed tear-filled eyes with the edge of her apron.

"Because I did fall asleep on Carter's shoulder in the boat

on the way back from the bowling alley. I was so tired. He woke me up when we docked and then walked me home."

"Oh." Aunt Millie covered her mouth with her hand.

"Is that all?" Her grandmother sat up straighter. "Not that I doubted your virtue. I knew you wouldn't let any man take liberties with you and it had to be something like that."

Lips pursed, Aunt Ethel scowled. "Well, it's still unseemly."

"Perhaps, but innocent as well." Her grandmother stood and turned to her aunts. "As for you two, perhaps a little less gossip and a little more card playing are in order."

"I'm sorry for doubting you, dear." Aunt Millie patted her shoulder.

Grandma Kate quirked an eyebrow toward her other sister.

Aunt Ethel's lips thinned. "I suppose apologies are in order, but you'd better be more mindful of appearances, young lady. Your choices reflect on those around you."

As her heartbeat returned to a normal rhythm, Emily took a deep breath. Aunt Ethel was right. While this wasn't a serious situation, another instance might be. She needed to be more careful when it came to Carter. Every decision she made affected the suffrage cause, and she couldn't let her feelings, however intense, harm that work in any way.

24

After reining in his horse, Carter climbed down from his phaeton. Life at the lake hadn't required the use of the sporty rig often, and he'd missed the feel of control while commanding it. He patted Curveball's chocolaty neck and secured the fidgety horse to the hitching post.

He sauntered toward the Yacht Club to meet Emily and plucked a single daisy from beside the path. Once again she'd sequestered herself with her suffrage club, intent on making this game with the Bloomer Girls her crowning glory. She'd worked so many hours in the last week, he'd almost forgotten what she looked like.

Her moss-green eyes and perfect smile filled his mind. Warmth fanned in his belly. He chuckled. Perhaps he remembered her after all. With any luck, he'd pry her away for a few hours.

Taking a seat on the rail of the fence, Carter waited until clusters of ladies exited the flag-topped building. He waved at the few he knew—Olivia DeSoto, Sally Nesmit, Marguerite, and Lilly. No surprise—Emily came out last.

She skipped down the steps, seemingly without a second thought to falling, and pride puffed his chest. In the last couple weeks, she'd changed. She appeared more confident, and he hoped he deserved a bit of the credit. The Lord knew she'd certainly changed him.

He hopped down from his perch and met her on the walk.

"For you." He held out the daisy. "Your favorite, right?"

"You remembered."

"Of course I did. The other day you said you loved its simple beauty." A rosy blush bloomed on her cheeks, and he grinned. "And I brought you something else too."

He pulled a folded paper sack from his pocket, opened it, and held out a lemon drop. Holding it to her lips, he waited until she opened her mouth before plopping it in.

"Mmmm. Tart and sweet. Thank you. I didn't expect to see you this afternoon. I thought you had a game in Glenwood."

"We did." They fell in step as they walked. "But they had to postpone it. Their pitcher broke his arm. So I'm all yours for the rest of the day."

Her eyes flickered merrily. "And that's supposed to be a good thing?"

Carter placed his hand over his heart. "You wound me."

"I don't think I could deflate your ego so easily." She giggled and fingered the flower. "I'm not sure I can spare—"

"Emily, you haven't had a moment to yourself all week." The acidic taste of frustration made his jaw tick. She hadn't made a moment for him either.

Lilly strode up beside the couple and plucked the tablet from Emily's hands. "Shoo."

"Excuse me?"

"You heard me." Lilly waved the tablet in the air. "Shoo. Get out of here. Go have fun. There's nothing on this list that can't wait until morning." Lilly nudged her with the papers. "And as long as we're talking about how you spend your time, you might consider setting aside a little for the Lord too."

"Lilly."

The hard-edged warning in Emily's voice surprised Carter. Perhaps he should ask Emily about it later. But for now he had other plans.

"You heard the lady." Carter swept his arm in a grand gesture. "Your carriage awaits."

❦

Emily popped a second lemon drop in her mouth. She sucked on the candy and waited for the sweet, sugar-coated outside to give way to the sour center.

Seated beside Carter in the phaeton, Emily grabbed the edge of the carriage as the horse picked up speed. Rolling Iowa hills passed by in a dizzying blur of green and brown, and a cloud of dust trailed behind them. She lifted her face to the wind.

Carter glanced in her direction. "Do you want me to slow down?"

"No!" Her cheeks warmed and she turned to him. "I mean, I like to go fast."

"I thought you would." He skirted a hole and directed the horse around a bend in the dirt-packed road. A straight stretch loomed before them.

Emily touched his arm. "May I drive?"

"Now?"

"Yes."

"I don't know, Emily. There are lots of ruts from the rain,

and Curveball here is still young and hard to handle. She's even scared of grasshoppers."

"Just tell the truth, Carter. You don't trust me." She swallowed the hurt.

"It's not that."

"Trust comes from proving oneself. That's why it's been so hard for women to earn the trust of men. If we are never given the opportunities, then how can we prove what we can handle?"

He shook his head and reined Curveball in. "I should never argue with you."

"Smart man."

After passing the reins to Emily, Carter leaned back in his seat. "Prove away, Miss Graham."

She snapped the reins, and Curveball galloped down the road.

"Can't you at least ease into it?"

"Tackle everything head-on, I always say." Emily didn't let the horse have her head, but she gave her more freedom than most would on the less than pristine road conditions. They bounced and jostled and even skidded a bit as they rounded another turn.

She glanced at Carter. He didn't flinch. Impressive.

Finally, she eased up and let Curveball continue at a gentler pace. "Do you want the reins back?"

"No, I don't have to drive. You're doing fine." He held another lemon drop to her lips.

She parted them and accepted the sweet treat. "You're not like most men. Did you know that?"

"Because I let you drive my rig? I knew you could."

"Actually, because you don't always have to be in control." She held out the reins to him. "I don't always have to drive either."

He slipped his arms around her and covered her hands with his own. "How about we drive together?"

His heated breath sent prickles down her neck, and she leaned into the strength of his arms. The clean, fresh scent of his soap tickled her nose. Although she kept hold of the reins, he controlled the horse now, and his calloused hands easily covered her own. She leaned against the wide expanse of his chest and closed her eyes. Was there a better way to ride?

They reached the crest of a hill, the steady drumming of Carter's heart against her back echoing the *clop, clop, clop* of Curveball's hooves. She caught a whiff of swine and glanced around for the pigpen. At the bottom of the hill, a sow lay in the mud, nursing her piglets. How could something so small make such a rancid stench? Phew! Her eyes began to water, and she turned her head into the sleeve of her dress.

The phaeton's wheel dropped into a hole with a *thunk*. Emily jerked and swallowed. The lemon drop wedged in her throat.

She yanked her hands from beneath Carter's and grabbed her throat. Heart pounding, she tried to suck in air. None came.

"Emily?"

She tried to answer.

Carter yanked the reins, and Curveball snorted in protest at the abrupt stop.

Eyes wide, Emily prayed Carter understood what was happening. Why couldn't she breathe? The corners of her vision grew fuzzy, and she frantically pointed to her throat.

Pushing her shoulders forward, Carter whacked her on the back with his open hand. On the third blow, the lemon drop flew through the air and landed on the dirt road.

He pulled her against him while she sucked in the rank, pig-scented air.

After several minutes, she inched away, but he continued to rub circles on her back. "You scared the living daylights out of me. Are you all right?"

She nodded and croaked, "Yes, thanks to you."

"And God." His chest heaved against her arm as he leaned close and kissed her temple.

"I'm sorry. I didn't mean to put a damper on our day."

"Don't apologize. I'm just glad you're okay." They remained on the side of the road for several minutes. Finally, Carter squeezed her shoulders. "Ready to head back?"

She nodded.

"Nice and slow. No more life-and-death experiences."

"Sounds good. I'm not ready to meet my Maker today."

Carter turned the rig around in an intersection. "Speaking of Him, what did Lilly mean about you taking time for the Lord?"

Emily stiffened. "Lilly's always got one hand on the Bible."

"And you don't?" His light tone grew serious.

"I have other things to do than read my Bible all day."

"Why did Lilly bring that up?"

Emily sighed. A now familiar surge of guilt nudged her. Why hadn't Lilly kept her mouth shut?

Carter gave her a halfhearted chuckle. "Is God getting about as much of your time as I am?"

She smiled weakly. "Sort of."

"And that's okay with you?"

"Carter, it's not like it will be like this forever."

"Really, Emily? Do you see yourself changing? Am I missing something?" He snapped the reins, and Curveball switched

219

from a walk to a trot. "Things will slow down as soon as the game is over."

"And what then? What's the next cause you'll take on? What's going to get your undivided attention then?"

"Carter, why are you talking to me like this? This hasn't been a problem before. One minute we're having a delightful ride, except for the almost choking to death part, and the next we're bickering like my aunts." She paused, tilting her head toward him. "Wait a minute. Are you jealous of my suffrage work?"

Carter slowed Curveball and directed the phaeton onto a side road. He reined the horse to a stop and turned to Emily, his caramel eyes darker than she'd ever seen them. Curling his hand around the back of her neck, he locked his gaze on her. "Maybe I am jealous. Maybe I had a glimpse of how it would feel to lose you. Maybe I want you to tell me there's nothing to worry about, because the more I'm with you, the more of you I want."

His words sent a blend of fear and joy rippling through her. Somewhere in the last few seconds, the conversation had flipped, and the unfamiliar ground left her more trembly than the lack of air had.

With soft pressure, he pulled her toward him, tracing her bottom lip with the pad of his thumb before claiming the spot with his lips.

He tasted of lemon drops. Sweet and tart. Warm and wonderful. The kiss deepened, and the explosion of feelings left her heart fluttering. His hands slipped to her waist, and he drew her closer.

She pressed against him, wanting and needing his touch.

A hunger awakened, and she realized she wanted more of him too.

Carter leaned against the railing lining the boardwalk, and Ducky squeezed in beside him. They both peered up.

The Great Lorenzo, a renowned tightrope walker, mounted the ladder leaning against a pole that had been erected on the beach near the Grand Plaza. Another pole nearly ten yards away stood in the water, and a thin rope hung taut between the two.

Carter elbowed Ducky's ribs. "I bet I wouldn't catch you walking any little ropes forty or fifty feet in the air."

Ducky laughed. "No sirree, but I bet it looks fun to you."

"I've been known to take a few chances." Carter shielded his eyes from the sinking sun. "But that's not really your way of doing things."

"I take chances."

"Eating the new menu item at the lunch counter does not count." Carter chuckled.

"At least I can tell a good risk when I see one."

"What's that supposed to mean?"

"I'm saying you have a habit of only risking stuff on sure things."

"Such as?"

"When you have to take a real chance, you sort of ignore it and hope it will go away before you have to make a decision. Like that baseball scout who visited college last year."

Carter clenched his jaw. Ducky's words hit home. The scout had professed an interest in Carter, but he hadn't followed up on it. When the man never returned, it made Carter's decision easy.

Why had he done that?

Not ready to face those demons, he turned his gaze toward the performer. The tightrope walker balanced a long pole in his hands. The crowd hushed. Slowly the barefoot man took his first steps on the wire. He teetered and the crowd gasped.

Carter clenched the railing. A funny feeling made his chest tighten. He'd never admit it, but he hated heights. Give him anything on the ground any day, but don't make him climb higher than the water toboggan slides in the lake.

"Halfway there," Ducky whispered.

Licking his lips, Carter inhaled slowly. He should have gone to see Emily instead of taking in this show. Then again, lately she'd been almost as scary as the high wire. That little buggy ride yesterday had put the fear of God in him—and he wasn't talking about the lemon drop episode. Never before had a simple kiss turned into so much more and left him on the brink of losing control.

He had to take a step back and look at this relationship. What if she wasn't the right one for him? And what about her walk with the Lord? Her close friends were concerned too, which confirmed his fears Emily might be in trouble in that area. He wasn't marrying anyone who couldn't love God and put Him first.

Marrying?

The thought sucked the air from his lungs. Is that what he wanted? They needed to slow down. They'd been moving awfully fast, and he didn't want to risk hurting her when he wasn't sure what he wanted. Maybe some distance would do them both good.

But was Ducky right? Would he let Emily slip away because he couldn't make up his mind?

He rolled his shoulders to release the tension. The tightrope walker reached the pole's platform, and the crowd cheered.

Ducky inserted his fingers in his mouth and released a shrill whistle. "Pretty amazing, isn't it?"

Carter nodded.

"And a little crazy."

"We risk takers are all a little crazy." Laughing, Carter knocked Ducky's hat off his head. Ducky lunged for it and caught it before it sailed into the water beneath them.

Ducky slapped the cap back in place. "You're more than a little crazy, Stockton."

The tightrope walker waved and started back across the wire, and the crowd again grew quiet. When he reached the midpoint, this time he squatted, bent his head, and somersaulted on the rope. In a fluid motion, he rose to his feet but lost his balance in the process.

Carter leaned forward on the rail as if he could help the man regain his footing. In horror, he watched as the Great Lorenzo teetered far to the right, and one foot lifted from the wire. The long pole dipped quickly to the left, and the bearded man managed to secure his footing once again. He stood still on the wire for several seconds before continuing his journey.

Cheers and applause exploded around Carter, and he joined in. The tightrope walker safely arrived at the platform, and the crowd continued to show its appreciation. The man waved and bowed deeply.

Carter understood the strange combination of feelings that must have been pulsating through the tightrope walker—both success and relief. Those same feelings filled his veins after pitching a winning game.

Only taking risks on sure things? Ducky didn't know what he was talking about. Every pitch was a risk. Standing up to Nathan was a risk. And courting Emily?

The biggest risk of all.

25

Even in Cottage Grove, the picnic area at Lake Manawa, the temperature seemed unbearable. Emily lugged two tables over and positioned them end to end for the meeting with her suffrage ladies. She adjusted her papers and rolled up her sleeves. She hadn't been this hot since—

Her face burned at the thought. Not since Carter's kiss yesterday. Fanning her cheeks with a tablet, she attempted to force her thoughts away from it. It wasn't proper to dwell on such things, but oh, it had been sweet—and moving. What a strange sensation it had been. The corners of her lips curled.

"And what's got you grinning like a schoolgirl with a crush?" Lilly sauntered up and bounced Levi on her hip. "Is it a crush on a certain baseball player?"

"Lilly, I've got work to do. I have to get ready for the meeting."

"Uh-huh."

"What's that supposed to mean?"

"You might as well tell me what's going on, because I'll

get it out of you eventually, and the others will be here any minute."

"I guess I have to talk to someone." She sat down at the table, and Lilly scooted in on the bench seat across from her, setting Levi on her lap. "Things with Carter have been going so well."

"And?"

"And I'm surprised by the feelings he, uh—"

"Stirs in you? Been kissing, huh?"

Cheeks aflame again, Emily waved the tablet harder.

"And now you don't know what to do with the feelings?"

"It's all happening so fast."

"Talk to him."

"I couldn't do that!"

"Emily, you're scared and thrilled all at the same time." Levi fussed, and Lilly handed him a dark purple rubber teething ring. The tot immediately stuck it in his mouth. "It's normal."

"But it's all so strange, Lilly. Should it be this . . . this exciting?"

"Falling in love is a funny thing, my mama always said. If you fall in it, you're bound to hit bottom, but if you slowly grow in it, as you both move closer to God, you'll move closer to each other."

Her pulse picked up speed. But what if only one of them was moving toward God? It wasn't like she didn't believe in Him. She simply didn't have time to spend on her relationship with Him right now.

And truthfully, she didn't have time to spend on a relationship with Carter either.

"I'd better finish up. I see some of the ladies coming." Emily stood and tickled Levi's chin. "You've got a wise mama too, little man."

225

The ladies went straight to work. Each committee had matters to attend to, and Emily flitted from one group to another.

Olivia arrived late, waving a telegram in the air. "I have urgent matters to discuss with this group."

Emily set down the schedule of activities in her hand. "What is it now, Olivia?"

"Where were you yesterday when the delivery boy tried to bring you this telegram?"

"When? What telegram? Who came?"

"The Pearson boy. He rode his bicycle all the way out here to the lake, and no one was at your cottage." She scanned the ladies and seemed to delight in their undivided attention. "But we all know where you were because we saw you leave with Carter Stockton. You were off courting instead of being available for important society business."

Emily reached for the telegram. "Give that to me."

Olivia waved it with a flourish out of Emily's reach. "Thankfully, I happened upon the telegraph office as the boy was relaying his sad tale and offered to deliver this myself." Finally, she relinquished her hold on the paper. "As you can see, the Bloomer Girls will be arriving a day earlier now, so we have to redo all our plans. That certainly would have been nice to know yesterday, wouldn't it, ladies?"

Emily's heart sank. She hadn't been available. And while this wasn't crucial to the cause, the next time it might be.

The ladies mumbled around her. Lilly passed Levi to the lady beside her and stood up. "Olivia, don't be so overdramatic. Emily has a right to a ride in the country as much as anyone else. In fact, I encouraged her to do so."

"But this will mean we'll have to move the whole parade up a day," Mrs. O'Neil whined.

Emily stepped forward. "Yes, Gertrude, it does, and it

226

means we'll have to be extra vigilant in getting everything arranged in the coming days. We'll need to see to accommodations for them. Perhaps some entertainment too. We are the hostesses, and I promise you I will be available from now on."

"What about your personal life?" Olivia lifted her eyebrows.

"This work comes first. No matter what." She sighed. Besides, she and Carter could use some time to cool off.

❧

The walleye's eye stared back at Emily. Lying on her plate beside the roasted potatoes and slivers of carrots, the grilled fish should have been appetizing. After all, she hadn't eaten all day, but the constant throbbing in her head and the horrendous temperature now robbed her of an appetite.

She glanced at Carter and noticed he didn't seem to be having trouble consuming the catch of the day, nor did any of the other patrons at the country club. After two days of putting him off because of her preparations, she had finally acquiesced and agreed to spend some time with him tonight.

Above them, electric fans stirred the humid, hundred-degree air. She glanced at the electric lights the Fish and Game Club sported, and winced. The pounding behind her eyes intensified, and she pinched the bridge of her nose.

Carter set down his fork and appeared to study her. He frowned. "How much sleep did you get last night?"

"Please, let's not start on that." Emily pushed a roasted potato to the other side of her plate. Maybe she should have skipped staying up half the night to read the new report from the National Woman Suffrage Association.

"Okay, then, what did you have for lunch?"

"I wasn't hungry."

"And now? That potato's doing more dancing than the folks in the next room."

"I have a bit of a headache." She cut a small bite from a carrot, eased it between her lips, and forced it down. "At least I'm here."

He folded his napkin and set it beside his plate. "Come on. I'll take you home."

"No. Let's finish our dinner." She touched his hand. "Please."

Sighing, he replaced his napkin. "Is your stomach bothering you? I can order you some soup."

She shook her head and broke off a piece of roll, buttered it, and nibbled the corner. "Did you see the Carnival Company's acts?"

"I caught the high wire the other day. You?"

"I saw the trick bicyclist. He was really something, and you could tell he loved what he was doing—like you and baseball." She speared another carrot. "Carter, why didn't you pursue your baseball career?"

He shrugged. "Funny you should ask. I've been thinking about that a lot lately."

"And?"

"And . . ." He took a swig of water. "I've been praying about it."

"You know that's not what I mean."

"But you'd have to agree, it is a good place to start."

"I suppose so." Her queasy stomach flopped. She turned her attention to the staring walleye. Why didn't they cut the heads off these things? "Carter, what would you do if you didn't think God wanted you to open that door?"

He sat back in his chair and took a deep breath. "If God didn't want me to do it, then I wouldn't."

"Even if you wanted it more than anything?"

228

"Yes. I'm not saying it would be easy, but if God closed a door to me, I would trust He had other plans."

"Why?" It was a simple question and one she'd asked her grandmother more than once. How did people know God had other plans? Better plans?

"Because He's God." He flaked a piece of the fish with his fork. "What's this about? Are you questioning your suffrage work?"

"No. Not really. I was just thinking."

"If you're having doubts, God might be trying to tell you something. Maybe you should take a step back and reevaluate your priorities."

She stiffened in her chair.

"Relax, Emily. I'm trying to tell you I think you're working too hard, and it has to stop."

"Carter . . ."

Waving his fork in the air, he silenced her. "First it was the suffrage speeches and the articles, and now it's the Bloomer Girls' game. Look at you. You've made yourself sick. It's too much."

"It's a headache, Carter. I won't die from it." Her voice softened at the concern in his eyes. "Sometimes it does feel like I'm running in circles, but it will be over soon."

His gaze fell to his water glass. He wrapped his fingers around it and squeezed until his nails turned white. "I hate seeing you like this, and it's getting worse, not better. I should have offered before, but do you want to pray together about what you should do?"

"No." The word came out too quickly, and she wished it back. "I mean, I will—when I'm alone."

He seemed to study her face, and then a sadness stole the light from his eyes. "Broken cisterns."

"What?"

"Look it up."

"Where?"

"The Bible." He chuckled. "You still have one, don't you?"

"What's that supposed to mean?"

"Nothing." Carter laid his napkin on the table. "Let's go before I get myself in more trouble."

She rose on wobbly legs, and Carter took her elbow, concern filling his eyes again. Once she was in his phaeton, the horse's pounding hooves only added to her agony. A thousand unrelenting hammers beat inside her head. She tugged the pins free holding her hat in place and set it on her lap. By the time they reached the cabin, she could scarcely keep the tears at bay.

Carter lifted her to the ground. "You okay?"

She nodded and he released her. The world tilted at an awkward angle. She swayed.

"Emily?" Carter's voice seemed far away.

Then he was gone and blackness swallowed her.

"What happened?"

"She fainted." Carter shifted Emily in his arms, pushed past Aunt Ethel, and hurried toward the cottage. "What room is hers?"

"You can't go into her bedroom!" Aunt Ethel's voice shook. "What will people say?"

"Good grief, Ethel." Aunt Millie pulled the screen door open. "This way, Carter."

He followed Aunt Millie as she teetered down the short hallway.

"Her bed is on the right. Was it the heat? Should I send for the doctor?"

"She had a horrible headache. The heat didn't help, and she's hardly eaten."

Emily moaned as he placed her onto the crisp, white sheets.

He positioned her head on the pillow and patted her cheek. "Emily?"

Aunt Millie handed him a damp cloth. "I'll get some fresh water for her to drink."

Carter pulled a chair closer to the side of the bed, then laid the cloth on her forehead. "Emily? Come on. Time to open your beautiful green eyes."

Emily's eyelids fluttered, lacy lashes dark against her pale cheek. "Carter?"

"Easy. You fainted."

Her gaze circled the room and her eyes widened. "You're in my bedroom?"

"Against your aunt Ethel's wishes." He took her hand in his own. "I'm sorry I upset you. Headache any better?"

"A bit."

"You scared me to death—again." He removed the cloth, dipped it in the nearby washbasin, and wrung it.

"Sorry."

"I'm getting used to it." He sat back down and replaced the cloth on her forehead. "I'd better get out of here before Aunt Ethel comes in and shoots me. On second thought, maybe I should let her, because then I'd have to sleep on that bed and I could keep an eye on you." He motioned to the empty one on the other side of the tiny room.

Emily smirked, but her voice came out weak. "You'd have to share with Aunt Millie."

Carter made a face and squeezed her hand. "You—rest. Sleep in tomorrow. Understand?"

Kate rapped on the door frame. "We'll take care of her."

Carter hopped to his feet. "I'm sorry, ma'am. I didn't see you earlier."

"I was down by the lake praying. Ethel summoned me." She placed a hand on his arm. "Thank you for taking such good care of her. She hasn't been doing a very good job of that herself."

"Grandma."

Glancing at Emily, Carter smiled. "That's going to change. Right, Emily?"

"Broken cisterns?"

A sense of accomplishment shot through him and surfaced in a grin. He'd made his point, and Emily obviously saw she needed to take a good long look at her life.

Maybe tightrope walking wasn't so bad.

26

With morning sunshine already heating the Manawa summer, Emily popped a nail head into her mouth and hefted a hammer in her hand. Around her, other ladies drove nails into rough bleacher boards with a resounding *thwack*. A few men had joined them, but more to laugh at their efforts than to lend aid.

She'd deliberately kept their plans from Carter, knowing he'd have his Owls there erecting the stands in half the time she and her girls could do it. Something kept her from telling him. Pride? No, more of a desire to prove they could do it without men. Besides, he wouldn't be happy to see her working after last night's little event.

Fresh embarrassment heated her cheeks. Good grief. She'd dropped like a tightly corseted fat lady into Carter's arms, and all because of a lousy headache. If she didn't find a way to show him she could handle her responsibilities, he'd never take her or her work seriously.

She pushed the sleeves up to her elbows as the hot sun bore

down on her. In another hour or two, they'd have the stands completed. In fact, this one already had three tiers.

Balancing on her knees, she eyed the spot she needed to secure and tapped the nail head. It didn't budge. Needing more force, she drew back her hammer and slammed it down, but it slid off the nail head and struck her thumb.

"Ow!" She threw the hammer onto the board and popped the throbbing digit in her mouth.

"Problems?"

She whirled at the sound of Carter's voice, thumb still in her mouth. Her dress caught on the rough board and her foot slipped. Arms flailing, she managed not to fall down the first tier but lost her battle with the side of the bleachers.

Carter caught her in midair. Instead of setting her down, he kept her cradled in his arms. "You okay?"

"Put me down."

"Answer me." His curls bobbed as he chuckled, eyes twinkling.

"I'm fine."

"Except for your thumb?"

"And my embarrassment." Heat rose from her toes to her nose. He'd carried her twice now? Aunt Millie might be buying her bust food, but Aunt Ethel had probably ordered her a medieval chastity belt.

"You deserve to be embarrassed. You're supposed to be sleeping in." He lowered her feet to the grass and held her waist until she was steady. "So, what's all this?"

"Extra seating for the Bloomer Girls' game."

"And you didn't think my boys and I would be willing to lend a hand?"

"More like take over," she mumbled. Emily picked up a long piece of scrap lumber. She turned and nearly slammed

234

the board into Carter's side. He caught it and took it from her.

"I'm doing fine." She fought to get the board back. A splinter sank into her palm, but refusing to cry out, she glared at him.

"Even so, I'm here to stay. Get used to it." He gave the board a yank.

"Why can't you let me do this alone?"

He cocked his eyebrow at her. "Why do you think you need to?"

"Ooooo." Chafing at his insolence, she jammed her fists against her hips. "Carter Stockton, I can do this."

"Listen, Emily, you can probably pound a nail as good as any man, but together we'll get it done in half the time." He slipped the board onto the framed spot and picked up the hammer she'd tossed. "And I have ulterior motives."

She raised an eyebrow and held out three nails in her hand. "Such as?"

"I want you to go to the game at four and then the tent meeting at seven tonight. We're playing the Atlantic Nine, and they're undefeated." He swiped the nails and drove the first one in with a single, solid stroke. When he finished, he turned and flashed her a cocky smile. "If you play your cards right, I might throw in dinner."

"You know I can't leave right now. I have to finish getting everything ready for the big game. I have an article due for the *Woman's Standard*, and I have yet to complete the book you gave me on the rules of baseball."

Carter crossed his arms over his chest. "This game is important to me, Emily, and so is the tent meeting. Besides, you need a break. I thought we talked about this." He marched to the other end of the bleachers. "Broken cisterns?"

"I didn't get to look that up yet."

"Now there's a surprise." His flat tone set her nerves on edge. With his sleeves rolled up, he flexed his well-toned muscles, tanned by hours in the sun, and drove the nail through the plank.

Emily pressed a knuckle to her lip. She wanted to go with him. He deserved her support—especially after all the support he'd given her. Then, out of the corner of her eye, she caught a glimpse of Olivia, holding court with her minions. If she went to the game, she'd certainly hear about it from them, and she was so tired of not measuring up.

Carter stood, pushed a damp clump of curls from his forehead, and followed the direction of her gaze. "Are you saying no to me because of her?"

"Of course not."

"Why do you care what she thinks?" He propped one foot on the bleacher and bent to tie his shoe.

His words grated. "Don't you care about your team's opinion of you?"

He straightened. "That's different."

"How?"

"It just is."

Her stomach coiled and the irritation burned. "Because you're a man?"

"Now you're twisting my words." He grabbed another board from the pile. "Besides, this is about you making time for important things. Not about me and my team."

"So, in your opinion, my to-do list consists of unimportant things, and only going to the game and attending the tent meeting is important."

"I didn't say that." He pounded another nail in the board.

"You didn't have to." Her pulse thundered. "Are you even

listening to yourself? First you want me to take it easy. Then when I prioritize my commitments, you tell me I'm doing it wrong because I'm not giving you your way."

Carter glared at her. "Why do you have to be so stubborn? It's only one night."

"Exactly. It's only one night, so you'll be fine without me."

❧

"Troubles?"

Carter turned toward his best friend as Emily marched to the other set of bleachers. "Morning, Ducky."

"Wasn't that your girl hightailing it out of here? You striking out again?"

"She's the most incorrigible, stubborn—"

Ducky laughed. "So you two have a lot in common."

"For that, you can get busy and help me." He tossed Ducky the hammer and indicated the joint that needed to be nailed in place. "She's overworking herself."

"She is one determined lady, but you knew that." Ducky drove the nail in the board. "So is there a bigger problem?"

Carter took a step back and surveyed their finished work.

"I'm worried about her priorities. A good Christian woman wouldn't—"

"Careful, Carter."

"What?"

"Of judging her."

"I'm not."

"Could've fooled me."

Carter walked to the water crock and downed a dipperful. "It's just that Emily says she loves the Lord, but I don't see God getting any of her time."

"Ask her about it."

237

"I can't do that."

"I don't see as you have much of a choice." Ducky took the dipper from Carter. "We've been friends long enough for me to know you could never marry someone who doesn't share your heart for the Lord."

"Whoa! I didn't say a thing about marriage."

"You didn't need to." Ducky doused Carter with the remaining water in the dipper.

Carter jerked back and wiped the water out of his eyes. Then he hefted the crock onto his shoulder. "Ducky Winslow, you are a dead man."

❦

Emily stood, pressed her hands to her aching back, and glanced at the early evening sun. If she hurried, now that her article was completed, she could catch the end of Carter's game. Not that he deserved it.

Then again, the morning of bleacher construction had poured over into the afternoon, and they wouldn't have finished the extra stands without Carter and his Owls. It had been nice of them to work so hard—not that Carter gave them any options.

His words still angered her, but she knew he'd spoken them in frustration. And she'd certainly said a few of her own. In the last few hours, her disposition had softened, and going to the game seemed an easy olive branch to offer.

After ducking into the cabin, she positioned a flowered straw hat on her head and inserted two mother-of-pearl hat pins to hold it in place. She glanced at her hands, now rough from the work. Her thumb still throbbed from the errant hammer strike, and it sported a deep purple nail. Gloves could cover it, but the unbearable temperature sent the thought into the trash bin.

"Grandma, I'm headed to Carter's game," she said once she was outside. "There's a tent meeting following it. We'll make it an early evening."

"After last night, you'd better."

"I love you too." She kissed her grandmother's cheek and hurried down the path.

Even with a faithful following, the Owls didn't garner enough fans to fill the new stands. A smile curled her lips. Her Bloomer Girls would.

"Emily!"

Greta Wilson waved at her from one of the new bleacher seats. Freckles sprinkled the blonde's nose, and her wide mouth took up too much of her otherwise pretty face. She motioned for Emily to join her.

Wanting to see the rest of the game, Emily scurried to the spot. "What inning are they in?"

"The bottom of the ninth."

Carter, standing on the pitching mound, glanced around. His sweat-stained uniform told her he felt the heat, and the day's growth of beard told her he'd had to hurry to make it to the game on time. He appeared to spot her, grin, and tip his head in her direction.

Emily's pulse skipped. "What's the score?"

"Three to two. The Owls are ahead." Greta glanced at her. "Where have you been?"

"I had a lot to get done."

She frowned. "I couldn't miss my Elwood for the world. I love to watch him. Have you seen how he can send the ball plumb out of the field?"

"He's very good." And so was her Carter. Good-looking too. No other player on the field had his solid jaw or broad shoulders.

Carter drew the ball back and hurled it over the plate. The batter swung, catching only air.

Emily applauded. "I have a new appreciation for how hard it is to hit that ball."

"Oh, I bet you do." Greta placed her hand on Emily's arm as if they were the best of chums. "And Carter is a wonderful pitcher—even if he's a bit bossy."

"Bossy? Carter?"

Greta covered her mouth with her hand. "Please forget I said that. Elwood would be furious with me if he knew I said anything."

"If you said anything about Carter? Or about Elwood? I'm sorry, but I'm confused, Greta."

"No, not about Carter. Well, not directly, anyway. I'm talking about the little bet he made."

Following the flighty Greta left Emily feeling light-headed. "Greta, who made a bet? Carter or Elwood?"

"Both of them, silly. You know. The one about you."

Emily's breath caught. "They bet over me?"

"You didn't know?" Greta's wide mouth bowed downward. "But I thought . . . I should have kept my mouth shut."

Emily drew in a shaky breath. "Greta, tell me the whole story, and start from the beginning."

"Please, let's forget I said anything."

"No, it's too late for that." Emily's firm tone told Greta there would be no more arguing the point. "Tell me everything."

Irritation gave way to anger in minutes as Greta relayed the story of Emily's hit. Emily recalled Elwood watching her that day and Carter's comment of catching her on first. Yes, he'd catch something all right. He'd catch her ire, and if she weren't a lady, he might even catch the heel of her shoe on his instep.

How dare he bet on her? And worse, how could he trivialize the importance of the Bloomer Girls' game by making Elwood dress up like a woman? Didn't he realize he would single-handedly make a mockery of the event?

Cheers erupted around her. She turned her gaze to the field, where the Owls hoisted Carter onto their shoulders. Another victory.

Enjoy your win, Carter Stockton, because you're about to lose a whole lot more.

Something was wrong.

And if Carter had to guess, that something had to do with him. The congratulatory peck on the cheek he'd anticipated from Emily never arrived, nor had any words of praise. Instead, Emily waited for him at the sideline, her face stony, while his teammates milled around, relishing their win.

"Out with it," he said as soon as he approached.

"Not here."

"Yes, here."

"Not now."

He raised an eyebrow at her. "Why not?"

Her gaze flitted to Greta and Elwood.

"Did Elwood say something to you? Upset you?" Carter clenched his fists. "Tell me what he did. I'll take care of him."

"And who'll take care of you?"

"What are you talking about?"

"Do you remember any bets you made? Perhaps ones involving my ability to hit a baseball?"

Carter's gut clenched as if he'd been punched. "It's not what you think."

"Tell me what you were thinking." She bit out the words.

"Because as far as I can tell, there wasn't a single intelligent thought involved."

"Elwood Taylor got to me. He was saying you couldn't do it." He fought to keep his voice low. "I knew you could."

"And so you bet on me?"

"I'm sorry, Emily. Honest." He took her hand in his. "And at least we're getting him back."

"By dressing him up like a woman!" Her voice rose, and other players turned toward them.

"Shhh."

She glared at him.

"Please."

Her green eyes flashed. "You cannot make him do that."

"Oh yes I can." It was over Carter's dead body that Elwood was going to get away with the rude things he'd said about Emily. No way. No how.

Emily jammed her fists against her skinny hips. "Carter Stockton, you are not going to ruin my Bloomer Girls' game. Either the dress goes or you do." Brushing past the gaping faces of Carter's teammates, Emily marched off the field.

Carter took off his hat and scratched his head. What in heaven's name had just happened?

27

Could things get any worse? Of all the people to be waiting upon her return from the Atlantic baseball game, Aunt Ethel was the last person Emily wanted to face. Didn't elderly women go to bed early? And wasn't this why Emily had spent the last three hours skipping rocks on the glassy surface of the lake until the sky had ribboned with color?

Her heart squeezed. On one hand, it was such a silly argument. Carter wanted to make Elwood Taylor wear a dress to the Bloomer Girls' game. On the other hand, the deeper subject of the fight was an impasse they'd not been able to breach. At its very foundation was his respect for her work.

Three more steps and she'd reach the screen door without having to talk to Aunt Ethel.

Her aunt cleared her throat. "Getting home a bit late, aren't you, Emily?"

"It's been a long night. I'm heading to bed."

"Don't you mean it's been a heartbreaking night?"

Emily stopped. How had Aunt Ethel been able to tell?

Aunt Ethel set down her knitting. "Problems?"

"I don't really want to talk about it."

"Come now." Aunt Ethel patted the empty rocking chair beside her. "I can see you're upset, and I'm not the ogre you've made me out to be. I do know a thing or two about men. Your uncle Leo and I enjoyed many happy years together."

Emily sank into one of the new wicker rockers beside her aunt and traced a curlicue on the armrest with her finger. "I don't think you're an ogre."

"Old-fashioned and stuffy?" The dying sun caught a brief smile on her aunt's sharply angled face. "I hope you realize I care a great deal about you—as if you were my own granddaughter."

"Thank you, Aunt Ethel."

"So, what happened? Did you have a tiff? I promise to listen without passing judgment. Or at least try."

What did Emily have to lose? She wouldn't be able to sleep for hours anyway.

Once she began, the words tumbled from her lips. To her aunt's credit, she did not interrupt.

"This is worse than I thought." Aunt Ethel heaved a long sigh and shook her head. "He loves you."

"What?" Emily gaped. "How did you get that out of what I told you?"

"Let me see if I got this right." Aunt Ethel peered over her spectacles. "Carter is angry with this Elwood fellow because he said unkind things about you, but you're angry with Carter because he's doing something about it."

"No, it's not that way. I mean—well, maybe it is, but not the way you think."

Aunt Ethel tsked. "Emily, you are a brilliant young suffragist, but you don't know a thing about a man in love."

"Why do you keep saying that? This isn't about love. It's about him respecting my work."

"You see it that way." She stood and smoothed her skirt. "But for Mr. Stockton, I believe it's about respecting you."

"And there's a difference?"

Her aunt emitted a rare chuckle. "Oh yes, Emily, there is. Good night, dear."

"That's it? No advice? No telling me what to do?"

Aunt Ethel gathered her knitting and peered over her spectacles. "You know what to do. You simply don't want to do it."

❦

And Emily thought she was stubborn.

Two days of baseball practice and Carter hadn't said a word to her.

Not one.

Even in passing.

The men whispered among themselves like gossipy old ladies. She heard them wagering on whether Elwood would have to wear the dress or not. She'd have marched over there and put an end to it if she hadn't heard the odds were in her favor.

Lifting the bat over her shoulder, she allowed a hint of a smile as she met the pitcher's eyes.

Hard as the dirt on his pitcher's mound, Carter's expression never changed. He fired a pitch. It flew by her so fast she felt the breeze, and it landed with a thud in Ducky's glove.

Emily blinked. His anger certainly hadn't cooled.

The next one sailed in even harder. Ducky grunted. "Easy, Stockton. This is only practice."

Carter glared. He'd made his point and he knew it.

More like what she was used to, the third pitch came in a bit slower and she connected her bat with the ball—a grounder right toward Carter. Without hesitation, she tossed the bat to the ground and raced toward the bag. Carter didn't toss the ball to the first baseman. Instead, he scooped up the ball and tagged her himself.

"You're out," he growled.

Maybe it was how hard the caramel in his eyes had become or how his voice seemed to be made of ice, but her eyes suddenly filled with tears.

No! She would not cry. She tipped her chin upward. "At least I tried."

"Since when did you care if someone tried to do something?"

Before she could respond, he turned and marched back to the pitcher's mound. Shoulders slumped, she trudged back to the bleachers.

How had things gone from bad to worse?

❧

Hoooot. Hoot. Hoooot.

Emily covered her head with a pillow. The barn owl outside her window needed to go back to a barn. For the second night in a row, he'd made sleep difficult for her.

Who was she kidding? The only owl truly keeping her from sweet dreams was over six feet tall and looked very good in a baseball uniform.

Giving up on chasing sleep, Emily sat up and jammed her feet into the slippers beside her bed. She snagged her crepe wrap from a hook and padded down the hallway to the parlor. It didn't take long to locate the matches and light the lamp on the table. Soon the pale light bathed the small room. Now, to find a book.

Emily ran her finger over the spines of each book in the case. Grandma Kate kept the bookshelf stocked with a blend of classics and new works: *Emma* by Jane Austen, *The Awakening* by Kate Chopin, *The Castaways of the Flag* by Jules Verne, and *Wee Willie Winkie and Other Stories* by Rudyard Kipling.

A ledger wedged between H. G. Wells's *Invisible Man* and Stephen Crane's *Red Badge of Courage* caught her eye. She recognized it as the one Carter had spent hours poring over. What was it doing here? It belonged on her grandmother's desk.

Emily tugged it free and set it down on the table. Then, returning to the shelf, she selected Rudyard Kipling's collection of stories and turned to *Baa, Baa, Black Sheep*. Maybe the short story of that title would be close to counting sheep.

She couldn't have been more wrong. The story of the two youngsters, Punch and Judy, soon made her rumbly stomach churn even more than before. In the story, Judy was treated warmly by her foster family in England, while Punch was miserably abused.

Emily closed the pages. This was not the light reading she needed tonight.

Her heart ached to reconcile with Carter, but she couldn't give in. This was too important.

But she missed him.

Longing for a part of him, her gaze fell on the ledger again. Maybe if she could see his handwriting, it would help.

She ran her hand over the leather binding. His hands had touched the same volume only this morning. She opened the pages to the last set of entries, which bore his familiar script in notations beside perfectly balanced columns. Her eyes clouded with unshed tears. One fell onto the page and smudged the ink. She blotted it with her palm and read the figures beneath.

One hundred twenty-seven dollars?

How could Grandma Kate have so little in her general account? Her grandma always liked to be flush. The stocks and money she held from Grandpa Ethan's experience in the silver mines more than supplied her grandmother's needs.

Or at least they had.

She flipped back through the pages. Other entries seemed odd. Large amounts subtracted without any notation as to why. Notes penciled in the margins about talking to Nathan.

Was her grandmother in some kind of trouble? Surely not. Carter would have said something. Perhaps this was the banking discrepancy he was working out.

She closed the book. It was really none of her business. Carter was taking care of this. He might be angry with her, but he thought the world of her grandmother. He would make sure it all got ironed out in no time.

Still, if the subject came up, she could ask him a couple of questions.

If he ever talked to her again.

❧

"I'm here to offer you a position on our club team."

Carter looked at the contract the scout from Des Moines handed him following the out-of-town game in Glenwood.

"You'd be one step closer to the majors, and you'd be playing with men who would appreciate that arm of yours."

A surge of pride swelled Carter's chest. This was it. What would Nathan think if he saw him now? Carter cleared his throat. "Mr. Gibbs, I'd be lying if I said I wasn't interested."

"We have a lot to offer. A salary of twenty dollars a month, lots of travel, meals, and a place to stay."

"When do you need to know?"

"Two weeks."

248

"Before or after the fourth?"

Mr. Gibbs twisted the end of his mustache. "Got a girl you need to talk to, huh? I understand."

Carter clamped his lips shut. His first thoughts had been of Emily, but right now that didn't mean much. What would she think if he left? Would she wait for him? It wasn't like they had any commitment to one another.

So why did his heart lurch at the thought of telling her? He hoped she'd come to her senses soon so he could talk to her about this offer.

"I'll give you until after the holiday. I'll be in Council Bluffs for a couple of days next week. I'm staying at the Ogden Hotel. After you read the contract, we can get together and discuss it." The scout stood and offered Carter his hand. "I enjoyed the game, and you'd enjoy being part of our team. I look forward to hearing from you."

"Thank you, sir. I appreciate your interest, and I'll be sure to let you know what I've decided as soon as I can."

⁂

Waffles.

Emily took one look at the checkerboard treat drenched in strawberry syrup and recalled Carter catching the bite that had flown off her fork when he'd first come to the cabin. He'd grinned but never said a word about it.

Her heart squeezed. Why did Britta have to serve waffles today, of all days? Carter had yet to say so much as hello to her, and tomorrow she'd have to face him at the tent meeting.

Outside, rain tinkled against the roof. Soft, but not comforting. Nothing was.

She sighed.

"Whatever it is, admit your fault and he'll forgive you."

Aunt Millie patted Emily's hand. "A girl like you can't be too picky."

"Millie." Grandma Kate scowled. "Emily is a perfectly wonderful young lady, and any man would be blessed to have such a caring soul by his side."

Aunt Ethel snapped her napkin in the air, then smoothed it on her lap. "Yes, but she does lack certain graces."

"And her womanly figure is a bit wanting," Aunt Millie added.

"I'm sitting right here." Emily downed the rest of her tea. "Why don't you talk about me being daft while you're at it? Besides, the two of you didn't like Carter, and now you're on his side?"

"I'm sure we could do better." Aunt Ethel sliced into her waffle. "But for the time being, in the interest of family harmony, I've acquiesced to this flight of fancy with the baseball player. When you tire of it, we'll step in and assist you in finding a truly suitable match."

Emily gaped. Flight of fancy? Truly suitable match? Hadn't Aunt Ethel said Carter loved her?

Aunt Ethel met her gaze. "When one has sincere affection for another, he or she does not let trivial things stand in the way of reconciliation."

"It isn't triv—"

Grandma Kate cleared her throat. "My dear sisters, Emily is perfectly capable of handling her own affairs. Now, dear, how are you going to pass the time with another day of dismal weather? Bible study?"

Emily laid her hand on the baseball rule book beside her. "No, the only book I have time to study is this one."

The book told her how to survive the game. Now, if only there was one that could tell her how to handle the players.

28

Biting her lip, Emily glanced out the window for the third time that morning. She didn't want to face Carter at Sunday's tent service, and while Saturday's rain had saved her from practicing with the team, today's bright sky offered no escape. He'd be there. Of that she was certain, and she still didn't know what to say to him.

Drawing on her gloves, she glanced at her reflection in the parlor's beveled mirror. At least the netted veil on her hat hid her puffy eyes.

A knock on the door startled her. She jumped, whacking her knee on a chair.

Her aunts and grandmother already waited outside, so who would knock?

The door opened and her brother stepped inside.

"Martin!" She wrapped her arms around his neck and squeezed. "Why did you come all the way to the lake to go to church with us?"

"I've been seeing your picture all over town on those Bloomer Girls' posters," he teased, "and it made me miss you."

Emily slapped his arm. "And to think for a moment I was actually glad you'd come."

"Nice hat." He lifted the flimsy veil, peered into her eyes, and frowned. "What did Carter do?"

"How do you know it was Carter?"

"Because I know you. Lost causes, injustices, and inequalities make you angry. Only people upset you."

Aunt Ethel called to them from outside.

She smiled. Saved. For now.

Martin held the door. "You can tell me all about it on the way to morning services."

True to his word, her brother pried the whole unsettling story from her as they walked. Like Aunt Ethel, he sided with Carter, saying Elwood obviously needed to be taught a lesson.

By the time she reached the tent meeting, irritation rubbed against her conscience like a pebble in her shoe. Why didn't they understand? She didn't need someone to stand up *for* her. What she needed was someone who'd stand up *with* her.

She stopped on the path as soon as she spotted Carter. Her heart hammered against her corset. Already seated beside Ducky, he wore a striped linen summer suit. Since he'd set his straw hat on the chair beside him, his tumble of curls had been freed to fall on his forehead.

Martin nudged her. "Where do you want to sit?"

Unsure, she glanced around. A row of empty chairs sat in the front, but she didn't want to parade in front of everyone. With Carter seated in the middle, it would be clear to all something was amiss.

"Let's sit in the back."

Aunt Ethel frowned but said nothing. Silently, the whole entourage filed into place, and she took her seat sandwiched between broad-shouldered Martin and plump Aunt Millie.

252

Ducky turned around and gave her an encouraging smile, like he often did before she batted. But Carter kept his eyes trained toward the front. Then, before Brother Greene stood to lead the first song, Carter swiveled in his chair and glanced at her. Her pulse quickened, but no winning smile followed his look. Not even a tilt of his head in acknowledgment.

Her heart capsized. Had she finally struck out with Carter Stockton?

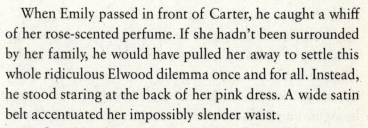

When Emily passed in front of Carter, he caught a whiff of her rose-scented perfume. If she hadn't been surrounded by her family, he would have pulled her away to settle this whole ridiculous Elwood dilemma once and for all. Instead, he stood staring at the back of her pink dress. A wide satin belt accentuated her impossibly slender waist.

He flexed his fingers. In the carriage, he'd held her waist, and his two hands practically touched when he spanned it. Forcing his gaze upward, he watched a few wisps of hair dance across her neck, blown by the breeze.

He tugged at his collar, twisted his neck, and muttered to himself about the unbearably hot breeze.

"Thank you for the wonderful sermon, Brother Fossen. It was truly inspiring." Aunt Ethel shook the preacher's hand. "Having a forgiving spirit is imperative for all of us."

Did she cast a look at him? He must be seeing things. Surely Aunt Ethel wouldn't know about their fight. If it were Aunt Millie or Grandma Kate, he could believe it, but Emily wouldn't confide in Aunt Ethel.

Anger still burned in his chest whenever he thought about Emily's ultimatum concerning him or the dress he planned to put Elwood in. Why couldn't she understand that his team-mate needed to learn a lesson? No one was going to mess with her when he was around.

Sidetracked by his thoughts, he missed the approach of Olivia DeSoto. She wedged into line, blocking his view of Emily. When she reached the preacher, she gushed over-the-top praise in an annoying singsong voice. As soon as Emily stepped beyond the tent, Olivia caught her. Emily waved the rest of the Graham family on.

Olivia gave Emily a syrupy smile. "I couldn't help but notice you weren't sitting by Carter Stockton. Has he grown tired of you so quickly? One too many accidents?"

Carter jolted. Although he and Emily weren't exactly speaking, he realized she would now have to answer for his stupid bet. He excused himself from his place in line and skipped speaking to Brother Fossen. Hurrying to Emily's side, he slipped a possessive arm around her shoulders. "Good morning, Mrs. DeSoto. Did I see that successful husband of yours come in with you this morning?"

"H-h-he wasn't able to make it. He wasn't feeling well."

"No, I imagine not. I saw him last night, and he seemed to have celebrated quite hard after our win." Emily elbowed his side, and he bit back a grin.

Emily smiled. "I do hope he'll be up and around soon."

Olivia flipped open her fan and waved it before her flushed cheeks. "He'd better be, hadn't he? After all, I do have my special tea with Mrs. Coggeshall tomorrow."

She emphasized the name, and Emily's shoulders stiffened beneath his hand.

"Olivia, if you'll excuse us, Emily and I would like to join her family."

He didn't wait for an answer but lowered his hand to the

small of Emily's back and nudged her toward where her family had spread a blanket.

"That woman!" Emily fumed.

"She likes to goad you."

Emily stopped. "Wait a minute. Why did you come to my rescue?"

"It's what we knights do." He chuckled.

"You're not getting off so easily, Carter Stockton. You haven't spoken to me in days, and we have a lot to talk about."

"I imagine we do." He glanced around at the churchgoers still thick on the lawn. "Let's talk somewhere a little less crowded."

They walked down the lawn, which sloped toward the water's edge. Around them, trees whispered and birds trilled their summer songs.

"What's going on tomorrow at Olivia's? I could tell it bugged you."

"A special tea. She invited every one of the members of the Council Bluffs Equal Suffrage Club except for me."

Carter raised his eyebrows. "And I take it you care?"

"Yes, I care. Her guest is Mary Jane Coggeshall, the former president of the Iowa Women's Suffrage Association and a close friend of Carrie Chapman Catt."

Carter stared blankly at Emily. *Catt. Catt. Catt.* Why was that name so important?

Emily rolled her eyes. "President of the National Woman Suffrage Association."

"Then go to the party."

"Weren't you listening? I'm not invited."

"Go anyway." He stopped on the lawn. "It's not like she'll kick you out in front of Mrs. Coggeshall."

The corners of her mouth curled. "I could, couldn't I? Wouldn't Olivia love it if I showed up at her door?"

"That's my girl."

Emily sat down on a fallen log stripped naked of its bark. While this spot was still visible to all, the cover of the cottonwoods made it seem less public. "Am I still your girl?"

"You've never stopped." He shucked off his jacket and sat down beside her. "But we've got something big to figure out here."

Emily's eyes lit, then the brief flicker dimmed. "I'm sorry you got upset when I pointed out the error of your logic."

He raised his eyebrows. "You're apologizing for my feelings and because I was wrong?"

She stood and smoothed out her dress. "Thank you for admitting that. Can we go now?"

"Not so fast." He caught her wrist and pulled her back beside him. "You are the most stubborn creature God ever placed on this earth, Emily Graham."

"Thank you."

"I didn't mean it as a compliment, and I'm not saying I was wrong." He shoved up his shirtsleeves. "No one—and I mean no one—is going to talk disrespectfully about you when I'm around."

She blinked and glanced in Olivia's direction. "I . . . I . . . don't know what to say."

"How about, 'Elwood can wear the dress'?"

"No. Not in a million years." She turned toward him, and the sun caught the golden streaks in her fawn-colored hair. "Carter, do you understand why I became so angry?"

"You weren't exactly forthcoming." He crossed his arms over his chest. He could be stubborn too.

"I know, and I'm sorry for that." She folded her hands in her lap. "The purpose of this Bloomer Girls' game is to show people that women are as capable as men when it comes to playing a sport, running a business, or making decisions. All those things so many believe we cannot do."

"And what does this have to do with Elwood?"

"Everything." She sighed. "Please try to understand. I know the Bloomer Girls will be performing. They'll play to the crowd and make folks laugh. But they'll play good baseball too. They do want to win. Our team, the Owls, will be playing serious ball against them. If Elwood dressed up, it would trivialize this whole process. It would make it look like the Owls went along with this only for the laughs and would make a mockery of the serious message. Does that make sense?"

Carter crossed his ankles. "Yes. I only wish you would have told me on Monday."

"Would you have listened?"

"Maybe." He chuckled. "Probably not. And for the record, Emily, I'm still not happy about the things Elwood said."

"And I appreciate that. Truly."

He nodded toward her family. "You'd better go eat."

"You're not going to join us?"

"I wasn't invited."

A wide grin spread across her face. "And why should that stop you? Come anyway."

Approaching the group, Carter could tell they all knew of his spat with Emily—even Martin. Peachy. Grandma Kate welcomed him and indicated the spot they had left open.

Aunt Millie squeezed his arm. "And we have cherry pie."

Well, at least he'd have pie to go with his crow.

He'd barely finished the last of his pie when the Warrington boy raced over. "Mr. Stockton! Will you play ball with us?"

Glancing at Emily, he asked, "Do you mind? It's kind of a tradition."

"Not at all."

"Martin, why don't you join us? I like to teach the boys a thing or two on Sunday afternoons. Usually we get an impromptu game going. I could use the help corralling the ruffians."

"Sure, why not?" Martin shrugged out of his jacket and rolled up his sleeves.

Carter tapped Emily's nose. "And before you get your nose out of joint, the girls could play too, but they're all in their Sunday best and I don't think their mamas would appreciate the offer."

Now both in shirtsleeves, Carter and Martin headed in the direction of young Carl Warrington. Carter recognized a few of the boys from the previous weeks, but the cluster continued to grow. Since the Owls' ball field was quite a jaunt from the place where the tent meeting was set up, they'd have to make do in the grassy area.

Martin glanced back over his shoulder. "Emily really wanted to come."

Carter didn't miss the incredulous sound in his voice. "She likes the game, and she's gotten pretty good at it."

"You don't have to pretend with me, Carter. I'm well aware Emily is clumsy, and she is too. We've been telling her for years. Emily has a lot of endearing qualities, but we all know gracefulness isn't one of them, and if you can't run around the bases without tripping, then, well, there's not much use in trying."

Clamping his jaw shut, Carter fought to keep from blurting out a response. Emily's family had been telling her she didn't measure up all her life. How dare they? Of course she believed them.

Carter released the breath he was holding, long and slow. "She doesn't trip, Martin. Not anymore." He paused. "But if she did, I wouldn't mind one bit."

29

Sitting on a patchwork quilt in the shade of a spreading oak, Emily cheered the boys on. They'd divided in half with Carter leading one team and Martin the other.

It was a pleasure to watch both men play alongside the boys and inspire their young team members. Right from the start, Martin organized his boys and kept them in line. He corrected their stances and yelled at them to keep going. The boys seemed to like him, but not the same way Carter's boys worshiped their leader.

Carter's team enjoyed every minute. Anything the pitcher said was treated like gold. Carter laughed with them, making each boy feel like he was a champion. He praised their efforts and accomplishments while providing tips, much like he'd done for her. They also played smarter and faster than her brother's team.

Shielding her eyes against the sun, she saw Carter hit a ball deep into the outfield. The boys on the other team scrambled to get it while he took his time running the makeshift bases. Only Carter would give a group of boys a chance to get him out.

Not Martin. When his turn came, he hit a line drive so hard the shortstop had to hop out of its way. Then, when the boys fumbled picking it up in the outfield, he stole another base. She rolled her eyes. Her brother liked to win no matter what the cost.

The game drank up the afternoon. Other spectators came and went, but one man remained on the edge of the field for quite some time. Although Emily had not been formally introduced, she recognized Carter's older brother Nathan from school. He lacked Carter's athletic build but had the same solid lines to his face and jaw. He also lacked Carter's sense of fun. Seriousness seemed to surround Nathan like a rain cloud.

Poor Carter.

Emily plucked a dandelion from the base of the tree. The once sunny yellow flower had aged and transformed into a ball of downy fluff. She held the dandelion up to her lips, made a wish, and blew the cottony seeds into the air. She'd be tempted to tell Carter her wish when the game was over, but wouldn't dare. Wishes, like her prayers, never came true.

⚬⚬⚬

As soon as he spotted Nathan, Carter wished he could sweep Emily to the other side of the lake before he was forced to make introductions. They already knew each other, of course, but only in passing. As the older brother, Nathan expected to pass judgment on any potential unions. And while Carter wasn't ready to make that leap, his heart kept telling his head the possibility was there.

"Mr. Stockton, will you show me how to throw a fastball?"

260

"And me how to hit better?"

"And when you steal a base, is it head first or feet first?"

The boys crowded around him, begging for more, cheeks and noses sunburned from the afternoon game. Carter tapped the bill of Carl Warrington's cap. "Maybe next week, boys. Right now I have a pretty lady waiting."

"Ewwww." Several boys stuck out their tongues.

Ruffling the fair hair of one of the youngest boys, he excused himself with a chuckle. It had been a long time since girls gave him the willies. And the one sitting in the grass blowing dandelions had the opposite effect entirely. He'd missed her and her kisses.

Beneath a wide-brimmed hat, her hair had blown loose from its tight bun, and wisps frolicked in the breeze. The mottled colors of the quilt added more whimsy to the sight. If he were an artist, he would have painted her at that moment. Natural. Pure. Beautiful.

She looked up as he approached, and a soft smile curled her lips as if she'd been caught. She ducked her head and tossed the dandelion stem away.

Carter held out his hand. "I hope you were wishing about me." He pulled her to her feet and kissed her flushed cheek.

"And why would I do that?"

Laughter bubbled in his chest. "Maybe I've already made all your wishes come true."

"I highly doubt that," a man's deep voice said from behind them.

Carter jerked around. "Hello, Nathan."

"Carter."

Deciding to get it over with, Carter sighed. "You may remember Miss Emily Graham from school. Miss Graham, this is my brother, Nathan Stockton."

Nathan tipped his hat. "Miss Graham, it's a pleasure to see the girl who's going to make my brother finally grow up."

"I have no intention of making Carter do anything, Mr. Stockton." Emily gave a polite smile. "I saw you watching the game. Weren't you impressed by how well he worked with those boys? He has a real talent for coaching."

"Boys will be boys." Nathan grinned and motioned toward the impromptu baseball field. "But he does have a propensity for playing games. How do you feel about that, Miss Graham?"

"What do you want, Nathan?" A familiar tightness spread over Carter's chest.

"Tsk tsk, Brother. You should know better than to answer for someone as forward thinking as Miss Graham." Nathan turned his attention back to Emily. "So how do you feel about the games Carter plays?"

"I'm more curious as to why you care."

"Touché." He stared at Carter. "Father wants you both to come for dinner."

"Tonight? We can't tonight. Emily has a lot to do before the big game against the Bloomer Girls."

"Yes, the game. Your idea, wasn't it, Miss Graham? Do you honestly think a woman can compete, say, in the banking world, when even the man beside you doesn't believe he can cut the mustard there?"

"I'll not have you speak to her—"

Emily's fingers dug into Carter's arm. "Mr. Stockton, I find you sorely lacking in both decorum and common decency. Are you so jealous of your brother's athletic abilities you cannot celebrate his successes? So threatened by him you cannot handle it if he does not fall into step behind you? I find it odd you believe he's the one who's childish and playing games."

Pride filled Carter's chest, but he kept his jaw set. "Nathan, tell Dad I'll drop by tomorrow and arrange something. Thank him for the invitation."

"I'm not your errand boy. Tell him yourself."

After Nathan marched away, Carter apologized for his brother's words. Emily would have nothing of it. "Our brothers have minds of their own. Look at mine over there."

Carter followed her line of sight and discovered Martin talking with Olivia's husband. "Your brother's consorting with the enemy."

She laughed. "I wouldn't call him the enemy simply because of who he chose to marry, but it does look like Mr. DeSoto made a miraculous, post-Sunday-services recovery."

<hr />

How Carter managed to convince Emily to meet him at the ball field on a Sunday, she'd never know. His weak excuse that they needed to make up for yesterday's washed-out practice didn't ring true for Carter's usual insistence that they all take Sundays off. The only Sunday they'd practiced so far had been on the day they'd ended up in the Kursaal.

It must mean she really needed more work than she thought.

Try as she might, she could not force her feet to move any faster. Carter would already be waiting for her at the field and wouldn't be pleased at her tardiness. Earlier he'd proclaimed he had no intention of losing to a bunch of women, no matter how talented they were.

"Miss Stockton." Elwood Taylor jogged up beside her. "Good to see I'm not the only one late. At least if I'm with you, Carter won't yell at me."

"I wouldn't count on that."

Elwood's face darkened. "Does Stockton raise his voice to you?"

Emily laughed. "Oh, heavens no. I only meant—well, you know how seriously Carter is taking this game."

"And rumor has it I have you to thank for not having to wear a dress to that game."

"Carter and I discussed it and came to a mutual agreement." She paused. "But how did you hear about that? We only came to the decision after church services."

"That's funny, Carter told me the other day."

Joy swelled inside her. He'd given in to her wishes long before they'd talked.

Elwood cleared his throat. "He told you I was against you playing, didn't he?"

"He mentioned it."

"I still don't think it's a good idea, but I have to say you're good for him." Elwood stretched his right arm across his chest, warming up as they walked. "Stockton thinks he has all the answers. You let him know he doesn't."

"And what about you?"

Elwood flashed a cocky grin. "Naturally, I know everything."

As soon as Carter spotted the two of them approaching the baseball diamond, he ran out to meet them. He halted on the path and a cloud of dust flew. He glared at Elwood. "Emily, is he giving you any trouble?"

"Absolutely not. Elwood's been a perfect gentleman."

The two men kept their gazes locked in a silent competition.

She pushed past both of them and looked back over her shoulder. "You two coming, or are you going to stand there all day acting like eight-year-olds?"

Before either man could catch up, she reached the field. The team gathered around her, each man grinning like he knew Santa Claus was about to arrive in his sleigh.

Emily searched the crowd for the familiar catcher. "Ducky, what's going on?"

Carter divided the crowd and came through with a box. "We got you a present."

"For me?"

"Well, we could make Elwood wear it," Digger said, elbowing Mac beside him.

Carter shot the boys a glare and held out the box. "Just open it."

The twine binding the cream-colored box gave way with only one tug. Emily lifted the lid off the box and passed it to Ducky beside her. Inside, a bright red *M* stared back at her. She traced it with her finger as tears filled her eyes. Her very own uniform.

"Do you like it?" Carter's voice held a note of concern.

She lifted it from the box and held the striped shirt to her chin. "I love it."

"There are . . . a . . . bloomers too." Carter's cheeks tinged with red, his coffee-colored curls flopping on his forehead. He took the hat from the box and stuffed it on her head. "There. Now you're an official Owl."

Emily pulled the cap in place. "Thank you. Thank you all so much."

"Well, let's not stand around here all day." Elwood grinned at her. "This is our day off."

She caught Carter's sleeve. "This was your idea, wasn't it?"

"We all pitched in."

"Carter?"

"Anything that makes your green eyes sparkle like that, well, I'd be a fool to say it wasn't."

She kissed his cheek. "Thank you. I'll make you proud."

"You already make me proud."

30

"I'm not sure about this." Emily stopped at the base of the steps leading up to Olivia DeSoto's large brick home. The wraparound porch, usually so inviting on most homes, seemed like a barrier between her and the women gathered beyond the front door. Her stomach clenched.

Lilly closed her parasol and hooked it on her wrist. "Uh-uh, young lady. You're going to march up those steps between Marguerite and me and walk into that tea with your head held high."

"But—" Emily turned to Marguerite for support.

"Don't look at me." Marguerite tugged on the hem of her sky-blue jacket, which matched her eyes perfectly. "I'm with Lilly. It was wrong of Olivia to slight you, and I can't wait to see the look on her face when she sees you here anyway."

"What if she makes a scene in front of Mrs. Coggeshall?"

Marguerite nudged her toward the steps. "She wouldn't dare. Now let's get on in there. We're late enough to make a grand entrance, but any later would be in poor taste."

Emily pressed a hand to her churning stomach. "Oh, I hope this is the right thing to do."

"It's going to be fine. You'll see." Lilly looped her arm in Emily's.

Marguerite flanked her on the other side. "Besides, what's the worst that could happen?"

Tripping on the first step, Emily clutched at their arms. "Do you even need to ask?"

The two friends laughed and climbed the steep stairs to the porch. Emily felt a solid object in the pocket of her skirt brush against her leg. The bust food. Aunt Millie had received a second canister and had thrust it into her hand as she left. Maybe she could throw it away while she was in town.

Marguerite rapped on the door, and an apron-clad maid opened it. She took Lilly's umbrella and said, "Welcome. The ladies are in the garden. If you'll follow me, I'll show you there."

Emily bumped the foyer table with her hip as she passed, and the crystals on the lamp jingled. She quickly stilled them with her hand. The maid jerked around, frowned, but said nothing.

Marguerite offered a reassuring smile.

Olivia's home reflected her pension for drama. Too many knickknacks and baubles littered the tables. The heavy scent of mint filled the air, and an immense grandfather clock, complete with a myriad of curlicues and swirls, gonged at fifteen minutes past the hour. They were tardy. Wouldn't Olivia like that?

With a sweep of her hand, the maid indicated the tea was beyond the French doors at the end of the dining room. The tinkle of teacups on saucers and the twitter of the ladies' laughter drifted in through the open doorway. Emily took a deep breath.

Lilly turned to her. "We'll go first, and you come behind us. It will be like a big surprise party."

As Emily's turn came to step onto the veranda, her stomach knotted. Some surprise. Parties were welcomed. She absolutely was not.

But she should have been.

The thought spurred her forward. She stepped onto the veranda.

"Emily?" Olivia's eyes widened.

"Good afternoon, Olivia." She crossed the open space to her hostess. "What a lovely home you have, and such a nice turnout."

Lilly nudged Olivia. "Aren't you glad Emily was able to come after all?"

"Yes, I figured my invitation got lost somewhere in the mail." She turned to the unfamiliar elderly woman seated at the table. "And you must be Mrs. Coggeshall."

She offered her hand. "I am, and you are . . . ?"

"Emily Graham, president of our local suffrage association."

"Oh, how wonderful! I certainly hoped you'd be here. I want to hear all about your idea for the game with the Bloomer Girls. Come sit with me and we'll talk."

Emily glanced back over her shoulder at Olivia. Fury sparked in her eyes, but she seemed to check her tongue. The ladies around her whispered, giving one another sidelong, knowing glances. A little thrill climbed in Emily's chest. With Mrs. Coggeshall's obvious approval of Emily's presence, Olivia couldn't say anything or she'd look like a fool.

"Now . . ." Mrs. Coggeshall pulled Emily into the chair beside her. "Tell me all about how you came up with such a brilliant idea."

The hour flew by as Emily shared her passion for women's

suffrage, her grandmother's friendship with Amelia Bloomer, and her commitment to the cause. After a while, she asked Mrs. Coggeshall to say something to the Council Bluffs Equal Suffrage Club that would inspire them to keep fighting.

The sixty-some-year-old woman stood and eyed the ladies gathered. "I will tell you all what I told the Polk County Women's Suffrage Society on the silver anniversary of that esteemed group. Twenty-five years has but deepened our conviction that reform is the need of the age. We only hope that the next generation of women may find their work made easier because we have trodden the path before them."

Emily marveled at how the women hung on every word spoken by the elderly suffragist. What would it be like to have devoted one's entire life to this work? Emily could only hope she had the opportunity.

After Mrs. Coggeshall answered nearly a dozen questions, the tea drew to a close. Emily thanked her and said goodbye before joining Marguerite and Lilly at the door. She had no intention of being the last to leave and risk being cornered by Olivia.

"Emily!" Olivia's grating voice rang out. She held up the canister of Sears Bust Food. "I believe this fell out of your pocket."

Cheeks flaming, Emily stared at the container. She could fess up, but not now after she'd made such a good impression on Mrs. Coggeshall. A thought tickled her conscience. "Oh, I brought that for you, Olivia. I'm glad you found it. Thanks for the invitation."

❧

Emily swiped the tears from her eyes as she clicked down the sidewalk beside her friends. Unable to contain her giggles, she pressed a hand to the stitch in her side.

"Did you see her face?" Marguerite sucked in her cheeks. "My face hurts from smiling so much."

Lilly dabbed her eyes with a lace-edged handkerchief. "Emily, that was perfect."

A new fit of contagious laughter erupted from the women, and Emily paused on the sidewalk to attempt to regain control of herself. She sensed the other departing suffrage club members staring at them as they passed, but she didn't care. Infectious laughter was one of the joys of friendship.

Lilly took a deep breath. "Well, since we certainly can't go home like this, what do you two say to some lunch? My treat."

"You don't have to do that," Marguerite said.

"Do you realize how good it feels to be able to be the one doing the treating?" She linked arms with Emily. "And how good it feels to laugh like this?"

Emily tugged her vest down into place. "But Ben is such a character. I thought he'd have you in stitches all the time."

"He's been away on business, and I can assure you, his parents talk to me as little as possible."

"Those old stuffed shirts." Marguerite stopped at the corner beside Lilly. After a buggy passed, they continued down the block toward Main Street. "Have you spoken to Ben about getting a house of your own?"

"It's a touchy subject. Their house is plenty big for all of us and my mama. Thank the good Lord she's there. She's so good with Levi, and even with the nurse there, I couldn't leave him unless she was around."

"My parents miss having your mother as their cook." Marguerite stepped over a puddle. "I don't think they realized how good they had it with her until they tasted Verla's cooking. Even I can make better biscuits."

Lilly raised one eyebrow. "I highly doubt that."

More giggles followed as the three crossed the last blocks leading to the café. Emily's stomach rumbled. The bells in St. Peter's, perched high on a bluff, pealed twelve times over the bustling city. No wonder she was hungry.

They reached an iceman's delivery wagon and paused to catch a cool breeze wafting from the back when he opened the compartment. Using enormous tongs, he lugged a block out of the back and carried it inside the ice cream parlor.

Emily glanced in the window. Ice cream would be almost as good as lunch. After all, they'd had cucumber sandwiches at Olivia's tea.

She stopped when she spotted Carter inside the parlor. Who was he speaking to? Nothing about his bowler hat or handlebar mustache seemed familiar. He pushed a set of papers in Carter's direction. Carter folded them and inserted them in his jacket pocket. The two stood and shook hands.

"Emily?" Marguerite held open the door to the café. "You coming?"

Emily hurried to the entry, guilt pricking her conscience. She'd been spying on Carter, but what were those papers, and what kind of deal had Carter struck with the man? Investments? But Carter didn't have any money of his own to invest. The family's money was all wrapped up in the bank and under Nathan's control. On one of their outings, Carter had alluded to some kind of allowance his father provided, and he'd said he received a modest sum playing for the Owls. He probably made a bit more from his work for her grandmother. Even with all that, it wouldn't be enough to make any kind of investment on his own.

Maybe he'd come into some other money. Her heart skipped, and she uttered a prayer before giving it a second thought. *Please, God, don't let this have anything to do with Grandma Kate's missing funds.*

❦

"You look like a princess."

Twirling to look at the back of the dress in the seamstress's full-length mirror, Emily frowned. "I don't know, Marguerite. With all this green, I hope I don't look more like a frog."

Lilly stepped forward to adjust the ruffle around the scooped neckline of Emily's dress. "It matches your eyes perfectly. Carter won't be able to take his eyes off you."

"Mary, you really outdid yourself." Marguerite thumbed through the seamstress's book of drawings she displayed in her shop.

Emily studied the dress. Was she being too critical? The moss-colored gored skirt with a short train was accented with dainty lace. She rubbed her upper arms. They were so bare, so vulnerable. Her cheeks warmed. Carter's hands would touch her skin.

But the dress did bring out the green of her eyes, and she loved the beadwork on the bodice.

"She's liking it," Marguerite said. "Look at the smile on her face."

"Do you?" Concern etched soft-spoken Mary's voice. "I so wanted you to be happy with it."

"Oh, Mary. It's lovely. You did a miraculous job." She twirled and swished the skirt in a circle. "I can't wait to dance in it."

"I'm so glad you like it." Mary continued hemming another gown.

Lilly fingered the golden silk. "Whose gown is that?"

"Mrs. DeSoto's."

272

"Olivia's?" Emily swished over. "It's gorgeous. It looks like spun gold."

Mary wrinkled her nose. "I wish it was for one of you three. She still won't like it."

Marguerite set the sketchbook on the table. "Why?"

"No dress is going to make her husband pay attention to her." She sighed. "I can mend about anything except broken hearts."

Emily stepped back. Surely Mary had misread the cues. Olivia, the belle of every ball, commanded attention. She didn't need to beg for it anywhere.

Still, her husband had been less than attentive at the play. And on Sunday, he'd not come to services with her. In fact, he was seldom with her anywhere. Could things not be happy at home?

Casting a glance toward Marguerite, Emily sensed her friend considering the same question. Guilt poked Emily in the chest. With Olivia always such a thorn in her side, Emily had never taken time to think beyond those nasty occurrences. Would that explain why Olivia did what she did? And had they all been so irritated by her that they'd failed to see the truth behind her actions?

Lilly placed a hand on Mary's shoulder. "Well, if she doesn't want it, I'll certainly take it."

"You should have ordered a new ball gown, Lilly." Marguerite carried the sketchbook over and flipped it open to the middle. "This one would be perfect."

"Sorry. No husband in town. No ball."

"You're not going?" Emily asked.

"Not unless I plan to dance by myself. Ben won't be back until late that night." She shrugged and then winked at Mary. "But I'd look mighty fine sitting in my rocking chair wearing that gold dress when he finally got home."

What was wrong with Nathan?

Carter slammed the ledger down on his brother's desk, and the sound echoed off the stone walls of the bank. "I know Kate Graham deposited funds into her account the other day, and now your clerk says they were never there!"

Nathan crossed his arms over his chest. "And where did these supposed funds come from? All of her savings are with us."

"Mrs. Graham is a savvy businesswoman. She has accounts in other places as well." *Thank goodness for that.*

"And you have a receipt of the transaction?"

"I told you she came in and took care of the matter herself. I don't have the receipt because she misplaced it."

"And I'm telling you if our clerks didn't record it, then she probably only thinks she made the deposit. When are you going to face the possibility that the old lady is daft?"

"As far as I'm concerned, Nathan, there's only one possibility." Carter jammed a finger on the mahogany surface of his brother's desk. "Something is going on right here—under *your* nose."

Fury seemed to radiate off his brother. "Get out. You're not going to come into my bank and accuse my clerks." He stopped suddenly and smirked. "For all I know, you're stealing the old woman's money and trying to blame it on my men. What is the family dandy living on since I convinced Dad to cut you off?"

Carter cut off?

Emily halted in the bank lobby. Her heart skidded. Had

she heard that right? She'd only heard the tail end of their conversation. And what a heated conversation it was. What was Nathan accusing Carter of? Blaming his clerks for what?

To the right of the entryway, the door to Nathan's office remained open. Carter leaned over the desk and appeared ready to come to physical blows with his brother. She strained to hear his hissed words while her heart told her she shouldn't be eavesdropping.

Carter whirled in her direction as he marched from the office. She froze. Their eyes met, and guilt flooded his face. Instead of greeting her, he slammed the heavy oak doors open and rushed outside.

Chest so tight she could barely breathe, Emily sank onto a chair, dropping her dress box with a thud onto the shiny, planked floor beside her. What was going on?

31

"Miss Graham, you just missed my brother."

Several minutes after Carter had departed, Emily looked up and found Nathan standing above her.

"Were you coming to discuss the missing funds from your grandmother's account too? As I told him, he had no proof the deposit was ever made. And if there was one, only those with permission could withdraw any funds. I stand by my clerk's records."

Emily blinked. Only those with access. The pieces were coming together. Besides Carter, only her family had access. Carter had been cut off. If he didn't make money somehow, he'd have to work at the bank, which he was loath to do. And then there was the business deal at the ice cream parlor.

Pressing her hand to her chest, Emily rose on shaky legs. Tears puddled in her eyes. Could he have pretended to care for her to get to her grandmother's money? After all, why would someone like handsome, athletic Carter Stockton fall for someone as clumsy and outspoken as she was?

"Miss Graham, are you ill? You look pale." Nathan sounded genuinely concerned. "I can send someone for my brother."

She waved him off and fled from the bank, her cumbersome dress box slowing her down.

Please, God, let me be wrong.

⊷⊶

Twisting her ankle to the right and then the left, Emily struggled to free her foot. She'd been in such a hurry to get across the street to meet the trolley, she'd not seen the hole between the paving bricks and the streetcar track, and now her heel was wedged in tightly.

Tears trailed down her cheeks, and she jostled the bulky box to her other hip. She wiggled her foot again, but it still wouldn't budge. She could slip the shoe off, but then what would she do? She couldn't hobble around in her stockings all the way back to Lake Manawa.

A wagon drove around her, and then two boys, chasing their spotted dog, ran by. She glanced around, half afraid someone would notice her predicament and half afraid they wouldn't. Several blocks away, the streetcar trudged in her direction. She gasped and worked her ankle harder. Why wouldn't the shoe move?

The streetcar drew closer, but she still had time. *Don't panic. Breathe.*

"Emily?" She turned to see Ducky. "What's wrong? Why are you standing here?"

She sucked in her quivering lip. "I'm stuck."

"What?"

"My heel is stuck. I can't move."

Ducky grinned. "Which foot?"

"My right one."

"May I?" He took the package from her hand, set it on the street, and then knelt at her feet.

Heat flooded her face, and she glanced at the streetcar lumbering toward her. "Please do."

Ducky lifted her skirt and placed one hand around the back of her heel and the other on her ankle. Her cheeks flamed afresh.

After wiggling her foot back and forth, he looked up at her. "I'm going to try to pull your shoe out. Put your hands on my shoulders to steady yourself."

She did as she was told.

"On three. Ready?" His grip tightened. "One. Two. Three."

He yanked hard and the shoe gave. She dug her fingers into his shoulders to keep from toppling.

"Easy." He held out his hand to support her as he stood. "Is it twisted? I can carry you."

"No. It's fine."

The motorman on the streetcar dinged his bell, and Ducky scooped up her package. "We'd best get out of his way." He kept hold of her elbow until they reached the sidewalk.

"Thank you, Ducky."

"Least I can do for Carter's girl." The streetcar stopped. "Headed back to the lake?"

She nodded and held out her hands for her parcel.

"Then you're in luck. Consider me your personal beast of burden since we're headed in the same direction."

Even though she preferred to be alone right now, she couldn't very well dismiss her rescuer. She stepped onto the streetcar and deposited a token in the glass box beside the motorman.

Ducky did likewise and followed her. "Do you want a window seat or an aisle?"

"You can have the window." He squeezed in place, holding the large box against his chest, and she settled beside him. "Is this your dress for the ball tonight?"

"Yes."

"Carter said you promised it'd be green. He's been talking about it matching your pretty green eyes all week."

"He talks about me?"

Ducky chuckled. "Nonstop."

"He's probably like that with all the girls he's—"

"Nope. Only you." Ducky eyed her. "Never seen him like this about anyone before, and we've been friends for quite a while now. I know you two have had your differences over Elwood and all, but you have something special. Hey, even an old hayseed like me can see it. He's drawn to you like a fly to a piece of cherry pie."

"Rhubarb."

"Excuse me?"

"Carter's favorite pie is rhubarb." Ducky's warmth was infectious, and Emily smiled. "Is cherry your favorite?"

"It sure is."

She twisted her foot beneath her dress. "Then I'll have to see if I can get Britta to make you one. It's the least I can do for you saving me today."

"As long as I don't have to share it with Carter."

Carter. What would he think when he heard about yet another of her escapades? And about what she'd heard?

"Do you know what Carter was doing in town today? I saw him, but he avoided me."

Ducky's thick brows drew together. "Emily, I know it's not my place, but I can see the doubt in your eyes. Carter's as straight an arrow as God made 'em, and the only games he plays are on the field."

"But you saw me earlier—things like that happen to me all the time."

He chuckled. "He said that too, and he says it keeps life interesting."

❧

Carter paced in front of the streetcar depot. With streetcars arriving every twenty minutes, where was Emily?

The next streetcar approached, stopped, and emptied. She wasn't among the passengers.

He checked his pocket watch again. He'd been back an hour, and he wanted to speak to her before the ball at the Kursaal tonight. With the way he'd stormed out, he'd be lucky if she didn't break their date altogether. He shouldn't have left like that.

He sat down on a bench and dropped his head into his hands. What a day this had been. Nathan always brought out the worst in him. Even though he'd prayed before confronting his brother, he'd let his anger get a foothold, and he hated that Emily saw him in that state. How much had she heard?

Checking his watch again, he noticed the next streetcar was late. The skin on his neck prickled. Maybe there was a problem.

Finally, the streetcar rumbled into view. He stood up. If she wasn't on this one, he was going to get his phaeton and head back to town.

Relief washed over him as Emily stepped down the steps. He hurried to meet her.

"Carter, what are you doing here?"

"Waiting for you."

Ducky stepped off behind her and passed Carter the box.

"Since you're here, you can carry her box. I gotta go spiff up for the ball."

Emily smiled at him. "Thanks, Ducky—for everything."

He nodded. "And you be careful and watch where you step."

Carter and Emily started down the paved path leading to the Grand Plaza. "What was that all about?"

"My heel got stuck, and thankfully, Ducky happened along."

"Stuck where?"

"Aren't we avoiding the real issue?" Emily stopped beneath a willow tree and faced him. "What was going on at the bank? And why did you leave so abruptly?"

"I was furious. I didn't want you to see that. Something about Nathan makes me so angry." He took her hand. "I'm sorry. I shouldn't have taken off."

"I was quite shocked."

"I know. How much did you hear?"

She bit her lip.

"You heard the part about Nathan convincing my dad to cut me off financially, didn't you?" He dropped her hand and shifted the parcel. They reached the Grand Plaza, and he placed his hand on the small of her back to guide her through the crowd.

Why did she have to know about the suspension of his dad's support? Now every time he took her somewhere, she'd be second-guessing if he had the money to pay. He did. He'd figured a budget from the day his brother had declared the news. And until he started courting her, he hadn't needed much extra, so his cookie jar was flush.

He took a deep breath. "I'm determined to show Nathan I don't need his money to make a name for myself."

"You two had some strong words. Nathan said it was over my grandmother's account."

"He told you?" His voice grew hard. How dare he concern her. "You don't need to fret about that. I'm taking care of it, and you have more than enough on your own plate right now."

"But—"

"No." The word came out unyielding, so he tried to soften it with a winning smile. "You worry about the Bloomer Girls, and I'll worry about the account discrepancy. Some clerk simply made an error. It may take awhile, but we'll get it worked out. Okay?"

Concern clouded her eyes, but she finally nodded.

He captured her hand and pulled her toward the bandstand. What could he do to reassure her? "Let's take a break."

"But I have to go home to get ready."

He sat down and tugged her down beside him. "So, you're still going with me?"

She smiled. "I have to go with you. You're the only one who will appreciate my green dress."

He chuckled and pulled her close. "You'll be gorgeous."

"Croak, croak," she mumbled.

"Emily, when are you going to start seeing yourself as beautifully as I do?" He kissed her cheek as Dalbey's band introduced their first song, "Ideal American" by William Chambers. The famous string and brass band struck up the tune. On their second song, they switched gears and announced an intermezzo piece, "Love's Dream after the Ball" by Alphons Czibulka. While Carter had never heard of the composer, he hoped by the end of the lilting piece, he'd owe the man a debt of gratitude for carrying all of Emily's doubts away on the melody. He only wished he were holding Emily right now on the dance floor.

As he intertwined his fingers with Emily's, warmth pooled in his chest. He studied her as she closed her eyes to enjoy the music. She truly had no idea how beautiful she was. Even more so inside. And in those moments when he'd waited for her, he'd realized something. He had a future now. He didn't need to keep his feelings silent any longer.

The last strains still hung in the air when he pressed his lips to her ear. "Emily," he whispered, "I do believe I love you."

32

"Don't fidget so."

Emily stilled while her grandmother finished buttoning the tiny pearl buttons on the chiffon gown. In the light of the cabin, the dress looked more ivy than moss green, and even Emily had to admit the soft flounces of lace draped around the skirt and train would be lovely when she danced.

With a man who loved her.

Her heart skipped, and she pressed her hand to her chest. The open neckline, which Mary insisted was in vogue, left much more skin exposed than her day dresses. At least the seamstress had been generous with the lace draped over Emily's shoulders.

Grandma Kate stepped back. "You're a vision."

"Thank you, Grandma." Emily adjusted the garland of fabric roses trailing from her left shoulder to her waist. "You don't think these are too much?"

"They look so real, I can almost smell them. You're only

missing one thing." Grandma Kate reached into the pocket of her skirt and pulled out a box. "Go ahead. Open it."

Fingers trembling, Emily took the gift and removed the lid. Diamond ear bobs sparkled against a swatch of black velvet. "Aren't these yours?"

"A gift from your grandfather." She pulled one of the pieces out and held it to the window. It glittered in the sun. "He gave them to me as an anniversary gift, and I want you to have them."

"Grandma, I can't."

She placed the ear bob back in the box and laid her hand on top. "Yes, you can. When you wear them, you can think of the love your grandfather and I shared."

Tears beaded in Emily's eyes as she slipped the ear bobs into the holes in her lobes.

"Carter told you he loves you, didn't he?"

Wide-eyed, Emily turned from the mirror. "How did you know?"

"You nearly floated into the house when you came home. And now your face switches from joy to terror in seconds." Grandma Kate smiled, the wrinkles crinkling around her eyes. "And what did you say?"

Heat infusing her cheeks, Emily licked her lips.

"Ah, he didn't let you answer. Smart boy."

"Grandma!"

The older woman waddled to the door. "It's good to make him wait a bit for your declaration. You should pray about it before you say anything. Affairs of the heart need to be placed in the hands of the Lover of our souls. Only God knows what is best." She tilted her head to the side to take in both ear bobs. "He's a good man, Emily. Don't be afraid."

Her grandmother slipped from the room. Emily sat down

on the bed and slid her feet into her black satin slippers. After easing her hands into her long white kid gloves, she took a deep, steadying breath. Fear tainted the thrill of Carter's proclamation, and the memory of the bank discovery wouldn't go away. What if Carter wasn't as good a man as everyone thought? And what about the deal she saw him making in the ice cream parlor? He hadn't mentioned a word about that.

But he'd said he loved her. Every time she replayed the words in her head, her heart danced. Surely her fears were unfounded. Even though she may not have said it at the moment, she knew one thing was true.

She loved Carter Stockton.

But when should she tell him? Maybe, like Grandma Kate said, she should pray about it.

Carter's deep voice carried through the open windows. Well, that answered that. No time to pray now. He was here.

With a heart ready to burst, she grabbed her fan, checked her hair in the mirror, and stepped toward her future.

❧

Robbed of his breath at the sight of Emily, Carter stood in front of the Graham cabin and let his gaze sweep over her appreciatively. Part of her hair was pulled up with a jeweled comb, which left the remaining soft tendrils trailing down her graceful neck. The green of the dress made her eyes gleam like emeralds.

Aunt Millie elbowed him in the ribs.

He jerked and swallowed hard. "Emily, you're stunning."

"Thank you. You look quite dapper yourself."

He grinned and tugged on the lapels of his dark tailcoat. With the white waistcoat restraining his chest from moving, the stiff collar and the bow tie strangling him, and the hot kid gloves making his hands sweat, he longed for his baseball uniform. Whoever designed these things had never been to Lake Manawa in late June.

"Shall we go?" He offered his arm and waited until her hand was tucked in the crook of it before he nodded to her aunts and grandmother. "Ladies, have a wonderful evening."

"You too." Aunt Millie giggled.

Aunt Ethel shot Emily a look of warning. "Try not to trip and ruin your new dress."

Grandma Kate kissed her cheek. "Make tonight special."

The walk to the Kursaal was less than twenty minutes from the Graham cottage even at their leisurely pace. The tailcoat kept him hot as a pot of soup, so Carter welcomed the hint of a breeze drifting off the lake. Hopefully it would help keep the second-floor ballroom cool tonight. If it didn't, he might have to whisk Emily off for a stroll.

As they approached the new snowy-white pavilion, he marveled at how it jutted out into the water. At nearly 180 feet in length, the Kursaal was now easily the biggest building on the lake. Only last week, workmen had completed the deck, which surrounded the building on all four sides, and yesterday he'd heard they'd put the final touches on the electric lights around the roof. Tonight for the first time, the lights would be turned on, and he couldn't wait to see Emily's face when they lit up.

"Something wrong?" Emily sounded concerned.

"No. I was thinking about the Kursaal." He flashed her a grin. "Think we'll have as much fun tonight as we did the first time we were there?"

She giggled. "I don't know, but I certainly look better."

"Different. Not better."

Strains of music floated from the ballroom into the air outside the opulent pavilion. Carter escorted Emily up the few steps leading to the Kursaal's double entry doors. He handed the doorman his tickets before they entered. They paused to take in the room, which had been only bare bones when they'd visited unchaperoned. He grinned. That night he'd held Emily's mud-dappled face and kissed her thoroughly. Tonight the mud was gone, but the desire to whisk her away to kiss her senseless remained.

He shook his head and focused on how different the Kursaal now looked. Trimmed in dark wood, the walls sported the same crisp white as the outside of the building. The floor had been polished to a gleam, and dining tables lined the walls. In the center of the first floor, a long table filled with refreshments had been arranged for this grand opening.

"Did you want to get something to drink before we go upstairs?" He eyed the beverages on a far table. "I think I see something you'd like."

"Yes, after the walk here, that would be refreshing."

Two lemon ices later, they made their way up the wide stairway. Emily hesitated at the door.

"What's wrong?"

"I should warn you I dance like I play horseshoes."

He raised an eyebrow. "I'll take my chances."

"But I can't dance with only you all night."

"Want to bet?"

Before she could protest further, he led her into the room and swept her into his arms. The woman who claimed she could trip over a chalk line danced and spun like a prima ballerina.

※

Something wonderful awakened inside her, and Emily let the music carry her across the floor. Giddy with love, she stopped thinking about the steps of the dance and started thinking only about the moment and the man who held her.

Carter spun her in a wide circle, and her dress swirled against her ankles. She giggled and he pulled her closer. Around them, other couples twirled, but she hardly noticed them. Colorful Japanese lanterns illuminated the room, yet they paled when compared to the glow in her heart. "I could do this all night."

"Good, because I intend to do just that."

When the song ended, he reluctantly released her to Ducky but claimed her only two songs later from another Owl for the next dance.

"Ladies and gentleman," the bandmaster called. "I've been told that if you'd like to see the first electrical lighting of the Kursaal, it will occur in five minutes."

Carter leaned close to her ear, and his breath made her quiver. "Ready?"

Whatever current there'd be outside, it would have nothing on the one he transmitted.

He led her down to a cleared area by the lake and stopped beneath a wide-girthed sycamore. "I heard we can see it best if we're off the decking."

The crescent-shaped moon smiled on them, and the stars winked in the sky over the rippling waters. Music and laughter blended with the chirping crickets and croaking frogs in a wild Lake Manawa symphony. Carter slipped his arms around Emily's waist, and her stomach fluttered. Leaning against his chest, she sighed. What a truly magical night.

They stood cuddled in the spell of the lake for several minutes.

"Ten, nine, eight!" the people began to shout. When they reached "one," a cheer went up, and a thousand lights outlined the roofline of the Kursaal.

The crowd oohed and ahhed, but the sight stole Emily's breath. She blinked. "It's so beautiful."

"You can see all over—almost like it's day."

Emily swatted a mosquito on her arm. "Apparently we aren't the only ones who like the lights."

"Let's get back inside."

Carter conveyed her to the deck railing and pressed a kiss to the top of her head. "I need to go check on something. Will you be okay out here alone for a few minutes?"

"Of course." She turned in his arms. "Where are you going?"

He tapped her nose. "I'll be right back."

The fears she'd laid to rest came to life like a nightmare as she watched him go back inside and speak to the man with the wide mustache from the ice cream parlor. She needed to stop this doubting. What kind of a relationship could they have if she couldn't trust him?

"Hi, Emily." Greta Wilson, dressed in a taffeta rose gown, joined her. "Elwood went in to get me a dessert. Is Carter doing that too?"

"He had something to check on." Emily sighed. She liked Greta, but her tendency to talk too much intruded on the magical feeling of the evening.

Greta placed her hand on Emily's arm. "You know, I admire you."

"Me? Why?"

"You're standing by Carter when even his brother thinks he's guilty." As usual, her words came out in a rush. "My brother says the clerks at the bank think this whole investigation Nathan Stockton is launching is ludicrous. But if Carter's guilty, Mr. Stockton says he'll have him arrested for stealing from your grandmother. Can you imagine having your own brother arrested?"

Emily grabbed hold of the railing. "Who's investigating it? Is there any evidence?"

"Only rumors. The bank manager, Mr. DeSoto, is the one doing all the checking." She raised her gloved hand to her lips. "You didn't know, did you? Why am I always telling you things I thought you knew?"

"It's all right, Greta." Emily forced her voice not to waver. "I'm sure Carter simply didn't have the chance to discuss the situation with me yet."

"Here comes Elwood, I'd better get back. Take care, Emily." She waved her fingers. "And I really do admire you."

Emily turned back toward the inky water. Her stomach roiled. She was such an idiot. Even Carter's own brother thought he was guilty. An investigation. Rumors of evidence. The contract. The money. The ledger. The lump in her throat grew with each thought, but it didn't hurt as much as the one in her heart.

She was in love with a thief.

❧

Balancing two pieces of chocolate cake, Carter zigzagged through the crowd. He made his way back across the room and out the door to the decking. He spotted Emily at the railing, handkerchief in hand, and came to a halt. His chest tightened. Was she crying? What had happened while he was gone?

He hurried to her side. "Emily? What's wrong?"

She spun toward him. "Did you ever really love me?"

"What are you talking about?" He stepped back. The two pieces of cake suddenly became a nuisance, so he set them on a deck chair. "Emily?"

Her lip trembled.

He took hold of her bare upper arms. "Emily, I asked you what you're talking about."

"My grandmother's missing money." She yanked away. "And don't pretend you don't know about it."

"I know about it." His gut twisted. He did not want to get into this here or now.

"And your brother thinks you did it. He's launching an investigation at the bank."

"I knew that too." He paused. Stupid Nathan. Why did he have to stir up all this trouble? "But what does this have to do with me loving you?"

A tear slid down her cheek.

"Wait. Do you think I'm guilty? Do you believe I've been courting you to get to her money?"

"Carter, the charade is over. Why don't you simply admit it?"

"After all this time, do you honestly believe I could steal from anyone?" Anger burned deep inside him and fanned to a consuming fire. How could she even consider these accusations? "Or that I'd hurt you or your grandmother in any way?"

Her silence and tears shouted she did.

Pain knifed through him. He loved her, and he believed she loved him.

"This is the excuse you've been looking for, isn't it?" He heard the hard edge in his voice. "You think you can push me away before I get the chance to hurt you. You'll go bury your feelings in a pile of work just like you always do. You're scared to love me, but you're too late, Emily Graham. You already do."

"I never said that."

His chest heaved. He wanted to hit something or throw something—or someone—over the railing. Scooping up one of the cake plates, he pitched it as far as he could into the water. Two faint plunks told him the cake and then the plate had landed.

Calm, Carter. Think. Breathe. Lord, help me.

"Did you pray about this?" he spat.

"It doesn't have anything to do with God."

"It has everything to do with God!" His voice rose, and he knew others were watching, but he didn't care. "Don't you get that yet? Don't you see all the social issues and busyness in the world will never fill the void in your life? I thought I could be the answer to your insecurities, but I can't. Only He can."

"This isn't about me, and it's not about God." She squared her shoulders, pain filling her eyes. "It's about you and your secrets. Take me home, Carter. I knew it could never work between us, and as hard as this is, I think we should end it now."

❧

Every step of the walk home hurt more. Had Emily made a mistake? No, this wasn't going to work. And while the pain almost crippled her, how much more would it hurt if she let this go on until the truth came out?

"The game?" she whispered.

"I'll keep my word. I always do." Carter stopped within sight of the cottage. "I'll watch till you get to the door."

"You don't have to."

"I said I'll watch."

Fresh tears sprung to her eyes at the hurt and anger in his voice. She wanted to scream it was all a mistake, but it wasn't. He couldn't have ever really loved her. Deep down she knew that. Not her. Not clumsy, plain Emily Graham.

With her feet as heavy as anchors, she trod the last part of the path and sank into one of the wicker chairs outside.

In the moonlight, she watched him turn and walk silently away into the night.

The first hot tear rolled down her cheek, and her chest squeezed. She couldn't breathe. It hurt too much. Like plate glass struck by a baseball, her heart shattered in a million tiny pieces.

33

"She said it was over between them, but she won't say why."
Kate set her teacup on the outdoor table. When she'd found
Emily sobbing on the rocker late last night, she'd barely been
able to pry that much from her. It had taken another hour to
convince her distraught granddaughter to go to bed. Only the
Lord knew how long it took for the poor girl to get to sleep.

"I don't understand. They left so happy." Millie speared
a healthy chunk of ham.

"Let's give her some time and space. Perhaps they will
reconcile."

"Or perhaps not." Ethel nibbled on her toast spread with
the thinnest layer of jelly. "You're not going to let her lie
around in her room all day, are you?"

"One day of doing nothing would be good for Emily." Kate
sighed. Her granddaughter needed to let God heal her now.

"Humph. Best cure for a broken heart is work," Ethel said.

"Or . . ." Millie's face lit up. "Another man."

"Oh, you may have something there, Sister."

"Ethel, Millie, you can't."

"Not yet, Kate. When the time is right." Millie turned to her sister. "Now, where did we put that list?"

The words on Emily's list swam before her eyes. How could she have any tears left after last night? Her chest felt heavy after all the sobbing, and her puffy eyes squinted in the glare of the morning sun. Even the yellow dress she'd put on didn't lighten the heaviness in her heart.

It was over.

Carter had used her and stolen from her grandmother.

Emily picked up her to-do list. If she kept busy, maybe the hurt would go away. At any rate, she'd not have time to dwell on it. Tugging on her netted gloves, she glanced over the fifteen things on her list and prayed they'd consume the day.

Her grandmother stopped at her doorway. "Emily, what are you doing?"

"Going out. I have work to do."

"Dear, you need to give yourself time to deal with your pain."

"No, Grandma, I have to keep busy." She pinned her hat in place and pulled down the gauzy veil. "I can't stay here all day."

Her grandmother cupped her cheek. "When you're ready to talk, I'm here."

Emily covered Grandma's wrinkled hand with her own, and fresh tears pooled in her eyes. "Thank you." She gave her grandmother's hand a final squeeze and rushed from the cabin.

With its rich Oriental rug and polished brass trimmings, the foyer of the Ogden Hotel invited the rich more than any of the other hotels in the city. The gas lights, complete with hundreds of sparkling crystals, glistened in the morning sun. Carter recalled the ballroom with the marble dance floor upstairs. Emily would love—

His chest tightened at the thought of her, and the spot beneath his eye ticked. Raw hurt and anger had battled most of the night in his mind, leaving him unable to sleep. Had she fared any better?

What had possessed him to think two people so different could make a go of it?

Determined to put that part of his life behind him, he approached the front desk and tapped the bell. Seconds later, a clerk dressed in a black jacket with shiny brass buttons asked how he could be of assistance.

"I'm Carter Stockton. Can you tell me what room Mr. Gibbs is in?"

The clerk checked his register. "He's in room 224. He said to send you right up. His room is at the top of the stairs and to the right, sir."

"Thank you."

Carter gripped the carved banister and mounted the marble-topped staircase two steps at a time. If he didn't get to the room soon, he might change his mind.

And today was a day of new beginnings.

Even from outside, the boat shop reeked of noxious glue. Emily wrinkled her nose and rapped on the door. In less than a minute, sandy-haired Tate opened it.

"Mommy, Auntie Emily's here!" he called inside. He turned

back to Emily and narrowed his eyes, then turned around and yelled again. "And she looks sick!"

"Tate, I'm not sick."

"Then why do your eyes look all red and spidery?"

Marguerite, catching the tail end of her son's words, scurried over. "Honey, why don't you go help your daddy in the shop?"

"You'll take care of Auntie Emily? Give her some castor oil?"

She ruffled his hair. "I'll see what Aunt Emily needs first, okay, sport?"

He tipped his chubby cheeks up toward Emily and held his nose. "It's not so yucky if you do this."

For the first time all day, Emily's lips curled. He waved goodbye and grabbed a toy boat from the floor before scampering away.

Marguerite stepped outside and pulled Emily to the bench near the door. "It's cooler and less smelly out here. What's wrong? Did something happen?"

Emily wrung the handkerchief in her hands. "I came to find out how you were doing publicizing the game here at the lake."

"We've been friends for years, Emily. Do you think I'm going to believe that? One look at you and I know it's not true. Is it Carter? Did you two have a falling out?"

Emily released a long, slow breath, but her voice still broke when she spoke. "Carter and I won't be courting any longer."

"Why? What happened?"

Lips trembling, Emily swiped at the tears escaping again.

Marguerite placed her hand on Emily's arm. "Let me go tell Trip I'm going for a walk with you for a few minutes, okay?"

Emily nodded. She needed to talk to someone.

Maybe Marguerite could explain how Emily had let all of this horrible mess happen.

34

Carter dropped the ledger on his brother's desk with a bang.

Nathan jolted, looked at Carter, and scowled. "What's this?"

"Kate Graham's records. They're spotless. If she was losing her mind, they would have shown that long before I took over."

"I already knew she wasn't senile." Nathan picked up his pen. "I spoke to her yesterday."

"Then you also know the problems were going on prior to my involvement in her financial matters."

"According to the two of you, yes."

Praying for a calm he didn't feel, Carter took a deep breath. "We've had our differences, Nathan, but you don't think I'm capable of stealing from an old woman, do you?"

"I'm not sure what you're capable of. How could I, since you won't work here?" Nathan stood. "That's why I launched the official investigation."

"With me as a suspect."

Nathan quirked a mirthless grin. "Well, it appears someone took the money, and as you pointed out, it's either you
or me."

⸎

Skirting her way through the crowd, Emily went over the
speech she planned to deliver on the steps of the pavilion in
half an hour. Oh, but it was hard to concentrate. Why had
she let Carter Stockton into her thoughts and her heart?

While talking to Marguerite had helped for the moment,
it did nothing for the Carter-sized wound that reopened
whenever something reminded her of him—the Midway,
the pavilion, the electric launch. Each place held a special
memory.

She inhaled deeply and hurried to meet several other suffragists. Neither Marguerite nor Lilly could come today, and
it wouldn't be the same without them.

Olivia nudged Sally Nesmit out of the way and faced Emily.
"I heard you and Carter are on the outs. If you're not up to
this, I can certainly take over."

Emily swallowed hard. "How did you hear that?"

"I have my ways. You poor dear." Fake sympathy oozed
from her. "No one would hold it against you if you decided
you couldn't speak today."

"I'll be fine, Olivia."

A few minutes later, Emily dragged herself up the steps and
slowly turned to address the crowd. Only a handful stopped
to listen at first, but more came as she went on. "Half a century ago, in Massachusetts, only properly qualified persons
could practice law. The Supreme Court of Massachusetts
decided a woman was not a person, and before Miss Leila
Robinson could even be admitted to the bar, a special act of

the legislature had to be passed declaring women as persons. But times have changed. Women are lawyers . . . and doctors and business owners."

A man jeered at her from the crowd, but Emily spotted a young woman at the foot of the steps. If only she could reach that one girl.

"In the last half century," she continued, "boys have been born who have become voters. However, women are still trying to convince men of their fundamental rights. Have our senators and representatives been elected by the people of the state? No. They've been elected by the men. Half of this state has not elected those men to represent them. If, in a republic, all are equal, how can this be justified?"

Emily caught sight of something flying toward her seconds before it splattered on the bodice of her dress and splashed wet bits on her cheek. A second red object struck her skirt and its contents burst open. Some crowd members gasped while others laughed. The stench of the rotten tomato made her stomach lurch. She wiped the dregs from her face and scanned the crowd for the culprit. She spotted the heckler Carter had once stopped and glared at him. If only Carter were here now.

Taking a deep breath, Emily focused on the young woman and drove her message home. "As God ordained from the beginning of time, men and women are to go through this world together. They complement one another—in the home and in government. Removing half the population from the decision-making process weakens us all. I urge all of you to sign the petition we have with us today asking our representatives to revisit this topic and give the women of Iowa a vote of faith."

Emily remained at the top of the staircase until the applause died away. She took a deep breath and joined her suffrage sisters at the bottom.

"Oh, Emily, are you okay?" Sally dabbed at the chunks of tomato clinging to Emily's yellow dress.

She nudged Sally's hand away. "I'm fine. I'll hurry home and change."

"And I hope wash." Olivia wrinkled her nose. "I am quite glad you did not take me up on that offer to speak in your stead."

Sally handed Emily a fresh handkerchief. "And you did such a wonderful job."

Emily noticed the young woman she'd been so focused on waiting by one of the benches. She excused herself and walked over to the girl, who had to be in high school. "Hello. Can I help you?"

"I'm sorry," the girl said.

"What are you sorry for?"

She started to speak and stopped. Blonde curls fell forward as she hung her head. "My dad threw the tomato. He got it from one of the lunch counters when he found out you were speaking today. He thinks women are weaker than men."

"I see." Emily glanced down at her red-streaked clothes. "It's not your fault. You didn't throw the tomato. Besides, there's no permanent damage—a little smelly vegetable won't hurt me. What's your name?"

"Priscilla Sawyer."

"So, Priscilla, do you think women are weaker than men?"

The young woman shrugged. "Men can lift more, but there are lots of kinds of strong."

"There certainly are." Emily smiled. "Listen, Priscilla, there's going to be a baseball game with women playing men. Have you heard about it?"

Priscilla nodded.

"Good. Be sure to come. Bring your dad too. He might see something that surprises him."

"Priscilla!" a man bellowed.

Emily whirled to see the burly man barreling toward them. He grabbed the girl's arm and yanked her to his side. "Don't be filling my girl's mind with your nonsense."

"Giving women a voice is not nonsense, Mr. Sawyer."

"Well, giving you a voice is. I'm tired of listening to your nagging already. No wonder you don't have a husband." He tugged on Priscilla's arm. "Come, girl. You're going home."

Emily watched them go, and her commitment to the cause grew tenfold. There was still so much to be done, and she had to make a difference for all the young girls like Priscilla Sawyer across the country. And without worrying about Carter Stockton, she could press forward unfettered.

The rancid smell of the rotten tomato again wafted toward her. Maybe she should forge ahead after a bath.

<hr />

By the time Emily approached the cabin, the familiar heaviness of last night had closed in around her. Tears made paths through the tomato smears on her cheeks. Never had she felt more alone.

"There you are, Emily." Aunt Millie toddled down the path toward her. "Oh my, what happened?"

"One of the men didn't like the color of my dress today."

"Oh dear." Her aunt looped her arm in Emily's. "We have to get you cleaned up."

"Why? What's going on?"

"We're trying to help you ease the torment in your soul, dear."

Emily raised her eyebrows. "And how do you intend to do that?" Stopping on the path, Emily saw exactly how her two aunts planned to do it, and he appeared to be the town's undertaker sitting in a rocking chair beside Aunt Ethel.

"Is that—"

Aunt Millie patted her hand. "No hasty judgments, dear. Dudly has an excellent job with a steady clientele, and he's dying to meet you."

A moan rose in Emily's throat. She held out her splattered skirt. "Look at me. Smell me. I can't meet anyone tonight even if I wanted to, which I do not."

"Now, dear, you can't very well turn him away. He came all the way from the city." She pulled her forward. "Besides, I don't think the bad smell will bother him one bit. In his profession, I would guess he gets used to horrible stenches."

What did Emily care if she offended Dudly Lynch? She didn't want to be courted by him or anyone else, and the sooner he learned that, the better.

With a sigh, she marched up to the paunchy middle-aged man and stuck out her hand. Dudly's handshake, cold and limp, made Emily wince. And the thick beard hanging off the man's chin did nothing to compensate for the lack of hair on his head.

"Hello, Mr. Lynch." Emily squared her shoulders. "I believe women should have the right to vote. I believe they are every bit as intelligent, talented, and able as men, and I believe they should say exactly what is on their minds. Don't you agree?"

"I . . . uh . . ."

"Good. So, here's what is on my mind." She tugged on her shirtwaist, ignoring Aunt Ethel's glare and Aunt Millie's gaping mouth. "I don't want to entertain a suitor right now.

I want to go inside and wash away my unfortunate meeting with a couple of tomatoes. Is that all right with you, sir?"

"Uh . . . yes . . . of course."

"And please forgive my aunts for dragging you out here. I would say I hope this turns into a profitable business trip for you, but given your occupation, please understand although I'd sometimes like to kill these two, I won't do so today."

35

Though stuffy and humid, Emily's bedroom remained a better option for her right now than the garden outside with her aunts. Poor Dudly Lynch. He probably left wishing for the silent company of the dearly departed.

But her aunts? No guilt there. They deserved what she'd said.

Sitting up in her bed, Emily heard footsteps in the hall. Hopefully Britta would arrive bearing something to eat, and she prayed it wouldn't contain tomatoes.

"Your aunts have not stopped talking about your little display this afternoon," Grandma Kate said from the doorway. She bore a tray with a sandwich and a tall glass of lemonade. Emily's favorite.

"I suppose you think I owe them an apology."

Grandma Kate smiled and set the tray on the nightstand. "Actually, no. I think they owe you one."

"Really?"

Her grandmother nodded and sat down on Aunt Millie's bed. "What do you think?"

"They don't understand I'm in control of my own life."

"That isn't necessarily a good thing, Emily."

"What do you mean?"

Her grandmother's lips curved in a soft smile. "How are you doing, sweetheart, truly?"

The softness in her grandmother's voice melted all of Emily's resolve. Fresh tears beaded on her lashes and escaped. "It hurts so much."

"Are you ready to tell me what happened?"

She couldn't tell her grandmother about the money yet. She'd know soon enough if Nathan's investigation proved his guilt. "I wish I could, Grandma, but I can't. At least not yet. "

"I understand." She stood up. "Emily, can I ask you something?"

"Yes."

"If your daddy was standing behind you, and he told you to fall back into his arms, would you do it?"

"Of course."

"Why?"

"Because he'd catch me. Daddy would never let me fall."

"But if he was on the other side of the room and told you to fall back, would you do it then?"

"No, he'd never be able to catch me in time."

Grandma Kate picked up Emily's Bible and wiped the dust from its cover. "God didn't move, Emily. You did." She handed Emily the volume and kissed the top of her head.

What did her grandmother mean? If she asked, Grandma Kate would probably tell her to think it through for herself.

When her grandmother reached the door, Emily blurted out, "Where does it talk about broken cisterns?"

Grandma Kate's smile widened. "Jeremiah, I believe. Read the whole book. You'll find it."

After her grandmother left, Emily set the Bible on her bed and picked up the sandwich. She'd look for the passage later.

❧

Having abandoned all hope of sleep, Emily crawled out of bed. She spotted the Bible on the nightstand and picked it up along with her wrap before padding down the hallway. She slipped into her gown and grabbed the lamp and some matches from the table. She nudged the screen door open, wincing when the hinges squeaked.

Outside, the cool night air greeted her, and she pulled the edges of the cotton gown tighter about her shoulders. She settled in one of the wicker rocking chairs and set the lamp on the table beside her.

Stars glittered in the night sky, and the silver sliver of the moon reflected off the ripples on the surface of the lake. Emily's breath caught. It was beautiful. When was the last time she simply sat and soaked up this gift?

In the stillness of the night, Carter's accusation haunted her, playing over and over in her mind. *"Don't you see all the social issues and busyness in the world will never fill the void in your life? I thought I could be the answer to your insecurities, but I can't. Only He can."*

Busyness. What did never-grow-up Carter Stockton know about busyness? If the only thing she was worried about was making herself look good to her brother, she'd have time to spend doing other things too—like read her Bible.

But God understood why she couldn't. Didn't He?

A profound emptiness, vast and lonely, swallowed her.

Carter had called it a void. Did he have a point? Was she trying to fill the empty places?

No. She had important things to attend to. Someone had to change the world, and since no one else seemed to be doing it, she was the one.

Still, it wouldn't hurt to find out what Jeremiah said about broken cisterns.

She struck the match, lifted the flue, and lit the wick. The lamp bathed the darkness with a warm glow. Opening the Bible to the book of Jeremiah, she started in the first chapter. God was calling the prophet into service. He told Jeremiah that Israel had left the devotion of their youth.

Her heart pricked. She closed her eyes and listened to the swashing of the lake's waters against the shore. In high school, she had been so devoted to the Lord and had been immersed in this very lake after a tent meeting one summer. Had she lost that devotion?

She looked back at the Bible. God told Jeremiah that Israel had forgotten all He'd done for them. Then she found the verse she was looking for. She read it aloud. "For my people have committed two evils; they have forsaken me the fountain of living waters, and hewed them out cisterns, broken cisterns, that can hold no water."

Digging cisterns was evil? How could that be? The Israelites were only taking care of themselves. They saw a need and met it.

She blinked. But God had always provided for them, and they knew it. The man-hewn cisterns soon revealed their brokenness. They'd never worked.

Emily's chest squeezed. Carter had seen her brokenness and tried to help, but he wasn't the answer.

Her thoughts whirled. Her work was important. Day after

day, she fought for women to have the right to vote, and some days the thrill of small victories left her feeling filled to the brim with pride and success. But, like the water in the broken cisterns, it seeped away and left her empty again.

What broken cisterns had she dug herself into? Her suffrage work? Her relationship with Carter? Had she put her hope in something that held no water? Did she have to give it all up? *Lord, please, no. I want others to see more than a clumsy girl when they look at me.*

And there it was. Her cistern—broken and empty—lying exposed before her.

Lord, forgive me.

❧

"Emily?"

Grandma Kate's voice crept into Emily's dream about walking the high wire. What was Grandma doing on the tightrope?

Someone laid a hand on her shoulder and shook her. Emily opened her eyes and found her grandmother's concerned face staring down at her.

"Have you been out here all night?"

Emily nodded and pressed a hand to the crick in her neck. The Bible fell from her lap.

"Broken cisterns?"

"Living water." Emily smiled, and then felt a prick. "I have a lot to give up."

Grandma Kate sat in the rocking chair beside her. "Emily, your thirsts come from God. He made you and put them there. It's not wrong to long for women to be treated fairly or to want a relationship with someone who loves you. But we get in trouble when we don't let God be the one filling us up and meeting our needs."

"Not letting Him catch us?"

"You moved away from God." Grandma Kate touched her hand. "He would still have caught you, but you made it impossible for yourself to believe He would."

"I feel so foolish."

"No, honey. Today you're who you wanted to be. God can mend our brokenness. In Christ, you know you matter."

Like a balm, the words flooded over Emily's bruised heart.

"Are you going to speak to Carter now? Tell him what you've discovered?"

Emily rubbed the ache in her neck, but it didn't ease the pain the mention of Carter caused. He'd been right about her. Had she been wrong about him?

It didn't matter. She was too late. The damage was done.

How much damage could Carter do with this one last act? He stared at his father's bank, where vice president Nathan handled all of the day-to-day affairs. The large brick building, solid and unyielding, seemed so much like his brother. His gut twisted. How would their father deal with discovering one of his sons had betrayed him?

Carter stuffed his hands in his pockets and squeezed the wad of cash. This was no time to stop. He had to do what he had to do, and everyone would know the truth soon enough. Taking a deep breath, he set his plan into action.

36

The heat of June melted into July and took with it Emily's hopes of seeing Carter again. Tear-filled nights turned into colorless mornings despite the white daisies and rainbow of zinnias blooming around her. Even at the few practices with the Owls he'd arranged especially for her, Carter was absent, although she doubted he missed the regular ones with his team. Still, he never wandered far from her thoughts or her prayers.

Prayers. In the last few days, she'd found a special time again with the Lord. Today she'd risen before her aunts or grandmother and quietly made her way to the beach. She walked along the far southwest corner of the lake where lily pads generously dotted the water's surface with broad, heart-shaped leaves and pale pink blossoms. A frog croaked and leapt from the bank, splashing into the water before her.

Emily glanced toward a castle-shaped cloud in the sky. *Lord, I'm trying something new today. I'm asking You to help put my day in order. I want to control it, but I'm giving it to You. The Bloomer Girls are coming tomorrow. I can think of a hundred things to check on, but I have no idea where to start.*

Gathering her skirt, she sat down on a thick log and leaned against the oak tree trunk behind it. She drew her knees up on the log and wrapped her arms around them. A doe and fawn froze in the clearing only yards from her. Finally, the deer sprinted away with her speckled fawn in tow. Emily smiled. She'd been at the lake over a month and had scarcely taken a moment to enjoy the wildlife around her.

Lord, I can't believe I'm going to say this, but slow me down. I've missed out on so much.

Including Carter.

❧

"This way!"

Digger Hall jumped off the side of the boardwalk and raced down the beach toward a pair of large rowboats.

Emily stopped on the pier. "Shouldn't we be practicing ball? The game's in two days."

"We rent the boats and do this before a lot of big games." Ducky held up his arms to lift her to the sand. "Carter thinks it breaks the tension. Besides, rowing is not only good exercise, it takes teamwork."

"Boys, it's nice of you to include me, but I don't know how to row."

"That's okay. Neither does Elwood." Digger laughed at his own joke.

Elwood glared at him. "You wish, Digger. We outfielders haven't lost to you infielders in the last three races, and no offense, Emily, but I don't want you on my team. Hate to ruin a good winning streak."

Several other team members pinned him with their stares.

"No offense taken." Emily scanned their faces and smiled. Only six of the regulars were present this morning. "Elwood's right. I'd only slow the team down. Why don't I just watch all of you from here?"

"No! You're part of the team," Ducky insisted.

Digger raised his eyebrows. "So where's she going to ride?"

"With me." Carter's voice boomed from the back of the group. She hadn't even noticed him approaching. The team divided to let him through. "She's playing shortstop, so she'll ride with the infielders. Digger, you can ride with the out-fielders."

Emily glanced at the regular shortstop and he shrugged. Carter brushed past her and climbed into the boat. The first baseman took his seat, leaving the one in front of Carter open. The rowboat tilted and wobbled as they climbed in, even though one end still remained on the shore.

"Get in." Carter's voice held no warmth.

Ducky stepped forward and offered his hand. "You heard the man, Emily."

"I really—"

"Get. In."

Emily glanced at Carter and blinked. As usual, coffee-colored curls escaped from beneath his cap and bounced on his forehead in the breeze. Seeing him made all the wounds bleed fresh.

Did she see a flicker of something in his eyes? Could he possibly still care? She shouldn't want him to—not after what he'd done to her grandmother—but she did. *Lord, help me be strong.*

"Emily?" Ducky waited until she placed her hand in his and then helped her step into the boat.

"Am I just going to ride?"

"No." Carter's voice, hard and terse, made her shiver. "You're part of this team—at least for two more days. You're going to work like the rest of us."

And then I'll be done with you for good. She heard his unspoken words as plainly as if he'd said them.

Ducky glanced at Carter and quirked an eyebrow before gathering the two oars from the beach. He handed them to Emily one at a time. "Put the pegs in those oar locks. There you go. Good work. Now hold on to them until we get going and don't let them fall in the water."

He went around to the front of the rowboat and shoved the stern off the sand. As soon as the rowboat was clear, he hopped in, shaking the boat in the process.

Emily gripped the sides and glanced at the other rowboat, already filled with the outfielders, waiting offshore. The infielders in her boat began to work together in practiced ease. Once the two boats were lined up, the oarsmen stopped.

"To Turtle Island and back." Carter readied his oars. "On your mark. Get set. Go!"

Unsure of how or where to start, Emily merely grasped an oar in each hand and watched them work. Oars slapped the water in a steady rhythm.

"Don't just sit there," Carter growled. "Start rowing."

"But—"

"Move your hands like this. Forward. Up. Pull. Down." He chanted from behind her. "Forward. Up. Pull. Down."

It took several tries to figure out Carter's pattern. When she moved the handles of the oars forward, the oars moved back. Then, by raising them up, the blades dipped into the water. Pulling required straightening her legs to keep her from sliding on her seat. When she pushed her hands down, the blades of the oar lifted out of the water, and the process repeated.

But despite Carter's continued chanting, she could not master the same rhythm as her teammates. Her oval rowing motion always seemed half a stroke behind. Finally, he switched to saying "pull" at the right times instead of all four movements. With time, she caught on and Carter stopped his reminders. Still, she forced her mind to concentrate while the others joked among themselves.

She glanced at the other boat only yards ahead. Her arms ached, but she pulled harder, determined to do as much as any man.

"We'll take 'em on the way back," Ducky announced after the other boat reached the buoy off Turtle Island first.

"Don't use your left oar!" Carter shouted.

Too late Emily realized the others had stopped using their left oar. She jerked and her oar popped from its lock. Caught by surprise, she let go of it. The oar toppled into the water with a splash, and she lunged for it.

Carter caught her belt. "Are you trying to dump us all?"

"No, but—"

The others in the boat had stopped rowing when they heard the commotion, and Carter used his oar to drag hers close. He bent over the side and retrieved it before passing it to her.

"Thanks, Emily." Sarcasm dripped from the third baseman's comment.

Emily reinserted the peg of her wet oar into the bracket. "I'm sorry."

"Stow it, Mac. We win as a team and we lose as a team." Carter dipped his oars back in the water. "Loyalty. That's what matters. Right, Emily?"

Emily's chest constricted, and tears burned in her eyes.

Refusing to cry, she dug the oars into the water in tandem with the rest of the crew, his words echoing with each stroke.

Anger and hurt churned inside her like the water displaced by the oars. Loyalty. He was the one who'd betrayed her trust. He was the one stealing from her grandmother. Did he expect that in the short time they'd known each other, she'd put him before her own family?

As Carter had said, she was an Owl for two more days, and right now it couldn't end soon enough.

❧

Leveling the Winchester at the shooting gallery targets, Carter eased the trigger back.

Ping! The cast-iron rabbit toppled backward, and Carter's lips curled. He cracked open the rifle and stuffed another .22 shell inside. He lifted the Winchester to his shoulder and sighted another target.

Ducky fired his first shot and missed. "So was that little display today to punish Emily or to let everyone know why you two are on the outs?"

The report of gunfire filled the building, but no metallic pings followed. Carter glared at his friend. "Someone's got to put her in her place and wake her up. She's only doing this suffrage stuff to be someone. It's all about her pride."

Ducky lifted his shotgun to his shoulder. "Anyone ever told you you're a hypocrite?"

"What did you say?"

"You heard me."

"You do remember I'm holding a gun, right?"

A chuckle resonated from Ducky's chest. "Shoot me if you want, but hear me out first." He pulled the trigger, hit the target, and set the little piano tune playing. "You say Emily's doing all the work to get the recognition, right? That it's all so she can be someone?"

Carter nodded. "She doesn't think she measures up."

"But you've spent your whole life trying to prove yourself, just like her. Think about it. You wouldn't marry her unless you could have it your way, when you were someone."

"I didn't ask her to marry me."

"Fine, but it doesn't take a genius to guess you would now since you have that baseball offer from Gibbs." Ducky reloaded his rifle.

Carter took aim on the moving cast-iron squirrel. His gut twisted in frustrated, angry knots. "Well, I couldn't very well marry someone on what I make as an Owl."

"And you didn't love her enough to work in the bank." Ducky fired at the squirrel first. It toppled backward.

"This isn't about me," Carter growled.

"Don't waste your breath. The truth is you didn't put your relationship with her in God's hands any more than she did."

Carter clenched the rifle in his grasp, his chest heaving. He'd prayed about things with Emily. He'd even begged God to open her eyes. But had he seized back control, wanting to look good to her and to prove himself to Nathan?

He laid the gun down on the counter. "I think I'm going to head back. I need some time to think before the game."

"And pray?" Ducky raised his eyebrows.

Even though suggesting someone pray should not cause violent outbursts, it took everything in Carter not to punch his best friend. Could Ducky jab the knife in any deeper?

"Remember, someone like Emily won't be around forever."

Apparently, he could.

37

Every member of the Council Bluffs Equal Suffrage Club stood outside the Rock Island Depot, along with most of the Manawa Owls. Carter had considered skipping the whole brouhaha, but his team expected him to be there, and the Chicago Stars would arrive any minute. He'd better be able to handle a few minutes with Emily. Tomorrow he'd have to handle a whole game.

He caught sight of her in the front of the crowd, her hand pressed to her stomach. He imagined the butterflies inside were in overtime. This whole thing meant the world to her. He inched closer.

"You look good in that uniform." Ducky gave Emily a reassuring smile.

She ran her hands along the bare flesh on her forearms that the shirt's cut revealed. Yesterday the boys had decided to wear their striped uniforms for the welcome, but Carter was pleasantly surprised she'd worn hers as well.

"Maybe I should have worn a dress. It's not like I'm a real baseball player."

Elwood chuckled. "But they don't know that yet."

Carter whacked Elwood in the stomach but didn't say anything. When Emily smiled her thanks, he looked away. The last thing he wanted to do was give her any wrong ideas.

The rumble of the approaching train shook the platform. The brakes shrieked and the train rolled to a stop with a steamy hiss.

"Would you look at that?" The awe in Emily's voice echoed his sentiments exactly.

The fancy Pullman Palace car housing the Chicago Stars rested before the Owl/suffrage club gathering. Rumor had it the special railcar cost ten thousand dollars.

A door swung open on the Pullman car, and the first of the Chicago Stars stepped out. Ducky hurried to the bottom of the steps and offered his hand. The female player, with her straw-colored locks hanging loosely on her shoulders, smiled and took the help he offered. She descended the steps with a bounce at the end.

In minutes, the first player was soon joined by seven other girls, all clad in loose-fitting red blouses, matching crimson bloomers, and black stockings. Two men in similar uniforms, clearly players, also joined them.

Finally, a slightly older man wearing a flashy summer suit stepped forward, removed his bowler, and swept it toward the ladies. "May I present to you the Chicago Stars—champion baseball club of the world!"

Emily's suffrage ladies applauded. Ducky nudged Emily forward.

Just as Emily took a step, Olivia DeSoto jutted out her foot. Emily stumbled. The younger male player on the Stars caught her and held her a bit too long for Carter's liking.

Emily regained her footing and took a step back. "I'm so sorry."

"It's okay." He chuckled and touched the bill of his baseball cap. "The girls are always falling for me. You okay?"

"I'm fine." Emily glanced at Carter.

Like a coward, he ducked his gaze again.

Her cheeks flamed as cherry as the Bloomer Girls' uniforms. Finally, she cleared her throat. "On behalf of the Council Bluffs Equal Suffrage Club, welcome to Council Bluffs. We're so happy you're here."

"It's our pleasure, miss." The younger male player cast a daring look at Carter.

Carter chuckled. These guys were good. If they could rile the Owls from the start, they'd have an advantage.

The older man nudged the younger out of the way and removed his cap. "I'm J. B. Olson, manager of the Stars. Thank you for inviting us to your fine city."

She nodded. "Thank you all for coming. We've prepared a picnic luncheon at Lake Manawa's Cottage Grove, and we hoped to have a parade through the city and around the resort in honor of tomorrow's game. Of course, you are all welcome to swim at the lake this afternoon as well. Mr. Olson, does that meet with your approval?"

"Perfectly." He plopped his cap back on his head. "Except for the swimming. We don't want to tire our team out before the game, or maybe that was what you had planned all along?"

"No . . . I—"

Mr. Olson laughed. "I'm only joshing you. The ladies can swim all they want. Lead the way, Miss Graham."

Outside the depot, buggies polished for the guests lined the street. Mrs. O'Neil, who was in charge of the parade, had draped garlands of flowers around each team of horses while they waited for the train's arrival. Emily explained to Mr. Olson that the girls could choose any of the available carriages in which to ride.

"What about me?" the male player asked from beside Emily. "Is your buggy full?"

She smiled at him. "No, Mr.—"

"Russell, ma'am. Hank Russell."

"I'm afraid I don't have a carriage."

Carter felt the pinch of jealousy but forced a smile. "Mr. Russell, you can ride with me up front, and Emily can ride in the back with—"

"Me." A dark-haired player held out her hand. "If it's okay with you. I'm Maud Nelson, pitcher and third bagger, and I can't wait to hear how this game is going to help the suffrage cause."

A broad smile curled Carter's lips. "In that case, it looks like we're all set."

"Carter, are you certain you want me to ride with you? I could ride somewhere else," Emily whispered as they walked toward his rig.

"Let's just get through these two days, Emily."

As planned, Carter led the procession down Broadway in the fancy buggy he'd borrowed from his father. Store patrons stopped and waved as they passed. Children hoisted on their daddies' shoulders waved at the visitors. But it was the girls dressed in their fancy aprons he noticed most. Their faces lit up when the Bloomer Girls' parade approached. How many of those girls yearned to compete like their brothers? Nothing had ever been off-limits to him as a man.

How many of the little girls would actually attend the game? Even if they didn't, Emily's plan was already a success.

She'd opened up the world of baseball to them. Council Bluffs would never be the same.

"Did Amelia Bloomer really live here?" Maud asked.

"Yes. We could show you where she lived if you like." Emily tapped Carter's shoulder. "Could you make a little detour to the Bloomer house?"

Carter nodded and led the entourage to 4th Street. He pulled the carriage to the side in front of the two-story home. "There it is. Dexter and Amelia Bloomer lived here. They're both deceased now."

"The Bloomer Girls at the Bloomers'." Maud rubbed her hands on her pantaloons. "Did you ever meet her?"

Emily nodded. "As a girl. She and my grandmother were good friends."

"I bet you're as thankful as I am not to have to wear a skirt to play baseball."

"The bloomers do make it easier to move." Emily smiled at Carter. "But they take some getting used to."

Carter chuckled and clicked his tongue. The horses clopped down the brick-paved road.

"I believe Amelia Bloomer would have loved to see all of you," Emily said. "Are you aware dress reform wasn't her only fight? She petitioned the Senate and the House saying that as the owner of several thousand dollars' worth of property, she was being taxed without representation. In her letter, she petitioned Congress for the removal of the burden of taxation—or for the removal of her political disabilities."

Hank Russell glanced over his shoulder. "She had disabilities?"

Maud rolled her eyes. "She meant, either don't tax her or let her vote."

"I bet she was a handful," Hank said. "I feel sorry for her husband."

"Actually, it was her husband who deserved much of the credit for her work in advocating women's rights," Emily said. "He was a very forward-thinking man. He believed in her, encouraged her publishing, and admired her mind. Not all men would do that."

"Only the special ones." Maud looked from Emily to Carter, and Emily stiffened.

Hank adjusted his starred ball cap. "Yeah, I don't know about you, Carter, but I've spent enough time around talented ladies to learn two things. Don't argue with them and don't get in their way. They'll do anything to get what they want."

Carter sighed. "Have to agree with you there, Hank. Have to agree with you there."

～⚮～

While taking the streetcar would have made the jaunt to Lake Manawa much faster, the steady trot of the horses' hooves in the parade of carriages drew attention wherever they went. Emily glanced at the noonday sun overhead. The slight breeze and cooler temperatures promised a perfect picnic.

Carter turned off the main road on Shady Lane. Oak trees canopied the street, and when they drew closer, the blue lake provided a backdrop for the Grand Pavilion, which marked the park's entrance.

"This is lovely." Maud glanced around at the buildings and Midway. "I never would have imagined something like this here."

"You mean in Council Bluffs as opposed to Chicago."

"Well." Maud laughed. "Actually, yes. No offense?"

Emily smiled. "None taken. I bet you see things all over. Where have you been?"

"This year?" Maud's eyebrows drew together. "Well, we're making our way from Kentucky to Oregon. We played ten games in ten days in Kentucky, several in Missouri, and now we're here."

"It must be hard to travel so much."

"It's an adventure and I'm doing what I love."

"Do you feel the same way, Hank?" Carter asked.

"Traveling with eight women?" He chuckled. "'Adventure' hardly covers it."

As planned, Carter led the parade along the service road circling the lake. Crowds of spectators covered the paths, and clearly used to such displays, the Bloomer Girls made a big show of waving to them and inviting them to the Independence Day game.

Carter slowed the horses as they neared the open area dotted with towering cottonwoods, sturdy oaks, and spreading maples. "We call this picnic area Cottage Grove. It's a popular place for businesses and clubs to hold their festivities, and it has a good view of the lake."

"But is there food?" Hank rubbed his stomach for effect.

Carter's lips curled. "With all the food these ladies have planned, I don't think you'll need to eat again for a week."

After Carter pulled the horses to a stop, he hopped down to secure them. Hank held up his hands to lift Emily from the carriage. Emily hesitated. Would Carter offer? And if he did, would she want him to help her down?

Hank's bright blue eyes sparkled mischievously. "I'm on the other team, but I'm not the enemy."

"I know that." Emily smiled and placed her hands on his

shoulders. When his hands gripped her waist, her stomach cinched. How odd it felt to have another man touch her.

Hank lowered her to the ground, then turned to help Maud down.

"Look out, food, here I come." Hank tugged on the bill of his ball cap.

Emily laughed and began walking toward the picnic area where tables had been set up and laden with goodies. "Carter's right. The ladies have been planning this for weeks."

"If you tell me there's fried chicken, I'll marry you right here on the spot."

"You don't want to marry me." Emily giggled. "I can't even cook."

"But I bet you can do a lot of other things." He quirked a knowing grin, revealing a handsome smile.

Heat infused Emily's cheeks. Why was Hank flirting with her, of all people? And why was she noticing his roguish grin in return? She glanced over her shoulder to gauge Carter's reaction to the baseball player's antics. The last thing she needed today was a fight between the two men.

Her heart grabbed.

Carter was already back in the carriage, vanishing without so much as a goodbye.

"Leave the poor girl alone." Maud hit Hank's arm. "You're making her blush."

"Emily, over here!" Marguerite waved to her. Marguerite's husband Trip and son Tate sat beside her on a large quilt spread in the grass.

Taking a deep breath, Emily plastered on a happy face. She refused to let Carter's disappearance put a damper on the day's activities. She'd worked too hard for this day, and she intended to enjoy every minute of it, with or without thieving Carter Stockton.

She turned to Hank and Maud. "Would you two care to join us?"

Hank grinned. "I don't know about Maud, but I'd love to."

38

Carter steamed away like a locomotive from the Bloomer Girls' picnic scene. Tomorrow Hank Russell would pay for all his flirting. He started to mentally tick off the lightning-fast pitches he planned to hurl in Hank's direction. Who knew? Maybe one would "accidentally" go wild.

Now again in town, he pulled the rig to a stop and tied the horses to the hitching post. Thoughts of Emily sent a confusing mix of feelings through him. His fury had ebbed, but the longing hadn't budged. And the twinge of jealousy Hank evicted surprised him. He hated leaving her today in the company of a man, but this appointment wouldn't wait.

Besides, he had to put her out of his mind. In truth, he had no say over who spoke to Emily or even who flirted shame-lessly with her. They'd gone their separate ways, and he had plenty of reasons for keeping his distance. Her lack of trust in God topped the list, with her lack of trust in him following right below. And no matter how much she made his heart jump, those two biggies would keep them apart forever.

Carter opened the door to the café, and the bell rang above the door. The young woman behind the counter smiled at him. He nodded back and found his lunch companion at a table in the back. Dressed in an impeccable dark suit, Jim Wilson fidgeted in his chair.

"Have you been here long?" Carter removed his hat and set it on the table. "I'm sorry if I'm late."

"You were helping with those lady baseball players, right?" Jim's hands shook as he spread his napkin on his lap.

"What's wrong?"

"Your brother isn't exactly happy with you right now. If he sees me eating lunch with you, it could cost me my position at the bank."

"Don't worry. He never eats here. Says their fried chicken still clucks."

Carter paused when the server came to their table and looked at Jim. "What'll it be?"

Jim took the special of the day, roast beef and gravy, while Carter ordered ham steak and mashed potatoes.

After the server left, Carter leaned forward. "What did you find out?"

"I did what you told me to. Every fifteen minutes I checked the ledger where we record all our transactions to see if the deposit you made had been altered in any way."

"And?"

"Before I came over here, I checked it again. The deposit had been changed from 350 dollars to 50. Someone had erased the three. Since there were only two people who'd gone near that book and one of them was me, I'm pretty sure I know who's taking the money from Kate Graham's account."

"Who?"

"Carter, you're not going to believe this."

He took a deep breath. "Try me."

❦

"You went to town in that!"

If Aunt Ethel hadn't been sitting down, Emily was certain she would have fainted. Beside her, Hank's chest rumbled against her arm. Traitor.

"You might as well parade around in your drawers and corset."

Emily's neck heated and her cheeks burned like coals. Had her aunt really mentioned a corset in Hank's presence?

He coughed.

Emily pinned him with a stare. If he laughed now, she'd punch him. The picnic with the Chicago Stars had been so enjoyable. Why did Aunt Ethel have to be such a dishrag about it?

The screen door banged open, and Aunt Millie toddled toward them. "Why, Emily, don't you look sporty. And just who is this, dear?"

"Mr. Hank Russell. Mr. Russell, meet my aunt Ethel and my aunt Millie." Emily caught the twinkle in Aunt Millie's eye. "Mr. Russell walked me home after the picnic so I could get my bathing costume."

Aunt Millie lowered her ample body into one of the wicker rockers. "I take it those Bloomerettes made it to Council Bluffs, then?"

"Bloomer Girls, Aunt Millie, and yes, they arrived in a fancy Pullman Palace car made especially for them."

"Oh my, that must be something to see." Aunt Millie picked up a crochet hook and a ball of yarn. "What was it like inside?"

"I didn't see the inside," Emily said.

Hank grinned. "If you'd like to, I can give you a personal tour."

"Excuse me." Aunt Ethel cleared her throat. "We were discussing Emily's selection of inappropriate apparel."

Confusion muddled Aunt Millie's countenance. "But I thought Emily was talking about the Palace car. You were, weren't you, dear? My mind isn't slipping. You know, Ethel tries to tell me it is, but I don't believe her."

Hank's chest rumbled again. Emily glanced at him. He was sucking his cheeks together too. If he didn't let it out soon, he might burst. Emily patted Aunt Millie's plump arm. "Your mind is perfectly sound."

The screen door creaked open, and salvation stepped out. Grandma Kate crossed the yard and sat down at the dining table. "Hello, Emily."

Emily quickly introduced Hank and explained how he'd insisted on walking her home.

"I take it all is in order for tomorrow's big game." She turned to Hank. "Are you ready to play Lake Manawa's talented nine?"

"Yes, ma'am, I believe we are. We haven't lost the last ten games."

"Didn't you notice her *clothes*?" Aunt Ethel's voice rose, and she pointed to the bloomers covering Emily's legs. "She wore them all around the lake and all over the city."

Grandma Kate beamed. "What an excellent way to promote the game, Emily. Marvelous use of advertising."

"And those Bloomerettes came in a Palace car," Aunt Millie said. "But Ethel interrupted, so I haven't yet heard what it was like inside."

Emily smiled. "We didn't see inside it, but I could tell Carter wanted to."

"Carter." Aunt Ethel stood and glanced at Hank as if she only now noticed his presence. "What did Mr. Stockton think of you gallivanting about in that?"

"Aunt Ethel, please."

"Didn't he give you the uniform, dear?" Aunt Millie asked.

Emily bit her lip. "The Owls did. I'm part of the team."

Hank smiled at Emily. "Ma'am, does it help to know that all of the Bloomer Girls are wearing similar uniforms?"

"Humph." Aunt Ethel crossed her arms. "I for one won't be attending tomorrow's game. It's nothing more than a burlesque show on a ball field."

Emily gasped and Aunt Millie gaped.

"Come sit down, Ethel." Grandma Kate placed her weathered hand on the chair next to her. "No need for theatrics."

"Theatrics? You've let Emily go so far, your son isn't even going to recognize his daughter when he returns from England. She carouses without a chaperone on the arm of a man he'd not approve of, she preaches women's suffrage at every turn, and now she's running around all creation in bloomers. What would he think of that?"

No one breathed. No one moved.

Finally, Grandma Kate smiled. "I think he'd be very proud of the young woman Emily has blossomed into—a woman who can think for herself." She stood and pulled Emily into a warm embrace.

Tears stung Emily's eyes at Grandma Kate's tender words and the reminder of her parents' absence. A lonely ache tugged at her heart. "Thank you."

Her grandmother cupped her cheek. "As for the game, I want a front-row seat. Ethel and Millie, you'll have to decide for yourselves on attending."

After Grandma Kate returned to her seat, Emily looked

from Aunt Ethel, whose lips were drawn in a thin line, to Aunt Millie. Caught between her two sisters, the plump aunt seemed reticent to answer. If only Aunt Millie had half the ability to speak her mind that Aunt Ethel did.

"I'm going." Her words came out soft as a whisper and then grew bolder. "I wouldn't miss something this important to Emily."

"So you're going to indulge Emily's foolishness as well? When all of this explodes, I hope you remember I told you so." Aunt Ethel tipped her nose in the air and marched back into the house, slamming the screen door in her wake.

Hank shifted nervously.

"Mr. Russell, I apologize for my sister's behavior." Grandma Kate laid her hand on Emily's arm. "Are you all right?"

"She'll come around, right, Grandma?"

Grandma Kate shrugged. "Either way, you have to do what God calls you to do."

❧

Waiting in front of the bank was not how Carter wanted to spend his afternoon. Finally, the St. Peter's bell chimed four o'clock, and Nathan emerged with William DeSoto. After exchanging goodbyes, the two men separated at the foot of the stairs and went in opposite directions. Carter followed the man he needed to speak to.

Quickening his steps, he matched the pace of William DeSoto. "Fine day, isn't it?"

"Why, yes, Mr. Stockton, it is, but your brother went the other direction."

"I know, but it's you with whom I'd like to speak."

"Me?" DeSoto stopped in front of a hat shop. Propped on

stands of various heights, hats of the newest styles in different shapes, colors, and sizes filled the window.

Carter turned to DeSoto. "You're one of the bank's managers, correct?"

"I am. Under your brother, of course, but you're already aware of that." DeSoto drew his hand down the length of his beard. "Oh, you're finally considering taking the position Nathan offered."

"As a manager, what exactly does your job entail?"

"I have a great many jobs such as opening new accounts, overseeing the records of deposits and withdrawals, and preparing statements for our clients."

"And it's that middle one I want to talk to you about. Overseeing the records of deposits and withdrawals." Carter glanced inside the window. The milliner, who seemed to have taken an interest in the two of them, had turned away. With a flick of his wrist, Carter indicated they should continue on.

"It's not that difficult. You'd get the hang of it quickly, I'm sure."

"I'm not interested in the position, but I am interested in how deposits and withdrawals are handled."

"Mr. Stockton, you're a suspect in Kate Graham's missing funds. I shouldn't be talking to you about this. I'm supposed to be investigating you. Is that what this is all about?"

"In a manner of speaking." He glanced in the window of the Five and Dime as they passed. "I made a deposit today into Kate Graham's account, and by noon the ledger had been changed. Ironically, you were the only one who had access to it."

"No, I wasn't. Jim Wilson was there."

"Except he was serving as my investigator." They reached an alley between two large buildings, and Carter yanked

DeSoto into the gap. He grabbed the man's lapels and tossed him against the brick wall. Before the banker could fight back, he pressed his forearm hard against the man's neck.

"Here's what's going to happen," Carter hissed. "Since tomorrow is the fourth, I'll give you until the fifth to get all of Mrs. Graham's money back."

DeSoto fought to break free. "You're out of your mind. Why would I do that?"

Carter shoved him back into place against the brick. "Because if you don't, I'll go to the police with what I know."

"And why would they believe you?"

"Do you want to take a chance they wouldn't?"

DeSoto's face reddened. "I'm warning you, you don't want to do this."

"Why?"

The banker didn't answer, and Carter leaned even harder against DeSoto's throat. Eyes bulging, DeSoto dug his hands into Carter's arm. Finally, Carter let up. "I said why?"

DeSoto coughed and his words came out hoarse. "I'm not admitting anything, but maybe someone's involved you don't want to hurt."

Carter's stomach wadded into a ball. "I don't want or need to know who that person is." He released his hold and adjusted DeSoto's lapels. "You and your partner get the money back by noon on the fifth, and we can make this whole ugly problem go away."

⁂

Haunting her like ghosts in the shadows of the night, Grandma Kate's words about God's calling kept playing over and over in Emily's mind. She punched her feather pillow and flopped onto her back.

Every time she turned around lately, it seemed someone was reminding her about God. God's calling. God's will. God's plans. *But Lord, what about my plans? What about the things I want? Aren't those important? And how am I supposed to discover Your plans for me?*

Aunt Millie's snores trumpeted in the tiny room, and for a brief moment Emily considered tossing her down pillow at her aging aunt. Instead, she hugged it against her chest. Maybe God did want her to continue her suffrage work. God had blessed her efforts so far. The Chicago Stars were here, the game was tomorrow, and if it worked as she hoped it would, it would open the minds of many citizens—at least here in Council Bluffs, Iowa.

Too bad the only difference she could make was in this little corner of the world. Suffrage was a national issue. How long would it be before a woman could vote for president of the United States?

The stifling air made sleep even more difficult to find. She threw off the sheet covering her. Was Carter sleeping any better?

Emily rolled toward the wall and attempted to count sheep. As she began to doze off, the sheep turned into baseballs, flying at her so quickly she had no hope of hitting them. Her queasy stomach knotted tighter than a tatted doily. Then she noticed the smirk on the hurler's face. Olivia.

It figured.

Emily's eyes popped open. What if this was all a horrible mistake? What was she doing playing baseball? Carter's reassurances did little to soothe her now. In a few hours, ready or not, she'd step onto the baseball diamond in front of a thousand people—and one man who could barely stand to be around her.

At last Emily decided to go outside and pray. That had to do more good than listening to Aunt Millie shake the room with her snores.

Not bothering with slippers, Emily padded into the parlor and slipped out the front door. The moon smiled down on her, and she easily made her way to the wicker rocking chairs.

"Hello, sweetheart."

"Grandma! You startled me." Emily pressed a hand to her chest, her heart beating wildly beneath it.

"Couldn't sleep? Nerves or heat?"

"Both. It's so hot I think the butterflies in my stomach are cooking."

Grandma Kate laughed. "Is it the game making you nervous, or the players?"

"What do you mean?"

"I mean you and Carter."

Emily dug her toes into the dewy grass. "Grandma—"

"You said you'd tell me what happened, and you've yet to do so. Now is as good a time as any."

The butterflies did a simultaneous nosedive. The money. Emily didn't want to have to tell her grandmother about that, but she deserved to know. *Lord, help me explain this.*

Emily took a solidifying breath. "Grandma, you aren't aware of this, but funds are missing from your bank account."

"Sweetheart, please tell me you don't suspect Carter?"

"I discovered it one night while I was awake and took a look at your ledger. I confronted Carter and—"

"About what?" Her grandmother placed her hand on Emily's. "Is that why you two have stopped courting? You think he's stealing from me?"

"I'm so sorry, Grandma. He was simply using me to get access to your money."

"Poppycock."

"Excuse me?"

"Emily, I do wish you would have spoken to me before you acted so rashly." Grandma Kate sighed. "The problem with the missing funds had been going on for a month before I elicited his help. I wanted an outside opinion on the matter. Carter has been helping me discover why or where they've gone missing."

Emily's breath whooshed from her lungs, and sweat beaded on her upper lip. When her breath returned, it came in ragged gasps as tears flooded her eyes.

"Let me guess. You drew the conclusion that the only reason he was courting you was to get to my money, and he got angry because you didn't trust him."

Hot tears of frustration trailed down Emily's cheeks and onto her cotton gown. Never had she been so angry with herself. Why had she jumped to conclusions? Why hadn't she trusted Carter? Why hadn't she prayed about it?

"Oh, Grandma. What have I done?"

Her grandmother took hold of her hand and leaned back in the rocking chair. "Nothing God can't undo."

Lord, I know I don't deserve Your help, but please, please fix the mess I've made.

39

Emily awakened to the pop of firecrackers breaking the quiet of the morning. She rolled over and moaned. The Fourth of July and boys—an obnoxious combination.

When she finally convinced her weary body to rise from the bed, she discovered that with morning came an unexpected clarity. She donned her uniform for the afternoon's game and pulled her hair into a bun, whistling all the while. Adjusting the baseball cap on her head, she offered a quick prayer of thanks to God for providing her with direction.

The screen door slammed behind her as she exited the cabin. Aunt Ethel looked up from her plate and scowled.

"Breakfast?" Grandma Kate asked.

She snagged a muffin from the table. "Where is Aunt Millie?"

"Taking muffins to the Hamlins. Mrs. Hamlin's rheumatism has been acting up. Where are you going?"

Emily swallowed the cinnamon-laced bite of her raisin muffin. "I'm heading to town to see Martin before the game and to convince him to come have a picnic with us this evening. I think he was keeping the implement company open until noon."

"That's an excellent idea." Grandma Kate poured Emily a glass of milk and passed it to her. "You've slept half the morning away already, so you'd better hurry or you'll be late to your own game. Perhaps you can convince Carter to join us for the picnic as well."

Emily smiled. "We'll see. I haven't gotten the go-ahead from God on that yet." After downing the milk, Emily kissed her grandmother's cheek. "I'll see you at the game."

While the streetcars arriving at the lake for the day were packed upon their arrival, Emily discovered she was the only person aboard as the trolley made its return journey to the city. She disembarked on Main Street and trekked to the large, brick Graham Implements building. A train whistled, followed by the familiar *chug-chug-chug* of a locomotive trying to pick up speed. She spotted it nosing its way from behind the Graham building, probably after making a delivery.

Emily wrapped her hand around the brass knob on the door and turned it. Good. It was open. Inside, she found the building mostly deserted. She smiled. Martin had probably given the majority of the employees a holiday, but of course he'd remained.

The building was four stories high, and Martin's office was at the top. Out of breath by the time she reached the top floor, she paused and waved her hand in front of her face. Being up here in the summer was crazy. Why didn't Martin take one of the offices downstairs?

Once she caught her breath, Emily traipsed down the hallway, preparing her speech for why he should come celebrate with them after the game. And perhaps, if she got the courage, she might speak to him about Carter too. Getting a man's perspective certainly couldn't hurt.

Loud voices echoed from the end of the hall. One of them belonged to Martin. She stopped. Maybe now was not the time.

"You take care of it!" Martin boomed.

"I'm telling you, Carter Stockton wants the money back."

Carter? She pressed herself against the wall and eased closer. She didn't recognize the other voice. Wait a minute. Could it be . . . ? If she could only get close enough, she might be able to see if her guess was correct.

"And how did he find out?"

"Apparently he made a deposit and had one of the clerks watching the books."

"Couldn't you blame it on someone else?" Martin growled.

"I messed up, okay? I was the only one there besides Jim Wilson."

The sound of Martin's squeaky desk chair signaled he'd moved. "But you said you didn't tell him about my part in this?"

"Yeah, but I guarantee I will if you leave me hanging."

Emily's pulse raced. What did Martin have a part in that involved Carter?

"William, take it easy."

That confirmed it. The second voice belonged to William DeSoto, one of the managers of the bank.

"We've got until tomorrow to hand over the money."

Martin coughed. "I don't have it and you know it."

"Well, I'm not giving him my share."

Silence in Martin's office emboldened her to move closer.

She jumped when one of the men struck the desk. Then Martin spoke. "I never should have let you talk me into stealing from her."

Emily gasped and her mind whirled. Martin was taking the money? But why?

"Too late for regrets. You're involved now, but I've got an idea," Mr. DeSoto said. "There's another way to handle this. Since Stockton's the only one who knows, if we take care of him, we take care of the problem."

"What? You are insane!" Martin's shouts made the walls shake. "It was bad enough to take my grandmother's money. We're not taking this any further."

Further? Knees weak, Emily clutched at the chair rail along the wall.

Inside the office, a chair squeaked. Then someone lifted a window sash.

"Give Stockton what you have." Martin's voice sounded farther away. Perhaps he was near the window now. Emily inched closer to hear. "Then tell him you need more time. That will give me the chance to confess everything to my grandmother like I should have done long ago."

There was a pause.

"What are you doing with that?" Martin's pitch rose higher and fear laced his voice.

Emily froze.

"Does your office have a key?" Mr. DeSoto asked.

"Yes, it's in my desk drawer." There was another pause, and Martin's voice took on the same tone he used as an employer. "William, don't be a fool. Put the gun away."

Gun? Emily's blood turned to ice. She heard what sounded like a drawer opening.

"Is this it? Good." Mr. DeSoto's footfalls moved closer to the doorway.

Needing to hide, Emily slipped into the empty office beside her brother's. To find her way, she slid her hand along the wall and brushed it against a cobweb. She cringed and yanked her hand away, bumping into a cast-iron umbrella stand. It rattled against the wall. Grabbing the stand, she righted it.

"What was that?" The walls distorted Mr. DeSoto's words.

"Not sure. No one's here except us," Martin said. "Let's talk about this, William. Listen to me, we've got to turn ourselves in."

"I'll take care of Stockton. And don't worry about it. You'll be locked in here, and our troubles will be over by the end of the day."

"You can't do this!" Martin shouted.

Emily heard a scuffle and then a loud thud. She exhaled. No gunshots. *Thank the Lord.* The office door slammed shut. Through a crack in the door casing, Emily caught a glimpse of Mr. DeSoto locking the door and jamming the key in his pocket. He stuffed the gun under his topcoat in the waistband of his pants. Then, after buttoning the coat, he squared his shoulders and looked straight at her hiding place.

She froze. Not a twitch. Not a breath.

After what seemed like forever, he finally shook his head and marched away.

Emily took a shaky breath, fighting tears.

He's going to kill Carter.

40

"How 'bout you, sir? Would you like a photo of pretty Miss Maggie Burke?"

Carter turned his head to watch the Chicago Stars' second bagger, Miss Katie Becker, flounce her way through the crowds, soliciting a collection of photos at a penny a picture. He chuckled. The attractive redhead batted her eyelashes at nearly every balding gentleman and soon had her stack gone.

"Wish I'd have told Katie to save me one of those." Reggie Wallace, the Owls' center fielder, swung his arm in a circle.

Carter frowned. "You're using Miss Becker's given name and they've only been here a day."

"It doesn't take long for some of us to woo a girl." Digger elbowed Fred Brunner.

"Knock it off." Carter playfully whacked the back of Digger's head.

"Why? There aren't any ladies around."

The mention of ladies sent Carter searching the crowd

again for Emily. His stomach clenched. Where was she and why hadn't she arrived?

"She'll be here." Ducky walked several yards from Carter and crouched to catch the warm-up pitches.

Carter hurled one toward Ducky. It went wide.

Ducky snagged it in his padded glove and threw it back in one smooth movement. "So, how many folks do you think are here? I've never seen so many at a game."

Carter glanced around. The Bloomer Girls' manager had had the temporary fence erected this morning around the field. He told Carter they carried it in a special compartment in their Pullman Palace car so no one could sneak in the game without paying. The newly made bleachers overflowed with hundreds of spectators. Patrons lined the fence and every spare space all the way to left field. At a nickel a person, the box receipts should make the Chicago Stars glad they'd made a stop at the lake resort.

He sent a curveball into Ducky's glove. "I heard there are eight hundred here at the lake today for the Omaha Butchers Association picnic. There has to be at least that many here at the game. Maybe more."

Across the way, he spotted the Bloomer Girls' pitcher hurling the ball with ease and accuracy to the catcher, Hank Russell. Should he go ask Russell about Emily's whereabouts?

Putting his frustration into his pitch, Carter sent a fastball into Ducky's glove.

The umpire glanced at his pocket watch and signaled the game to begin. Cheers rent the air, and Carter's stomach lurched as he jogged to the pitcher's mound. He turned and spotted Emily's grandmother and aunts—both of them—sitting in the front row of the new stands. If she'd gotten cold feet, they wouldn't be in attendance.

Something was definitely wrong. This game meant everything to Emily, and nothing short of a disaster would keep her away. If she didn't show by the fourth inning, he'd go find her—wherever she might be.

❦

Beating on the door, Emily tried to rouse some kind of response from her brother inside. "Martin! Martin!"

She heard a moan, and her heart raced. Shaking the doorknob in vain, she tried to calm herself. *Think. Think. Think.*

Please, Lord, show me how to open this door.

The umbrella stand!

After scrambling into the next office, Emily hefted the iron stand into her arms and carried it into the hall. Then, wielding it like a baseball bat, she swung at the lock. The impact jarred her arms and shoulders, and the doorknob clattered to the floor.

She stuck her finger in the hole left by the knob's shaft and pulled. Her heart sank. The door remained locked.

She peered through the keyhole. Martin lay sprawled on a floral rug.

"Martin!" She beat on the door. "Martin!"

Could she pick the lock? Martin had showed her how to do that once. Pulling a pin from her hair, she inserted it into the hole. She wiggled it around, listening for the clicking of the pins inside.

"Emily."

"Shh, Martin. I'm trying to open the lock." Something poked her hairpin from the lock, and she tried to push it back in. Frustrated, she leaned her shoulder against the door. Suddenly it opened and she tumbled inside. She looked up into her brother's face. "Martin! You're awake!"

"Barely."

"How did you—"

He held up the skeleton key, then swayed.

Emily jumped to her feet and looped her arm around his waist. After helping him to his chair, she examined the welt on his head. Now that the danger for him was past, her anger began to flame, mingled with deep hurt and pain. She pushed the feelings down deep. She'd have to deal with them later.

"I'll get a doctor."

Martin caught her hand. "You need to find Carter. William DeSoto wants to kill him."

"I know. I heard everything." Disappointment filled her voice.

"All of it?"

"Yes."

Martin rubbed the back of his neck. "I could explain, but there isn't time."

Tears clouded her vision.

"Go. Find Carter and tell him what happened. I'd just slow you down. I'll get the sheriff and tell him everything." He squeezed her hand. "And Emily, I'm sorry."

<hr />

The scoreboard read 3–3 in the bottom of the fourth inning, and the Owls were taking the field as Emily fought her way to the entry gate.

"I'm one of the Owls." She pointed to her uniform. "I need to get in."

"Listen, ma'am. I'm not a fool." The old man shook his head. "The Bloomer Girls are the only ones with ladies on their team."

347

Carter spotted her and hurried to meet her, his face etched with concern. "Where have you been?"

"Tell this man to let me in and I'll tell you."

"She's one of us, Charlie."

"Is that a fact?" Charlie opened the gate and she squeezed in.

"I can see you're not hurt, so come on. Let's go. You can tell me later where you were for the last three innings."

"Carter, you're in danger." She grabbed his shirt.

"What?"

The umpire blew his whistle.

"We've got to get started. Are you sure you're okay?"

She refused to relinquish her hold. "Did you hear me? I know you didn't take Grandma's money, but William DeSoto did, and he wants to hurt you."

"Nothing's going to happen to me out here in front of a thousand people."

She dug her nails in his arm. "He wants to kill you, Carter!"

"Are you two lovebirds going to talk all day or play?" Elwood shouted.

"We'll talk to the sheriff as soon as this game is over. I promise. It's going to be fine." He squeezed her hand. "Trust me. I want you to enjoy this game. You've worked too hard on it not to."

Still unsettled, Emily reluctantly took her place as shortstop. Her eyes darted around for any sight of William DeSoto in the packed stands. Surely Carter was right. He'd be safe here, and they'd see the sheriff after the last inning.

Mac McSorely, third bagger, walked over to her. "I'll cover you as much as I can, but there's only so much even I can do. So keep your eyes open. You're an easy target."

Emily's pulse pounded. "They'll try to hit in my direction?"

Mac laughed. "Yeah. Wouldn't you? Remember, if you catch anything, throw it to first."

After he returned to cover his base, Emily wiped her sweaty palms on her bloomers and jammed her hand into the padded leather glove. *Please, God, don't let any balls come to me, and please let Martin find the sheriff and stop Mr. DeSoto.*

Her thoughts jumped to Olivia, and her heart grabbed. What would Olivia do when she heard about this whole affair? *Please, God, help her get through this ordeal too.*

By the end of the inning, God had answered at least one of her prayers. Between Carter and Mac, no balls had reached her. Emily took a deep breath. Now, if she could just survive being at bat.

Along with the rest of the Owls, she jogged in and sat down on the bench. Ducky slid over so Carter could settle into the spot beside her.

"Mac, you're up after Digger," Carter called.

Graceful yet athletic Maud Nelson, the Chicago Stars' pitcher, stepped onto the mound while Digger swung his bat several times before stepping into the box. After raising her hands above her head, Maud fired a fast one over the plate.

The spectators cheered at the strike. On the next ball, Digger connected, making it to first despite the stellar throw of the Stars' pretty left fielder, Maggie Burke.

Emily scanned the crowd. The packed stands thrilled her, but the success of the day was overshadowed by the threat to Carter's life. Would William DeSoto try to kill him? When? How?

Carter was right. He wouldn't do it out here in the open.

He gave her a halfhearted smile, and she relaxed a bit. After the game, they'd work it all out. Warmth spread across her chest when she spotted both her aunts and her grandmother sitting in the front row. Aunt Millie waved. Had they been worried about her?

Mac swung and missed. The Owls jeered at him until Carter silenced them. On the next pitch, he made it to second on a line drive. Fred Brunner then connected and sent a fly into left field. Maggie Burke pulled it down and managed to hold Mac at second. Yeula Robertson covered third base and picked off Digger.

Now with two outs, Carter called for the team to step up. Ducky's grounder got him to first.

"Okay, Elwood. Bring 'em home."

Elwood waved to the crowd as he stepped to the plate and eyed the Stars' pitcher. Maud's first two pitches landed with a thud in the catcher's mitt without Elwood tensing a muscle.

Carter stood up. "What do you think you're doing?"

"They're girls, Stockton. We've got to take it easy on them."

"They deserve a good game, and we're going to give it to them."

Elwood swung a few times and stepped back to the plate. He nailed the next pitch and cleared the bases. The crowd roared, with several men breaking out their revolvers and firing blanks in the air.

"Can they do that?" Emily asked Carter.

He flashed her a grin. "They've been doing it the whole game. After all, it is Independence Day. You're next, Emily."

She wiped her sweaty palms on her bloomers. "I suppose it's too late to quit now."

"You'll do fine."

Stepping to the plate, she smiled at Hank.

He grinned back from beneath his mask and punched his fist into his glove. "Well, I daresay you're the prettiest Owl out here."

"That's not saying much." She chuckled and stepped to the plate.

Maud lifted the ball in the air and sent it sailing toward home plate. Emily's stomach tightened and she swung, catching only air. She looked at Carter.

"Choke up on the bat. You can do this."

Heeding Carter's words, Emily inched her grip toward the bat's nose and leaned forward over the plate.

On the next swing, she connected. She dribbled a slow roller toward Maud and raced toward first base. When she landed on it only a second before the ball, she stared victoriously at Maud. The pitcher grinned. The crowd cheered and a thrill surged through her. Even Olivia DeSoto applauded—

With William DeSoto looming beside her.

The sight of him made her shiver.

With Carter up next, Emily prepared to run. On the second pitch, Carter hit one over the fence. The guns started going off as Carter jogged down the baseline toward her.

Frantically, he waved both hands, signaling her to run. She took five steps and glanced at the stands. Her heart stopped. DeSoto, like a few of the other men, had his gun out and aimed at the field, except his was pointed directly at Carter.

She spun around and raced back toward first base, screaming for Carter to get down. The crowd roared. He couldn't hear her.

He appeared to shout at her, motioning for her to run the other way.

She wasn't stopping for anything. With her eyes focused solely on him, she tripped on the edge of first base and stumbled. Carter awkwardly caught her, and together they toppled to the ground and rolled in the dirt.

41

Emily shook her ringing head and blinked away the stars behind her eyes. Laughter from the crowd drowned out Carter's words.

He lifted her to her feet and kept a firm hold of her arm. "Are you okay? What was that all about?"

"William DeSoto—"

"Emily, I told you not to worry about him."

The disbelief in his voice hurt more than the knot forming on her head. As the Bloomer Girls began to converge on them, she pressed her hand to it and winced. The high-pitched fury of panicked voices made her squeeze her eyes shut for a moment.

Yeula raced over and held out her open palm. "I thought they were shooting blanks out there!"

Carter stared at the bullet. "Where did you find that?"

She pointed beyond first base. "I felt something whiz by my cheek. What kind of game is this?"

"Easy, Yeula." Maud punched her glove. "Does this have anything to do with your tumble?"

Emily nodded. "Someone shot at Carter." She turned to him. "It was William DeSoto. That's why I ran back. I saw him aiming at you. I was trying to warn you, but I tripped."

"And your little accident probably saved my life." He touched the purpling area above her temple. "Let's get you off the field."

"What about Mr. DeSoto?"

"I'll take care of him."

❧

As they approached the benches, some of the Owls joined them, along with the umpire. Carter filled them in as he scanned the crowd for the man who'd shot at him. His insides burned as he thought about what DeSoto had done. What if he'd hit Emily or one of the Bloomer Girls?

Then he spotted the coward lurking in the shadows of the stands, directly down the first-base line. When their eyes met, DeSoto took off through the crowd, pushing and shoving anyone in his way.

He turned to Ducky. "Take care of her." He burst into a run after the corrupt banker.

❧

Emily didn't give Ducky time to stop her. She sprinted after Carter, only to be passed by most of her Owl teammates. DeSoto shoved his way through the spectators standing off to the right of the field. When he finally reached an open space, Carter tackled him.

Carter planted his knee in DeSoto's back and pinned the banker's arm behind him. The teammates skidded to a halt at the scene.

DeSoto fought to get up. "Get this guy off me before he breaks my arm!"

"Taylor, you take him." Carter stood up, pressing his knee harder into DeSoto's back in the process, and pushed a clump of sweaty curls from his forehead.

With a firm grip on DeSoto's collar, Elwood hauled the banker to his feet. "Stockton, maybe you missed your football calling. What'd this guy do?"

Still out of breath, Emily held out the bullet. "He shot at Carter after his last hit."

"He tried to kill you?" Elwood gave the man an angry shake. "That wasn't very neighborly. Stockton can be annoying, but shooting a decent pitcher on the Fourth of July is downright un-American."

Questions flew from the various Owls, and finally Carter held up his hand. "I promise to explain it all later. All you boys need to know is I found out he stole money from Emily's grandmother at the bank, and he wanted to stop me from telling the authorities."

Ducky turned to Emily. "How'd you get involved?"

"I went to see my brother and overheard him talking to Mr. DeSoto, who planned to kill Carter because he had figured his whole scam out."

"Your brother?" Surprise followed by relief washed over Carter's face.

Emily's eyes widened. Was Carter still so angry with her that he'd be glad her family was suffering? "That makes you happy?"

"No, I'm sorry. You must be devastated. But I thought *my* brother was involved."

"Afraid not." Martin walked up with the sheriff. "It was me, but I'm owning up to my mistakes." He draped his arm around Emily and hugged her. "I'll do whatever it takes to set things right."

After convincing his teammates to return to the game, Carter explained to the sheriff what had happened and how he'd discovered the bank manager's involvement.

"Mister, it looks like you're under arrest." The sheriff grabbed DeSoto's upper arm and turned to Carter. "I'll take care of him. Meet us at the Manawa jail after the game to give your statement. It'd be good to have someone from the bank there too."

"I'll find my brother," Carter said, placing his hand on the small of Emily's back.

The sheriff nodded. "Come on, mister. Let's get you to your new home away from home." He paused. "Who's that?"

For the first time, Emily spotted Olivia hurrying toward them, her eyes wild with worry. "It's Mr. DeSoto's wife. I'll speak to her."

"She can visit him in the jail after four, but don't let her show up earlier." The sheriff walked away, pushing his prisoner before him, with Martin walking behind.

Emily took in Olivia's frantic expression. Gone was every shred of the woman's usual composure. Something unfamiliar tugged on Emily's heart. Olivia needed a friend, so could God be trying to tell her it should be her?

She turned to Carter. "You'd better go back to the game."

"I'm not leaving you to handle her alone."

"Carter, I think God's calling me to help her—if she'll let me."

"God's calling you?" He quirked an eyebrow. "Why do I get the feeling we have a lot to talk about?"

"More than you know."

355

"I know my husband! He wouldn't steal money or hurt someone."

Emily drew Olivia away from the crowd to the shade of a grove of trees. She laid her hand on Olivia's arm. "He tried to kill Carter. I saw him and I heard him planning it beforehand."

"You're lying." Tears filled Olivia's blue eyes. "Please, Emily, tell me you're lying."

"I wish I was, but you were standing next to him. Where was his gun pointed?"

Olivia pressed a hand to her mouth. "He can't do this to me. What will people say?"

What will people say? Her husband had tried to kill someone, and the only thing Olivia could think of was her public persona? Emily took a deep breath. *Lord, what do I say to this woman?*

"Olivia, let's take one day at a time."

"He betrayed me! You don't know how it feels to be betrayed by someone you love."

"Yes, I do know." Martin's image formed in Emily's mind. Never in her wildest dreams had she suspected him. But Carter? The thought pierced even now. "And worse, I know what it's like to betray the trust of someone I care about." Emily glanced toward the crowds, again on their feet cheering and setting off their guns. "We'd better get you out of here before the game is over. There will be a lot of questions."

❧

Following the game, Carter arrived at the Manawa jail with both his father and Nathan. He glanced at Emily and Olivia sitting in straight-backed chairs. Dank and musty, the small jail wasn't a fit place for ladies.

The Bloomer Girls had won and destroyed his perfect season. He smiled. It didn't matter anymore, but he hadn't even had the chance to tell Emily what a success the game had been.

A thought hit him like a medicine ball to the gut. Someone was going to have to tell Emily's grandmother that her grandson had stolen from her. He swallowed. That someone was probably him.

"Okay." The sheriff dipped his pen in an inkwell. "Let's get down to business. Miss Graham, why don't you start?"

Carter cleared his throat. "Maybe I should do that, sir. I've been investigating this for a while."

The door swung open, and Martin entered, his face pale and drawn, with his grandmother on his arm.

Kate's gaze swept the room and rested on Emily. "Sheriff, I'd like a word with you and Mr. Stockton in private, if I may."

The sheriff sighed. "And you are?"

"Mrs. Graham, sir. It is my money in question."

"Ma'am, if you don't mind waiting outside, we were about to begin."

She stepped in front of his desk. "I'd like to speak to you, sir—now."

Carter chuckled. She was a hard woman to say no to. A lot like her granddaughter.

"You heard the lady." The sheriff flicked his wrist, indicating everyone should leave.

When Nathan made no attempt to follow the others, Kate looked at him. "Aren't you going?"

"You said you wanted Mr. Stockton to stay."

She nodded to Carter. "That Mr. Stockton."

"But I'm—"

Angus Stockton inclined his head toward the door. "Come on, Son. You do not want to argue with Kate Graham."

She turned to Emily. "And this private meeting doesn't include you either."

"But Grandma—"

"No buts, dear. Trust me."

42

A contrite Martin sat beside Emily on a bench at the Grand Pavilion, watching fireworks explode in the air.

Emily couldn't believe her ears. Somehow her grandmother had convinced the sheriff not to file charges against Martin or William DeSoto for the theft of the money.

"Grandma told the sheriff that technically the money was mine all along since she'd given me unlimited access to her accounts."

"Why did you do it, Martin?"

A brilliant burst of red and yellow cascaded above them. Martin waited until the colors faded. "It was all about pride. I made a bad investment, and the business hasn't been doing so well. I didn't want Dad to come back and see I'd failed."

"And now?"

"And now I have to live with knowing I failed a bigger test—a test of character—and the people I love like you and Grandma are all aware of it." His voice barely above a whisper, he added, "Can you forgive me?"

Emily looked at the sky and watched the trails of a white Catherine wheel spin into space. "Yes. I understand a little something about wanting to measure up in the eyes of others." She sighed. "What's going to happen to Mr. DeSoto? He still tried to kill Carter."

"Carter offered not to press charges against him, but the sheriff said the state still had to." He squeezed her hand. "He wants you to come in tomorrow and give your statement about what you heard."

Emily sighed. "I'll have to go early."

"Plans?"

"Carter and I have a long overdue talk."

"Are you going to work things out?"

"I'm not sure we can. We live in different worlds and want different things. Besides, I really made a mess of our relationship and hurt him terribly."

Martin draped an arm around her shoulders and hugged her against his side. "After today, the one thing you should be sure of is God is great at fixing our messes."

❧

An unfamiliar female voice chirped outside the cabin and paused Emily's morning toilet. As she peeked out the window, her heart stopped.

Mary Jane Coggeshall was here. Here. Right at her grandmother's cabin.

Emily stuffed her stocking-clad feet into shoes and grabbed her hat. Placing it on her head, she quickly stuck the pins in, poking her scalp in the process. She exited the cabin in record time, careful not to let the screen door bang shut.

She pretended to act surprised when she approached the table and found the woman she so greatly admired having tea with her aunts and her grandmother. "Mrs. Coggeshall, how delightful to see you again. To what do we owe the pleasure?"

"I've come to talk to you, actually."

"Me?" Emily sat down.

"After our meeting, I was so intrigued by your unique idea concerning the Bloomer Girls' game that I took the liberty of writing Carrie about it."

Carrie Chapman Catt? Had Emily heard that right? Mrs. Coggeshall had written to the president of the National Woman Suffrage Association about her?

"Carrie wired me back immediately. She feels you are a perfect fit for a new position she'd like to begin on the national level."

Emily swallowed hard. "Me?"

Mrs. Coggeshall smiled. "We'd like a younger woman such as yourself to go to college campuses and recruit the ladies in the student body to the cause. We believe your creative ideas would be the perfect way to get the attention of these young coeds."

"Me?"

"Oh, for heaven's sake." Aunt Ethel set her cup down. "Can you say something more intelligent than that?"

Aunt Millie twittered. "I believe the cat has her tail."

"Her tongue," Aunt Ethel corrected.

"Are you sure? I was certain the saying was 'a cat has her tail.'"

"She doesn't have a tail."

"Sisters." Grandma Kate glared at them.

"What do you say, Miss Graham?"

Everything in her wanted to shout yes. A chance to work on the national level and to make a difference everywhere was her greatest wish.

But what about Carter? That Sunday watching him play ball with the younger boys had brought a new wish to her lips for a future that might include him.

The thrill of the moment faded like last night's fireworks.

"When do you need to know? I really need some time to pray about this."

"I understand." Mrs. Coggeshall stood and handed Emily a piece of paper. "This sheet tells you where you can wire Carrie. She asks that you let her know by the end of next week. She also said to make sure you know you'd make a most welcome addition to the team."

Emily got to her feet. "May I walk you back to the dock?"

"No need. I have a driver waiting on the service road." She paused. "Sometimes this fight seems so long and arduous, but when I meet young women of vision like yourself, I'm filled with hope. God bless you, Miss Graham."

Emily watched her go, then stared at the paper in her hand containing the contact information for Carrie Chapman Catt. The pulse in her temple pounded, and she pressed her fingers to it. Smiling through her tears, she turned toward her grandmother. "How am I ever going to decide?"

◦◦◦

"Nathan?" Carter quickly tucked in the tails of his shirt. "What are you doing here?"

"Can't a man come to take his brother out for breakfast?" Nathan swept his gaze over the Owl Club rooms that several members of the club called home during the summer, and frowned.

"He can, but you don't."

"I am today. Hurry up."

Carter chuckled, slipped into his striped jacket, and grabbed his hat from the hook. "Okay, let's go."

Nathan led him to the Grand Pavilion, and they found a table in the open-air section. Both men ordered plates of biscuits and gravy, which were delivered immediately.

Carter forked a bite of biscuit drenched in the creamy gravy. "So what do you want to talk about?"

"Your future." Nathan took a swig from his coffee cup and held up his hand. "And before you say it's none of my business, hear me out."

"Okay." Carter leaned back in his chair. "Shoot."

"As you know, there'll be an opening at the bank now."

"I've been thinking about that. Maybe it's time—"

"No, it's not." Nathan paused. "I watched you at the game yesterday, and I had to finally admit something to myself. You're good. Really good. Then I talked to Ducky, and he said you've been offered a contract by a man named Gibbs."

"But I'm not so sure it's what I want now."

"Because of Emily Graham?"

"Her work is here. I can't ask her to leave." Carter took a swig of coffee. "Don't you think I can handle the bank job?"

"I have no doubt you can. If I had doubts before, your handling of Mrs. Graham's affairs disproved them admirably. I apologize for implying you couldn't handle the job and for accusing you of impropriety."

A little grin escaped. "So what's the problem?"

"You'd hate it." Nathan folded his napkin and set it beside his empty plate. "I wanted you to be there, but I wanted it for myself. Something inside me said if my little brother followed in my footsteps, then I must have done my job right. After yesterday's game, Dad pointed out that raising you was his job, not mine, and he'd done it quite well."

Carter chuckled. "So, I don't belong in the bank, and I don't want to leave this place. Any suggestions?"

"Actually, what if I told you Dad and I came up with an idea that would let you play baseball and be a businessman?"

"I'd say I might be interested in hearing what you have in mind."

❧

After speaking to the sheriff, Emily checked her watch and headed to the bandstand to meet Carter.

Dalbey's band struck up a brassy tune as soon as she arrived. She stood behind the park bench–style seating and searched the area for Carter. Not seeing him, she moved away from the bandstand and found a quieter bench to ask God to help her make the right choices.

All her life she'd wanted to make a difference, to rise above being the girl who tripped over her own shadow. And now that her dream was within her grasp, she wasn't sure what to do with it. Taking this job meant leaving her grandmother, aunts, parents, and Martin. Worst of all, it meant leaving Carter.

But she still didn't know where she stood with him. Would he want her back after the things she'd said? Carter had incredible skills. If they married, would that keep him from becoming who God wanted him to be?

She shook her head. Married? Where had that thought come from?

Lord, I gave my life to You all over again. I want to follow Your will, but You're going to have to help me see what it is.

Suddenly two hands covered her eyes and a man spoke behind her. "Guess who."

"Hank?" She giggled.

"You wound me." Carter came around to the front of the bench and dropped down beside her. "I really don't like that guy."

"You don't?" Emily flashed Carter a smile. "He was rather sweet."

"So is molasses, but I don't care for that either."

"You were jealous?"

"Me?" He held his hand over his chest. "No, of course not."

She raised her eyebrows.

"Okay, maybe a little." Carter stood and pulled her to her feet. "So now that you've made me humiliate myself, are you ready to have some fun?"

"Fun?" He kept hold of her hand, and she couldn't bring herself to pull away. "Aren't you still angry with me? We have a lot to talk about, and I have something important to tell you."

He led her to the path. "And we can do that at the rink."

Emily halted. "You're taking me skating? You really are still mad at me."

"What can I say? I need a good laugh."

"So you're already planning to laugh at me."

"*With* you. Not *at* you." He captured her hand and tucked it in the crook of his arm. "Besides, I was only joking about skating. I have something else planned."

"What is it?"

"All you have to do is come with me."

"What about our talk?"

He held up a finger to her lips. "Later."

Emily walked beside him in silence, not daring to bring up the topics wedged between them. Had Carter really forgiven her for doubting him? And how would he take her news about Mrs. Coggeshall's offer?

Carter led her past the Grand Pavilion filled with patrons and buzzing with activity. Dalbey's band continued to pipe a tune, and the flowers in the many planters burst with colorful blooms like last night's fireworks displays. Some families picnicked on the neatly mowed lawn, and one of them had set up a game of croquet.

Her heart squeezed. She'd miss this place if she left. Six summers on these shores. Here love grew, families played, and people enjoyed all life had to offer. Would she be able to return next year? How big would Marguerite's Tate be by then? Or Lilly's baby Levi? And where would Carter be?

The lake beside them lapped at the rocky shore, and she glanced at Carter. He merely smiled back. Were they ever going to talk? At least he seemed to have forgiven her already.

When they reached the Yacht Club, Emily's curiosity grew. They passed beyond that, and Carter led her toward the boat shop owned by Trip, Marguerite's husband. Marguerite greeted them at the door. "Ready to go sailing?"

Emily turned to Carter. "You know how to sail?"

He shook his head. "Trip and a couple of his friends are taking us out. I arranged it earlier today."

Marguerite led them to the shop area, through the large doors in the back, and onto the boat dock. Trip waved and hopped off the deck of his *Endeavor*.

He hooked his arms around his wife's waist. "We're all set."

Emily nodded toward Marguerite. "Are you coming?"

"I'm afraid she's been docked for a while." A broad, dimpled grin broke out on Trip's face. "I'm not letting her near a sailboat."

"Letting her?" Emily's blood pumped. How dare Trip tell Marguerite she couldn't participate in something she clearly loved! Well, he wouldn't get away with it as long as Emily was there. "You're not *letting her* go out?"

Marguerite laid a hand on her arm. "Emily, it's okay."

"No, it's not okay. He should not be telling you what you can and cannot do. You are as capable a sailor as he is—or at least that's what you've said—and he has no right to take that from you on some overprotective whim."

Laughter seemed to start in Trip's belly, rise to his chest, and explode from his lips. Carter soon joined in.

Emily's jaw dropped. "And what, gentlemen, is so funny?"

"I'd have to agree with everything you said." Trip chuckled again. "She's probably a better sailor than I am, and I shouldn't tell her what to do, but I've got to think of the baby."

"Baby?" Emily's gaze dropped to where Trip's hand now rested. "You're . . . that's why . . . oh my goodness." She covered her mouth with her hand, and tears filled her eyes. "You're going to have another baby."

"Finally." Marguerite pulled Emily into a hug. "But God's timing is always perfect."

Emily stepped back and dropped her gaze to Trip's shoes. "I'm sorry, Trip. I jumped to conclusions."

"Jumped?" Carter chuckled. "You took a flying leap on that one."

"It's not a problem." Trip faced Carter but tilted his head in Emily's direction. "You sure you know what you're getting into?"

Carter patted her hand. "I sure hope so."

"Then let's get you on board."

❧

Emily seemed different.

She had yesterday too, but unable to put his finger on why, Carter simply watched her as the sailboat traveled over the soft swells of the lake. The crew, consisting of Trip and three mates, went about their work. They left Carter and Emily alone in their seats in the ship's stern. Emily used a lace-edged handkerchief to dab at the spray hitting her face, then glanced at him. Her lashes drooped shyly over her slightly freckled cheeks.

"What's wrong?" She raised a hand to her bun and tucked an errant strand behind her ear.

"Nothing's wrong. I was admiring the view."

She smiled and swept her hand toward the shore. "The view's out there."

"I happen to like the one I was enjoying."

Her cheeks blossomed, but then she sighed. "Carter, we need to talk."

"I know." He draped his arm around her. "You said you had something to tell me, and I have some news to share with you too."

"That's not the part I meant."

"I know that too."

She licked her lips and inhaled deeply. "I need to apologize for doubting you and to tell you that you were right."

The sailboat leaned slightly to the right, and Carter tightened his grip on Emily. "I like how that sounds."

"Don't get used to it." She swatted his arm. "I'm being serious."

"So what was I right about?"

"I was building a broken cistern, trying to fill myself up. Even though I never felt like I was good enough, I was prideful in my own way."

His heart did a little jig. So that's why she seemed different. God's touch had a way of changing His children.

"You wanted people to acknowledge you and make you feel worthy. I think we all do that." He flicked the annoying mop of curls from his forehead. "I was prideful too. I didn't speak to you in love, and I said some hurtful things."

"I accused you of stealing from my grandmother. You had a right to be upset."

One of the crewmen unlashed some lines.

"Boom coming across," Trip called out.

As instructed earlier, they both lowered their heads until the sail had swung to the other side.

"I could have told you what I suspected, but I was afraid my brother was the one doing the stealing. He and I don't see eye to eye on everything, but he's still my brother. I was hoping to persuade him to put the money back, and then I'd tell your grandmother I found the error."

"But that wasn't prideful."

"No, the prideful part was not wanting to look bad in your eyes and not trusting God to work out a way for us to be together."

Tears pooled in her eyes. "You could never look bad to me."

"Excuse me?"

"Well, at least you won't ever again."

"That's good to hear." He winked at her. "So, before I share my news, tell me yours."

"Well." She shifted in her seat so she could face him. "You're never going to believe what happened. This morning I got a visit from Mary Jane Coggeshall."

"That suffrage lady from Olivia's tea party?"

Her eyes dancing, Emily nodded. "And she was so pleased with the idea of the Bloomer Girls' game, she contacted Carrie Chapman Catt, the president of the National Woman Suffrage Association."

"Honestly?"

"And Mrs. Catt wants me to come work on the national level." Her smile widened further. The wind picked up, and she held her hat on with her hand and raised her voice over the noise. "I'd go around to colleges and try to recruit young women to the cause. She said they need someone like me with innovative ideas."

The news punched him hard. His chest heaved, but he forced a smile. Emily wanted this. It was her dream. He should want it for her. But how could he?

The sailboat heeled deeply to the left. Emily lurched forward and Carter grabbed her arm.

Emily clutched at his grip. "Thank you for catching me."

"I'll always catch you."

The words tripped in his throat. It wasn't true. She was leaving, and he couldn't—rather, he wouldn't—catch her before she left for Washington DC. It wouldn't be right to steal her dream.

"So what did you want to tell me?" Her eyes still sparkled with excitement.

"Never mind. It's not important."

43

Not important?

Under star-filled skies, Emily sat on a park bench beside Carter, watching a hot-air balloon inflate on the open field outside the Grand Pavilion. The thickness of his voice when he'd spoken those words haunted her.

As the balloon inflated, its breathtaking, vibrant colors contrasted with the darkness of the night, making the craft appear to glow. Soon it would lift, and she wished it could carry the heaviness that had descended between the two of them after she'd shared her news.

"It's beautiful."

"It is."

She removed her hat and set it beside her on the bench. In a few minutes, the hat would have blocked her view of the balloon's ascent.

A chasm of silence settled between them.

Long.

Sad.

Painful.

And oh so vast.

Her eyes filled with hot tears. He didn't love her enough to stop her. He hadn't told her not to go. If he wanted her to stay, he should at least say so.

Carter squeezed her hand. "Emily, do you really want to go?"

A tear hung on her lashes for a second, then made its way down her cheek. The wind blew across it and cooled the narrow streak. "Yes and no. Does that make sense to you?"

"Completely."

The hot-air balloon, now filled, lifted into the air. As it rose above the trees, the red, yellow, and blue stripes were backlit by the balloon's furnace. Several stories in the air, the pilot released his harness and dropped from the balloon. Seconds later, his parachute opened and he floated to the ground while the balloon continued on without him.

"Pilotless?" Emily turned to Carter. "What will happen to the balloon?"

"It'll fall eventually. Then someone goes and picks it up."

Falling eventually. She'd fallen. God had picked her up, and here she was flying pilotless again, only days after telling Him He had control of her life. Even though she'd told Mrs. Coggeshall she needed time to pray, she had yet to ask the Lord what she should do.

She squeezed Carter's hand. "Can we pray together about whether I should go to Washington DC?"

"Now?"

"Yes. I don't want to wait."

"I'd like that." The thickness in his voice was back when he spoke. "Lord." He paused and she heard him swallow. "I don't know what kind of plans You have for Emily. She's such an amazing woman, and You placed the desire to change the world in her heart. Maybe it's selfish, but I don't want to let her go. Not now. Not ever. I love her. I made some plans, but I didn't include You either. So here we are, asking You to help us make our paths straight."

He finished the prayer, and Emily swiped the dampness from her cheeks. He loved her.

The voices of the other balloon watchers faded as she pondered his words. Her emotions whirled like a tornado. *Lord, I'm Yours. For whatever You want me to do. Stay. Go. Marry Marion Wormsley. Thank goodness You don't want that. But I have to know.*

Carter stood and pulled her to her feet. He wrapped his arms around her waist, and she leaned against his chest. Her aunts would be mortified, but it felt so good to be in his arms. So safe. He would catch her. She knew it.

They watched the hot-air balloon climb farther into the inky sky. "Carter, what was your news?"

"It doesn't matter now."

"It does to me." She tipped her face to his.

"My dad and brother want to invest in a baseball team I would manage."

"That's wonderful!"

"A Bloomer Girls' team."

She dug her fingers into his arms. "Are you considering it?"

"I already started making a list of places where I can recruit."

"But what about the major league?"

"I realized I like teaching and coaching more. When I was with those boys and teaching you, I loved every minute. I had an offer for a club team in Des Moines, but I turned it down already." He took a deep breath. "I was hoping my wife and I could manage the Bloomer Girls' team together. I thought you could travel the country with me and preach suffrage to every crowd we draw."

She gasped.

"Emily, I've been trying to be noble and not ask you to give up your dreams. I'm praying this is what God wants me to do and that I'm not being selfish. But I want to marry you. You're a great catch and I don't want to let you go. I want to take a chance on us. Please tell me you do too."

She opened her mouth, but the words stuck in her throat.

He rested his chin on the top of her head. "I understand. You want to go."

"No!" The word finally broke free. She jolted her head up, and it struck Carter's chin.

He jerked back.

"I'm so sorry. Are you okay?"

His chuckling broke the quiet. "I guess I'd better get used to that."

"Life with me can be threatening to one's health." Her heart twirled. "Can you handle that? I'm headstrong, stubborn, and I want my way far too often. I hate the word *obey*, and I can give Independence Day a whole new meaning."

"Are you trying to scare me? Because it isn't going to work. I'm aware of those things."

"Then do you know this?" She placed her hand on his whiskered cheek. "I love you, Carter Stockton. I love how you want to follow God, I love your trustworthiness, and I love the tumble of curls on your forehead."

"Is that a yes?"

"That, my love, is a grand slam."

With a whoop, he lifted her from the ground and spun her in a circle until the dizziness in her head matched the dizziness in her heart. He set her down and she stumbled. Instinctively, he caught her, and then before she'd regained her balance, he lowered his lips to hers.

Excitement and joy, passion and love all fought for her heart, swelling inside her until she feared she'd burst. Was this what it felt like to hit a ball out of the park?

She doubted it.

This had to be much better.

Author's Note

The turn of the century marked many changes for women. Before then, the lives of most women centered on the home. As a wife and mother, the woman spent much time doing such things as cleaning, sewing, and cooking. By 1900, the industrial society was drawing more and more women out of the home and into the workforce. These women had more freedom than ever before. They were exploring a new world full of possibilities.

The Bloomer Girls' teams are a product of this time period. They crossed the country playing against men's teams from the 1890s to 1934. Hundreds of teams including the Chicago Stars, the All Star Ranger Girls, and the Philadelphia Bobbies provided entertainment for the crowds while showing the world they could hit, field, slide, and catch as well as any man.

Maud Nelson (born Clementia Brida) not only pitched for the Chicago Stars and other teams, she was also a scout, manager, and owner. Her forty-year baseball career should make her a household name, but because she worked with women's teams, history records little of her. Even the newspapers of the day record the Bloomer Girls' teams more as spectacles than the serious athletes they were.

Although Iowa was one of the states leading the fight for woman suffrage, the women of Iowa would not receive the right to vote until 1919 (ratified in 1920) along with the rest of the country. It is odd that a state that gave the movement such leaders as Elizabeth Cady Stanton, Mary Jane Coggeshall, Amelia Bloomer, and Carrie Chapman Catt was unable to pass a state amendment granting women the right to vote prior to that. In addition, Iowa was known for its progressive attitude toward women. For example, Iowa State Agricultural College (now ISU) was coeducational from its beginning in 1869.

Can you imagine the excitement of these women, who worked tirelessly for the right to cast their vote, dropping a ballot in a ballot box for the first time? I like to think Amelia Bloomer and the other suffragists who had already passed on would have rejoiced in heaven on such a day.

Acknowledgments

Special thanks to . . .

My editors Andrea Doering and Jessica Miles, for their encouraging words and excellent eye for detail.

Baker Publishing Group, for their outstanding work from cover art to marketing to sales. It's a privilege to work with all of you.

My agent Wendy Lawton, for sharing her wisdom concerning the publishing industry.

Shannon Vannatter, Brenda Anderson, Dawn Ford, and Marlene Garand, crit partners extraordinaire, for their honest critiques and devotion to making my work better.

Judy Miller and Laura Frantz, my dear writer friends. This journey would not be the same without you both.

The Scribblers, for keeping me accountable.

My extended family and church family, for praying for my writing ministry daily.

My children, Parker, Caroline, and Emma, for being the joy of my life and for being excited about each story I write.

My husband David, the love of my life. "Thank you" hardly seems adequate for all you do for me.

Most of all, my Lord Jesus Christ, the Giver of gifts. I pray my work brings glory to You always.

Lorna Seilstad is the author of *Making Waves*. She lives in and draws her setting from her home state of Iowa. A history buff, antique collector, and freelance graphic designer, she has won several online writing awards and is a member of the American Christian Fiction Writers. *A Great Catch* is her second novel.

LORNA SEILSTAD IS SURE TO MAKE WAVES!

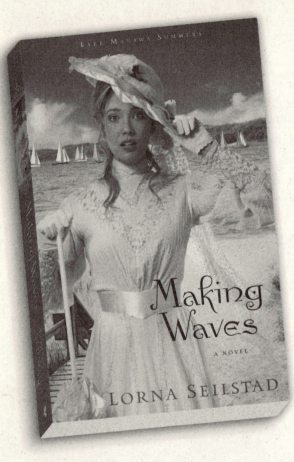

"You'll set sail on a wonderful adventure in Lorna Seilstad's new series set at Lake Manawa, Iowa. Her quick wit and captivating characters are mixed into a little-known slice of history that will keep you turning the pages and wishing for more when the story ends. Fortunately, there's another book to follow. I can't wait!"

—Judith Miller, author, *Somewhere to Belong*

Available Wherever Books Are Sol

"If you're looking for an awesome writer and a story charged with romance, you don't want to miss *A Hope Undaunted*."

—Judith Miller, author of *Somewhere to Belong*, Daughters of Amana series

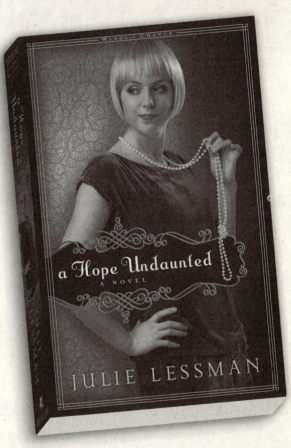

Kate O'Connor is a smart and sassy woman who has her goals laid out for the future—including the perfect husband and career. Will she follow her plans or her heart?

ML   7/11